OUT OF THE
CRUCIBLE

MARIAN WELLS

OUT OF THE CRUCIBLE

BETHANY HOUSE PUBLISHERS
MINNEAPOLIS, MINNESOTA 55438
A Division of Bethany Fellowship, Inc.

Manuscript edited by Penelope J. Stokes.

Cover illustration by Dan Thornberg,
Bethany House Publishers staff artist.

Published by Bethany House Publishers
A Division of Bethany Fellowship, Inc.
6820 Auto Club Road, Minneapolis, Minnesota 55438

Printed in the United States of America

Library of Congress Cataloging-in-Publication Data

Wells, Marian, 1931–
    Out of the crucible / Marian Wells.
       p.   cm. — (Treasure quest)
    Sequel to: Colorado gold.
     1. United States—History—Civil War, 1862–1865—Fiction. I. Title. II.
Series: Wells, Marian, 1931–   Treasure quest books.
PS3573.E492709   1988
813'.54—dc 19
ISBN 1-55661-037-8 (pbk.)   88–21121
                                               CIP

Books by Marian Wells

The Wedding Dress
With This Ring

Karen

The STARLIGHT TRILOGY Series
  The Wishing Star
  Star Light, Star Bright
  Morning Star

The TREASURE QUEST Series
  Colorado Gold
  Out of the Crucible

CHAPTER 1

J ust what I expected." Matthew Thomas shoved his broad-brimmed hat back on his head. The dark-skinned man riding beside him in the Oberlin town square edged his horse close and waited. Matthew threw him a glance and added, "A college town with all the trimmings. See the campus over yonder in the trees? Look at the church. Even *it* fits the image—white frame with a belfry and a cross." The black man nodded silently.

"William, let's find something to eat and then drop this message at the office of Samuel Ward."

"The honorable Samuel, friend of the slaves." William's eyes shone with pride as he nodded, "Yes, sir, only a step away from being a slave himself, and now he's set on freeing us all."

"William, hush your talk. These trees might have ears."

"You have no need to remind us," William shuddered. "No man just escaped forgets the whip. No takin' chances here with the law." He glanced at Matthew. "Still might slip over to Canada. Least when my Mattie comes, I will."

The man paused, then turned troubled eyes in Matthew's direction. "I hear something, Matt. This college town may not be as nice as you think. I hear a crowd comin'. They're rumbling like upset bees."

Matthew cocked his head. Listening to the clamor of baying hounds, the shouts and cries of a mob, he said, "We'll know in a minute; they're coming fast." He looked at the man's fearful expression. "William, don't wait. Head up behind the college. If you can't take the mare into the trees, drop her and get out of town. Could be students having a good time, but no sense taking chances."

William shook his head. " 'Round here, these students don't have that kind of a good time. Too serious, those hounds." With one more quick glance, William headed down the street.

The crowd appeared. Matthew narrowed his eyes and watched. They were coming upwind. Making himself relax, he held his mount steady. "Easy, old girl. They'll not catch a scent here, so William is safe for now." The mare continued to fight the bridle, rolling her eyes at the baying hounds.

Settling back in the saddle, Matthew studied the mob. "Without a doubt there's two distinct groups," he muttered. He continued to speak in soothing tones, "You needn't give away the game. They'll never guess you to be an abolitionist horse at heart if you'll just settle down and act like a gentleman's mount."

The mob split and settled around him. He eyed the red-faced men. The ones with the hounds were grim-lipped and hard-eyed. The ones with the shiny sheriff badges were sullen, shrinking into their collars, away from the others.

Matthew's heart went out to them. He had guessed their story. It had been repeated over and over across the northern states—lawmen forced to comply with a law they detested.

As he waited, Matthew muttered, "So it's old John Calhoun's Fugitive Slave Act, just as I guessed."

As the group approached, he studied the faces of men sworn to cooperate by allowing these hunters to reclaim runaway slaves for their masters.

Turning to look at the crowd just beyond the square, Matthew's eyes quickly picked out the dark faces in the midst of the youths. They were freed slaves mingling with the students. Close to them, he saw plain-faced, determined women marching along behind their menfolk.

Beyond them was another group. Matthew spotted black suits and rough workmen's garb; but it was the expressions on the faces that nearly made him chuckle with glee. They were angry. He turned back to the men with the dogs.

"Let me guess," he drawled. "You've come here with neat papers describing a man who wants freedom more than life."

"A nigger, a slave, not a man."

A low growl rose from the crowd. Matthew said, "Bounty hunters. Looking for human flesh to sell beyond the river."

"They call it the Fugitive Slave Act, mister." The voice came from the middle of the crowd. "I don't know who you are, but don't sidle up with the likes of them. Around here we don't go with the Act. Freedom for all mankind in Oberlin, Ohio!"

The cheer became a chant. As the men with the dogs slipped away, the men with the badges moved forward. "Go back to your homes." Their voices became braver. "It's no trouble we want. Law and order will be preserved. And the law says a man is entitled to his property. We can't buck the law."

"But we can!" the chant came. "Tell us the name of the man, and we'll see he's safe."

A man wearing a black frock coat stepped up on the edge of the watering trough and waved his arms. Matthew recognized the lawyer he had come to see. Slipping off his mare, he tied her to the hitching post and started toward the crowd.

Samuel Ward was saying, "Quiet! We're acting like hoodlums, and on top of that, those bounty hunters have slipped away. We've got to keep them under surveillance. You men spread out, and make it quick."

Abruptly he stopped and turned at the sound of a horse coming fast. They watched the youth riding hard as he came into the square. Circling his horse in front of Ward, he cried, "Oh, Mr. Ward. There's men with hounds and guns. They have John Price on a horse. I saw them riding fast for Wellington."

"Wellington!" The crowd took up the cry. "They got him! They'll ship him over the river. They'll stick him on the train and send him home."

A heavy voice rose above the crowd. "The next train heading south leaves at nine o'clock tonight. Let's go after him. 'Tis no time for legal matters. You lawyers go home; we'll handle this. Men, get your horses!"

Matthew elbowed his way toward Ward. "Samuel! I've a packet here for you from Duncan."

The harried man turned. "Where are all you Underground Railroad men when we need you?"

Matthew handed him the packet. "Seems to me you're doing fine."

"One of these days there's going to be a battle. Not one little gunshot; every rifle is coming out, and there'll be war."

Matthew hesitated. "Are you talking about Oberlin or the whole country?"

Ward faced him soberly. "I was thinking about people—the deaths, the destruction. But you can't measure the cost of freedom. I suppose it's bound to happen. What I want to know is, where will it end?"

Matthew headed out of town, back the way he came. He was still mulling over the man's question and measuring it against his own hurt when he heard the shouts and thundering hooves behind him. The riders swooped down on him. "Freedom—ride for John's freedom."

For the one moment he hesitated, and at that moment his memory threw out the pictures, one by one. He saw Harriet Tubman's face, ebony black and stern, heard her voice ringing in his ears: "Death is better than slavery."

An old picture from out of his childhood showed a black woman lying in the dirt, her hands and feet spiked to the ground. She writhed while the bullwhip laid wet red slashes across her naked back. Matthew winced. That old picture refused to dim with age.

He saw the auction block: black arms reaching toward black arms, and being pulled away. He saw a tiny face with sorrowful eyes and swelling bruises.

Matthew dug in his heels. He reached Wellington on the tag end of the crowd. He could see the train waiting at the station, puffing slow clouds of steam into the air. The riders were pouring down the street. "The hotel!" came the shout. "They're holding him there."

He wheeled his horse down the street to join the crowd. On the top story, behind a lighted window, Matthew saw black arms and a glistening face pressed against the glass.

"Let my people go, let my people go." The chant changed to a song. " 'My Lord's writing all the time, Oh, He sees all you do, He hears all you say. My Lord's writing all the time.' "

"Give us a hand." The murmur came in Matthew's ear. He turned and followed the man around the building, through the bushes.

" 'My Lord's writing all the time . . .' " The words faded away, but the rhythm throbbed in the air.

In the thick woods behind the hotel, he faced the dark shadows, heard the murmured voice again, "Our men are chasing the bounty hunters across the river. There's one guard upstairs stuck in front of that door. He has a mean look besides a gun. He doesn't know, but he's a-guarding an empty trap."

"I saw—" Matthew began.

Firm fingers pressed. "He's a free man. In the dark those people don't know. Neither does his guard. John's over here. Ward said you'd escort him to the promised land."

Dark shadows moved, Matthew heard a gentle nicker; then a warm, dark hand reached for him. Emotion flooded through Matthew's voice. "My friend, come along; you're safe now. At least as long as I'm alive, you're safe. Here we come, promised land."

A week later Matthew returned from Canada. Picking up his horse in Oberlin, he rode back the way he came. When he crossed the Pennsylvania line, he headed down to the farm on the shore of the Ohio River. It was late afternoon when he dropped his mount at the stable. Shouldering his pack he headed for the wharf. And all the time he kept his eyes carefully turned away from the big house up the hill.

"Matthew, Matthew Thomas! Wait for me." He turned to watch the woman striding purposefully toward him. Her long calico skirt twisted around her ankles as she cut through the stubble of the cornfield. When she stopped in front of him, her flashing blue eyes were on a level with his.

Giving her a twisted grin, he said, "Well, I can guess who you've been talking to."

He watched her shove at hair the color of corn silk as she said, "You're right. I've just been talking to your wife."

"Amelia, I'll tell you for the last time, keep yourself out of the quarrel. I've made up my mind, and I'll brook no interference from you."

"Matthew, you can't be serious! People don't just tear apart lives with so little reason."

"Amelia, cut it out! You've stuck your nose in my affairs just one time too many."

"For the sake of all that's holy, Matthew—"

He laughed cynically. "You're a fine one to be talking about holiness. Amelia, you'd make a mighty poor Sunday-school teacher. I don't feel any need to listen to your arguments. What's done is done."

He saw the defeat in her eyes as she whispered, "Don't be a fool; don't throw your life away—as I did." He could see she was waiting for a response. He gave her a twisted grin. With a sigh she asked, "What will you do?"

"It's home for me." He swung the sailor's bag over his shoulder and said, "I've played this game for too long. I'm going home to act out the part of my father's son. Does that answer your question?"

"Making all of this a lie, a sham. Matthew, what a step down you are taking! You've been moving slaves over the Underground Railroad; that's a life-or-death situation even for a white man. Now you say you're going back to the plantation, back to watch these people live out their lives in bondage."

He wiped his hand across his face, suddenly bone-weary. "You may say that, but you've little idea of what's going on in my heart. I feel as if I'm being torn into two different men." His voice had brooded over the words; now he looked directly at her and said, "I'll never forget this place, but—"

Following him down to the wharf, she gave a nod at the riverboat anchored in the middle of the channel. "Sweet Chariot," she mocked, "comin' for to carry me home."

Without a backward glance, he stepped into the rowboat and

pushed off. Dipping the oars into the river, he headed toward the steamboat waiting beyond the sand bar. The sun caught fire from the brass nameplate on the dark polished wood. "*Golden Awl,*" he murmured, "the caboose on the Underground Railroad. Are you surrounded by angels, or will this trip mean the end for you? But God help me! My stomach will take no more. I've seen the last slave chained and mutilated. Maybe home will blot the memories."

Matthew pulled himself up the rope ladder and faced Clancy. "You skipper this trip?"

"Aye. Duncan's gone north." Mike Clancy looked over the boat railing. "Stewart will be taking the rowboat back. All your gear aboard?"

Matthew faced the question in the man's eyes and hesitated. "Yes," he said slowly, "and I guess you've heard of the trouble. I won't be coming back with you."

Mike tipped his cap and turned. "Gotta go build up a head of steam if we get outta here tonight." He added, "Way things have been going lately, it'll be the Lord's grace if any of us make it back."

Matthew paused to look out over the river, and to the house up the hill. He could see light in the windows. With a sigh he forced himself to look west. The clouds had been mounting all afternoon; it was no wonder this September evening darkness fell abruptly.

The moon was but a hazy circle in the sky. With one last glance up the hill, Matthew carried his gear to the small cabin in the bow of the riverboat.

Back on deck he went to help Clancy. The man looked at him. "So you're going home?"

"Back the way I came. Clancy, I'm going home for good. I don't suppose you'll understand this. See, a person can get twisted in his thinking until nothing seems right."

The man slanted a shrewd glance at him. "Too many doin' your thinking for you? Been there myself. I guess a man's got to own his thoughts. Matters not how good or bad; they gotta be his property."

Matthew turned and leaned over the rail, watching the foggy moon rise over the Ohio River. "For better or worse, this decision is mine," he muttered to himself. "And I will have to live with it forever."

CHAPTER 2

The cheval mirror caught the bright Mississippi sun, throwing a bar of intensified light at the marble fireplace and bits of crystal lined along the cherry wood mantel. Struggling into the brocade jacket, Matthew stepped up to the mirror to adjust his cummerbund. He heard the timid tap on the door, and called, "That you, Coly? Come."

"Oh, Massa Thomas, didn't know you were dressin'; I just come to tidy up." Coly's dark arms cradled a pile of snowy linen. As with all the house slaves, Coly's head was topped by a white cap. Its starched frill nearly hid her dark eyes.

He turned as she said, "Beautiful you are. Those fancy clothes for tramping in the barn?" There were troubled shadows in her eyes. Thinking of the many times during the past year when he had brushed aside her timid questions, he shook his head slowly.

Coly carried the linens to the bench under the window and then came back to the mirror, her hands resting on her bony hips. "Like an angel of light you are. That pretty brocade and the blue sets off the white right well. You partying in the middle of the day?"

"No. Coly, why don't you wait until tomorrow to change the

bed linens? No sense doing it twice." Seeing her quick glance, he added, "I need to see Father. Most likely I won't be here after tomorrow."

Trying to read the dark expression in her eyes, he saw something like mingled sorrow and excitement on her face. "You going up the river like last time?" she asked.

Matthew hesitated as he wondered about the conjectures going on in the slave's quarters. Stalling for time, he crossed the room to look out the window. Finally he answered, "Coly, you and I both know there's been a heap of questions floating around. I suppose now is the time to answer them."

"Massa, I don't know if the others—"

"Don't worry, Coly. I'm not going to report the talk to Mother. Let's be honest. You've practically raised Olivia and me. Seems you deserve to know some of the details. And I have an idea you have a few things to tell me."

Her dark eyes were watchful as Matthew continued. "I know my ugly disposition's scared you off for the past year. Sorry, Coly, but I've had some thinking to do. Don't know that I've made any decisions, but I do know which things are pushing me into the corner. If I don't kick out at them now, I'll be in a position where I can't be anything except a calf in a halter."

She still hesitated. Matthew prompted, "You ask the questions."

"Well," the black woman began, "ever'body knows you and Missy ran away with that fella with the boat. We knows why. And we knows it about killed your mother. Like a ghost she was. A proud lady like that cain't live with that distress."

"Coly, I did what I had to do, but I won't listen to your accusations where Mother is concerned. Shall we just leave it all as it stands?"

"Massa! Mississippi's outta the Union now, huh?" Her defense was down, and he saw the terror in her eyes. "We gotta know. Is there goin' be war?"

"How can it be otherwise? Lincoln is too strong to be manipulated the way Buchanan was."

She wilted for a moment, then whispered, "They said you went off to work the Underground Railroad."

"We did. Need I tell you we were headstrong youths running after more excitement?"

"No, Massa, we figured such. We heared you both got married, and that was something your mother didn't like."

"Well, with Olivia—I think Mother was relieved to know Duncan made an honest woman out of her. And me?" His grin was twisted. "She didn't like her little boy growing up. Childish pranks? Well, you know she says 'boys will be boys.' But when it came to marriage—no girl would be good enough." He added bitterly, "She was glad the marriage fell apart."

Softly Coly said, "Them shadows I see, Mr. Matthew—you ain't happy."

"No. That's one reason I've got to go. I aim to make it right, if that's possible."

"Shouldn't be hard." Her affectionate grin was wide.

Shaking his head, Matthew muttered, "You don't know the half; it's nearly impossible."

She waited. Finally she whispered, "The good Lord hears us. Now we pray for it to come together." In a moment she added, "You still in the railroad business?"

"No. It's a difficult situation," he said slowly. "There's good and bad in it, Coly. My mind's in a muddle. I've been listening to many voices. Some say Lincoln's the answer. Some say he isn't. Some say matters have gone from bad to worse. The only thing I know for certain is the whole South has come out of the cage like a tiger, and I'm left wondering which corner I'm in."

He started for the door and turned. "Coly, no matter what happens from now on, nothing's going to be easy for anyone."

There was one last plea in her eyes. She whispered, "You don't think President Lincoln will set us free?"

"He says he won't. The war talk says fighting will be to preserve the Union. And they think it will be a brief battle. I'm thinking that's wrong." He closed the door behind himself and walked toward the stairs.

At the head of the stairs, Matthew paused to admire the gentle curve of polished mahogany spiraling down into the main hall. For a moment nostalgia for the quiet, peaceful years swept over him and he shook his head sadly.

Where the stairway turned, a mirror curved into the wall. Looking toward the mirror with a twisted smile, Matthew mimicked his mother's softly accented voice with a line he'd heard since childhood. "It's of the finest diamond dust. Note the carving. A French dealer found it for me. Supposedly it once reposed in Marie Antoinette's villa—on the Riviera, or some such place."

Matthew's smile was still twisted as he started down the stairs. With another dozen steps, he knew he would face his reflection in that mirror. Now he saw the dim image of polished boots and spotless white trousers. The cummerbund came into view. It had been pure impulse, but it set off the brocade smoking jacket nicely. He paused. Only his youthful thatch of unruly brown curls ruined the dignity of the picture. He met his own mocking smile and saluted smartly. "Good practice," he murmured. "I have a feeling it'll be needed, sooner or later."

He took the last of the steps in a boyish leap. Across the hall the library door was closed. For a moment he chewed his lip, feeling like a guilty schoolboy again.

"Son, come in." The voice was quiet and controlled. That was encouraging. He opened the door and saw his father's eyebrows arch slightly as he took in the glory of Matthew's clothing. "You have an appointment?"

"No, I was coming down to see you." His father came from behind the desk and slowly removed his spectacles, waiting expectantly. Matthew said, "I believe it's about time we have a serious talk, Father. I've been home for over a year. You and I both know it just isn't working out."

"Has it ever? Since law school you've been a stranger in your own home. Matthew, you know Harvard was for the intention of preparing you to take over the plantation. As my heir, Shady Oaks is not only your heritage, but also your responsibility."

As his father spoke, Matthew had the sensation that his words were spilling past a year of restraint. "It has always been my intention that the traditional values of our lives pass on down through the generations. As my father did, I've left the plantation better than I found it."

He paced the room and faced Matthew again. "We've more land, and even our tenant farmers are more dedicated to our values. The soil is better, the cotton yield is one of the best in the whole state. When this political mess is straightened out, I fully expect to realize an unprecedented demand for our cotton."

"Political mess?" Matthew questioned. Feeling like a stranger, separated from his father, viewing objectively the scene in front of him, Matthew watched the old white-haired plantation lord move stiffly to the fireplace.

Even a stranger could see that Cornelius Thomas and his wife Sally Ann were of the old school. Matthew glanced at leather books lettered in gold, silver decanters and crystal goblets, paintings bearing proud signatures, oriental carpets, and velvet draperies shutting out the view of the black people who had made this life possible.

For one moment the room overlapped with the vision of black people marching through the night—silently, fearfully intent on the North Star in front of them.

Matthew faced his father. Studying the watchful, lined face surrounded with white hair, he felt a rush of sympathy. *How could they be expected to think and act apart from the beliefs that had seen them through the past half century? They have put their minds in a box. For them, there is no other way to regard life.*

Matthew continued to wonder at his detachment as the store of thoughts garnered in his mind began to demand a hearing. "Cornelius Thomas, plantation owner and country gentleman. How could you raise a son like me?" His voice gentled. "By rights you should be able to depend upon seed of your seed. Father, what has gone wrong?"

Cornelius's voice was tired as he slowly said, "It's these times."

"Slavery versus states rights, the Constitution and the abolitionists, even John Brown and the South Carolina breed?" Matthew sighed and shook his head miserably. "Not the times. And I'm guessing you knew this would be the result when Olivia and I rebelled and ran away from everything that you hold dear."

"Actually, I hoped you two would tire of your adventure and come home. I see the events of these past months have made it impossible for your sister to return. I suppose I'm just grateful she married." Matthew winced and his father added, "After watching you, I am beginning to fear you haven't really changed your ideas."

"Since Major Anderson holed in at Fort Sumter, we've all known there's no backing out of the situation," Matthew brooded aloud.

"I wish to God I could take back some of the past!" The words burst from the old man.

Astonished, Matthew looked at him, and when he saw his father's eyes, a sympathy unknown to Matthew gentled his voice. "Are you referring to your part in the Democratic convention in Charleston? Father, we all know the stink. It was foul from the beginning; an underhanded attempt at coercion to gain political advantage. How could it result in anything good?" He saw the bright spots of color on his father's cheeks and stopped.

Cornelius straightened. Coldly he said, "Son, there's no sense in going back over it. I know your law education has given you an insight I lack, but the convention—it's over."

"I never could figure out why you delegates thought the election of a Republican would solve problems. It simply brought Senator Douglas down on you." Matthew tried to keep his voice calm.

"And now, with Lincoln as president—if he isn't shot first—" Matthew winced, and for a moment his father hesitated. "Son, it's wild talk, but possible."

"Everything has gone wild."

"Is that why it's all soured with you? Matthew, I had hopes when you came back, full of that talk about doing your duty to family and the South. I thought I had my son back; now I wonder."

"Father, I wonder too. For a time I thought I'd gotten my head on straight; now I don't know."

"What happened there in Pennsylvania to change your mind?"

For a moment Matthew froze. When he relaxed and shoved his hands into his pockets, he said, "It wasn't just one incident. I suppose it was a culmination of many." He faced his father.

"For one thing, I was surprised by the emotional climate up

North. For years we've been hearing that the only civilized people in the United States were all in the South. That's not so. I met gentle people who really cared about others. Surprisingly, I found some of the abolitionists seeing our way. They're in favor of separation. They think the only way we'll settle the problem is to split the Union."

"What else influenced you?"

Matthew paced the room. "You know about my marriage going bad. I suppose that was the key thing pushing me into making a decision."

"About what?"

Matthew took a deep breath. "I've told you one of my schoolmates had been putting the pressure on me. He'd seen the handwriting on the wall and he let me have a full dose of responsibility to home and the South—let me know that if this whole problem escalated into war, well, I'd be needed here and I'd better get back home while I could." Bitterly he added, "He filled me full of the horror stories about the North using me and my money to further their cause. It was enough to make me feel like a rotter. Now I regard his talk as nonsense."

Cornelius walked back to the desk. He placed his spectacles on his nose and shuffled among the papers on his desk. "On the contrary, he sounds like a level-headed young man. Of course he was right to make you aware of your responsibilities. Son, I understand your feelings more than you realize. Even taking off for the North on your self-righteous errand of mercy, although I can't say I appreciate your dragging off some of my most valuable slaves. You know—" Abruptly he closed his mouth and sat down.

Gently Matthew said, "Thank you, Father. Of course, you know we're still poles apart on the issue, and that I haven't changed. There's absolutely no way we can agree on the issue of helping the slaves escape to Canada."

His face twisted in a grin. "Look at it this way. Since I'm your heir, it all boils down to the fact I was throwing my own money away!"

Cornelius's face reddened and his anger rumbled through his words. "I'm not dead yet! But you're right—we can't agree. Now, come here and listen to this."

He waited until Matthew sat down across the desk from him before he reached for the newspaper. "Just snatches I'll read. It's from the *Pleasant Hill* newspaper. This is a copy of the speech intended for the governor of Maryland. When he refused to listen, it was delivered to the citizens of Baltimore, on the evening of December 9th, just last month. And it was one month after Lincoln was elected President of the United States.

"The gentleman, a Mississippi commissioner, says, 'Secession is not intended to break up the present government, but to perpetuate it.' Matt, this fellow says our going out of the Union is only for the time it will take us to win our rights. We must have slavery or our economy will collapse." Cornelius pounded the desk to emphasize his words. He rattled the paper and continued, "He said the country has been agitated by the question of slavery for the past twenty or thirty years. That's so, but at the time the Constitution was written, the South tried to gain their just recognition as being in favor of slavery. You know, Matthew, the Bible supports slavery. Under God, we are living as responsible Christian people."

"Father!"

"Now, hear me out, son. The Commissioner says the plan is for the southern states to withdraw from the Union for a time. If the Union wants us badly enough, they'll give us the rights we are entitled to—namely the freedom to have slavery."

"Father, you have it here in this state! But you have to consider that the expansion of slavery to every territory and state is against the wishes of the nation at large. In addition, it is contrary to the Constitution we have sworn to uphold."

"What do you mean? We don't have freedom until we are free to take our property into every part of the nation without the threat of having that property taken away from us." He rattled the paper again. "Not a one of us really wants separation. But it may be necessary. Like a wounded soldier, sometimes it takes amputation to heal."

Matthew got to his feet and paced the room. "Any red-blooded man would go to great lengths to avoid an amputation. But I agree that perhaps secession is necessary. For good; not as a temporary measure."

"It breaks my heart, but—" The door to the hallway creaked open. Matthew turned as his mother came into the room.

Smiling and nodding her crown of white curls, she pointed to the table before the fire. "Jacob, place the tray there. Cornelius, all this serious discussion demands a little refreshment. Too bad we're not more in the mode of the English, with their afternoon tea. Hottentots we are. But nevertheless, I've brought you some blackberry wine to sustain you both."

"Sally Ann," Cornelius protested as he got to his feet, "you know I don't like those cloying sweet wines. My dear, sit down; at least you'll enjoy the stuff. I'll break out the brandy."

"Now, Cornelius, you know Pastor has been preaching against the evils of hard liquor. For the sake of the boy—"

"Mother, I think I'm already too corrupt to be tainted by Father's indulgences. Please, have a seat."

Cornelius nodded at Jacob and Matthew went to sit beside his mother. "Matthew, I am deeply disturbed by all this. I couldn't help hearing that argumentative note in your voice. Now, my dear, let's talk about this like civilized people." She paused, and Matthew forced his attention to her words.

"You've been home from your mad wandering for over a year. We've watched you flit around without design. You've gone from overseer of the plantation to the position of attorney, which Mr. Hanagan was so gracious to give you—and by the way, you've your father to thank for putting in a word."

"Yes, Mother, but I flitted into that contrived job as overseer of the plantation by displacing the longtime employee who, by the way, had to station himself at my elbow in order to keep the whole plantation from falling apart. Mother, please!"

She dabbed at the tears on her cheeks and added, "Matthew, you know we want more than anything else to make you happy. Unfortunately, we've managed to have the most headstrong children in the whole parish. I've long given up on the hope of having my daughter close to home. How I would love to raise my grandchildren! But then, her disastrous marriage will probably never produce grandchildren."

"Disastrous? Well, I don't think the pair in question feel that way about it. I think Duncan is just what Olivia needs; they appear happy."

Matthew paused to chuckle and shake his head. "You were right in calling us headstrong. But, Mother, it was Olivia who always had the good ideas; I just tagged along."

"Was that the reason for all this?"

"Sally Ann, it takes sons longer to grow up. Let the boy be. At some point he's going to have to make up his own mind and learn to live with the consequences of his actions."

Slowly Matthew got to his feet. "Mother, Father, that's exactly why I came down here. I wanted to tell Father what I've been thinking. It is time for this fella to begin making decisions and sticking with them."

"Matthew," protested his mother, "the decisions you've made, I'm just grateful you haven't stuck to them. Take for instance—"

"My marriage? That is the principal reason I wanted to talk to Father. It's taken a lot of pondering, but now I'm certain, I want—"

"A divorce? Of course, Matthew." She touched his hand and looked into his face. "I've talked to Pastor about that. No reason, in this day and age, that it can't be arranged speedily."

"Mother." Matthew tried to calm himself with a deep breath. For one moment he waited, and the sureness of his decision made him grin. "I'll not bore you with the details of my marriage, but I am absolutely certain that if I can possibly convince my wife I still love her, and if she will have me back—well, that's what I want."

"Son," Cornelius said softly, "we want your happiness, but I think it will be best for you to wait until all this is over."

Matthew faced him. For a moment he was silent. Slowly he said, "Sir, deep down you really do expect this action of secession to escalate into war, don't you? I'd guessed that was the mindset of the South. But then, I suppose I agree that's the only possible solution."

"I don't see how it can be avoided. Son, we—the South—need you desperately."

"It won't take long," Sally Ann said brightly, "and then you can get your bride and bring her home."

"Mother, Father, you don't understand this whole situation. My wife is Creole, and I know that offended you. But you have not yet begun to be offended. You see, her father was a slave, sired by his master!"

The next day Matthew left the house at dawn. The January mists were still heavy and cold in the Mississippi valley. Just a few degrees from freezing, they lay like spun cotton close to the ground. From the distant river came the monotonous toot of boats, weaving a melancholy farewell through Matthew's mind, and that message made him shiver.

He threw one last glance at the dark, silent house. His heavy heart echoed the forlorn message of the riverboat whistles, and he tried to remind himself that the dawn would bring hope. He turned his mare and headed down the trace toward Natchez.

It was midmorning when he reached the city. On the bluff overlooking the water, he studied the line of fashionable inns and businesses with a shudder. His heart was still sore from the final conversation with his parents, and he found the city held too many memories. For Matthew, even his growling stomach made the risk of meeting an acquaintance at the inn out of the question.

He dug his heels in the mare's sides and turned down the lane to the shacks bordering the edge of town. There the prostitutes and river thugs would present unfamiliar faces.

At a smelly gray shack, Matthew ordered his breakfast and settled back with a mug of coffee to warm his chilled hands.

An old man with a toothless grin sidled into the shack and sat down beside Matthew. "Got some nice wine I'll share with you for the price of victuals."

"Not interested, old dad, but I'll buy you some breakfast." Matthew waved to the barmaid.

"Where you be off to?" his guest asked.

While Matthew hesitated, another man came into the shack. "Busy place, Tillie," he addressed the woman. Matthew eyed the coarse woolen jacket and greasy cap as the fellow nodded and sat down at the table. "Looks like you're traveling," he said to Matthew. "I suppose you've passed the last kisses around at home and are heading for the Army."

"Army? So it's getting that bad?"

The toothless wino dug into his breakfast and spoke around his mouthful. "It's that Mr. Lincoln. Brung us all into war. Best thing the country could get is fer him to stop a shot."

"Don't blame Lincoln for the troubles," Matthew said heavily. "I saw the newspapers. His platform states he's for free soil in the territories and noninterference with slavery. What more can you ask of a fellow? Seems to me we ought to give the man a chance." Matthew slanted a glance at the burly fellow at the end of the table. "I don't go along with this jumping the gun on the man and getting all hotheaded when there's no reason."

The fellow turned and rested his arms on the table. "Seems fer a man that looks like he has a lick of sense and a bit of book learning, you're just a bit too free with your opinion. I say Lincoln stinks and I back my friend here."

"Mister, you've a right to your ideas," Matthew said through tight lips, "but so do I. I say give the man a chance. Might even be that he can teach us a few good things if we give him a following. I hear he's not the least namby-pamby, and that counts with me. If we go pushing out front with the idea of fighting, I have a feeling we'll get set back on our heels."

The stranger hunkered into his coat and quickly finished his breakfast. When Matthew finally detached himself from the bleary-eyed talker, the sun was pushing toward noon.

Turning down the alleyway to his mare, Matthew nearly collided with two men ranged on either side of his skittish mount. He stopped and studied the pair. "Well, fellow," he addressed his breakfast companion, "so we meet again. Admiring my mare?"

"No, waiting for you." There was a click. The fellow grinned and waved his knife. "We take exception to your talk about Lincoln, but we're inclined to give you a chance to repent. Don't like cutting up a lad, especially one who's going to be a first-rate soldier in the Confederate Army. I'm Lieutenant Clark; this here is Sergeant Adams. Like I said, welcome to the Confederate Army. That is, unless you'd rather be cut up a mite and dumped into the river."

He waited until Matthew nodded. "Come along, then—we're headed for Texas."

CHAPTER 3

M atthew Thomas! Old buddy, I'll be whipped for a nigger if
I'm mistaken." The ocean of gray uniforms around Matthew shifted slightly. A few curious faces turned toward him as Matthew wilted into his uniform and allowed his gray cap to slip forward on his nose. With the supply wagon still in front of them, the crowd surrounded him, carrying him forward. Even as they shifted and passed around him as they pressed for the supply wagon, the call came again. "Matt!"

Matthew shoved his cap back and looked at the escape route opening in front of him. He considered, then muttered, "There's no escape in an army camp. Better face the music." With a sigh he turned.

The gray crowd rippled and Matthew watched the cap swim against the current. Coarse, reddened features backed by steel-gray eyes surfaced in front of him. "Herm Wadle," Matthew said slowly. His guess had been correct. The voice hadn't changed; neither had the hungry, cunning eyes. The crowd carried them along, pressing too close for a handshake.

Herm gestured with his chin. "Let's get away from the supply wagon. They ain't got nothing. No letters this trip. Newspapers are long gone. Didn't say nothing anyway. News travels faster on the wind." He paused for a chuckle.

He studied Matthew carefully with questioning eyes as he said, "We oughta know all about that. Our esteemed President Lincoln was elected on November 6 and by the 7th, everybody in the country knew it. 'Twas nearly that fast when we found out our gang fired on Fort Sumter," he crowed. His thick shoulders shoved an opening in the advancing pack of soldiers. He edged in front of Matthew, eyed him and said, "Long time no see. Heard you'd come home."

The crowd thinned and Matthew led the way to the one spot of shade on the riverbank. Overhead the oaks twined their branches, creating an oasis of muggy shadow. It was only slightly cooler than the sun-baked parade ground, but they had escaped the clamor of the troops.

Herm shoved his cap back and asked, "How long you been here, old buddy?"

"Since February. Just after Texas seceded from the Union."

"So you didn't get in on the big battle to take over the Union forts."

He was still chuckling as Matthew said, "Guess that was the whole idea of our being shipped this direction. All the way over we were being pressed with battle plans. Our captain had it all laid out. First we were to head north to Fort Arbuckle and seize it in the name of the Confederacy. Got there and found out they were more'n willing to hand it over and go along with secession. Next we headed for Fort Wichita, just over the hill and a little northwest. They were mighty glad to join up, too. We marched here to Fort Lancaster."

Herm nodded, "Same here. I understand they're startin' to move regiments out. Sending them back across the river. I figured on being sent too, but for some reason—"

His voice trailed away as he studied Matthew with a puzzled frown. "What's next?"

"Just rumors. Heard we might be going to Fort Bliss." As Matthew lifted his cap to mop away the perspiration, he met Herman's amused grin.

"Hard life fer a fella like you," Herm drawled. "Now, us poor whites cut our teeth in the middle of the cornfields, gnawing on wormy cobs—"

"Cut it out," Matthew said roughly. "I'm sick of hearing about how tough you've had it. It's all I've been fed since I joined the Army the end of January."

"Give me a chance to ask you why ya didn't come around waving banknotes and offerin' to give me the privilege of taking yer place in front of the line—fer an honest price, of course, the going rate."

Matthew resisted the urge to push his shoulders straight as he looked up at the loose-featured lad. Despite the uniform, the familiar lock of hair still hung in his eyes. Softly he said, "Herm, seems impossible time's gone so fast. Was it more'n yesterday we hunted squirrel and 'possums on the trace?"

Ruefully Herm nodded. " 'Twas a sight more fun pretending to be river pirates running away from the law than totin' guns across Texas now." He stopped to grin before adding, "We're kinda forced to keep on with the game here, even when we're tired of it."

The two men were silent, lost in their separate reveries. Matthew's thoughts were filled with the gentle memories of plantation life. Back then, the days Herm had referred to, the most arduous tasks Matthew had known were grooming his horse and keeping the setter's hair free from burrs. Glancing at Herm's sober face, he guessed the memories his boyhood companion was having.

For the Wadle family, home was a weathered gray shack that scarcely blocked the path of wind-driven rain sweeping through the Mississippi valley. They were called the poor whites back then. In those days the rich river bottoms were prized by the tenant farmers. But more often than not, the small farms were scratched out of the sections deemed worthless by the plantation owners.

Matthew reflected on the poor living the small plot of land provided the Wadle family as they struggled to support themselves and their children.

As he studied Herm's weathered face, he saw that time had stamped a new cast to his features. It seemed, since their young days, the carefree expression on his friend's face had grown into a mask of defeat. What had happened in his life to mark out a permanent cynical twist on his face?

In the moment Matthew found himself wondering, he was ashamed. Somehow it seemed he had stepped across forbidden boundaries. He could nearly hear his mother's gentle voice reprimanding him for asking the prying personal questions. *Matthew, one must not ask. We take care of our people. However, there are limits. You mustn't forget you are a gentleman. Some will take advantage of your position.*

Matthew spoke huskily. "Herm, you know I look back on the times I spent with your family as being special. I remember your mother always had a word for me. And chitlins or dried apples. Back then us young'uns always seemed to have time for fishing. I must admit the schoolhouse down the hollow looked like the greatest of fun."

"With a teacher who couldn't hardly write her name and didn't know sums?" While Herm questioned, Matthew saw the sharpness in his eyes had been replaced by shadows.

When Matthew turned to go, Herm said, "I heard tell most nearly all the foot soldiers are poor boys. It's the plantation sons who are officers." He paused again. "Most paid out to have us fellas take their place. How come you didn't?"

Matthew shrugged. How could he explain that the words he had poured out in defense of President Lincoln had been responsible for his abrupt induction into the Confederate Army? And that some inner code of conduct that he didn't quite understand made him more comfortable with being a soldier than an officer?

But the man's question had plunged him back into the differences. Looking into the gray eyes, he knew Herm wouldn't understand. For him life was simple, a matter of money and land and pigs.

They parted and Matthew walked slowly back to his regiment. He was still thinking of the differences and was uneasy. He muttered, "What is it in me that demands more than land and pigs? There's a great deal to be said for the simple life, one circumscribed like Herm's, by acreage and stock."

"Sergeant Thomas?" The clipped words were delivered in the direction of Matthew's left ear. They were sharp with distaste and impatience, and he knew the reason.

He turned with a salute. "Colonel Peters?" The man's eyes narrowed with the same old questions, and Matthew met the look by setting his face in expressionless lines. He waited.

"You will stand guard last watch." He waited for Matthew's question while his mouth slowly twisted down in scorn.

Matthew offered a small smile and nodded, "Yes, sir."

The man's curiosity surfaced. "I cannot understand why a Harvard educated gentleman would choose to be aligned with tenant farmers and jailbirds when he could be commissioned with honor— or could he?" Before Matthew could formulate a reply, Colonel Peters added, "Seems a design for suicide, so honorably cast as to appear as martyrdom."

"That's right, sir." Matthew watched the man turn away with a snort of exasperation.

He grinned at the fellow standing in the tent opening, who said, "If yer thinking up ways to get the colonel's goat, you've dun it."

Matthew squinted up at the youth. "Tim, what he doesn't know yet is that colonels get shot, too."

Tim nodded. "Guess you heard we're moving out. That boat ride down the Mississippi was the nicest part of army life. Rumor has it we'll be heading out in a day or so. Going to join Baylor at Fort Bliss. It's going to be action for us, and they ain't telling us what or where. Matthew, did you hear of any fighting goin' on in Texas?" Matthew shook his head. As Tim turned away, Matthew saw the white line around his mouth.

"Tim, I don't think you like the idea of fighting any better than I do."

"I don't. But they were saying back home that the best way to get this job done is to push as hard as we can. Only thing I can't understand is what we're doing in this end of the country. I expected to be sent east."

Matthew shrugged, "I don't know, but I had heard we were coming this way. Don't know that I had much choice, but I am mighty glad to be heading west."

"How come?"

Matthew hesitated. Speaking carefully, he said, "I've been wanting to see the country for some time. Might want to settle here when it's all over—the war." He paused, adding, "It seems our movements are being kept quiet."

Tim was still watching him with that strange expression when Matthew went after his mess kit. The sun was setting, and the muggy heat began to ease. As evening quiet moved through the camp, supper fires mingled their smoke with the mists rising from the river.

While he worked preparing his meal, Matthew became conscious of the sounds unheard during daylight hours. There was the distant clink of metal coming from the corrals. Matthew recognized it as the sound of horses' harnesses backed by the music of Spanish spurs.

The river whispered past, nearly hidden by the counter melody of dipping oars and the clunk of rafts loaded with hogsheads gently drumming against each other.

Matthew finished his meal and carried his pan and coffeepot down to the river. The cooking fires burned low. He watched soldiers surround the rings of fire like gray boulders, silent and unmoving. The picture of apathy caught at him as he stepped away from the circle of light.

Between Matthew and the river the larger tents of the officers had been pitched. Tonight their flaps were up to catch the evening breezes, while smudge fires smoldered out their smoky threat to the mosquitoes.

Cutting behind the tents to avoid the smoke, Matthew pushed into the tangle of bushes. He had nearly reached the river when his boots crunched on a rotten piece of wood. He heard the crack of wood, but his attention was on the dark spot that suddenly set the bushes to dancing.

Reaching for his knife, Matthew moved sideways, peering into the shadows. "Please, Massa, don't! I's just getting scraps they threw out," the voice murmured up from the bush beside Matthew's boots.

Sheathing his knife, he pulled the branches apart. Keeping his voice low, he asked, "Why are you doing that? Don't they feed you?"

The ebony shadow nodded. "I jest can't see food being wasted, there's always—" Matthew squatted down until his eyes were on a level with the black man's. He could see the man was trembling. Matthew touched him and the fellow pleaded, "Please, couldn't you just keep this secret?"

Matthew deliberately made his voice heavy with meaning as he said, "Aren't you the fellow who works for the colonel? I don't know many slaves as scared of a whipping." The man's head dropped, but he didn't answer. Matthew said, "Could it be there's more at stake?" The man's body jerked.

Slowly Matthew got to his feet. "Perhaps we'd better go see the colonel. You're Amos? You know there's talk—"

Amos dropped his head and Matthew waited. He heard the desperation in the man's voice as he said, "Massa, possibly—you wait until morning to say such as you must?"

Matthew pushed. "So they can get away? Amos, it's strange to have a black man volunteer to cook for an army officer who's in this war to ruin your chances of freedom forever. How many are out there?" He felt the man wilt. Quickly Matthew said, "Go. If you're coming back, make it during the third watch." The man hesitated and Matthew added impatiently, "Get the food; I'll watch."

Slowly Amos went back to dig in the heap of garbage. For the first time in months, as Matthew stared at the black back, he prayed. *God, I can't avoid it, can I? I am tired, sick of all this, and it's just beginning. Is there ever a right way in a mess like this? I wish I knew.*

The man stood up beside him. His eyes were gleaming spots in the surrounding darkness. Wearily Matthew said, "Yes?"

"They's sick. I sure need some quinine."

"They? What are they doing in Texas?"

"Same as the others." Matthew stared at him, nearly daring him to say the words. "Following the star."

He sighed, "Come third watch; I'll have it."

"They's gotta go now." Without answering Matthew turned away. His lips twisted painfully as he headed for his tent. He visualized the horror on his mother's face if she were to know where her bottle of quinine was headed.

When he returned to the bushes, Matthew held out the bottle and then drew it back. "Better show me where they are." Amos hesitated, glancing at the bottle and then at Matthew. It was easy to guess his troubled thoughts, but Matthew waited.

When the dark shadow moved away, Matthew followed. His

tired mind still juggled the words the Negro had said. He badly wanted to ask their destination, to warn them how impossible it was to go in wartime.

Down around the embankment, in the moist, spongy ground, there was a cave. Matthew saw the line of bright eyes watching him. "No wonder you need quinine," he muttered. Crouching down in their midst he said, "You gotta stay away from the river as much as possible. How you going to cross the Mississippi?"

Amos answered, "Won't until it's little enough to hop."

"So you're going straight north. I'd heard of the route."

A voice spoke out of the shadows. "You know Duncan?"

"He's my brother-in-law. What do you know about him?"

"Word gets around. Ain't none of us who don't know the names of those to trust."

Matthew spoke hesitantly, nearly afraid of his words. "It's a long way, no matter which route you take. Best you head for Minnesota, but that means a hard walk. I can give you names, but with the fighting going on, I don't know what the situation will be." He paused, adding, "In wartime, they shoot." In the silence Matthew addressed the man who seemed to be the leader. "You read?"

"Yes, sir."

"Here's a paper with names and directions on it." He turned away, then paused. "Go with God." As Matthew slipped away into the darkness, he heard the faint shuffling of movement behind him. *They will escape*, he thought. *But I can never escape the horrors of this war—or my part in it.*

CHAPTER 4

L ike fleas on a shaggy dog's back," Matthew muttered. From his vantage point astride his horse, it seemed the troops were spread all across Texas.

Since leaving Fort Lancaster, they had been steadily heading northwest. Day after day they rode, crossing the lowlands, green and rich with farms and forest, before moving into the high arid desert.

Matthew watched the brown cloud of dust hanging over their route and shouted to the man beside him, "Nothing like I've ever seen before. With all the soil so poor it floats in the air, I doubt it's worth fighting for."

The fellow grumbled, "When we get to Fort Bliss, you be sure you tell Baylor that. Well, at least we see the country."

Matthew settled back into his own thoughts. "Sergeant Thomas," the mocking voice addressed him. Matthew glanced up at the rider.

"Herm Wadle, did you get a promotion?"

"Naw, but I should. Any fella from Mississippi who can choke down his hardtack buttered with dust deserves being made general without delay."

"I'll recommend you for the promotion," Matthew grinned, adding, "I understand South Carolina could use a few good men right now."

"What you heard I ain't?"

Carefully Matthew closed his lips over his slanted view of the war news. He considered the man beside him and said, "Well, I suppose you've heard all about Fort Sumter, so that's old."

Herm drew his horse even with Matthew. "Bet I heard one you didn't." He leaned close. "Secretary of War, Floyd, and Secretary of the Navy, Toucey, did dirty deeds." He chuckled before he added, "Wonder who's behind it? Anyways, the gentlemen in question have been robbin' the North. Toucey stripped ever' vessel he could get his hands on. Those he didn't strip have just sailed right outta sight. Then Floyd's found to be emptying arms and ammunition outta the North. Heard Floyd took ever' arsenal he could get his hands on, and shipped the goods south."

Matthew looked at Herm's deliberately doleful expression and carefully bit his tongue. Recalling his last day in Mississippi made the hair on the back of Matthew's neck rise in alarm as he remembered the gleam of the knife in the hand of the ruffian in Natchez. "I guess they win some, lose some," he muttered with a shrug.

Herm rode off. Matthew watched him go and reflected on the wary look in the man's eyes. *So, maybe a friend isn't a friend, sometimes. And maybe the Confederate Army isn't comfortable with me.*

The troops continued across the state of Texas, mile after dry mile. The time rolled up to June, and Fort Bliss appeared on the horizon, as desert dry as San Antonio had been humid and green.

Here the Rio Grande River cut south through Texas, her course lined with greenery. From a distance even Matthew had to admit the river looked like a heaven-sent oasis. But on his first opportunity to view the river from its bank, Matthew studied its wide expanse of shallow muddy water and muttered, "That water's not deep enough to wet the hooves of my mare. How do they expect to run a fort off it?"

The soldier standing beside him said, "'Tis nearly July. You should see it in the spring. That's why the fort isn't built any closer."

Within a week of their arrival at Fort Bliss, the rumble of activity escalated into a stream of excitement. Matthew felt the excitement on the day he watched the activity on the parade ground. The news had spread. "Baylor's leading us into battle. We're marching north."

Matthew turned to see Tim, who had brought the news. "How much more north is there in Texas?" Matthew asked.

"Not a speck," the officer beside Tim said. "You wantin' to know what's going on? Baylor's called out the troops for three this afternoon. Be on the grounds and you'll hear all about it." He grinned at Matthew, carefully spit a stream of tobacco juice, and walked away.

That afternoon, with Herm on one side of him and Tim on the other, Matthew listened to Lieutenant Colonel Baylor outline his plans. Pacing the parade grounds with his hands clasped behind him, Baylor said, "We have reached the point of embarking on our principal objective. Our fort lies just south of the border of New Mexico Territory. In the name of the Confederacy, we will march straight north, claiming the federal forts as we go. I do not anticipate any great difficulty. New Mexico is known for its gentle people and divided loyalties. Men, no doubt by now you have surveyed your ranks and realize there are four hundred and fifty of us to take the territory.

"In the eyes of the New Mexicans, we will appear to be four hundred and fifty Goliaths. Now, this is the plan. We will march north and cross the mountains eastward to Fort Craig, which will be our principal target. We plan to occupy it immediately.

"There are several other insignificant forts lying in our path, namely Forts Breckinridge and Buchanan. Also Fort Fillmore. They will probably afford us a battle and we will approach cautiously. Men, prepare your arms. See to it that your mounts and your equipment are in the best condition possible. We will leave at daybreak." With a sharp salute from his first lieutenant, Baylor nodded and dismissed the troops.

On the first evening of their march, Herm settled back against his saddle and complained, "We got cheated. Them first two forts, Breckinridge and Buchanan, won't even fight. By the time we get there, even their dust will have settled."

"You're mighty eager to fight," Tim said as he stirred his mess over the meager fire.

"Could be," Herm muttered. "Could be the way I've been raised. Can't say the place is worth a fight; might be why they took off."

Tim slanted a glance at Matthew. "You on picket tonight?"

"No, I drew tomorrow night."

Tim was silent for a moment. He glanced at Herm and said, "Me too. I understand we'll be close to Fort Fillmore then. Might be a tricky watch."

Herm picked up his saddle and strolled away from the fire. With a troubled frown Tim watched him go. "That fellow bothers me. At the most unexpected times I find him underfoot, listening."

Matthew chuckled, "I don't think you need worry about Herm. He's too easygoing to be a talebearer."

"Might be you trust your fellowman more'n you ought," Tim said with a troubled glance at Matthew.

The New Mexico nights were warm and dry. That first night on the field, while the men spread their bedrolls on the bare ground, Herm complained, "What about the night critters? I hear these rattlesnakes like company at night."

"'Taint no worse than at home, 'cept water moccasins aren't fond of warm blankets," came the amused voice from across the fire pit.

During the night Matthew awakened to every movement of the picket's boots. Staring at the moon until sleep would come again, his imagination supplied pictures to go with tomorrow's plans. He tried to visualize pointing his rifle at a man, pulling the trigger.

Perspiration broke out on Matthew's face and he rolled over. Tim was watching him. He spoke softly. "They're saying we'll see action tomorrow, for sure."

"I hope the enemy is inclined to run," Matthew rumbled quietly, "I'm a pretty good shot with a rifle, and I don't like putting lead into a fellowman."

At noon the following day, when they stopped to water the horses and rest, Baylor addressed the group. "Men, we'll reach Fort Fillmore about the time they're blowing out the lamps. Here's my plan. We'll hold back until nightfall. Let 'em get into that first deep sleep, and then we can make camp."

Baylor's prediction was correct. When he called a halt late that afternoon, the setting sun pressed against the backs of the men, while the final rays touched the crude adobe fort on the eastern horizon.

He spoke softly. "We'll wait here. I'll call off the names of the men who'll handle the mounts; there's water and feed a mile behind us. After dark we'll move in closer. Then it's cold grub and sleep for all except the pickets. Meanwhile, Thomas and Daly, take up your watch. Get as close as possible and report back midway through first watch."

Matthew saluted and picked up his rifle. He headed up the slope with Tim behind him. From their position the land sloped downward, gently running toward the river bottom. Scrub cedar and piñon covered the rocky hills, affording suitable coverage for the troops.

Tim stopped beside him. "Matthew, let's work our way along that ridge; we should be close enough to spit in the river."

Matthew nodded and watched Tim load his rifle. They exchanged a glance and turned to move through the trees on the backside of the slope.

There was still light enough to see the details of the fort when Tim and Matthew picked their position and settled in to watch. The air was cooling rapidly and the night sounds became amplified. When they heard a call, Tim stood up and murmured, "Coming from the fort. Sounds to me like it's a woman. Sure enough—look, Matthew."

"I can see something that appears to be a bright skirt," Matthew murmured. Looking at Tim, he said, "Do you suppose there's families down there?"

Tim poked his arm. "Look at that." Leaning forward, the two watched the line of tiny figures streaming toward the bright patch. "Young'uns, sure as I live," Tim murmured.

"Sure is; the men must have their families with them," Matthew said slowly. "Tim, that's a real problem. Baylor's intention is to fire on a fort full of men too sleepy and befuddled to defend themselves."

He saw the sick expression in Tim's eyes. "Tim, let's hope to God that the commander of this post has his wits about him."

"Guess we'll know that come nightfall when the pickets are placed. What'll we do if there's only a sentinel?"

There was a crunch in the underbrush. Matthew slipped back

into cover and waited. Tim saw Colonel Baylor and stood up. "Sir!" Matthew stepped out and saluted.

Baylor demanded, "What's going on?"

"Not a thing, sir," Tim murmured. "There's families down below. We watched their mamas call them in. Seems—"

Hastily Matthew added, "The fort looks harmless. I'd imagine we could ask for surrender right now, without a shot being fired."

Baylor's jaw tightened. After a moment of silence, he answered with cold, level words, "We'll stick to our original plan. Just before daybreak we'll move in. This is too good to miss." He turned on his heel and left the hillside.

Slowly Tim said, "Matthew, you make a lousy soldier. Didn't they tell you that officers don't like enlisted men telling them how to run the war?"

"I wasn't thinking," Matthew muttered miserably. "It was those little tykes down there. Tim, it's bad enough to scare them, but the way Baylor has it figured out, someone's going to get hurt. It could be their mamas or papas. It could be them."

Roughly Tim said, "Sit down and eat your cold beans. We've a long night ahead."

The last cow had voiced her complaint and the only sound was from the peepers along the river. Matthew and Tim passed each other on their stealthy lap along the ridge. Tim murmured, "Close enough to pitch a stone in their dooryard."

"Might be a good idea. Right now seems something is necessary." Tim kept on his course around the ridge.

When they passed again, Tim said, "Can't alarm them. It's against orders. They shoot fellas for such in wartime."

On the next lap Matthew asked, "Do they shoot fellas for not pulling the trigger when there's a little child in his sights?"

Later Matthew said, "Not going to be moonlight much longer."

Tim turned. Roughly he said, "All right, let's go. Better stack the rifles here. And don't walk so fast; we have all night, nearly."

Matthew led the way, muttering, "See if you can spot the sentinel; we can talk to him."

"No, he'll shoot at these uniforms. But there he is." Tim pointed and for a moment they watched the leisurely pacing of the man with the rifle.

When he turned and paced to the far end of the adobe wall, Matthew said, "Now!" Quickly they passed through the open gates and pressed against the wall. A dog approached. He sniffed their boots and wagged his tail. Matthew sighed with relief. Leaning close to Tim, he said, "I'm heading for that cabin. You keep the dog happy."

Matthew pounded on the door, waited and pounded again. A thick voice answered and the door was pulled open. Quickly Matthew slipped through. "Sir, don't show a light. I'm wearing a Confederate uniform and it's imperative to keep quiet."

There was a muttered oath and the man's hand fastened around Matthew's arm. "Take it easy," Matthew murmured. "I'm with Colonel Baylor's regiment, up from Fort Bliss. We've been watching you since sundown. His plan is to attack at daybreak. Now you know, let me and my buddy get back up the hill. We'll hold our fire until you're out in force."

The shadowy form rumbled, "How do I know this isn't a trick?"

"I guess you have to trust me. Think of any reason I'd warn you this way?"

In a moment the man released Matthew's arm. "Guess I'm not premature in thanking you. How'd you get past the sentinel?"

"Walked. He doesn't know we're here. My buddy is keeping the dog company."

The man sighed. "Think you can get out the same way?"

"Yes. That's necessary if we're to make it back up the hill before the fireworks start."

The rumble came again. "You're on your own, buddy. Hope you make it."

The dog had tired of Tim's presence. Matthew could see him heading toward the corral. Tim stepped out of the shadows and murmured, "Sentinel's on the other side. Let's go."

The first light of dawn showed the line of gray uniforms. Matthew saw Baylor's white grin and heard him shout, "Charge!" The horses streamed down the slope.

Halfway to the fort, the adobe walls erupted with gunfire. Matthew and Tim held back and watched Baylor's forces hesitate, break, and stream toward the river. Dryly Tim said, "Guess we didn't take Fort Fillmore after all."

CHAPTER 5

Amy Gerrett leaned her head against the cold windowpane and tried to see down the road. She was humming a flat, miserable tune as she looked at the humps of rough road and piles of mine tailings that made up Oro City.

In the silent cabin she turned to look at the old clock ticking out in a relentless fashion. "Lost my partner, what'll I do? Skip to my lou, my darling." She finished her song with a sigh and added, "Oh, Daniel, hurry home!"

As an added measure, she lifted her face and cried, "Oh, Lord, won't you please make him hurry home?" Amy's request ended in a shaky giggle as she got to her feet, adding, "And I said that like there weren't all those verses about waiting on the Lord."

Impatience carried her back to the window, but she needed to dab at the tears in her eyes before she could see. Under the dim shouts of the miners, the thump of the stamp mill, and the clunk of empty wagons going down the hill, she heard a crunch in the crushed stone of the path.

Eagerly Amy peered through the scrap of a window. A dark figure was coming up the road toward the cabin. Amy's heart leaped as she pressed against the window to see clearly. Then with a disappointed gulp, she muttered, "That's not Daniel coming; it's the nosy old lady from down the gulch."

Quickly she yanked her collar straight, smoothed her hair, and scrubbed at the tears on her face. "Dear Lord, here I am, trying to make a good impression on all these gold miners and that Mrs. What's-her-name is going to catch me crying like a baby. Bet she never missed her husband. But then, I'll bet she didn't marry him at eighteen."

Amy waited at the door as the heavyset woman trudged up the path. "Morning, Missus Gerrett." Those shrewd eyes sharpened and Amy knew they didn't miss a thing; not her red eyes nor the messy trail of ash on the floor.

Amy concentrated on the woman's hand, seeing the grubby knuckles and dark-edged nails as she slowly said, "Mrs. Withrop, I've been meaning to return your call all this past week." She waved at the ash. "But I haven't even finished my housework."

"A body can't be too busy with husband gone most of the time." She sniffed, then added more kindly, "Seems the church could see fit to keep a preacher in one spot instead of trying to spread him around like butter scratched out so thin there ain't no taste. I know it's the way of the church, but I don't approve."

Amy walked back to the window to hide the tears in her eyes, but she answered briskly, "I'm glad someone besides me objects, but I don't think it will make a speck of difference." She turned with a forced smile. "Have you noticed the view from up here? I like having our cabin halfway up the side of the hill. This way we miss most the racket the miners make. But it seems we're the first to know every time a chunk of gold is uncovered."

"Racket? Think this is bad; wait'll they get another stamp mill to goin'. A body gets to feelin' like all his innards are jumpin' when they smack that ore."

The last of Amy's tears had dried and she sighed with relief. As the scene in front of her caught her attention, she mused, "It's a pretty color, even if it's just tailings from the mines. All those piles of bright dirt spilling down to meet the green trees makes a nice picture."

Mrs. Withrop chuckled and moved to the window. "A year ago

when me and my man came into the gulch, I pretty near went crazy. I sez, 'Hank, will you look at all the gold they're wastin'!' I was ready to unload the wagon right then and go to scooping up that dirt. Colored bright as gold and copper, it was. I figured it was the real stuff. Hank just laughed at me, sayin', 'Lettie, use yer head; if there's gold in that, then they won't be athrowing it away.' "

"They've taken a big share out of the mountains," Amy said. "It's been a good strike right from the beginning. Daniel says that's why they named it California Gulch." With a shake of her head, she added, "According to reports, some say the best days are over."

Amy turned quickly to see the effects of her next words. "I'm of a mind to get a pick and do a little mining myself while Daniel's gone. It sure tears at me sometimes, watching all the others haul out the gold ore. I'm wondering what's under this cabin floor, hoping and wanting a hunk of it for myself."

Mrs. Withrop's eyebrows nearly met the frizzle of hair on her forehead. "Seems carnal for a preacher's wife to be wantin' gold."

Amy sighed and moved away from the window. She thought of her dwindling supply of tea and slowly said, "Could I offer you a cup of tea?"

Lettie shook her head. "I came up to see if you wanted a ride into town, if'n you can call that sorry settlement at the mouth of the gulch a town. Hank needs to go after supplies fer the mine, and I'm of a mind to go along if I have some company. A decent woman feels outta place on the streets with all the fancy ladies."

"Don't suppose there's goods to be had that are worth the trip," Amy reflected aloud. "Right here in Oro City it seems the goods are better—cheaper too. Daniel says he heard they're not expecting the settlement down there to amount to much. There's nothing to it except a few cribs and boardinghouses mixed in with the saloons. Same as you see anywhere."

She paused, then added, "At the rate they're taking gold out up here, I suppose the miners will see they keep the businesses going down that way. Up here there's not room to do much more building of anything. It's such a narrow little gulch. The mines and diggings fill all the free space. Daniel said they named it Oro City because the gulch isn't big enough to hold more'n a name that size."

"Gets mighty lonesome, havin' him gone so much." It was a flat statement. Amy nodded.

Quickly she said, "Yes, I'd like to go down the hill with you, even if there's nothing new to be seen. Are you ready to leave now?" Mrs. Withrop nodded and Amy went after her shawl. It was a new heavy one. Just a few short weeks ago, before they left Buckskin Joe, Daniel had insisted on buying it.

The memory made her choke again. She hesitated, wanting suddenly to be alone, to go back over those fearful and precious days in Buckskin Joe. Fearful? Shaking her head, her lips silently formed the word: *Mother.* She smiled to herself as she followed Lettie out the door.

They walked down the rocky trail to the roadway. Lettie pointed, "Hank's turned the wagon around. Makes him uneasy, tryin' to switch around on these narrow tracks. Might be my nerves agettin' to him. Mind sittin' on the gulch side?" Amy shook her head and crawled in after Lettie.

The narrow road the miners had hacked out wound down the side of the mountain. When Mr. Withrop guided his team close to the edge of the road, Amy could see the creek tumbling far below them. She exclaimed, "Look at the mine tailings! Since I last came this way, they've drifted down to the stream bed."

Lettie nodded, adding, "And up ahead they're sharing that torn-up bank with the sluice boxes."

Just below Amy could see a miner bent over a cradle. She watched him yanking the handle back and forth as he scooped water and gravel into the hopper. Lettie nodded at the man. "Them diggings are pretty poor for him to be going through the dirt again."

"He's working close to the sluice box; I suppose he's hoping they've missed some," Amy said.

Hank mused slowly, "'Tis a bad sign when a fellow wastes his time picking over the rubble." He hauled on the reins, pulling his team close to the mountainside. An empty ore cart came banging and clattering toward them over the rough road. They could hear the teamster shouting at his mules. In a moment he clattered by and Hank flicked the reins again.

Two miles farther down, the mouth of the gulch widened and the valley lay before them. While Lettie's running comments kept pace with the clatter of the wagon, Amy nodded. Lettie's voice disappeared into the back of her thoughts as she admired the wide mountain valley stretching out before them. With the changing season the landscape had become a quilt pattern of blue, green and winter brown.

The distant mountains seemed adrift in the early spring mist. She studied their rearing snowcapped peaks and shivered. Was Daniel somewhere in those snowy canyons? "Beg your pardon?"

Lettie was waving her arm for attention. "More cabins and shanties every time I come here. Hank, is that the supply place over behind the saloon? There's wire and tools stacked up."

He nodded and Lettie added, "Well then, you just drop the missus and me right here. We'll walk up and down the street and look in the shops." She nodded at Amy. "Wouldn't hurt to check out the store. My, don't them hams look good hangin' there?" Amy turned away from the cold view of the mountains and followed Lettie out of the wagon.

The spring snows had left the pocked road landscaped in lakes and valleys. The two picked their way to the line of loose planks teetering across the mud puddles. "A rickety boardwalk for the customers," Amy murmured, pulling her shawl tight against the bitter wind. Coming off the mountains the wind swirled down the street, rattling the clumsy shingles and banging loose shutters.

They started their walk down a street lined with shanties of milled lumber. The green cut lumber was already curling and gaping away from the supporting timbers. Amy said, "A poor place, isn't it? Makes you feel poor yourself. Like life's going downhill instead of up."

Lettie blinked and frowned. In a moment she nodded at an unpeeled log building, saying, "Shabby? Least they don't look ready to blow away. There's a new hotel, two-story. Guess that's a good omen; means they're expecting the place to grow. I 'spect they're lookin' for a fancy name to stick on it."

Amy tilted her head to look up. "The hotel? There're curtains at the windows on the top floor."

"No, the settlement. Curtains? They're lace. Uppity."

As they faced into the wind to begin their walk down the street, the door to the hotel opened. A couple stepped onto the boardwalk in front of them and started down the street. As Amy bent her head against the wind, she saw the man pull the woman's arm through his. *Gentleman*, Amy thought, eyeing the man's white broadcloth suit. She studied the tall white hat he wore and frowned.

Why does that white hat seem familiar? Is there someone in Colorado Territory I know with a hat like that?

Abruptly the woman laughed and tilted her head toward the gentleman. Her voice seemed low and teasing as she made her reply. Amy had turned to follow Lettie into a shop, but she hesitated long enough to glance at the couple. The woman's face was hidden, but the laughing sentence she threw at the man caught Amy's attention.

"What's she saying?" Lettie whispered. "Sounds foreign."

"It is," Amy murmured, glancing at Lettie. "And it caught me by surprise. I have no idea what she's saying."

"Well, come on." Lettie tugged at her arm. "Hank won't want to wait on us, and we haven't started looking yet."

Amy and Mrs. Withrop wandered through the general store, studying the picks and shovels hanging from the rafters next to the hams. Before moving on to the housewares, they admired the shiny stacks of tins containing peaches, imported marmalade, and fancy tea biscuits from England. They found a bundle of lace, but there was not a bolt of unbleached muslin in the store.

Lettie fingered the mirrors and ribbons, saying, "Get the idea they didn't stock the goods with housewives in mind."

When Amy turned away from the jumble of tin buckets, she saw the other woman in the store. There was an amused smile on her face as she listened to Lettie. Giving her another quick glance, Amy moved close to the woman.

"Oh, I know you!" Amy studied the pert face under the plumed bonnet. It was the tawny skin that attracted Amy's attention and confirmed her guess. "You're Crystal Thomas. I'm surprised to see you here."

As Amy spoke, her mind began to record the differences. The woman was beautifully dressed. Her face seemed serene and confident.

Most certainly, she no longer resembled the cook who had worked for Augusta Tabor. Even her speech seemed different. Feeling poor and shabby in her cotton frock, Amy began wondering about the changes she saw in the woman.

Crystal caught her eye; her gentle smile seemed to mock Amy as she turned away to finger the pile of lace. "I've torn my petticoat. No, my dear, I no longer work for Augusta. See, I guessed your question. The plain-bones life of a kitchen grub wasn't to my liking."

The words slipped out before Amy could stop them, "You're so different. I'm sorry, that was rude. Aunt Maude would die if she heard me." Wistfully she added, "It would be nice to see you in church."

Amy studied the golden velvet cloak and the plumed hat. Crystal's eyes met hers again. For just a moment Amy saw a hint of uncertainty there, but there was something else, a dark shadow. It was a shadow that pulled sympathy out of Amy before she had time to think. She stretched her hand toward the woman, but Crystal straightened her shoulders and said, "Might say I've changed my habits a little. Just don't seem to find time."

"I'd heard the preacher acquired a wife; didn't guess it was you." She backed away and fluttered her hand. "Might see you around. Please don't give my regards to Father Dyer. I can't take his brand of reproach." She hesitated and then swirled out the door. Amy looked after her, wondering about the hesitation and the lonely expression in her eyes.

Bemused by this new Crystal, the memory of the last time she had seen the beautiful woman with skin the color of Augusta's cream-filled coffee caught at Amy's thoughts. It had been at Lizzie's funeral. And as Father Dyer quoted Scripture, Crystal's lips had moved silently, following the words while her face glowed. Amy whispered the words that were read that snowy, miserable afternoon: " 'I am the resurrection and the life; he that believeth in me, though he were dead, yet shall he live.' "

Obviously Crystal's face didn't reflect those thoughts now. Amy shivered.

"Ya took a chill?" Lettie was asking, bringing Amy back to the present.

"I suppose it's just thinking. Sometimes you get to depend on someone—something. And it fails." She looked at Lettie and tried to explain, "It's like a board in a bridge giving way. Makes it scary to walk across the bridge, thinking what if one breaks under you."

Lettie blinked and said, "Hank's awaiting on us."

When Crystal Thomas walked out of the store, the wind caught at her cloak. She ducked her head and hurried toward the hotel. The wind whistled down the street and moaned around the buildings. Crystal shivered. In this strange place of shacks and log buildings as dreary as the wounded hillsides surrounding the mining camp, her isolation seemed more real than the old velvet cloak around her shoulders.

In the hotel lobby she looked at the round iron stove and the line of benches bordering it. As cold as she knew her room would be, it was preferable to the company of the men huddled around the stove, eying every movement she made.

She started toward the stairs. "Mrs. Thomas. Here's a note for you." It was from Lucas Tristram. So he would see her at dinner. With a sigh of relief, Crystal hurried to her room.

When she closed the door behind herself and leaned against it, she slowly murmured aloud, "So you don't like the room? So it leaks cold air like a sieve, and the little stove barely melts ice. Crystal Thomas, you got yourself into this. Curiosity as usual. Now decide for yourself. Is Tristram's proposition worth the risk? You be his lackey, and he'll help you find your husband. Or at least that's what he says he will do. Have you ever known him to keep a promise? He played you false last time. Do you really trust him?"

Crystal shivered and pushed her cold hands against her face. "The question is, do I really want to see my husband again?"

But that was foolish. She reminded herself, "Why else are you here?" Crystal slowly hung her cloak and pulled out the warm dressing gown. She was still mulling over the events that had dropped her back into Lucas's life as she poked wood into the little sheet-metal stove.

Rubbing her hands briskly together, she wandered restlessly around the room. The scrap of lace was on the bed. Looking at it she murmured, "Might as well get this petticoat repaired now. Who knows when I'll find time again."

The wind was lifting to a howl, causing the log hotel to creak under its onslaught. "At least I don't need to share the common room with the other women," she said, thinking of the drafty room under the eaves where she had spent her first night in Oro City.

Crystal pulled out her sewing kit and found scissors and thread. Placing them on the chair beside the stove, she unbuttoned her frock. "Oh, terrible," she murmured with a shiver. "I'll be grateful for spring. Undressing long enough to do my mending is misery."

She had hung her frock and was pulling off the petticoat when she heard the door creak. With a gasp of surprise, she whirled around.

The man stepped inside and closed the door. "Lucas! I'm dressing."

"I noticed. And it's the loveliest sight I've seen for a long time. Don't let me disturb you. After all, if we're going to have all this time together, you'd better get accustomed to my popping in and out."

Crystal gasped and reached for her dressing gown. "I refuse to have you here. Please leave."

He grinned as he watched her pull the robe in front of herself. "Lovely. I didn't remember. But I've always liked skin that color. Creole, aren't you? But a little dark."

"You know very well, Lucas. And I remember the last time this happened. How carefully designed it was! Bursting into my bedroom just as my husband came up the stairs. You had only enough time to remove your waistcoat while I stood there like a ninny in my pantaloons."

Her voice hardened as she said, "After months of pressure, it was that incident that finally broke my husband's resistance. How much were you paid for him? You might as well confess; you and I both know how desperately the South needs every man, every dollar."

The smile was still mocking, but the light in his eyes cut through her anger and left her trembling. "Get out—now, or I'll scream!"

"And you think that would bring someone to your aid? Crystal, you are very mistaken." He reached for the robe. As she turned to scream, he struck her across the mouth.

CHAPTER 6

The spring dusk had begun to paint a misty pink across the sky when Hank stopped the wagon in the lane leading up to the lonely cabin. Slowly Amy slipped down to the ground. "Thanks. It helped the day to pass."

"Could be the parson's back," Hank said. "Seems I see his horse."

Amy stretched to tiptoes. "Yes!" Her voice broke as she turned to run. Bursting into the cabin, she paused. Daniel was on his knees in front of the little stove, shoving wood into the crackling fire.

"Oh, Daniel!" He caught her up close, but not before she saw the melancholy lines on his face. She whispered, "You've missed me as badly as I've missed you." It wasn't a question; it was confirmation of her own feelings. Slowly she touched his face and burst into tears.

Pulling a bench forward, Daniel gathered Amy close to him. "You're cold. Where have you been?"

"Oh, Daniel, I'm so sorry I'm such a baby." She stopped, gulped and took a deep breath. "I was with the Withrops. We rode down to the settlement. You must have gone right past us."

"I saw his wagon."

Amy rubbed gently at the wind-chafed redness of his face. "Has the weather been bad? It snowed here. I worried so. Sometimes I feel like you'll just drift out of my life and I'll never see you again."

His eyes were studying her curiously and she could guess at the questions. "I know. You wonder why I feel this now, when before I spent all my time running away from you." She shook her head. "Daniel, I honestly don't know. But I guess back then I feared more'n I'll ever be able to put into words. Maybe I was afraid to love. But now—Daniel I can't understand why."

She gave a shaky laugh and added, "I suppose we've had the strangest start to married life that ever a couple could have. A year ago I didn't think I'd ever see you again. We met, married, and then—"

"Everything fell apart for me when you took off."

"Daniel, it did for me too. I can admit it now. A silly spoiled baby. At least that's what I wanted to be. I had some strange ideas about marriage."

"Like what?"

"That once we were married you'd spend the rest of your life running after what I wanted. I guess," she added slowly, "these past weeks when I've been alone so much, I'm learning to think straight. Marriage is love and hungering after each other, but it's more, isn't it?"

"You say it."

"Learning to think the other person's needs are more important than your own."

Daniel frowned and lifted her face. The frown disappeared as he studied her eyes. "I have some learning to do, too. Maybe learning from you. Amy, I have my own problems, of learning to trust both you and God in a deeper way."

As she snuggled into his arms, she began thinking of Crystal. Seeing the woman had reminded Amy of the lonely time in Buckskin Joe. She was ready to talk about Crystal and those fears when Daniel lifted her face and kissed her.

When she got up to prepare their supper, he said, "I saw the folks."

Amy frowned. "Wherever have you been?"

"Oh, I didn't leave the circuit. I met Mother and Father just on the other side of Granite. They said Dyer's been at them to go down and look over New Mexico Territory. Says he's had the place on his mind for a year now, fretting because the church hasn't ventured into the area yet."

He threw her a quick glance. "I spent the evening talking to them. Your father has given up his charge in Central City. They were on their way to New Mexico."

Amy turned slowly. "The church and the circuit? You mean Father is no longer pastor of the church?" She couldn't keep the shock out of her voice.

"Of any church. I'd guessed he would feel he must."

He came to Amy as she turned back to the stove. Resting his hand on her shoulder, he watched the play of expression on her face as she pondered his statement. Glancing up she said, "Is it because of Mother?"

"Of course," Daniel said. "He didn't want to put her through the kind of scrutiny the bishop must use. You know, Amy, it's an awkward situation, not only for your mother, but also for the church. It isn't often a pastor has a former dancehall girl for a wife."

Amy winced. She stirred the beans simmering on the stove as she listened. He added, "You and I know enough of the facts to let us live easy with the situation. But it could be painful for them to be forced to justify their actions in the past and now."

Amy nodded. "Father feels partly to blame because he didn't forgive her years ago."

"And Silverheels—I mean, Mother—insists all the buffalo in Kansas wouldn't have kept her home." He paused. "I think all the circumstances—your finding her, the smallpox, even the revival meeting in Buckskin Joe was the Lord's grace, helping her make the recommitment both to God and your father."

"To any outsider the story would be ugly. Daniel, she's my mother. She's caused Father and me a great deal of hurt. You've been reminding me that when the Lord forgives, we dare not do otherwise." She glanced up at him. "But thinking of the genuine love I feel for her now, I'm certain the Lord has put it in me."

She stirred the beans and added, "I suppose one of these days,

I'll get over being so glad she's back that I'll want to begin asking questions."

Daniel spoke slowly. "I have an idea that would do more harm than good. Amy, for your sake as well as hers, let Mother decide what should be said and when. Let's respect her silence now. No matter what, we must try to keep from judging her by the past. Better our questions go unanswered than to allow ourselves to be warped by her past." Amy nodded as he added. "Otherwise you'd have no peace over the situation."

"Silverheels," Amy mused, "the beautiful madam, with her jewels and fancy clothes, with her men friends. How could she be content now?"

"Can't you believe in the changes that have happened in her? Amy, you can't live forever judging her by what she's done in the past; you've got to trust her—we all must."

Abruptly Amy's head jerked. "But isn't that what you were doing?"

Daniel frowned. "What do you mean? When?"

"You looked . . . unbelieving when I said how much I missed you when you were away."

After a moment Daniel admitted reluctantly, "I suppose. Amy, sometimes our finally being together seems like a dream, and sometimes I'm afraid to believe you've changed this quickly."

Amy bit her lip and went to the shelf to lift down the plates. He saw her face and apologized, "I'm sorry. You were right. I was judging by the past."

She whispered, "Will our todays always be shadowed by that horrible time?"

He hesitated, then asked, "Have you so easily given up the need to have security on your terms?"

She looked into his brooding face. "Daniel, is that fair? You don't understand, to a woman, having a sense of security is important. There are things we need so badly." Amy sighed heavily as she thought of the rocking chair she wanted, the rug and a new kettle.

Finally she tilted her chin at Daniel. "I'm not complaining. It's just this gnawing inside." Now the words burst out. "If somehow we could have a piano, I'd think heaven was on earth."

He smiled down at her and she recognized it as the special smile reserved for her.

"If you ever use that smile on someone else, Daniel Gerrett, I'll use the broom on you." He was grinning now and she sighed with relief.

"And Mrs. Gerrett, if you'll sit on my lap just a moment before you dish up the beans, I'll tell you why I am smiling."

She came, whispering, "Daniel, I must confess. I feel that way too. Nearly afraid our happiness will evaporate. Sometimes when you're gone, I get to wondering if all this is real. Then the happiness is almost scary."

Holding her close with his lips against her neck, he nodded. When he lifted his head, he grinned and said, "I am going to make certain that one of these days you will have a piano. I may have to dig gold in all my free time, but a piano you will have. I'll seal that promise with a kiss."

"Oh, Daniel!" She swallowed the lump in her throat and pushed away the nagging thought that Daniel was dreaming dreams as frothy as hers. Amy lifted her face. "Love," she whispered as she desperately determined to think of nothing except these brief days alone with Daniel.

"What are you thinking?" he asked, pressing his face against hers.

"Time," she murmured. "It seems to fly when you're here and drag when you're gone. Will it always be like this?"

"I hope not."

As she got to her feet she sighed, thinking, *I'll just have to hang on to what I have—the Sabbath. Only the Lord knows how hard it is to release him on Monday morning. For five days he doesn't belong to me. He eats some other woman's cooking and sleeps in a stranger's bed. I don't know when he's sick, or whether he's had to outrun the Indians. He's not my husband; he's pastor to the mining camps.*

Daniel came to stand beside her. "Amy, I don't like being gone all week. Sure, I'm busy except when I'm riding the trails, but at night I wonder how your day has gone. I miss you too."

His words made it easy for her to admit, "I'm not charitable. I want you home, and when you are gone, I find nothing to do except count the days." She faced him. "I know your schedule. I try to imagine the places you go. This week it's Twin Lakes; next week will be Granite and Salida."

On Sunday Amy stood watching the early morning sun stream through the window, and thinking how quickly the weekend was over. As she turned back to the table and the pile of dirty dishes, the sun was warm on her shoulders. A feeling nearly like contentment wrapped around her as she looked from the sunshine pooled on the table to the steam rising from the teakettle.

Wiggling her shoulders in the warmth, she went back to her task of stuffing a chicken for dinner. Nodding toward Daniel, she said, "It's clear and springlike this morning. I don't believe we'll need a fire in the church today."

Daniel raised his head and closed the Bible. "That is so." He studied her curiously. "What are we celebrating? Can't do that too often—there aren't that many chickens."

"I don't think you get fed very well. You come home looking thinner than ever."

In a moment Daniel came to the table. "I'll help. Amy, next week when I head down Granite way, would you like to go along? You've been invited by the folks in every place I've stopped. In addition, the horse Mother gave us could use a good workout. Right now the trails are safe. It's too early for the Indians to be up to their tricks."

Amy grinned up at him. "Daniel, my dear husband, you don't have to beg! That would be wonderful. After these weeks of being alone, even horseback sounds like a treat."

After she put the chicken on to cook, she took up her shawl and followed him out the door. This morning she smiled and nodded contentedly all the way to church.

Today it didn't matter that the Oro City church was only a deserted log cabin, swept and lined with crude benches; nor did it matter too much that most of the miners continued pouring ore into the sluices on the Lord's day. Daniel was here and in another week they would be riding the trails together.

On the bench beside the Withrops, under cover of her spreading skirt, Amy counted the days until they could be on the road. She must remember to ask if there would be a home for them to stay in each night.

Monday morning Daniel headed his horse down the gulch just as the sun cleared the mountains. His breath left a rim of frost on the muffler Amy had tucked under his chin. With one hand he loosened it while he flicked the reins against the horse's flanks.

When he turned out of the gulch, he could feel the sun warm on his back. The horse loped down the road, cutting along the edge of the settlement at the mouth of the gulch. "Gee haw!" Daniel heeded the shout behind him and yanked on the reins as the Denver stage surged out onto the road.

He watched the long whip snap across the backs of the horses as the coach took the corner, swaying dangerously close to the rocky edge. Shaking his head, he muttered, "There's going to be an uncomfortable trip for that bunch. Pity the pressure's on the fellas to the point they take risks when they shouldn't."

With the road to himself, Daniel hunkered down into his collar and allowed the mare to set her gait. "Well, Father Dyer," he muttered, addressing his absent mentor with a wry grin, "there's virtue in riding shank's mare, but I get more prayin' and sermonizing done when I don't have to watch where I put my feet."

It was nearly noon when Daniel caught up with the stage. Rounding a curve on the narrow mountain road, he straightened and pulled back on the reins. The stage was tipped, leaning against the side of the mountain. The driver and some of the passengers were huddled around the team.

The wind caught the open door of the coach and banged it as Daniel slipped from his horse and approached the group. The youthful driver lifted his white face, saying, "Aw, the thing's dumped."

Shaking his head in sympathy, Daniel asked, "Team down?"

"One of the lead mares. Think we'll be hard up to save her."

"Can three horses pull the stage?" Daniel turned at the soft question. The plumed velvet bonnet was tilted toward the driver. Daniel studied the wine-red velvet of the woman's cloak and matching bonnet before he turned away. He had stepped close to the driver and had his mouth open to question the youth when the men around the stage-coach moved. He heard the sharp whinny then the dull report of the rifle.

For a moment they were all silent. At last the cold cutting wind throwing snow and dust against the bottom of the stage released the silent, motionless group. The woman shivered and Daniel said, "We'd better get the stage back on its wheels."

The driver looked around the group of sober-faced passengers, and his shaky grin added weight to his words. "It's getting cold. Better give it a try before we all freeze."

The chubby red-faced dandy pulled at his lapels and said, "Looks to me like the accident smashed a wheel on the rocks. Besides, there's only three of us to set that thing upright, not counting the young lady."

She turned her bonnet toward Daniel as he spoke. "I'm headed Twin Lakes way—" He hesitated and peered at the face shadowed by the bonnet. "I could contact the livery stable."

The bonnet faced the driver. "I would like one of the horses to ride with the gentleman. I must be in Twin Lakes before nightfall."

"Ma'am—" he protested feebly.

She added, "Besides, I'll freeze waiting in this cold."

In the end, Daniel watched the two male passengers crawl into the tilted stagecoach. Shortly afterward the driver galloped down the road on one of the horses. Daniel was left to wrap a buffalo robe around the woman and lift her onto his own mount. He said, "I'll make do with one of the team. I know my mare's gentle."

His hunch was confirmed as he helped the woman mount, but he said nothing until they had left the stagecoach behind. Then he turned to the woman riding beside him, "Crystal Thomas, formerly coveted queen of the Tabor boardinghouse kitchen. I am surprised to see you here."

She added words to his thoughts. "And you are wondering why I am here and what—"

"Fabulous gold mine you have found." He saw the flush spread across her cheeks. Gently he added, "And why is it imperative you reach Twin Lakes before sundown? Your cloak impresses me as being adequately warm."

She was still silent, and Daniel was surprised. The words crowding Daniel's thoughts came out. "You have a beautiful voice, Miss Crystal Thomas, but more than that—I watched you at revival services in Buckskin Joe. I decided you had a beautiful soul. I can't believe my impression was wrong. Now I'm wondering why you haven't filled the preacher's ears with your explanations—for all of it."

She turned troubled eyes Daniel's direction and softly said, "Thank you, Parson. And it's Mrs. Thomas."

They were on the outskirts of Twin Lakes when she said, "I thank you again for not pressing me for answers. Now I beg of you. Please forget you've seen me. My life—" She paused to bite her lip. As they rode toward the livery stable, she added, "I won't ask you to believe me, but sometimes things are not what they seem."

"Lovely cloak," he murmured.

"Would you believe it's ancient? Perhaps not. Well, good day, Parson."

On Monday, after Daniel left Oro City, the clouds rolled in over the mountains and it began to snow. Amy tried to shake off her dismal mood by chiding herself as she went about her tasks. "The first of March, and you're expecting weather like June."

By midafternoon she wrapped her shawl around her and headed down the gulch to the Withrop cabin. Lettie met her at the door, dabbing at her poor red nose. Amy explained, "Yesterday Tom Allen told me there was a new family in the gulch. I'm not certain of the cabin. Do you know anything more? He said their name's Morgan and they live close to the mouth of the gulch."

Lettie rubbed her forehead and sighed. "Hank told me about them. Live off the road a piece. Mentioned they had a wagon with blue lettering on the side. Hank said it looked like their rig was patched up with bits from a freight wagon. Had a mite of trouble getting here," she added, making her way back to the fire.

When Amy sat down beside her, Lettie picked up a coarse sheet of paper and handed it to Amy. "Hank brought this home today. Seems someone's been passing these things around to the miners."

Amy studied the paper. "A solicitation for money to buy arms! These names, Jefferson Davis, Robert E. Lee." She looked at Lettie.

Slowly she said, " I recognize these names; every one of them is from the South. From the states that have seceded from the Union.

"Lettie, these people are secessionists—they're all against the Union! What are they doing in Colorado Territory? I've been listening to war talk like it was something happening in a foreign land. Now this puts it in our dooryard. It's scary. Are they trying to get our money?"

Lettie nodded. "Can't imagine where the notice came from. Surprises me. Didn't think there were southern sympathizers around these parts. Makes you feel the fighting is getting too close."

Slowly Amy spoke her thoughts aloud. "The slaves. I really feel sorry for them. I can't understand why we must be divided and fight. Why don't they just let the slaves go free? Lettie, I read the newspaper. There're people dying. Some women are losing their husbands, and children their fathers. War. Can the South believe slavery is this important?"

Lettie shook her head and shrugged.

Amy left the cabin and started down the road. The snow had begun in earnest. She huddled into her shawl and wished herself home. As she walked, her thoughts were taken up with the things suggested by the handbill. The frightened expression on Lettie's face made her uneasy. *Secessionists in Oro City!* Like Lettie, she shivered.

Walking slowly, still lost in thought, she was only vaguely aware of the growing cold and increasing snow. When she heard the wagon rattling up the hill, her feet were too numb to obey the command to hurry.

Stumbling to the side of the road, she heard the shout and curse from the driver. She also heard another voice pitched to a gentler tone.

The wagon stopped. A man jumped down and came quickly to her side. "The snow's getting bad. If you're going up the hill, we'll give you a ride." The man added, "This is dangerous; in another few minutes you'll not be able to see the edge of the road."

Bewildered, Amy hesitated and looked around. The snow was falling like lacy saucers, tilting, drifting, and swirling in the wind. The man took her arm and led her to the wagon.

"Home, yes. And I'll be grateful," she said with a shiver. "It isn't far. It's the parson's cabin."

The man bent over her. "Amy Randolph. I thought there was something familiar—"

She pushed back the shawl and rubbed melted snowflakes out of her eyes. "Lucas Tristram," she said slowly. "Colorado Territory is a small place, after all. Have your mining interests taken you this far afield?"

"Certainly," he said with a laugh. "Did you expect me to grub gold in Central City all of my life? But the most astounding thing is to find you here. I declare, has the parson gone off and left you to your devices again? I can't believe he has any real appreciation of the fairest of the ladies." His voice was mocking and Amy studied his face. That twist to his smile hinted of bitterness. He was still angry with her.

The cursing driver spoke, and his voice made Amy more uneasy. "Ah, Lucas, so you know the lady. Church, huh? It is a shame you've neglected your duties since you've been in the lovely city of Oro. Ma'am, you need to stir up your husband to make a call on this parishioner. He should be good for a generous donation, if nothing else!" The man laughed heartily, and Amy and Lucas continued to study each other. Unexpectedly Lucas's expression softened, catching Amy off guard at the moment she had been trying to remember what it was that first attracted her to this man.

Speaking thoughtfully, with his face still close to hers, Lucas said, "You're right, Mac. I do need to remember my church."

In a small voice, Amy said, "Here's the cabin. Just let me off at the path."

"I'll walk with you to the door." Lucas lifted her down, swinging her clear of the icy mud puddle.

He followed her into the cabin and looked around. It was easy to guess he was comparing his house with this. There was a confident, amused expression on his face.

"My dear." He bent over her hand while she resisted the impulse to snatch it back. "I can't forget the wonderful time we had together, and of your generosity to a lonely bachelor. If I am restrained from expressing my gratitude to you, then surely I will be allowed to give a gift to the church?"

Thinking of the poor, shabby building they called church, Amy gasped, "Oh, Lucas, you are kind! Most surely! Anything you do for this church will be deeply appreciated."

With another bow, and words Amy didn't hear, Lucas left. Amy was musing, *Gift*. There was a wry smile on her face as she thought of the multitude of things the small church could use.

By morning the snow had transformed the trees and mining camp into a rolling mass of whiteness. Amy had only begun to worry about Daniel when she heard the knock and the shout.

When she reached the door, Father Dyer was leaning his snowshoes against the cabin. "Come in; Daniel's gone to Twin Lakes."

"I know. Met him on the trail yesterday. Don't happen to have the coffeepot on, do you?"

"Come have some. I suppose you're headed up to that old, cold cabin."

He shed his coat. "It's as snug as yours. Did Daniel tell you that your father's going to New Mexico?" She nodded and went to pull the frying pan over the fire. He continued. "After you two left, I kept them around for a few days while we talked over the situation."

"Daniel said you had. Was it about Father's church—"

He shook his head. "I'm talking about New Mexico. I've been wanting to go back to the territory for a year now. Can't get the people off my mind. Never have seen a race of people so beat down."

"Race?"

"Mostly Spanish folks down that way. A few Anglos and lots of Indians, too. The people up from Mexico are an oppressed bunch. Little children needing lots of attention, schooling. Sad-eyed little ones." He continued musing aloud.

Amy carried the plate to the table and brought the coffeepot. "Eggs! I'd forgotten what they look like. I hope you're taking good care of those egg machines. Mighty cold for critters."

After Father Dyer finished his meal, he leaned back and said, "I've a gift for you, and I'll sing for my supper." Fumbling in his pack, he pulled out a small dirty object and placed it before her.

She touched the blackened side and exclaimed, "A crucible! Do you think I should be digging for gold?"

He chuckled, "To the contrary. I've done my share of digging, and I thought this would serve to remind you of my recent success. See, the speck there in the bottom—that's the record of my last assay."

Amy said, "It looks like a tiny dot of gold."

"It is. Collected it up Blue River way. Had a sack of rich-looking ore which nearly broke my back totin' it to Fairplay. How do you like the assayer's report? The fella gave me the cup to remember him by." Dyer chuckled. "After this, I don't think he expects me to come back."

While Amy rubbed her fingers over the smoky surface, Father Dyer spoke again. "Kinda reminded me of a hymn and I want to sing it for you." Amy nodded as she continued to pick at the gold in the bottom of the cupel. Giving Father Dyer a quick grin as he tilted his head to bellow out the words, she continued to examine the gold.

When he reached the fourth verse, Father Dyer's voice dropped and gentled. Slowly Amy placed the crucible on the table and faced Father Dyer as he sang, " . . . *my grace, all sufficient, shall be thy supply. The flames shall not hurt thee; I only design thy dross to consume and thy gold to refine.*"

When he sat down and picked up the last piece of bread, Amy said, "I'm not certain, but I think you're trying to tell me something."

"Just keep it and look at it every once in a while. Maybe it'll preach a better sermon than I ever did." He stood up and reached for his coat.

"I'm not faulting you, Amy. Could be it was the Lord who made me think of you when the fella gave me the crucible. For what reason, I don't know. It's certain, a high-spirited gal like you will have some adjusting to the circuit-riding pace."

Amy watched as he headed out the door. After he was gone, she stood there for several minutes, fingering the tiny crucible. The sides of the cup were blackened with ash and dirt, but in the bottom the speck of gold glowed.

CHAPTER 7

S o this is the town of Twin Lakes!" Amelia Randolph exclaimed. Turning to her husband she added, "I wish there were time to see the lakes before we begin our trip to New Mexico."

Eli pulled her hand through his arm. "Might be when we come back. Watch your step—you nearly walked in front of that wagon."

"Thank you," she said stiffly, glancing up at the man beside her. She measured the years in Eli's dignified gray hair and stern face; she saw only occasional brief glimpses of the young man he had been. He was still a stranger. She murmured, "Less than a month we've been together. How do we bridge the gap?"

"What did you say?"

"Just thinking out loud. About us. Sometimes I think I know you. But it's been so long. Eli, am I a stranger to you, too?"

He hesitated, "Would it be better if I said yes? It is nearly like a resurrection. Of ways of thinking, and talking. Sometimes you say words that are so familiar that the years nearly disappear. Like my name. You stretch out the sound in a way no one else has ever done."

They walked in silence until she asked, "Father Dyer seemed to side with you on leaving the church right now. Are you really content with that decision?"

He was studying her from the corners of his eyes. There was a slight frown on his face as he said, "Amelia, I'm getting close to the age when they start sticking old preachers on the shelf."

"It's odd," she murmured, "that this should line up with the time you decided to rescue me."

"Do I detect a hint of bitterness today? My dear, if you're looking for reassurance, you have it. I haven't changed my mind. I still want you back, and you'd best settle into the rut and stop fussing over it."

"Like an old hen." As Amelia said the words, she realized they lacked the humor she expected them to have.

"Pardon," the woman stepped in front of them and turned. "I'm sorry, I didn't mean to cut you off." She bobbed her head and rushed down the street.

Amelia stood speechless and Eli tugged at her arm. Glancing at him, she said softly, "Oh, Eli, sometimes this is hard. I know that woman and she didn't recognize me."

Slowly Amelia touched her scarred face. Eli pulled her close, "My dear, she scarcely gave you a glance. Now, I need to go to the livery stable and see about a new harness. Do you want to come?"

Amelia had been watching as the woman walked down the street and entered the hotel. She turned to Eli and said, "I treated that woman badly the last time I saw her. Now the Lord reminds me I need to apologize."

"Then go before it becomes an impossible burden. I'll meet you later at the wagon." Amelia nodded and hurried after the woman.

At the desk she asked, "Will you tell me where I can find Mrs. Thomas?"

The clerk nodded and said, "She's in her room. Second floor, number twenty."

When the door was pulled open in answer to Amelia's knock, the woman said, "I beg your pardon."

"Crystal Thomas, you don't recognize me. It's Amelia."

Crystal's hand went to her mouth and she murmured, "Dear

Lord, have mercy. I hear Amelia but—" First she looked at the tight wad of hair and then the scars.

Amelia stepped into the room and closed the door. Her voice trembled as she said, "You were one of the fortunate ones."

"The smallpox got you. Oh, Amelia, I am so sorry. Please come sit here with me. I see this means it's all over." Her eyes met Amelia's and slipped away. "May I give you some money. I know you must be—"

"Destitute because I can no longer sell my beauty? Crystal, I am not destitute. If I were so inclined, I could have maintained the board-inghouse. But you see, my husband has found me and now we are back together."

"My dear, I am happy for you." The words were stilted.

Amelia reached out to touch the tawny hand. "Your voice gives you away. Crystal, I want to tell you about it. You've known me long enough to guess going back to my husband was impossible. In Penn-sylvania I made certain you understood that.

"Impossible," she mused. "But the Lord is gracious. I know you left Buckskin Joe with the Tabors, before the epidemic was bad. I didn't. When I finally recovered and saw myself in the mirror, I nearly wished myself dead."

"I read the newspapers. You were something of a hero. They said you stayed to nurse the men when all the other women fled." She paused. "You said you nearly wished to die?" Amelia could see the pity in Crystal's eyes.

Amelia considered the question and lifted helpless hands; how could she explain the agony behind the words? She stated flatly, "I wasn't ready to meet God. Crystal, you know I'd thrown out all my beliefs. It was impossible to believe God would forgive my sins when I just kept on disobeying Him. You know how I lived before and after Pennsylvania. I know you were simply too good a friend to throw me over. But that was what I deserved."

Slowly Crystal said, "I remember the two of us struggled through some very uncomfortable times in Pennsylvania."

"Yes, we did. I remember how you tried to convince me that all the good I was doing in the movement was an attempt to appease

God. You said all my righteousness was self-made and that it was filthy rags in God's eyes."

"You were very angry." Crystal added, "But at the same time I was hardheaded, confident I would never fall into sin the way you did. Now—" She stopped and looked down at her hands.

Amelia touched Crystal's folded hands as she hurried on, the words spilling over each other. "Now I've come to apologize. Crystal, it was partly our quarrel in Pennsylvania that made me turn you away in Buckskin Joe when you came looking for a job. I could have made room for you at the house, but I couldn't face all the things you stood for."

Crystal looked up, puzzled, as Amelia explained. "Your shiny face singing hymns in my kitchen was just more than I could tolerate."

Amelia tried to force a smile, but found herself blinking at tears. Hastily she said, "I'm not trying to justify my actions. I only want your forgiveness, even though I don't deserve it."

"Of course you have it." Crystal's voice was flat. She got up and moved restlessly around the room.

Amelia watched her for a moment before saying, "Crystal, I've been running on about myself. Now I see you're having troubles too. Is there anything I can do for you?"

The Creole woman turned quickly. "I don't suppose so." Her smile was bitter as she straightened her shoulders and said, "Your confession reminds me of how far I've slipped from the tender mercies of the Lord."

The mocking words caught Amelia. Looking more closely at Crystal, she asked gently, "Would it help to talk?" The woman shrugged. Amelia pressed, "I remember you and your husband were having serious problems when he left Pennsylvania. When you came to Buckskin looking for a job, I was still too angry and selfish to ask about that time."

"I don't know where he is," Crystal said dully. There was silence while Amelia tried to recall those final days in Pennsylvania. Crystal took a quick step and squared her shoulders. "Amelia, you might as well know. I've sold my soul in an attempt to find out where he is. Isn't that ironic? Now my pride has me down to groveling in the dirt because I want—wanted him so badly."

She turned away, adding, "Of course, all of that is beyond consideration now."

"What do you mean?"

Amelia watched Crystal's agitated pacing until the woman pressed her hands to her cheeks and looked at Amelia. "Do you remember Lucas Tristram?"

Amelia frowned with the effort to recall those days. "The gentleman your husband knew at Harvard? And isn't he the fellow who came to Pennsylvania? How did he know you were there?"

Crystal shook her head. Amelia continued. "I remember he spent a great deal of time trying to talk your husband into leaving the Underground Railroad. We all laughed. We were all so confident it would never happen."

Bitterly Crystal said, "Of course you laughed. No one thought he would want to leave. But the talk of the South seceding from the Union got his attention. Then Tristram used home and family and deep southern loyalties like a knife." She turned away. "Even wives are expendable. Especially this kind of wife."

Looking at Crystal's rigid back, Amelia pushed tentatively for more information. "I remember hearing rumors of some big problem between the two of you. We dared not ask, because obviously you were crushed by his leaving."

"You mean you hadn't heard that he caught me in adultery?"

"Crystal! Not a one of us believed it enough to give you the pain of our questions."

Crystal took a deep breath and asked, "Did you also know that Lucas Tristram discovered that the slave from Louisiana, the man I took to Pennsylvania, was my father?"

"Benjamin was your father?" Amelia steadied her voice and said, "Crystal, we all knew that you had brought him to Pennsylvania. I suppose we should have wondered why."

Crystal's words cut in. "At first it was his desire to keep our relationship hidden. I agreed, not foreseeing a reason to regret that decision. How I wish it could have been otherwise!"

When she saw Crystal's agonized face, Amelia touched her and asked, "But what could Lucas do with that information?"

Crystal wandered restlessly around the room. "Amelia, it was my fault. I was a fool to think the story could be hidden. See, my husband didn't know."

"My dear," Amelia whispered, "now I understand. Please, don't hold it against him. He's too fine a man to allow this to ruin your marriage."

Crystal was shaking her head as she said, "Love does strange things to people sometimes. My husband knew I was Creole. I left it at that, simply because I loved him too much to risk telling him any more of my story. I refused to consider the consequences of my actions. See, his family is from Mississippi, and he's heir to a cotton plantation. Of course you know it takes slaves to run a plantation."

"Crystal! Are you forgetting your husband was involved in helping free the slaves? I watched him and Duncan stealing in with their boat loaded with slaves. They risked their lives for those people."

Crystal nodded, musing, "And he was terribly caught up in the cause. He is a compassionate man and he cared deeply about those people. I think he would have given his life for them if it had been necessary."

She straightened and looked at Amelia. "Don't forget, he's also southern. I'm from the South and I know what it's like to be twisted by these strong, strong loyalties. He deeply loved his home and family. If you remember, while we were in Pennsylvania the talk of war had started. Amelia, you know yourself that we listened to some of the abolitionists say the only solution was to split the Union.

"With rumors like that going around, for my husband to consider cutting the relationship with his family was a kind of death. I could understand that." She added, "Did you know that he and his sister were caught in a childish lark when they were swept into the movement? They hadn't intended to be part of it all."

Amelia glanced up. "No, I didn't. That surprises me. You are helping me begin to understand your husband, but I can't say I'm in sympathy with his decision." Amelia mused, "This I'll admit, they were both devoted to it."

"But when my husband realized the South was on the verge of

seceding from the Union, he began to listen to Lucas and question himself as to where his loyalties really lay. He was a torn young man when Lucas pushed him over the brink."

"How?"

For a moment Crystal covered her face before saying, "One afternoon while I was dressing, Lucas came to the house to see me. I asked Mycinda to have him wait in the upstairs parlor while I dressed and to tell him I would come to him there. He must have seen my husband approaching, because he burst into my bedroom, catching me undressed. Before I could collect my wits, he ripped off his coat and tie. That was when my husband walked into the room."

"Oh, Crystal! Surely he couldn't believe that of you."

Her voice was cold as she added, "He did when Lucas completed the picture of my integrity by revealing Benjamin as my father."

Feeling powerless to comfort, Amelia watched Crystal pace the room, twisting her hands in agony. When she came back to her chair, Amelia asked, "And you don't know where your husband is now?"

"I've never made an attempt to contact him through his family. Naturally, with the circumstances being what they are, it is impossible to force myself on him or the family."

"And you've determined to accept life without him?"

Crystal straightened her shoulders and lifted her chin. "No. I told you I had sold my soul in an attempt to discover his whereabouts."

"That frightens me. Please explain what you mean." Amelia studied the frozen features of the woman opposite her, feeling her heart sink as Crystal began to talk.

"After I left the Tabors, I tried to find employment in Denver City. I finally ended up working behind the desk at a hotel. Lucas Tristram found me there. Immediately he began waving a tempting flag under my nose. He said he knew where my husband was."

Crystal shifted uneasily on her chair, her voice dull as she said, "With that he led me on. He was very confident and forthright with me. He told me he'd been commissioned by some southern gentlemen involved in the new Confederacy. His job was to investigate and submit a detailed report of activities in Colorado Territory."

"What kind of activities?"

"The South wanted to know how much support Colorado would give to the Confederacy. There had been rumors both for and against supporting the cause. Also, they asked for a detailed report on the gold mines. Location and the amount of gold being taken out." Crystal looked at Amelia. "Of course it is no secret that the South is in dire straits financially. Also, Tristram let it slip that there is someone in the area who is making plans to invade Colorado."

"You mean actually attempt to take over the territory?" Crystal nodded and Amelia asked, "Have you any idea who it might be?"

"No."

Amelia got up to wander around the room. When she stopped in front of Crystal's chair she said, "I nearly hesitate to say this aloud, but it seems a duty. Crystal, if you could pass this information along to Governor Gilpin, well, you'd be doing a very patriotic thing. Even more, if you were to find out just who is planning to invade Colorado and when, well—"

"I have no intentions of being involved any longer." Crystal's voice was cold as she made the statement and got to her feet. "My plans now are to finish up some business and then to leave the territory for home."

"Home," Amelia said slowly. "Are you telling me that you intend to return to New Orleans? You led us to believe the decision to seek out your real father had closed the door at the home of your adopted parents."

"Not after I do what must be done. I've had communications with them this past year. They would never turn me out if my life is in danger." Crystal walked to the door. "Amelia, I have a stage to catch in several hours. It has been good to visit with you."

She opened the door, and slowly Amelia walked toward it. She had nearly stepped through when she stopped and turned. "Crystal, I am having a very strange feeling—as if the Lord is warning me. What is going to happen?"

Slowly Crystal's hands crept to her throat while her eyes widened with alarm. Amelia shoved the door closed. "I'm not leaving here until you tell me what your intentions are."

Crystal walked quickly to the window and turned. "Amelia, it is nothing that concerns you at all. Please leave; I mustn't be delayed."

"What did you mean when you said you'd sold your soul?"

Her face twisted into a tortured mask. "Just another foolish thing I've done. I'm committed too deeply to back out."

"With Lucas? And you've agreed to help Lucas sell out Colorado?"

"I didn't say—" She wilted. "You figured that out. All right, Amelia, I'll tell you. I intend to meet Lucas in Denver. I sent him a letter telling him I will help him get the information he needs. But I don't intend doing it." She stopped and took a deep breath.

"Amelia," she cried wildly, "I don't know why I'm telling you this. You don't need to know all of my plans." She started to walk away from Amelia, and then she turned back and lifted her chin. "I'm going to kill him."

Amelia caught the back of the chair. Taking a deep breath, she watched Crystal's ashen face as she gently said, "Please, Crystal, tell me about it."

For a long time the woman was silent, motionless. Finally her shoulders drooped and she leaned against the window frame. Her voice was a whisper. "He raped me. Do you understand? I am nothing. He has broken my last hope, my last reason for living. Now my husband will never have any place in my life."

Amelia was trembling as she stepped forward and put her arms around Crystal, whispering, "I love you. God and I won't let you destroy yourself."

"Amelia, help me! I need you desperately."

The afternoon sun had slipped away from the window when Crystal finally lifted her tear-stained face. "Thank you. I—guess it isn't the end of life. Now I feel strong enough to go on."

"What do you mean 'go on'?"

"With my plans, of course. Amelia, please go now."

Amelia crossed the room. Pushing back Crystal's hair, she cradled her face against her, saying, "You're too precious to waste yourself like this. Can you believe God has a great love for you?"

Her lips twisted. "That once again He is pursuing me?"

"Just as He did me," Amelia said softly. "Chased me until I

couldn't run anymore. At one time I didn't think I'd ever be able to surrender to His seeking love again. But Crystal, that's part of God. He never gives up on us. We're never too far away from Him to be forgiven and restored. I know firsthand."

After they had been silent for a long time, touching Crystal's face, Amelia murmured, "I need to know; what are you going to do now?"

Crystal pulled away and smiled bitterly. "What do you suppose? Lucas is expecting me. In less than an hour the stage will be here."

Amelia asked, "What will happen if you fail to meet Lucas?"

Slowly she said, "He's revealed his plans to me. That puts him in an uncomfortable situation. Since Tom Pollack cleaned the Bummer Gang out of Denver City, Colorado Territory has become known for dealing harshly with lawbreakers. You know how extreme Governor Gilpin has been. He's solidly behind Lincoln and the Union." Slowly she added, "I think Lucas will be very worried if I don't show up."

She looked into Amelia's face. "You mentioned talking to the governor. You said those things about being patriotic. Do you suppose I would dare do that? I would be a fool.

"He hurt me, Amelia. Beat me. My face was bruised for a week. He would do it again. He will kill me—if I don't kill him first."

For a moment Crystal pressed clenched fists against her face. When she dropped them she said, "I've thought, wondered what I could have done differently. Now I am wiser. I should have kept my door locked."

Amelia gasped, "Crystal, I'm afraid! Please, don't go to him! Just leave the territory as quickly as you can."

For a moment Crystal hesitated. Fear flitted across her face and then she whispered, "You don't understand, Amelia. I have nothing to live for. And this is worth my life. You might say that if this is to be my life's biggest sacrifice, it will be worth it."

Amelia's face was still rigid with horror as Crystal paced the room and then stopped in front of her. "I've told you this in confidence— don't betray me. Look at it this way. I'll be doing more than killing that man. Count it as my bid against slavery." Her lips twisted as she turned.

Walking to the door, once again Crystal opened it and waited.

The smile on her face mocked the pain on Amelia's. She said, "Now I insist. Please leave."

As Amelia passed through she whispered, "Crystal, I'll be praying that the Lord brings you to your senses before it is too late."

CHAPTER 8

On the Monday morning Amy and Daniel left Oro City, the housewives were hanging out their wash, and the ore in the sluice boxes was rushing down across the riffles.

When they reached the mouth of California Gulch, Daniel tugged at his reins, waiting for Amy to catch up. "Are you going to be comfortable riding on that saddle?"

"Most comfortable," Amy replied. "Back in Kansas, with the cousins, I rode bareback. This sidesaddle is rocking-chair comfortable. Besides, it's a mighty poor female who can't stand a horse for a week." She slanted a glance at him before adding, "If I could wish for more, it would be some of those new fangled bloomers the women are wearing so they can sit a man's saddle." At his expression, she added hastily, "Oh, I know the bishop would have apoplexy, and I wouldn't want that to happen."

"Well, I'm relieved," he said dryly.

"Oh, Daniel, isn't it a beautiful day? Look at the misty mountains and the line of green along the creek. It puts me in mind of a painting."

"It is nice. And if you feel that way about it, this week will be almost as good as a honeymoon."

"Well, I doubt it," she teased. "If we're sharing cabins with your parishioners, you daren't pass me a kiss."

He chuckled and pointed. "Look, the snow's melted except for the drifts under the trees."

"Could those possibly be pussy willows this early?"

"Not up here." He grinned. "It's dried leaves still clinging to the branches. Should have fallen off long ago."

It was only fourteen miles to Granite, the first town on their circuit. They rode lazily along the route, enjoying the early spring day. At midday they stopped to eat while the horses grazed and drank of the icy creek water. The sun had warmed the boulder on which they leaned and for a time they dozed.

When Amy stirred, she looked at Daniel, saying, "Can heaven possibly smell better? That wet, fresh growing smell mixed with the willow smell is good enough to save and put in a bottle."

Daniel nodded and bent over her. "I'm going to kiss your sun-burned nose; then we'd better move on." She sighed with regret as she lifted her face to him.

In the middle of the afternoon they reached the outskirts of the little mining town built along the creek. From the road they could look down on the community, which seemed to be stretched along the creek in a haphazard manner.

Amy looked at the line of log cabins and said, "Seems substantial, like they've taken time hereabouts to think of the future."

"But notice, these cabins are new. See that shack? Most of the places looked like that last year. There's been a new thrust of activity around here. New mines."

"Daniel," Amy said, hugging her arms, "I'm excited. I've listened to you talk about these places. Suddenly this all is part of me. The people. I want to know them."

As they cut down the hill into town, Daniel pulled back on the reins, slowing his horse. "I should warn you. Granite is a strange place. I can't quite figure it out. People are closed-mouth and clannish."

He looked at her, shrugged and grinned as he said, "Father Dyer has the reputation of considering not one hamlet too tough or small for his best efforts. Every time I ride into this town, I recall him saying that."

After supper that evening, the townspeople began to crowd into the little cabin to hear Daniel preach.

Studying the faces surrounding her, Amy began to understand Daniel's statement. With curiosity, she watched the silent line of unsmiling women as they sat down on the benches in the tiny cabin.

The next morning as they rode out of Granite, Amy bobbed her head in the direction of the cabin and shivered. "Daniel," she murmured, "you described the town as strange. That it is. Where were the men? Is it only the women who attend services?"

He nodded and she continued. "I've never seen such people; I'd believe they've never smiled. Did you feel as if they were frightened? I don't think they enjoyed the singing. Every one of them knelt for prayer, but their mood made them seem desperate."

"Yes, that is so," he said reluctantly. "I've heard rumors about the place. On the other side of the mountain they talk of an outlaw band hiding out hereabouts. I was told to not pry."

When she looked up, he was grinning at her. "Don't worry. Not many of the places are like Granite. You'll love the next little burg. Only a couple of families live there, but they're easy to love. I'm not certain they've gotten around to tacking a name on the town yet."

The following day they moved on. As their route dropped steadily down out of the mountains, the grass beside the road became green and thick. Amy pointed to the willows along the creek. "Daniel, we've caught up with spring! Look at the little pussy willows. I remember them from Kansas."

Suddenly she looked up and said, "I forgot to tell you about the strange handbill Lettie gave me. She said Hank brought it back from the mine. It seemed to be a plea from the South for money to buy arms. It mentioned Jefferson Davis and Robert E. Lee. The whole thing sounded confident—like we'd be glad to support the Confederacy. Daniel, is war really getting that close to us?"

"I don't know, Amy. I do know that everywhere I go it's the first subject people begin waving in front of my nose. I can't believe the secessionists have any designs on our territory, for all the talk."

"What designs could they possibly have?" Amy looked around in bewilderment. "I can't believe anyone would want the territory."

"There's gold," Daniel said heavily. "Lots of gold, and it would help finance a war."

Amy nodded in agreement. "Lettie says Hank hears plenty of war talk from the miners. She says he comes home angry at what he's hearing. He told her most of the fellows are just uneasy, but some are openly saying they support the secession, and that their cause is bound to win."

Amy rode past Daniel to look at the clutch of flowers growing beside the road. "Don't lean over so far," he called. "You'll fall on your head."

While he grinned down at her, she asked, "Aren't these wild irises?" He nodded, and she continued. "You know, you promised me wild irises along the creek at Oro City. All I've seen along that creek are mine tailings."

"I'm sorry. While I was in Buckskin Joe those miners made a liar out of me. First thing I noticed was the pile of rock where the flowers grew last year." Then he added, "We're dropping down out of the mountains. Enjoy the iris while you can. Pretty soon we'll be in the arid part of the territory. It's going to be too dry for irises down there."

That evening, before they could dismount at the cabin where the services would be held, a jolly-faced woman bounced out the door. "Parson, we're going to have revival. I feel the shouting beginning down inside. I've been promising the miners you'd be here tonight. Come have your supper."

She watched as Amy allowed Daniel to lift her from the horse. Amy smoothed her frock and said, "Mrs. Pepper, Daniel's told me about this place. Says besides the fact you are the best cook on the circuit, this place rests easy in his mind. I've been told the people here are of a mind to come to worship. You know it isn't that way all over. The biggest excitement in California Gulch is the gold."

"Well, there's plenty of that around here," Mrs. Pepper said, adding, "but there's also been some hard times, enough to remind the people they gotta have the Lord to see them through." She paused and a twinkle started in her eyes. "Besides, soon as they start slipping out of the habit of coming to services, I goad them on with the 're-member whens.' Yes, without a doubt most people need a good nudge regularlike."

The next day the morning sun was slanting into their eyes as they turned onto the road. "Mrs. Pepper made certain her prediction of revival was right, didn't she?" Daniel chuckled as they rode out of the little community. He smiled down at Amy, "I also have the feeling she'd given the promise to everyone else. At least there was a good group."

The trail narrowed and Daniel rode ahead. Amy was glad to be alone with her thoughts. She recalled Mrs. Pepper's declaration. *Why did she tell me I needed to pray down the joy of the Lord?*

Moving her shoulders uneasily, she flicked the reins and caught up with Daniel. Giving him a quick glance, she wondered, *Was it possible Daniel ever felt the tug to be something different than he was? Did he ever desire anything desperately?*

As she continued to study the face of the man who was becoming increasingly precious to her, she knew one thing was certain. Nothing must ever bring the old hurt back into Daniel's eyes. No matter how dear her desires, it was impossible to consider anything that would hurt him afresh.

But as she thought of her big desire, she settled contentedly down in the saddle and chuckled to herself. *Thank you, Father Dyer! I'd never have thought of it if you hadn't given me the crucible.*

She mused over the memory of the little crucible with its growing stack of gold nuggets, and she hugged the secret to herself. *One of these days, my husband, I'll spill out my big pile of gold nuggets that I've been fishing out of the creek while you're riding the circuit.* There were many things that they needed, but the piano was top on the list.

That night a stranger came into the worship services held in the crowded little cabin beside the Arkansas River. Daniel stood to preach just as he walked in. Daniel's hesitation and the question in his eyes alerted Amy. She watched him study the man. Later she drew a deep breath of relief as she began to understand Daniel's questions. He thought the man was a secessionist. Without a doubt Lettie's talk had triggered the questions. But the man wasn't there to cause trouble.

She was standing beside Daniel when the stranger mentioned Fort Garland.

He said, "We're the most neglected bunch in the territory. No chaplain for a handful of soldiers kept on duty just to run off the Indians and outlaws. No glory in that."

Daniel was nodding. "I'll come. We're this close and without a big need to get back to the gulch. Father Dyer will be there a couple of weeks. I'll just go on down now."

"He's a soldier?" she asked later. Daniel nodded. Her voice was low as she said, "His face was so hard and dark."

"But it didn't stay that way. Amy, as I preached I could see the yearning in his eyes. It was that which compelled me to say yes."

"Where's Fort Garland?"

"Straight south of here. Not as far as New Mexico, or even the mountains by Raton."

The man whose cabin had been serving as meetinghouse said, "Best way to get down there is by way of the sand dunes. Pretty good road runs along the flatlands, and it's fast. You oughta be able to get there in two, three days at the most."

"Indians?" Amy asked.

"Naw, no more'n usual. A few Utes. Plenty of places to stay along the way."

On their second day of travel, after studying the sagebrush and clumps of greenery as spiked as a cluster of swords, Amy said, "Daniel, this part of the territory is different; this is drier, sandy. It's getting pretty close to being desert, isn't it? For a time I thought all of Colorado was mountains and plains. And the people we're seeing. Somehow I got the idea all the people of Mexican descent lived in Pueblo."

"Not so. Remember, these people moved into the area before the territorial lines were drawn. They are just as much a part of Colorado Territory as we are. See these little brown houses? Not many trees around, so the people brought with them their way of doing things. The houses are made of sun-dried brick—mud, if you please. They call it adobe. In the winter the houses are much more comfortable than our log cabins. And in summer they're cool."

It was nearly sundown when they saw the smudge of buildings

centered in the middle of the high plains. "Fort Garland," Daniel said with a nod toward the line of adobes. "This is a first for me, too. Traveling this far south, I mean. The fort is impressive. How do you like that high adobe wall surrounding the place?"

"Frightening," Amy murmured. "It makes me wonder why it is necessary."

He replied, "Indians. We'll be there before dark if we move on," Daniel said, flicking his mare with the reins. Bending her head against the wind, Amy followed.

"Hallo!" Amy jumped and looked up as Daniel slowed his mount and veered toward a lone horseman. After a gasp of surprise, Amy followed.

The man was wearing a uniform. At her approach he touched his hat and nodded. Amy could see the insignia on his uniform. *Colorado Volunteer Army.*

Addressing Daniel, the man said, "Fella, I recognize you. I'm Chivington, lately of your outfit—now the Army's my field. Do I get the impression you're headed for New Mexico?"

Daniel leaned across his horse to extend his hand. "No, Major Chivington. I'm glad to meet you. I've inherited a cabin you've used in Oro City. Thanks for the books."

"You're welcome to them, fella. Have a feeling my days of using them are limited." For a moment his face saddened and then he smiled. "But decisions made must be honored. You can't coil up life like a rope and toss it out again, in a different direction if you please."

He lifted his head and turned his sharp eyes on Daniel again. "I'd appreciate a few prayers. The troops are headed into confrontation with the rebels in New Mexico."

Amy straightened and leaned across to look at the major. "Sir, what do you mean? Surely not war."

He nodded. "A frantic call for help. Dispatch from New Mexico informs us the Confederate Army is moving up from Texas. They've been taking the Union installations, fort by fort. Information indicates they're headed for Fort Union. That's the biggest and last stronghold before they're into Colorado Territory." His smile was crooked. "We're headed New Mexico way to help out Canby. There's no way of getting around it. We fight them there or we'll be meeting them on our own ground in a couple of weeks. It's the Colorado gold fields they have their eyes on. Colorado gold to fight their war."

"War," Amy said slowly. "Now it is here. We'll be having war in our own Colorado."

"Only over my dead body," Chivington said soberly. "We'll have a big fight in New Mexico, but Colorado? Not while I'm alive."

He lifted his hand in a salute. For a moment his smile was half mocking. "Parson, now's not a good time to carry the gospel into New Mexico. Better avoid Raton Pass." With that warning, he wheeled his restless horse, and dug in his spurs. Silently Amy and Daniel watched the cloud of red dust grow and hide him from their sight.

As they started to turn their horses, Amy gave a gasp. Reaching for her husband's arm, she cried, "Daniel, what about Mother and Father? You said—" She watched the dismay move over his face. "It's bad, isn't it? Even you're thinking it's all Chivington says."

He glanced down at her trembling hand and spoke as if he were thinking aloud. "He said Fort Union; the folks were headed that direction. Their plans were to go down through Las Vegas and Santa Fe." He took a deep breath. "Yes, Amy, it's bad. Bad enough that if it is at all possible to put you on a stage for Denver, I intend to ride after them."

"No!" Amy gulped, fighting back the tears that threatened to fall. "We can't afford a stage, but besides that, Daniel, I've no intention of leaving you. I'll go too. What if they've been caught in all the fighting? You'll need me. Besides, if it's that bad, I'd be in the middle of the fighting before you get back."

She saw him hesitate, chew his lip. Despite the dark expression in his eyes, he nodded.

CHAPTER 9

L et's ride on," Amy said impatiently.

Daniel dropped his hand. He had been studying the squat adobe fort sprawled across the horizon. "Go on?" Shaking his head, Daniel said, "Sweetheart, I know you're anxious, but we can't ride day and night. For one thing, I wouldn't want the wrong people to get to wondering where we're going in such a hurry. Chivington made it clear we weren't to talk about his mission."

Touching Amy's hand, he added, "Let's stay here at the fort tonight. I'll hold services according to plan. I'll also look at the army maps and get information about the trails."

Slowly Amy said, "This is frightening—like a bad dream. At home the war talk was easy to ignore. I mean, we're so far from Washington and even farther from the South where the fighting is going on. Now all of a sudden it's here."

Daniel nodded. "But, Amy, don't get in a panic over it. It's going to be two armies fighting it out, probably somewhere out in the middle of the desert. We've little chance of getting close enough to be involved.

"My guess is we'll have all the protection we need if we stick to the well-traveled routes. From what Chivington said, we'll have to avoid Raton Pass through the mountains."

He paused, then added, "We also need to get all the information we can about the location of the Confederates."

"Why did he tell us to stay off Raton Pass? You said Mother and Father traveled that route." She read the answer in his expression. Slowly she said, "I guess I can add up the facts. Chivington, Colorado Volunteers, and Raton Pass. You said we need information—about the fighting going on right now?"

He nodded and Amy began shaking her head as he added, "It would be better for you to stay here."

"With all these men? Daniel, I just refuse to let you go without me."

He studied her face before admitting, "I guess you'll be just as safe with me. If Fort Union falls, Fort Garland stands a good chance of being attacked next. I'd rather have you where I can—" His grin was strained as he added, "Now you've got me thinking war. Besides, it's easier for just the two of us to be dodging an army. At least two won't kick up as much dust as a thousand troops do. And even in war the clergy are given special consideration.

"Let's move out." He turned his horse and headed for the adobe fort.

That night during the evening services, while Amy led the singing she watched the serious eyes of the young men. Their sober gaze made her heart heavy with dread. *Daniel, it is serious*, she thought. *More than you think. Look at their eyes. They know what is going on in New Mexico, and they're thinking hard about eternity.*

As Daniel stood to preach, she watched the men lean forward with elbows on knees. From her seat behind them, she studied their knobby-knuckled hands and the slender young shoulders hunched with tension.

The attentive spirit of the young men caught at her throat, and she found her mood lining up with theirs. *War. Mother and Father are somewhere in the middle of it all. What is it like to know my fellowmen are ready to kill for gold—for a cause I can't understand?* She rubbed her chilled arms as she looked at Daniel.

Daniel echoed the word back. "Gold. If only men would guard the treasure God has put within them. The Divine has created us with the potential for fellowship with himself, and we hold this treasure lightly. There's not a miner alive who would sit by and let someone walk off with his bag of gold nuggets."

Later she and Daniel crossed the parade grounds to the quartermaster's cabin where they were to sleep. The moon had risen, and in the cold light the adobe fort seemed strangely isolated and lonesome. A coyote raised his mournful yipping from a distant hill. The horses in the corral snorted and shifted uneasily. Amy tightened her grip on Daniel's arm.

Inside the tiny chamber she watched Daniel spread their blankets on the floor. With the last one in place, he leaned back to look at her, asking, "What were you thinking tonight? I saw you shiver as those young men came down to pray."

"War. Daniel, it's frightening. I was thinking it must be terrible to be a soldier, knowing each day dawns with the possibility of riding out to meet a foe. No wonder their eyes were serious, and that they were so attentive. I wonder that they ever manage a smile. And now we're going down there."

He quirked an eyebrow at her. With a strained grin, he asked, "A risk? Isn't all of life a risk? Is it so different for them?" His voice dropped to a brooding murmur. "Granted, the stakes are higher for them, but still, each one of us faces risk in our daily lives."

He slanted a glance at her, trying for a lighthearted grin as he spoke. But she saw the question in his eyes as he said, "How do you young women so bravely dash into marriage knowing you must face childbirth? Far too many women die for their loving."

She looked up into his brooding dark eyes. "Daniel," she whispered, going to kneel on the blankets beside him. For a moment she couldn't answer; then slowly she began. "Children. Of course I want them. I'm not thinking about the risk. It is a threat we live with unheedingly. Daniel, to think on all this makes a body nearly afraid to draw another deep breath. Do you worry about our loving?"

"I don't think worry is the word, but I'm aware of the danger. Amy, I don't know how people like Lizzie can laugh through life. But isn't living for the Lord Jesus Christ really a matter of doing our best down here and then leaving the rest in His hands? Even life and death? Childbirth or war? The question isn't whether we live or die, but whether we end up satisfied with our lives when the end comes."

He brooded on. "The Bible tells us we have no control over the length of our life. And God knows about childbirth and war, so that makes the other thoughts such as the dread and fear of death seem just plain out of line. Unless, of course, the Holy Ghost is pointing out a man's need of salvation. In that situation, there's no way a man can escape the dread without dealing with his need."

In the morning as they left the fort behind, Daniel said, "I had a chance to look at the map. It's straight south for us. The first settlement we'll reach is San Luis. It'll be Catholic and Spanish. Even if they could understand us, I doubt we'll be given a voice, and I doubt they're looking for an itinerant preacher anyway." He added, "According to the map, from there on down into New Mexico, the other settlements are too small to be called towns."

"But Father Dyer preaches to any man he can back into a corner long enough."

"Not to the Catholics who can't speak plain old American."

The morning was crisp. Frost had outlined every bush and blade of grass with brilliance, reminding Amy it was still the middle of March.

During the days that followed, the miles before them slanted down out of the high mountain country. Cedar and piñon gave way to sage and mesquite, while rocky paths disappeared into sandy trails. They rode rapidly toward the border separating the two territories and discovered the lowlands were pleasantly warm and dry. The trail before them was clear-cut, marked by a line of scanty vegetation worn thin by the hooves of animals.

Nodding at the trail, Daniel said, "This morning a fellow told me a bit about New Mexico. Seems there's a gent by the name of Maxwell who just about owns all of the southeast quarter of the territory. They tell me he's a white man, known pretty much as a fair dealer and interested in both the Mexicans and Indians.

"They also told me an Indian agent by the name of Arny has

pretty much finalized plans for an Indian reservation, using part of Maxwell's land grant. A small part."

"They're starting to talk reservation here too?"

Daniel nodded. "Times are bad for them." Impatiently Daniel added, "They can't glean a living off the land now. We've helped abuse the land and ruin the game herds, so they've every right to be unhappy. But it's easy for the white man to forget the facts when it's his house being burned and his family murdered." He shook his head. "Now the government is scratching hard to make peace and settle the Indians on tribal lands. I don't agree with the methods, but I don't know better how to do for them. Without reservation land, they'll starve."

The following day they rode into New Mexico Territory. Daniel said, "There's no longer a need to pretend to be only missionaries for the Methodist Episcopal Church, going about our business. Amy, from here on out, we'll stretch leather until we get to Santa Fe. Then we'll start asking questions."

"About Mother and Father?" He nodded, and she persisted, "Heading into Santa Fe means we'll be close to where the fighting is. Maybe closer to the Confederate Army than Mother and Father?" His nod was abrupt.

As Daniel said, they stretched leather, and there was no longer opportunity to talk much while their horses trotted side by side, pausing occasionally to nibble at the grass along the trail.

Under the hooves of the horses the fine soil was beaten into a stifling cloud that drifted and settled, coating them from head to toe. In an attempt to avoid the dust, Amy stuffed her blond curls into Daniel's old hat.

On the following day, they stopped to water the horses at midday. While they waited, Daniel said, "I have an idea. Let's have something to eat while I tell you about it."

While Amy opened the pack of food, he said, "Sweetheart, what would you think of wearing this other pair of trousers?"

She thought about it. "Because I am a woman and you think it will make people guess me to be a fellow? Do you think it would make me safer? And what about a fellow on a sidesaddle?"

"It wouldn't be obvious from a distance. Up close, nobody in his right mind would mistake you for a man anyway, sidesaddle or no." He grinned affectionately and winked at her.

"Seems to me, Daniel, we're more harmless looking just the way we are." She saw his face and rushed to him. "Don't worry, my husband. Remember, these are the risks. Two days ago, you were talking brave talk about trusting the Lord, even in these risks."

She watched the lines of strain on his face as he said, "It's different having a wife along."

"I should hope so!" Finally he grinned and reached for her. In a moment she pushed away from his kisses, saying, "I have a big desire to wash the dust off my face."

He hugged her, not wanting to disappoint her, but he knew they needed to push on. "Could be a waste of time. Anyway, we'll reach Taos before sundown. Tonight, if we're fortunate, we'll find enough water for bathing."

"What is Taos?"

"Indian pueblo. They told me that at Fort Garland. My dear wife, we're both going to learn something new this trip. I've not yet seen an Indian pueblo. Father Dyer saw it on his visit, said it was very old. They told him it's been inhabited for hundreds of years."

"Pueblo?" she questioned as she divided the meat and bread.

"About like a bunch of Indian huts stuck together and stacked on top of each other. Adobe."

By midafternoon they were into the foothills of the Sangre de Cristo Mountains. Fir forests darkened the slopes and deep canyons. Daniel had been riding ahead. Now he turned his mare and came back to Amy. "Sangre de Cristo." His tongue poured out the liquid phrase. "Father Dyer says it means the atonement blood of the crucified Christ. I don't know the significance of the name in connection with the mountains."

The trail led deeper into the awesome canyons. Amy whispered. "Daniel, I can't help wondering where this is taking us."

"Well, for one thing, look up ahead." He turned to point upward. In front of them, the sun slanting between the mountains spread light across a block of brightness. At first it seemed an illusion, but as Amy studied it, she saw its dimensions and bulk. It was very real, rearing up between the screen of trees sketching out the river course.

Slowly Amy murmured, "Giant blocks. Could it possibly be—"

"Taos pueblo." They continued their ride in silence as they followed the winding trail through the rocks and trees. When they broke out into the clearing, the late afternoon sun struck them full in the face.

Daniel led the way toward the final crude bridge separating them from the pueblo. Curiosity had Amy leaning forward in her saddle. She had nearly forgotten her fatigue and thirst as she croaked, "Daniel, that pueblo is as big as a mountain! Those poles—are they ladders going up to the flat roof?"

Daniel nodded. "Don't see any doors on the ground level, do you? The second story seems to be a courtyard area. I see more ladders going up to the next level."

"Five stories," Amy counted slowly, adding, "The last level has a ladder sticking out the roof." She reached for his arm and pointed at the line of Indian children gazing at them from the opposite bank. "Look at the darling little children. They have such big black eyes!"

Daniel chuckled. "It's your hair and brick red face that's making their eyes big." He added, "Let's just stay on the main road and ride through to the little village.

"You notice there aren't any mamas and papas around trying to be friendly. Even if they were to appear and offer a room on the top floor, I've been warned against spending the night in the pueblos." At Amy's quick glance, he added, "Besides, tonight might be the night I take up sleepwalking."

The village they entered was crowded nearly on the heels of the pueblo. Daniel murmured, "It's obviously Spanish; there's not a white person to be seen."

While they rode slowly down the one short street, a covey of children began to follow, screaming incomprehensible sentences at them. Amy winced and shifted uneasily, but Daniel's puzzled frown disappeared.

He began chuckling. As he smiled and nodded, he said. "See, Amy, that little fellow is pretending he's a sleepy bird. I think he's offering us lodging." Daniel slipped off his mare and Amy followed.

They tied their horses to the hitching post beside the community well and turned to follow the grinning child.

The houses lining the street were all of adobe, as well as the wall circling each home. Amy nearly fell over her feet as she strained to see everything at once. "Oh, look! Daniel, slow down and look. It's so different. What are those pretty red things hanging beside the door?"

"Strings of chili peppers." Daniel tugged at her arm and they followed the dark-haired youngster through the courtyard.

"So strange," Amy murmured; "not a scrap of green grass. Daniel, it looks to me like they've *swept* their yard!" She pointed to the line of scratches in the hard-packed earth.

Daniel nodded. "Come along; I don't want to lose the fellow. As Amy followed him, she noticed the plain brown adobe house in front of them had a bright blue door adorned with a string of chili peppers. The house was as flat-topped as its pueblo neighbors, with tiny windows recessed in the thick dun-colored walls.

She was still looking around when a pleasant-faced woman came out, smiling and nodding as she gestured toward another door. They followed her into the tiny room. Amy turned slowly, while Daniel pulled out coins and offered them to the woman.

"I think it is well we have food and blankets," Amy said as the woman closed the door behind her. She went to peer at the fireplace. "If it weren't for the smoke-blackened wall, I'd have named it anything except a fireplace."

Daniel crossed the room. "Looks like part of a beehive stuck there in the corner. Interesting the way they've stacked wood on end. I suppose that's the way it's to be burned."

"Whitewashed, everything in the room," Amy pronounced before tilting her head to look up. "Oh, except the ceiling. A strange one it is. Daniel, it looks like the outside of a thatched roof."

During the following days Amy and Daniel traveled through one small village after another as they circled down through the mountains.

One afternoon Daniel said thoughtfully, "Amy, I've been seeing something new today, and it's making me uncomfortable. I think it's fear. The people we're meeting today seem uneasy and not very friendly. From the expression in their eyes, I get the feeling they know something we don't know. I wish I could communicate with them, let them know we are friends."

"Are we?" Amy asked soberly.

"I wondered how they felt," he admitted. "I've wondered about the fighting that's been going on. From what Father Dyer's told me, the people are accustomed to having someone's thumb in their back. He was of the opinion they wouldn't know how to behave if the thumb was gone."

That next week, one evening at dusk they reached the outskirts of the large village spread at the foot of the mountains.

Daniel murmured, "It must be Santa Fe. Look at the trees. They've been planted here; see the difference? I'm guessing this place is old and well established. That fits the description I was given. At Fort Garland they told me there's a fort in Santa Fe. The commanding officer at Fort Garland didn't know whether it's still in federal hands."

Amy pointed. "Look over that way. See all those buildings and corrals? There's also a big bare spot in the middle; could it be—"

"Fort Marcy," Daniel supplied. "I believe you're right."

"Why don't we go down there?" Amy asked. "We'll be safe in a fort."

Daniel shaded his eyes and continued to study the line of buildings. Slowly he said, "I don't know; there's something about that place—I just don't know. Let's ride into town instead. If the Confederates were to start delivering shells that direction, I wouldn't want to be there."

"Shells? Are you talking about a cannon?" Amy asked. "In the beginning all this didn't seem real. Now you're worried about a cannon. What next? Daniel, what shall we do now?"

He shrugged. "I've no idea except to suggest we ride into town and see what we can find out."

Dismay kept Amy silent as she studied his face, and fought back the desire to suggest going home. *But we still haven't found Mother and Father. They might be in danger if the war has moved this close. I can't be a baby now.* She nodded and said, "All right, Daniel, let's go."

As they started down the canyon road, the red ball of the setting sun abruptly disappeared behind the bank of tree-covered hills. Amy glanced uneasily at Daniel as he led them through the cluster of small adobes and wound down the trail into the middle of town.

There was only one woman in the shady square. As they rode closer, Amy saw she was drawing water at a well in the square. As they rode across the cobbled plaza, the clop of the horses' hooves was amplified, echoing from the ring of adobe buildings surrounding the square.

At Daniel's nod they slipped from their mares. Taking the reins in his hands Daniel turned to study the surrounding buildings. Evening shadows were quickly spreading across the square. The long, low line of buildings seemed to have linked hands like stoic family members ready to repel strangers.

Daniel still held their mounts as he walked toward the woman pulling her bucket of water to the stone wall. Daniel's horse caught the scent of water and snorted.

The woman turned. Slipping the reins to Amy, Daniel went forward to meet her. In careful, slow English, he began his request. She interrupted. "Sir, I speak your language." Amy listened to her slow, musical sentences, admiring more than understanding the words. When the woman stopped and waited, Daniel came back to Amy.

"Amy, she can offer us lodging. I think we'd better take it. She says Fort Marcy has been taken by the Confederates. I think she guessed we aren't sympathetic to the southern cause. I'm not certain this is a good idea, but—"

With her voice low, Amy slowly finished the thought, "We've no choice."

CHAPTER 10

When Crystal reached Denver City, she went first to the post office and then to her hotel. The one letter waiting for her was from home. Opening the envelope, she murmured, "Dear Mama, how faithful you are."

Crystal quickly read the letter. "So war is pushing at your precious New Orleans," she said, folding the letter carefully, then unfolding it again. "How sorry I am for your sakes. How desperately I wish to rescue you. Unfortunately this war must happen if we will be whole again." With another glance at the pained writing, she dropped the letter on the table.

After settling into her room and changing her frock, she picked up her cloak. Already her thoughts were on the interview with Lucas. As she walked to the closed door, she thought of her last encounter with him, and with a shiver of fear she turned away.

Slowly she dropped the cloak on the bed. Looking down at the cloak and the bulge of the tiny silver-handled pistol, she murmured, "Crystal, you are a fool to let your passions rule!"

But in the next moment the memory of that night surfaced and she clenched her fists. "Never will I be happy again until I see him dead!" She tossed her head. "Fool or not, I'll worry about that later." For one moment she hesitated, seeing a fleeting image of Amelia's face.

Quickly she turned away from the memory of that face, those haunting words, and her lips twisted as she said, "I'll never believe God was watching over me that night. This problem I will handle my way." With a bitter smile, she turned to snatch up the cloak.

She started for the door when the tap came. "Crystal, it's me." She recognized the voice and took one second longer to gather courage before she opened the door.

"Lucas, you may come in, but you are to leave the door open." Her voice was icy as she met his amused eyes.

"You've become quite the prude."

"Just cautious. Never again will I trust you." She turned away as he entered the room and dropped into the chair.

"Who's the letter from?"

"You've no right to ask, but since you have, it's from my mother."

She saw the curiosity as he said, "I hope you find her well."

"As well as can be expected. At the time of the writing they were expecting to be under siege. The Union ships were approaching the gulf. Mama says they've seen gunfire in town."

He leaned forward. "Then you are all the more committed to the cause," he exulted.

She caught her breath. A smile crept over her face as she began to think along with him. Turning to look at him, she admitted, "My parents are very precious to me. How could it be otherwise? Right now, I would do whatever is best for their safety."

"Then you are ready to cooperate with me?"

"I am ready. But, Mr. Tristram, it will be on my terms. Never again are you to force yourself on me. You started this proposition as a business venture. I know how much you are to profit if it is successful. We will just keep it as a business deal. Only a fool would let emotion tangle the skein of an enterprise as important as this."

His eyes sparkled as he grinned at her. "My dear, you are more than beautiful when you are indignant. I'll respect your wishes. And it will be convenient to do so. I find it necessary to make a quick trip south to Santa Fe. Meanwhile, here's a summary of the items you are to handle while I am gone."

He got to his feet with the sardonic grin still in place. His eyes twinkled down at her as he added, "I'll miss you. I hope to find you in a better mood when I return." He stepped toward her and Crystal swung around to the open door.

The New Mexico dusk deepened into twilight. Amy watched the dark-skinned woman slip back into the shadows. She waited there with her jugs of water while Daniel led the horses to the watering trough. When the horses finally lifted their dripping muzzles from the water, the woman beckoned and led the way.

They followed behind her as she slipped quickly through the darkening streets. To Amy it seemed the whisper of the woman's bare feet blended her into one quiet shadow after another. In contrast, their horses' hooves clopped loudly against the packed earth, the sound echoing from the line of silent adobes.

Just beyond the town square, the woman abruptly turned and cut down a heavily wooded slope. Catching her breath, Amy pulled her horse even with Daniel's as he nudged his mare into the path. The last of the sky's light disappeared as they wound their way through the trees, following a trail that had become only a pale slash in the woods.

When they broke out of the trees, the moonlight outlined the scene in front of them. As they crossed a meadow, Amy could see a low cluster of huts, circled by an adobe wall. When the woman turned to wave them on, they slipped from their horses to follow her toward the enclosure.

Pointing to the grassy meadow just beyond, the woman said, "The horses, they'll be safe. Hobble them." She waited for Daniel to follow her instructions. When he returned she walked quickly across the darkened courtyard.

Trying to keep her in sight, Amy stumbled through the dark. Momentarily the darting figure was outlined against the pale adobe. "Hurry!" Daniel murmured behind her. She reached the door as the woman opened it. The rasping hinges had Amy shivering as she followed Daniel inside. A light flared, revealing the woman kneeling on the hearth.

When she got to her feet, Amy struggled to understand her torrent of broken English. Her final words were, "You will be safe for the night. I do not know about tomorrow. I must ask my husband. But perhaps you had better move on tomorrow."

Daniel held out the coins. "Thank you. We too must decide, but I would like to talk to your husband."

"I send him."

They watched her leave and Amy asked, "What did she say?"

"I don't know. We'll have to hope her husband speaks better English."

Daniel had just untied their pack when the man slipped through the door. "My wife says you must speak to me."

Although as square and swarthy as his wife, he spoke with scarcely an accent. The two men hunched down by the fire, while Amy leaned against the wall.

She studied the stranger as Daniel said, "Tell me about this place. Is it Santa Fe?" He nodded. "Your wife says the fort has been taken by the Confederates. How does this affect you?"

Amy watched as he shrugged slowly with uplifted hands. "I do not get involved in white man's affairs. There is a war between the United States and the Confederates. I do not understand it. Our people do not see it of much importance. What does it matter who wins? Aren't we all one big people? I think I live happily with any, no matter his color or speech."

He grinned and rubbed his fingers together. "I work for the soldiers; that is why we speak like gringos. The money is the same; the people act the same. Why worry?"

Daniel sighed and asked, "How do the soldiers treat the people who do not agree with them?"

The man's smile disappeared. "If they wear a uniform, they are put in jail. If not"—he pulled down the corner of his mouth and lifted his hands—"they look the other way. I think they would rather not be bothered by people. That isn't the important thing."

"What is?"

"Land, gold. This is their talk all the time, saying, if they have many on their side, if they get the gold, they win. People. I do not think they like to hurt people, not the young soldiers. The young ones sing sad songs and talk long into the night about home and pretty girls."

As the man started out the door, he turned. "One thing that bothers us. This army is telling things to the Indians. You understand? We all try to live together without fighting. Now the Indians are listening to the Confederates and are joining in the fight with them. I think they feel strong when the soldiers are here. That makes us very unhappy."

He left and Daniel closed the door tightly after him. Amy began to pull out the pan and the supply of cornmeal. As she prepared their supper, Daniel spread the blankets and then came to sit beside the fire.

Finally he spoke. "That man has sharp eyes; from his talk, I gather the idea he doesn't miss a thing. I was thinking, while he talked, his easy grin and that shrug didn't seem to go with the eyes."

Softly Amy whispered, "Daniel, are you seeing too much in everything? I *feel* a strangeness here, but there's really nothing to—" She sighed, unable to explain the vague uneasiness she did feel.

Daniel continued as if he hadn't heard. "We know two things. Mother and Father crossed Raton Pass, and we know their destination was Las Vegas. Between those two places lies Fort Union. The Confederate Army could be moving that direction right now." He paused, then added, "Strange that Santa Fe seems so peaceful. If the Confederate Army is making a show of occupying the town, these people don't seemed disturbed."

"While that man talked," Amy said, "I had the feeling he wasn't showing us much of anything except his big smile."

Daniel nodded, saying, "That's so. In addition, we know nothing about the situation between here and Las Vegas. Today we found out Fort Marcy has been taken by the Confederates—but what does that mean?"

Amy shrugged, "I can't guess. But, Daniel, could not knowing be dangerous for all of us?" She continued slowly, saying, "We could walk right into the middle of the Confederate Army. What will they do to us?"

"I can't believe they'll do anything. The clergy has always received respect." He mused, "But we've been seeing fear on people's faces for the past two days. That tells me something, and I'm not certain what."

"Isn't it possible they know something about the fighting that made them fearful?" Amy asked as she stirred the cornmeal.

"The fighting that has gone on south of here?" Daniel questioned. Then he shrugged much the same way the swarthy man had. "Maybe we need to forget about the fighting and just take the fella's word. He said the troops didn't bother the men who weren't in uniform."

Amy took a deep breath. "And you're a parson. So I guess we're safe, and tomorrow we can begin to look for Mother and Father."

"Triple safe. I have my wife with me." He came to tousle her hair and kiss her ear.

The first ray of sunshine had drawn a bright square on the splintery floor when Daniel propped himself on his elbow and leaned over Amy. "I've been thinking. Since we're so safe, might be a good idea to linger around a day or so. Get some idea of where the troops are right now. Could be helpful for several reasons, since we'll be heading toward Fort Union."

Amy yawned and stroked Daniel's face. "What's the other reason?"

"The possibility of some unexpected surprises on the trail I'm not interested in having. Also, I'm going to be making inquiries about a middle-aged parson and his wife traveling in this end to the territory."

Amy had just finished washing the dishes when Daniel returned. "I've discovered our lady's name is Dolores; her husband is Manuel. More coins in the palm made us welcome for a few more days. But I still have the feeling our being here makes them a little uneasy."

"Then why did she invite us?"

"Money, plus the old habit of making everyone welcome." Daniel came to help her fold the blankets. "I think it would be wise to go back to the town square. Let's walk; we may have a better chance to get acquainted."

"I'll take this jug for water," Amy said, picking up the pottery vessel. "My bathing and the dishes took the last of the water."

"Lady, begging your pardon, but I'd be glad to carry it for you."

"You! A beanpole with maple leaves for hair—" Amy squealed as Daniel picked her up in his arms and swung her around.

"Water lady. How I wanted to tease you like this back then, but I didn't dare touch your hand with Aunt Maude lurking in the bushes."

"Oh, Daniel, my beanpole! You are terrible to talk that way." She wound her arms around his neck as he tried to set her on her feet.

"Would be almost too easy to forget why we're in New Mexico, at least for today."

"I would like that," Amy murmured. "It seems life has just thrown us back in the middle of everything all too soon."

"I promise you, my sweetheart, when we find the folks—when we can breathe easy over them, we'll have some real time to ourselves, even if we have to climb Pikes Peak to be alone."

Amy smiled up at Daniel. "Silly, huh? We are forgetting we have the rest of our lives to be together."

The sunlight was sparkling on a spring-fresh day when Daniel and Amy walked into Santa Fe. Looking down the street, they saw wagons pulled by mules clopping toward the town square. The men and women and children swarming through the streets scattered as the wagons approached.

"Most of them are Mexican, aren't they? Look at the beautiful dresses, all that embroidery. Aren't the children darling, those black eyes and—"

"Bare bottoms," Daniel chuckled. "The fashion speaks well of the climate."

Amy stopped abruptly. "Last night I wondered why the town seemed so strange, even frightening. Daniel, do you remember? Last night there wasn't anyone on the streets except Dolores. I wonder why? It was only early evening."

"That is so," Daniel said slowly. She noticed his troubled frown was back. But then he smiled and reached for her arm.

As they walked farther he said, "Looks like the town square has been turned into a market. Only they call it a plaza instead of a square."

"Oh," Amy whispered, "look at the embroidery! Daniel, please, just for a few minutes," she pleaded.

"Go ahead. I'll keep my eyes on your sunbonnet," Daniel murmured as he turned to scan the crowded plaza. When he looked back he saw Amy mingling with the women around the stall draped with colorful shawls. Spotting the line of wagons and weary mules on the far side of the plaza, he headed for them.

As he approached the wagon loaded with heavy barrels, the driver pushed his dusty hat off his forehead and turned. The man was white, and his steel-blue eyes narrowed when he saw Daniel. "Nothing here for the market; this is supplies for the fort."

"Come in over the Santa Fe Trail?" Daniel asked.

The man gnawed at a plug of tobacco before drawling, "Hardly. The Feds got it under guard. Came up from Fort Bliss." With a quick hard look at Daniel, he turned away.

If he'd spelled Confederacy I wouldn't have been better informed, Daniel thought, deliberately slowing his steps as he sauntered to the well before he turned to study the mass of people. His eyes sought out the bobbing pink bonnet in the midst of the embroidered shawls.

"Interesting old building, isn't it?" The voice came from behind him. Daniel turned and felt the shock coursing through his body. The speaker continued. "*El Palacio Real.* It's called the Palace of the Governors, and I'm certain it was of palace proportions when it was built. That was in 1610. One of the curious old places tourists seek out. Parson, I'm surprised to see you here. Has the Methodist Episcopal Church ventured into New Mexico or"—the man hesitated—"is this a pleasure trip?"

Keeping his voice even, Daniel responded, "Lucas Tristram, I believe. To answer your question, the church is always seeking new territory, and this is hardly a pleasure trip."

"I'm relieved to hear that," the man's eyes mocked Daniel. "Since Fort Marcy has been taken and Albuquerque is in enemy hands, I would suppose New Mexico isn't much of a pleasure right now."

Daniel nearly questioned the statement, but from the corner of his eye he could see the pink sunbonnet bobbing closer. Hastily he said, "It's always good to see someone from the territory. Have a pleasant journey." Quickly he extended his hand and then strode rapidly toward the bobbing bonnet.

Amy saw the handshake. She stopped in the shade of the oaks, blinking with surprise as she studied the square shoulders covered by the smooth broadcloth. Was it possible? What was Lucas Tristram doing in New Mexico Territory? As Daniel approached, she was ready to ask the question of him, but she saw his frown and his tightly compressed lips. Her heart sank. *Must Lucas always shadow our lives?* she wondered. Quickly she led the way out of the market.

When she slipped her arm through Daniel's and smiled up at him, she recalled Daniel's encounter with Lucas in Central City. Less than three months ago—hardly time enough for Lucas's barbed remarks to have disappeared from Daniel's mind.

Silently they walked back through the woods. Amy bit her lip. There was something else. The gift. Lucas had promised to do something for the church in Oro City. Her heart sank as she remembered her impulsive acceptance.

Of course I should have consulted Daniel before accepting. She prayed, *Please Father, don't let it be something that will hurt Daniel.*

Daniel stirred as if suddenly recalling her presence. "Oh, sorry. I've been thinking I should visit Manuel again and try to get a little more information."

"More? What did you find out today?"

"That the Confederates have taken Albuquerque and the Federal Quartermaster has fled. That north of here the Santa Fe Trail is still in the hands of the Union, and the only supplies reaching the Confederates are coming in from Texas."

"Daniel," Amy said slowly, "while I was looking at the shawls, I overheard two women talking. They were white women and they were angry because the Indian agent here in Santa Fe has given all the food supplies meant for the Indians to the Confederates."

"Amigo." It was Manuel, smiling as he faced them on the trail.

"Manuel!" Daniel exclaimed, "I want to speak with you."

"And I wish to speak to you." He fell in step with them and politely asked, "Have you had a good day visiting the sights of Santa Fe?"

"Yes, we have, but I have heard some things that bother me," Daniel said.

The smile disappeared from Manuel's face. "Amigo, the forest may have ears. Do you wish to talk about it later?" Daniel nodded and the man continued. "I will come to you."

They reached the edge of the clearing. With his lazy smile in place, Manuel turned into his house.

When supper was over and the fire had settled into rosy, glowing coals, they heard the thump on the door. Amy moved toward the door. Sharply Daniel said, "Stay there. I'll answer it."

With a shrug she went to pull the benches close to the light of the fire. Manuel came into the house. "I have another white amigo—Hal." Amy turned to watch a slender man limp into the house, wincing with pain.

He was nearly as tall as Daniel, and much thinner. The thick thatch of hair on his head shone like silver in the pale light. Amy saw the perspiration on his face as he lowered himself to the bench and dropped the crude crutch beside him.

"My friend Manuel told me there was another gringo in camp and since time is heavy on my hands, I thought I would pay a visit."

Daniel settled on the opposite bench and Amy said, "I will make coffee."

"Please, ma'am, I won't impose. I've brought a jug of housewine. Manuel's house. Not bad at all."

"Feel free to accommodate yourself," Daniel said. "I am an elder in the Methodist Episcopal Church, and we—"

"So, a parson!" The man's keen eyes brightened. "We will have more in common than I supposed. I enjoy the books myself. Do you read the classics? I must introduce myself. Please call me Hal."

It was very late when Daniel closed the door behind their guests. Amy watched his face as he came back to the fire. "Daniel, you look very strange. What is troubling you?"

He glanced up. "That man. I am wondering what he wants. And who he is. This, my dear wife, was the most baffling evening I have ever spent in the pursuit of nothing."

"Poor man," Amy murmured as she moved the benches away

from the fire. "He seemed so pale and ill. I can't believe he could enjoy himself enough to stay half the night. Do you suppose he has an injury to that leg? It was hard to tell."

"That was my guess," Daniel said, adding, "and neither do I understand his visit."

"At times I had the feeling he was testing you—like a teacher would. Do you suppose he is wanting to offer you a position as pastor of a church—"

Daniel laughed. "A big one in a city far from Colorado? Amy!"

"Daniel, I am only guessing, I—"

He caught her close. "There, don't cry. I know. You'll grit your teeth and determine to be happy in Colorado. My dear. My brave little dear, don't pretend so hard!"

"Daniel, it isn't pretending—I am trying! And Colorado is beautiful."

He cuddled her close and whispered, "I tease when I shouldn't. No more tonight. It's late and you are tired. Come, my precious one, tomorrow will arrive all too soon."

It was early when Daniel awakened. Thinking of Amy's tears, he turned to look at her. She was sleeping peacefully, with one hand cupped under her cheek. He smiled and yawned.

The sky had just begun to lighten, and Daniel was considering more sleep when he heard the crunch of footsteps outside the door. He turned his head toward the window and saw the shadow outlined against the sky.

Moving cautiously he eased himself out of the tangle of blankets as he heard the scratch at the door. "Amigo!"

"Manuel!" Daniel scooped up his clothing and slipped through the door. "What do you want at this—"

The man was shaking his head, murmuring, "Come."

As Daniel pulled on his clothes, he asked, "Where? I'm not leaving Amy alone." The man moved his head impatiently and pointed to the farthest cottage. "I'll get Amy."

"I'm here." Her voice came from the doorway and Daniel saw she was shrouded in a blanket. "Is Hal sick?"

Manuel hesitated, then nodded vigorously. Turning, he set off across the courtyard and they followed.

In the dimly lighted cottage they could see the white-haired man propped into a sitting position on the bed. He spoke as they entered. "Daniel, Mrs. Gerrett, I am sorry to trouble you this way."

"You're ill, we'll be glad to help—"

"No, there's nothing to be done." He struggled to lean forward. "You were very patient with me last night. It wasn't a game. All of this was because I am beginning to realize I need an ally. Forgive me for taking so much of your time." He winced as he added, "This leg is taking too long to heal. I hoped there would be more time together, but I am afraid not . . ." His voice trailed off.

"You're dying!" Amy dropped to her knees beside him.

"No, my dear Mrs. Gerrett, I'm not dying. It's—" He paused and looked at Manuel.

After the man slipped out the door and carefully closed it behind himself, Hal continued. "Manuel is my guard. He will alert us." Again he hesitated; then he apologized, "I didn't expect troop movement so soon. I was hoping—but it has been a year now, and they are getting impatient."

He looked up into Daniel's face and said, "I was injured at the battle of Valverde in February. They don't know I'm alive. Unfortunately, I can't run my own errands."

"They?" Daniel questioned. "Do you mean—"

"The Confederates. Daniel, may I entrust you with a message? You have a legitimate reason to be heading for Las Vegas and I'm in dire need of a messenger." He shifted his body and winced. "I can tell you of a trail that will put you through safely and quickly. But more than anything, I need someone who can be trusted."

"I don't quite understand," Daniel said slowly.

"I've been informed of new troop movement. Under Sibley, that traitor to the Union. Scoundrel! Briefly he was commanding officer at Fort Union last year.

"As soon as he and some of his prime officers heard of the battle at Fort Sumter, they pulled out. Taking as many of the enlisted men as they could, they went to Richmond. Now he's back and in charge of the Texas Volunteers."

The man shook his head ruefully and added, "I can thank him for the hole in my leg. Now, this old soldier is down, but still fighting. Boy, will you be my legs and carry a message for me?

"The welfare of New Mexico and Colorado territories will depend on this getting through. No blue uniform would have a chance of surviving the mission, but a Methodist Episcopal preacher will do just fine."

Back in their hut Amy and Daniel faced each other. Daniel watched Amy tighten the folds of the blanket around her neck. His attention was on that white-knuckled hand grasping the blanket as he said, "Amy, I don't know what to do with you. I'm convinced—"

"You'll do nothing except take me along, just as you have been doing. He needs help and we must find Mother and Father."

"They will be found. We're all in the middle of this war now. Mother and Father, as well as the two of us."

"War," she shivered. In the next moment, she dropped the blanket and began dressing quickly. "Daniel, we have cold beans and bread; shall we eat as we ride?"

CHAPTER 11

Daniel finished tying the bedroll to Amy's mare. He turned as she came out the door and carefully closed it behind her. "You need not be so quiet." He jerked his head. "Hear that? Sounds like half of Santa Fe is shooting it up in the plaza."

Amy stopped and cocked her head. "I do hear something. But it sounds like men cheering. Do you suppose it's a fiesta?"

"I don't know, but let's have a look before we take Hal's trail out of town." He lifted Amy into the saddle and watched as she shook her wide skirt over the tips of her shoes. "Maybe those bloomers wouldn't be a bad idea after all."

"What would the bishop say?" Amy teased. She leaned over to touch his face. "No matter—skirts and sidesaddles are a small price to pay." He studied her serene face and recalled the tears of the previous evening. He was still shaking his head as he followed Amy into the woods.

The clamor from the town plaza grew in intensity as they entered the village. Daniel drew even with Amy and leaned toward her. "Amy," he kept his voice low, "I don't like what I'm seeing."

"Where are all the people?" she whispered. "The streets are empty. Are they all in the plaza?"

He shook his head. "That's bothering me, too. Let's turn down this lane. We can approach the plaza from behind those trees." He led the way. When they reached the end of the lane, the clamor of voices abruptly ceased.

Glancing quickly at Amy, he guided his horse into the plaza. An array of backs faced him. The significance of that line of gray shoulders registered at the same moment he saw the focus of their attention.

Slowly, majestically a flag was being hoisted over the Palace of the Governors. Caps were snatched off and every face was lifted. Daniel studied the flag. The brilliant red field was slashed by a blue cross studded with thirteen white stars.

Amy's mare nudged close to his and Daniel muttered, "Let's get out of here; that's the Confederate battle flag. Just go slow. Act as if it isn't important."

As they turned their horses, Daniel could see the line of townspeople clustered around the well. Black lace mantillas were crowded close to the faded cotton of peasant frocks. Most of the faces wore a pattern of mild curiosity and something nearly like indifference.

Keeping their horses to a slow walk, they crossed the square to the lane. Just as they left the plaza, an excited rumble moved through the line of gray-clad soldiers. Daniel glanced over his shoulder. A cortege of Confederate officers appeared under the portico of the palace. "Let's move out," he murmured.

Amy flicked the reins and turned her white face to Daniel. As she nodded, he saw her press her lips tightly together. Daniel nudged his mare into a trot and they headed up the steep road toward the mountains.

The clamor of the crowd was behind them when Amy pulled her horse even with Daniel. "I really didn't believe all I heard until I saw that flag. Daniel, those men were cheering as if it were the most wonderful thing in the world."

"To them it is. A conquered city, people in submission—that's the story of war."

"And we're in the middle. Daniel, if we stayed they would have forced us to—"

"Accept? Never." He was shaking his head as she flicked the reins again and rode out in front of him. He watched her force the horse into a lope before he fell in behind her.

Just after midday they stopped to water the horses and to rest in the shade of the fir forest. Daniel came to sit beside Amy as she prepared the bread and beans.

"Daniel, Hal didn't tell us much, did he?"

"No, but I think there's a reason. I'm guessing he was an officer from one of the forts in the area, and from the looks of him, I'd say he's fortunate to be alive."

Her voice dropped as she poured water into the cups. "And if they catch him?"

"I have a feeling Manuel will keep that from happening." From her expression, he knew she wasn't satisfied.

Later she asked, "The message—did you read it?"

"No, but he said it described troop movement and gave recommendations, including the use of this trail we're on."

"Why is that important?"

"He expects the Confederate Army to be lining the road between Santa Fe and Fort Union within another week."

"How long will it take us to get to Fort Union?"

"This trail winds back through the mountains and then follows Apache Canyon down until we join the Pecos River. I'm guessing, from the information he gave us, that it'll take three or four days to get to Las Vegas."

"And the troops can get there in one day of hard riding? Then why—"

"That's the whole point. We're leaving now—ahead of the troops. Hal estimates we have at least a week in which to deliver the message. It shouldn't take us that long. You saw the men today—they were celebrating. That's encouraging."

"What were they celebrating?" Her voice was heavy.

Daniel could only shrug as he said, "A victory. They've taken Santa Fe, as well as Albuquerque. It's a short step to Colorado now."

That night they slept under the stars. Conscious of Amy's restless tossing, Daniel pulled her close and asked, "Afraid of all the night critters?"

"I can't help thinking—of all that's going on." Her eyes were dark shining spots in her pale face. "There aren't slaves here. The people are content. They just seem bewildered by it all. Why shoot and fight? Daniel, doesn't it matter what the people want?"

"Yes, it matters, but we're only guessing that they hold the same values we have. It's possible, just like Manuel said, that they don't care who controls the territory."

Thinking of the people they had been seeing, Daniel reviewed the impassive faces. "I don't like this, their acceptance without a fight." Moving restlessly on the hard ground, he said, "Peace and a decent life don't come easily. From here it looks like war is a hard thing, but peace is harder to come by. You have to want it with all your heart and then be willing to work to make it last."

"Peace inside as well as out," Amy murmured sleepily. And in a moment she spoke again. "Yes, peace is hard to come by."

When her gentle breathing indicated she was asleep, Daniel was still staring into the night, wondering about her final statement. *Why do I link that thought with Lucas Tristram?*

The following night they found an abandoned cabin beside the trail. The afternoon had been cool with a touch of moisture in the air, and Amy was more than happy to follow Daniel into the tiny log cabin.

As Daniel built a fire in the crumbling clay fireplace, he said, "We're getting close to the Pecos River and nearly to the point where we break out of the mountains. According to the map Hal drew for me, we're at the point of crossing the Santa Fe Trail, before it circles to join Santa Fe."

"What does that mean for us?"

"If his calculations are correct, we've avoided the roadblocks the Confederates have set up around Santa Fe."

"Will we have time to search for Mother and Father in Las Vegas?"

"Certainly—that is why we've come. Hal suggests we all head for Fort Union together. He's inclined to believe there could be fighting along the way if any of the federal troops from Fort Union have started for Santa Fe."

"Who gets the message in that event?"

"If there's fighting on the trail, the message has lost its importance. In any event, we'll worry about delivering it only after we find the folks.

"Amy, you realize the situation, don't you? If they aren't in Las Vegas, we must head for Fort Union." She ducked her head, and gently he added, "Tomorrow we can start asking about them."

In the morning when they left the cabin, there was a crystal finish on all the grass. Daniel nodded toward the shining foliage. "We're higher than I thought. Looks like we came near to having a hard freeze. Guess winter isn't over in the mountains."

"Daniel!" He turned at her sober exclamation and looked the direction her finger pointed. "Isn't that dust hanging over that hill?"

"Could be. I'm going to investigate." Quickly he slipped the reins over the mare's head and mounted. Nudging her with his heels, he rode up the rocky incline. Amy had only time enough to pace the square of level ground in front of the cabin before he was back.

"Amy, it's gray uniforms, headed this way. It's a big bunch, and I'm guessing they're bent for Fort Union. Come on."

"Where?" she cried.

"Ahead of them. We've got to hope they slow down when they hit the hills." Daniel slipped off the mare and went after Amy's horse. By the time the horses were saddled, Amy was there with the bedroll.

"Ride!" Daniel wheeled his horse and watched Amy move out ahead of him.

At midday Daniel pulled over and signaled to Amy. "Let's take time to rest the horses. There's enough underbrush here to hide us. We'll be safe even if they do catch up with us."

"Daniel, why are we trying to keep ahead of them?"

"We're riding for our lives right now. I'm not happy with the idea of being found carrying that message."

"You think they would shoot us!"

"No, never. I can't believe that of a fellow American. But we've a job to do. Who knows what failure will bring?"

Slowly she said, "What happens if—"

"We won't be separated. But in the event we're stopped, that message isn't very well hidden in my pocket."

"Give it to me, Daniel—I'll hide it in my stocking." He hesitated a second, then handed it to her.

"Amy," he pleaded, "I don't think we're in real danger, but if anything should happen, don't come after me. Promise?"

"That's foolish; why I'd never consider—"

"Amy, promise."

"Daniel, of course. If it will make you rest easy about me, I promise, but still—"

"If you've finished eating those dried apples, let's get moving."

Within the hour they broke into a clearing. Daniel signaled Amy to stop. "According to the map, we're at Johnson's ranch. Hal indicated they are secessionists. He said avoid the place, no matter what happens. Let's cut around through the trees and pick up the trail again.

"From the map it looks like the next spot he's marked is Glorieta Pass. It's up through the mountains. We've got a hard ride ahead of us."

It was late afternoon when Daniel signaled another stop. "Daniel," Amy said, "this is terrible land. We can't make any time! The big rocks and boulders have us cutting around in circles more often than we ride a straight trail."

Daniel nodded. "I know. I hope the troops behind us are having the same problem. I've been listening and looking for signs we're being followed. My hunch is the grays stopped for the night at Johnson's ranch. I'm going to check it out from that hill over there."

Amy slipped off her horse and watched Daniel guide his mare up the steep slope. When he disappeared from sight, the silence and heavy afternoon shadows pressed in upon her. She paced back and forth in front of her browsing horse. Tension was knotting her neck muscles. She pressed her hands against her stomach. "Lord, are you still here?" she whispered, fearful of raising her voice. "In a spot like this, it seems unlikely. I'm trying to remember that you promised you'd be with us forever. Even when we don't feel—"

Daniel came crashing down the mountainside. She ran toward

him. He slipped off the horse as she threw herself at him. "What's wrong?"

"Oh, Daniel, this is terrible! I—" She stopped and gulped. Pulling herself away from his sheltering arms, she took a deep breath and said, "Just being a baby. I was scared to death I'd never see you again. It's so lonesome here."

She caught her breath again. Daniel studied her face before saying, "I didn't see any signs that we were being followed. And I could see far enough down that dusty trail to be satisfied. Amy, there's a stream on the other side of this hill. Let's go find a place to camp. These horses are going to need rest if we're to make good time tomorrow."

Daylight was streaking wide bands of coral across the sky when Daniel slipped out of the blankets and began to pull on his boots. When Amy stirred he murmured, "Just going to walk around, see what I can see."

She sat up and looked at him with wide, questioning eyes. "Amy, I'm just checking. I think we're well ahead of them. Get us something to eat and then let's be moving on. We still have dried meat and apples, don't we?"

She nodded. "There's pancakes left from last night. Daniel—" He bent to kiss her. "Never mind," she said, "just hurry."

"No fire, understand?" He touched her chin as she nodded.

After setting out their meager breakfast, Amy rolled up the bundles to be fastened behind the saddles. Suddenly Daniel came flying down the slope, leaping boulders and bushes.

She jumped to her feet. With her hands pressed to her throat, she waited. The frown on his face cleared as he glanced around. "Wondered if you'd made a fire. From up the mountain, I spotted either smoke or dust."

"On the mountain?" she asked.

He nodded. "Could be a cabin over that way."

"It could be something else," she whispered. "Daniel, what do we do?"

"Eat." He grinned and settled down on a rock. "Afterward we start moving out. Don't act so guilty. We're harmless travelers. If we're stopped, we've nothing to hide—except that message. Besides, coming from that direction, it's probably a settler."

Finally Amy managed a smile. But they ate in silence and quickly prepared to leave. The sun crested the mountain in front of them and warmed their faces as they rode toward the mountain pass.

They had been riding most of the morning when over the jangle of metal and the creak of leather punctuated by the snort of the horses, Amy began to hear another sound. She glanced at Daniel. He was hearing it too. His face was grim.

He pulled close to Amy and said, "There are men coming. A lot of them. Follow me." Yanking on the reins, he forced the horse off the trail and up the sloping mountainside.

When Daniel stopped, they were well above the trail, looking down at the cloud of dust moving their way. Daniel slipped off the mare and led her, trembling and snorting, into the shade of the piñon. "A steep climb old girl," he murmured, rubbing the horse's nose. He tied the reins to the tree and lifted Amy down.

"It was bad," she said soberly. "From the way we rode, I'm guessing you really do think there's something to fear."

"Just not taking chances. Let's leave the horses here and go watch the road."

"Do you suppose this is Glorieta Pass? See, ahead the trail seems to drop off down the mountain."

"Looks like it," he murmured, squinting at the dust cloud. "You know, it could be Indians. Guess it's a good idea to get off the road when you don't know who's coming."

"Daniel—" He turned and squinted in the direction her finger pointed. "The dust is down over there now."

Quickly he came to her. Studying the surrounding mountainside he said, "Amy, I don't know what's going on, but I aim to find out. Stay here. I'm going to climb higher. It's possible—"

Amy ran after him, "Daniel, don't leave me!"

He took her hand. "Run!" Boosting her over rocks and then dragging her by the hand, Daniel plunged through the trees.

When they reached the crest of the mountain, they stood panting, looking over the sharp decline. From east and west the two clouds of dust rose against the intense blue sky and spread slowly toward each other.

Amy shivered against his arm. "What is it?"

"I don't know, but I think we'll find out very soon."

"I can hear horses." He nodded. The distant pounding of hooves changed into earth-trembling force. "Daniel, there's lots of them. More horses than I've ever heard on a trail."

Daniel tensed and leaned away from the sheltering rock. The dust cloud far down the mountain erupted into a streak of blue. "That's federal forces! Amy," he groaned, "those men are the United States Cavalry!"

"Daniel, they're headed right for that other cloud of dust. And we know that's the Confederate Army."

When she stopped, Daniel added, "Amy, there's not one thing we can do about it."

They were still staring at each other when they heard the explosion far below them. Together they watched the gray cloud drift above the trees. Daniel said, "Gun smoke. Howitzer. The Confederates are firing on them with a mighty big gun. No wonder they were so slow on the trail."

Another explosion drowned out his words and Amy pressed against him. "Oh, Daniel, let's go! Let's get out of here."

"Go? We're safer up here. That is, as long as they don't move that artillery any closer. I'm going to look."

He moved away from her and eased around the rock. Far down the slope he could see the two field pieces in the middle of the road. As he watched, the line of blue men hesitated briefly; then with horses rearing and plunging, the line split in two and charged up the sides of the mountain.

Amy came to press against his arm. Together they watched the huddled gray mass back away from the guns. The explosion flattened Amy and Daniel against the rock. Slowly the canyon filled with acrid smoke and dust.

When the smoke began to clear, Daniel exclaimed, "The bridge is gone!"

For a horrified moment, Amy was afraid to look. Daniel said, "Do they know—" The question changed to a whispered cheer. "Bravo! Amy, look at those horses leaping Apache Creek."

"Oh, Daniel," she gasped as she began to see through the smoke. "Those men down there are wounded. That horse—it's wounded, too. Daniel, they need help!"

As Amy's voice broke, Daniel pushed her face against his chest. "Not now," he murmured. "We couldn't do them any good right now." Amy huddled with her face against Daniel, flinching with every new outburst of gunfire.

Daniel finally stirred and spoke. "I think the Feds have them in retreat. The howitzers are gone, and the last of the cavalry has disappeared. Looks to me like they're taking care of the wounded. I see soldiers being carried away."

"Let's go," Amy moaned, still not looking down the mountain.

"Wait a bit," Daniel replied. "There's bound to be action down on that trail, and I don't want us run over. We'll need to get back to the horses as soon as possible, but for now let's stay here."

"Should we do something about the wounded?"

"Their men won't leave them, and they're better prepared to care for them than we are." He paused and listened. "I think troops are moving back this way."

"It's nearly dark," Amy said uneasily.

"And I think it's time for us to go looking for those horses. Now, while we can still see where we're going."

Amy's knees were still shaking. She looked up into Daniel's face and tried to smile. The smile he returned didn't touch his eyes and she found herself blinking at tears. "I'm sorry, Daniel. It's just that I've never been around anything like this."

He slipped his arm around her as they started down the slope. To Amy it seemed to take forever to get down the mountain. "Are you certain we came this far?" she questioned.

Daniel nodded, "Farther. And if we don't find the horses before dark, it will be nigh impossible."

"I'm hurrying as fast as I can."

Just ahead, they could hear the whinny, the restless stomping. "Over that way, Daniel. I heard them."

"Yes, I did too," Daniel murmured, "and something is upsetting them."

As they approached, they could hear the voice. "Take it easy, darlin's—we both need to find a drink o' water."

Daniel sucked in his breath. Amy gasped, "We don't even have a gun!"

"Halt! I've got my gun pointin' at you."

Daniel moved ahead. "Whoever you are, we're friends, and these are our animals."

There was just enough light for Amy to see the gray-clad figure sagging against her horse. There was blood on his coat. She could see hardly an area was free of the dark stain.

As Daniel walked up to the man, he attempted to lift the rifle with his left hand. Gently Daniel said, "It takes two hands to fire a rifle. Besides, we don't have a gun. I'm a parson. Would you like us to take you back to your camp?"

Wearily the man shook his head. "I just came from there." He paused, took a deep breath and said, "Parson, if you really are one, listen—I don't intend to go back. I'm sick of war."

CHAPTER 12

The three of them stood looking at each other while the silence stretched between them, stretched until Amy could no longer endure it. The man in the gray uniform swayed.

She left Daniel's side and strode toward him. "Well, I guess I'll be doctor," she said crisply; then biting her trembling lip, she added, "Sit down and let me see what can be done."

His dark frown fled. "Ma'am, I think it's just a flesh wound. It sure burns, and I lost some blood, but—"

Daniel paced three steps and returned. "Better attend to the matter at hand. Mind if I just set that rifle aside?"

The man tensed and then, as if the last of his strength fled, he slowly eased himself down on a rock. Daniel took the gun and propped it against the nearest fir tree.

Hands on hips, Amy studied the man while she questioned Daniel, "Shall we build a fire?"

"No!" both men exploded.

Astonished, Amy looked at Daniel. He tried to grin, saying, "How many guests can you handle?"

"We need hot water."

Daniel retorted, "We need to find water and shelter." Now he faced the man. "Are you absolutely certain you don't wish to be returned to your unit?"

The weary face turned toward them again. It had begun to remind Amy of a cornered animal, wounded and held at bay. Daniel spoke gently, "We want to help. Believe it or not, the war we're fighting doesn't involve guns."

The night shadows were deepening as the man hesitated. Finally he stated, "Absolutely." Giving a weary sigh the man said, "Name's Matthew Thomas. They call me Matt."

"Daniel Gerrett and my wife, Amy." The words were terse and Amy waited, guessing more would follow. "You make it hard for a fellow—"

"To trust an enemy? Parson, I just don't have a clear enough head to sort it out. After I was shot it was easier to run than think. Let me get my strength and then I'll be off. Don't want to cause problems."

Amy's words crowded in over Daniel's. "Problems? You are neither friend nor foe. You're an injured man."

And Daniel was saying, "Seems right now the thing I want most is to give you a hand." He paced to the horses and back. "The rest we can forget about. If you want to talk some time in the future, well, I'll oblige you by listening."

Amy heard his sigh. Under the fir trees the shadows hid their faces from each other, but Amy sensed the sympathy building in Daniel. For a time the only sound was the restless stomping of the thirsty horses.

Daniel moved to untie the horses. "Surprises me the horses didn't break loose with all that commotion." Amy watched as he struggled to untie the leather reins.

Matt said, "There's a stream down over the next slope."

Daniel nodded, saying, "Guess it'd be wise to water 'em and come back. Camping next to a stream is asking for visitors."

Daniel took the jug from Amy, adding, "Might be a little fire will pass notice tonight. We need the light. The odor of black powder's still heavy in the air; that'll help hide the smoke." He stopped, and Amy bent her head to listen. The muffled pounding was horses, and they seemed to be coming closer.

Dryly Matt said, "The Feds are going home. If they'd stayed at Fort Union, we could've had the place."

"You're sorry." The iron in Daniel's voice surprised Amy.

The man's voice was soft, muffled. "No."

By morning the man was flushed with fever. Amy watched him shivering and moaning in his blanket beside the fire. With a worried frown, she looked up at Daniel. He said, "It isn't that serious yet. A flesh wound like that is bound to have a fever."

"We need to get him to a doctor," Amy said anxiously. "It's a terrible wound, and I don't know how to care for him."

"I don't think it's a good idea," Daniel murmured. "I don't think we've seen the last of the fighting." He looked down at her. "Amy, one thing that's significant. About the folks. The fighting isn't taking place in town, so I'd say they're still safe."

"We can be grateful for that."

She touched his arm as he asked, "Will you be all right if I leave you with him?"

"What do you mean?"

"I think I need to do as much scouting around as possible. Seems to be the only way I can get a handle on what's happening." She nodded and sighed. Daniel bent down to kiss her, saying, "If there's no activity today, and our man is well enough to travel, then tomorrow we'll head over the pass and north."

"North? Mother and Father—"

"Amy, we have a prisoner."

It was late afternoon when Daniel returned. He glanced at the man still shivering beside the fire before he dropped down beside Amy. She looked at his sober face. "You're very tired."

He nodded and said, "Went down to Apache Creek. I guess it was what you could expect—dead horses, fresh graves in the meadow. No sign of either army."

The man on the blanket stirred. Turning his face he said, "Don't think they've pulled out. They'll hold their own and call for reinforcements."

Daniel's voice was full of regret as he addressed Matthew. "The losses must have been heavy, from the signs."

"I expected that," he muttered, turning his face away.

Daniel's hands hung limply between his legs as he continued to watch the man. Amy spoke softly. "I cooked some beans and rice with jerky, but he wouldn't eat."

With a sigh, Daniel got to his feet and said, "Amy, I know of only one thing to do. Unless we ask the Lord to intervene, this man's not going to make it. He needs a doctor's help. I'm fairly certain he has a bullet in there."

Amy slipped her hand in his, nodding as she pressed her face against Daniel's sleeve. When they knelt beside the man, he opened his eyes. His voice was slurred, tinged with bitterness as he said, "Do you think your God answers prayers for the enemy?"

"Maybe He doesn't see you as right or wrong, even good or bad, just a human in need of help."

"Saint or sinner? Parson, aren't you failing in your duty? I thought preachers were to press the sinners to confession before they prayed for their bodies."

"If you have a need to pray for forgiveness, that'll be the first consideration; otherwise, we'll get on with asking Him to touch the fever and help us get you out of here."

In the morning, when Daniel rolled out of his blankets, Matthew was sitting on a log by the dead ashes of yesterday's fire. He lifted a pale face as Daniel came to build a fire. "Sitting here, listening to the birds, makes man's intrusion on this earth a profane thing."

Daniel threw him a quick glance as he knelt to pile pine cones and bark. "I don't have that kind of book learning. I just go by the Bible, and that indicates man is more important than the rest of God's creation. Important enough for God to give first-place consideration to him."

"Then you think God will forgive this other kind of profanity?"

"You mean the fighting? Why don't you just say the killing that's going on between brothers? A fellow told me a while back that the Confederate is just as God-fearing and certain he's in the right as we are. After listening to him, I had to admit had I been born and raised in the South, I'd likely feel that way, at least in the beginning."

Matthew looked startled. In a moment he said, "The surprise is that you northerners fight in good conscience."

Daniel straightened and protested, "But I wouldn't keep—"

"You're feeling better." Amy stood beside the crackling fire, trying to shake the wrinkles out of her gown. "I hope you will eat today."

Matthew blinked. "Why, I do believe I would like something. The need to be up was bigger than my analysis of the situation."

While Amy wondered if he was referring to their prayer, Matthew continued. "It's humbling to have your enemies care whether you are well enough to eat their grub."

Amy went to prepare the cornmeal gruel, feeling nearly comfortable with the morning and with the sight of the two men sitting on the log talking.

The bubbles were exploding on top of the yellow sea of porridge when she dropped her spoon and turned. Matt and Daniel were listening too. "The Army?" she asked slowly.

"I think so," Daniel replied.

Just as slowly Matt added, "Sounds like it's coming up from the Johnson Ranch. That's our forces." Amy eyed the rifle leaning against the fir tree, and Matt turned a crooked grin her direction as he said, "Don't worry. I'm done with fighting. I just want to slip out of the territory as soon as I have the strength. That is, if you'll let it happen."

Amy looked at Daniel, remembering he had called Matthew a prisoner.

Daniel got to his feet, saying, "We'd better eat that cornmeal porridge while we can. Could be we'll be in the middle of the second installment of this battle."

For Amy the day was suddenly dimmed; even the busy chirping of the birds seemed diminished. They ate quickly and in silence. By the time they finished the last of their breakfast, the pounding hooves had passed.

Thoughtfully, Matthew spoke. "I heard just two shots, not enough to add up to a battle. Now those horses are at a full gallop, riding like they have business on up the mountain."

While Amy washed and repacked the dishes, Daniel brought fresh cloths to dress Matthew's wounds. She heard him murmur, "Certain you can sit a horse today?" She turned away as Matthew groaned and nodded.

Daniel came to her, saying, "Let's head out. You and I can ride together and Matt can use your horse. Fella, hope you don't mind a sidesaddle."

"Daniel, we can't ride toward the pass."

"I know. It's Las Vegas for us."

As they mounted the horses, the distant crack of gunfire began. Daniel hesitated and his arm tightened around Amy. When the second round began, Matthew winced. "Might be best for us to stick to the trees," Daniel muttered.

Matthew nodded. "I'd suggest we push straight south from here. We'll avoid the road and come out somewhere on the other side of Johnson's ranch."

Daniel gave him a quick glance and Matthew explained, "That's headquarters for us."

"I'd been warned to avoid the place," Daniel muttered. "But I don't want to spend the day wandering around in the mountains, either."

"We can pick up the Indian trails just up the canyon from the ranch," Matthew offered. With a wry twist to his smile, he said, "I'm not certain how long I can keep my nose out of the dust."

Daniel nodded and nudged the mare with his heels as they turned to follow the line of trees.

The sun was directly overhead when the sound of rifle fire faded into a dull distant boom. Amy noticed the terrain seemed to be changing. They halted on the edge of a rocky bank overlooking the Apache Creek, trying to get their bearings.

Daniel pointed to the thick brush covering the low land. "Might be a good idea to cut up the slope behind us. We need the cover of the trees."

Matt nodded and fell in behind their horse.

Daniel murmured, "As soon as we get around this hill, let's stop and rest."

"I've been watching Matt," Amy whispered. "I'm afraid—"

When Daniel stopped in the shade of the trees, Matthew moved his horse closer, saying, "There's dust hanging over that valley. I'm guessing there's a bunch coming through. Maybe we'd better wait."

"I've been watching too," Daniel admitted. "But I've about lost hopes of seeing who it is. They just dropped behind that bluff."

Amy had been looking beyond Daniel as he talked. Now she gasped, "Daniel, I think I see some men on the top of the bluff. Look!"

"I'm looking. Horses, and blue uniforms."

As they watched, the line of blue grew across the top of the bluff. For another moment the line was motionless, and then like a fall of blue water, it washed over the brow of the hill and plunged down the incline. For a time there was only the thunder of hooves. Now shouts filled the air. Abruptly they heard the deafening roar of cannon.

As the sounds continued, the three watched the distant fringe of trees. Finally Daniel shouted, "Let's move higher! I can't believe my ears."

Matthew plunged ahead and they followed. From their new position, they could see the ranch stretched out below. In the distance was the ranch house and barns. In the foreground they saw a milling mass of animals and a huge circle of wagons.

As they watched, smoke began rising above the trees. Amy looked from one vast column of smoke to the other. "Daniel, what has happened—what are they burning?"

"Wagons! There are burning wagons and stock spread all over that ranch. Those fellows have been shooting horses and mules. Look at that, Matt. What do you make of it all?"

Slowly, heavily, the man replied, "Supply train. I'd heard there was one stationed at Galisteo. I wonder why General Pyron brought it in here." He turned to face Daniel. "That's a loss the Confederacy can't afford. I have a feeling you Yanks have won this round of the fight."

Amy had been watching the road below. She poked Daniel's arm. "Look, there's a man leaving on horseback."

"Heading up the mountain," Matt added. "That's one of our men." Slowly they dismounted and settled down to watch.

All afternoon the glow of the fires was visible in the clearing while a pall of smoke spread over the valley below. Finally Daniel went to spread blankets for Matthew. Soon he was asleep. Amy came to Daniel, whispering, "What do we do now?"

"Camp here until morning and then go into Las Vegas," Daniel said heavily.

CHAPTER 13

Daniel and Amy moved away from the sleeping soldier and settled down to wait. By late afternoon, Matthew joined them as they watched the ranch. As dusk fell, the fires began to die down. Just before darkness took over the valley, they saw a movement in the trees between them and the ranch. Daniel murmured, "There's someone on the road."

They saw a lighter shadow and heard the sound of hooves pounding across stone. There was a sharp crack of a whip and they saw the desperate dash up the road. Matthew spoke heavily, "Another one made it out."

Amy blinked at the tears in her eyes as she watched the rider's dash for freedom. It was the despair in Matthew's voice that reached her. For a moment the barrier between North and South was gone as Amy looked after the fleeing soldier. "Poor lad," she murmured.

During the night Amy lay wide-eyed and bleak, listening to the sounds of movement on the road beneath them. As horses pounded up the hill while others passed down, Amy sensed Daniel's sleeplessness too. She visualized those blue and gray uniforms, some moving slowly, while others galloped through the dark. Occasionally, she heard a song sung in a heavy monotone. The sounds continued throughout the night, and Amy guessed Matthew slept no better than she and Daniel.

In the morning they saw Matthew's ravaged face, and Amy listened to Daniel's terse comment. "It would have done them no good; you couldn't lift a rifle."

Under the shadow of his silence they packed up and prepared to leave. But when they rode out from under the sheltering trees, a rifle was pointed at them. "You're under arrest. As an enlisted man of the United States Army, you are in my custody until I hand you over to my commanding officer. I am obligated to warn you, if you attempt to flee, I shall shoot." The rifle wavered slightly as it pointed at Matthew.

"I am an elder in the Methodist Episcopal Church—"

" 'Tis a good story, sir," the youth said gruffly, moving the rifle Daniel's direction. "But I'm not blind. I recognize a Confederate uniform when I see one. The lady can go, but you must come with me."

Amy shook her head violently and said, "I'm staying with my husband."

The soldier shrugged and motioned them forward. "Let's get going. It's a long ride." Instead of turning down the canyon toward Las Vegas as they intended, the rifle nudged them forward, up the mountain toward the north.

Amy looked over Daniel's shoulder and blinked at the tears in her eyes. "Never mind," he murmured, "we'll just trust God to work it all out according to His plan." He squeezed her tight.

"Mother and Father?"

"We're all in His hands. Amy, I guess I've never been in so tough a spot. One where I couldn't do a thing to help out the Lord. Guess now's as good a time to start as any."

"Start?"

"Learning what it really means to trust. We're powerless to do a thing for ourselves." Amy nodded and pressed her fingers to her lips.

It was nearly noon when their guard waved them to a halt. When they turned to face him, there was a cocky grin on his face. "We're now approaching the battle site. Because there are still personnel from the Confederate Army on the grounds, and I don't want them to feel obligated to attempt a rescue, we'll cut through the ravine to your right."

"Confederate?" Daniel exploded. "Do you think we're spies?"

The soldier waved his rifle. "One shout or quick movement and I will shoot you." He nudged Matthew. "Lead out, cut around that hill, and drop down to the next canyon. You'll see Pidgeon's ranch just ahead. Turn in there and proceed to the house."

Amy glanced at Daniel and he grinned down at her. "Don't look so dismal; we're on safe ground now! Hopefully Chivington will be there, and we'll soon be free to go our way."

Daniel faced the soldier. "You said battle site. What do you mean? We saw the battle at Johnson's Ranch."

The cocky grin was still on the youth's face. "There was a confrontation between Confederate Colonel Scurry and his men of the Texas Volunteers and Colonel Slough, my commanding officer, of the United States Cavalry. Must admit, Scurry was doing just fine until he got word that Chivington had done him in. Wiped out the supply wagon. Heard there were eighty supply wagons and around thirty head of horses and mules. Took about seventeen prisoners. A couple got away."

There was silence as they rode down the canyon, following the dry stream bed which led them out onto the wide plateau. "Strange contrast," Daniel murmured in her ear. "Look at the cows grazing like there's not even a fly to pester, but those horses—"

She looked. Bone weary, thin, they stood huddled in the pasture in a private group. "The poor things," she whispered; "they aren't even interested in grazing."

As they rode up to the ranch house, Daniel murmured, "It's obvious the barn has been turned into a hospital." Amy's glance shied away from the wagon loaded with long, blanket-wrapped objects. She saw Daniel's sober face as he lifted her down.

The rifle nudged Matthew as he slowly slid off Amy's horse. "Be careful!" Amy snapped. "He's injured."

Their guard leered at Amy. "Not many who ain't." He waved his rifle at them and jerked his head toward the door.

When they faced the uniformed man across the kitchen table, Amy's heart sank. Daniel said, "Sir, may we speak to Major Chivington?"

The man's tired face sharpened into a questioning frown. "I don't know where you picked up the name, but he isn't here."

He turned to the grinning soldier. "Looks like you've done your duty for the day. Report to Weston."

Facing Daniel he said, "I'm Colonel Slough, in charge of this offensive. I'm willing to listen to your story, but obviously your friend's story won't carry much weight since he's wearing the uniform of a Confederate soldier. Why were you carrying a rifle? Be careful what you say. It's a Perry, a breechloading carbine, just like the rest of the fellows from Texas are carrying."

"Sir," Matthew protested, "I was trying to steal his horse when he caught me."

"You were holding him prisoner?"

"Well, actually, no," Daniel said. "I couldn't make up my mind to turn him over. It seems—"

"And yet you want to talk to Chivington." The man's eyes were cold. "Well, you'll probably get the opportunity. Our detachment is leaving for Fort Union in the morning."

Late that evening, locked in a tiny room at the farmhouse, Daniel comforted Amy. "Dear wife, there's nothing to worry about. I'm certain we'll be delayed, but as soon as we see John Chivington, we'll be freed and ready to leave for Las Vegas."

"I hope you're right," she murmured into his shoulder. "I'm sorry about Matthew. I guess being in his company has nearly made me feel different about the other side."

"I know," Daniel whispered, "but this is probably not the best place to discuss it."

Flanked by the United States Army, two days later they rode into Fort Union. Looking at Daniel, seeing the concern on his face, Amy tried to smile. She murmured, "I can nearly feel important, being under guard like this. A dignitary. Daniel, do you suppose one of these days we'll laugh about this?"

He turned from scanning the terrain and smiled. "Most likely. Right now I'm looking forward to a decent meal."

"And water enough to bathe!" Amy straightened in the saddle and grinned up at him.

"Meanwhile, look at the strange shape of the land."

The guard beside Daniel said, "Since you're a prisoner, I might as well tell you; that's the famous star fortification." While Daniel winced, the guard continued. "They built an underground fort—well, they started anyway. Everything's under ground." He was silent for a moment before adding, "A good idea, but I understand it isn't the most comfortable place to live. Fact is, look at the tents. I guess the fellows would rather camp outside."

It was late when they were finally escorted up to the old log fort. Amy and Daniel watched Matthew being led away, and then they stumbled across the parade grounds with their guard leading the way. As he opened the door of the crude log cabin, the guard said, "Good thing you have your bedroll. Someone will be along with grub in a while. Don't try any fancy footwork. We're under orders to shoot first and ask questions later. These are war times."

He started out the door and then turned. "In the morning you'll be allowed out on the grounds, but under no circumstances are you to leave the fort. There's a well on the far end of the parade grounds. One of the officers' wives will tell you where to obtain supplies. Your case will come up for consideration at the convenience of Colonel Slough."

The urgency in Daniel's voice reached through Amy's dreams. "Sweetheart, come see. Now I understand why they say the desert is beautiful."

With the blanket wrapped around her, Amy came to blink sleepy eyes at the dawning world. "Daniel, it's all pink, even the soil—and those strange rearing shapes. They must be rocks."

"Sandstone, I think. It is colorful." He turned to point southeast. "Except for that line of dark blue mountains. Look at the green to the west. Must be a river. I've been hearing children, so there must be families here."

He squeezed her against him. "Good morning, Wife." After a quick kiss, he added, "Do we have any cornmeal? I prefer your cooking to what we had last night."

"We need water; I'll dress."

"I'll bring water and wood for the stove."

Amy had just pushed the last hairpin in place when the door opened. "Daniel—" she said as she turned. With a gasp she stared at the woman. "Mother!"

Crying and laughing, with their words tumbling over each other, Amy hugged her mother while Amelia explained. "We never did get to Las Vegas. Your father—"

"We were so worried!"

"Amy, I can't believe you're here."

"Where is Father?"

Daniel pushed in between them. "Accident—he has a broken leg. I found her at the well and we came back for you. Let's go."

They cut across the parade grounds and headed for the little log cabin at the end of the road. "These cabins are all alike, just big enough to hold a bed and stove," Amelia murmured, "but we have the distinction of having the one next door to the prison."

Amy stopped abruptly. "Daniel, do you suppose that's where they put Matthew?"

"Without a doubt."

"I don't suppose they've even dressed his wound."

Amelia moved ahead to push open the door of the cabin. Amy flew past her, "Father, surprise!" She threw herself at the man in the bed, "Oh, you're so pale."

"He's had a lot of pain," Amelia said gently, as she took the pail of water and carried it to the stove.

"What happened?" Daniel asked as he pulled a bench close to the bed.

Eli, looking flustered and concerned, released Amy. "Daughter, dry your tears. I'm not dying. There, there," he patted awkwardly.

"We've been worried," Daniel began. "When we heard about the Colorado Volunteers moving into the territory, we decided we'd better come looking for you."

Eli nodded gravely. "War talk. Heard about Chivington coming. Quite a switch in assignments, going from being a clergyman in the Methodist Episcopal Church to leading a volunteer army. Last night for the first time we heard about the battle at Glorieta Pass."

"We've just come from there. Matter of fact—"

Amy broke in, "We've been trying to find you. First we went to Santa Fe. That didn't seem to be the thing to do—" Her eyes were signaling Daniel and he frowned.

"Amy, I don't think we need to worry about the letter anymore."

"Maybe you should deliver it anyway. Then they'll know we're not spies."

Eli pushed himself into a sitting position. "Spies!"

Amy studied his pale face and said, "Just mistaken identity. I'm certain it will all be taken care of as soon as Daniel has a chance to explain to Major Chivington." Quickly Amy turned to Amelia. "What are you going to do now?"

"We can't do anything until that leg heals enough for your father to travel."

"Daughter, you're uneasy," Eli said. "Are you thinking I might be having some secessionist ideas since the family all came from Missouri? Well, rest easy. We're solidly behind the Union."

But Amy had closed her eyes. She was thinking of the events of the past two weeks. The faces of Dolores and Manuel were backed by those nameless figures in gray uniforms with rearing horses and blasting cannon. The parade of faces continued to move through her memory—Hal and Matt and then the stranger desperately lashing his horse as he flew down the road. Amy jumped to her feet and turned away from the bed.

Amelia moved to the stove, saying. "Amy, come help me. I'm going to make some breakfast for us. Seems a treat is in order. How about some fried cakes with maple sugar? Daniel, have you had a good cup of coffee since you burned your fingers grinding the beans for me?"

Suddenly Amelia was holding on to her, saying, "Amy, sweetie, what is it?" For a moment Amy relaxed against her mother, feeling Daniel's hand firm on her back.

"She's seen a lot of life since we left Colorado."

The room finished its swaying. Amy straightened and squeezed Amelia. "Life? I didn't expect to be dumped in the middle of war." She gulped and added, "I guess I'll—" She glanced at Daniel and remembered what he had said about trusting the Lord. She added, "I guess we will be fine now. I'm hungry and it's good to see you all."

For one more second Daniel's eyes were filled with concern, and then he grinned.

CHAPTER 14

Amy sat beside the bed, stitching up the rip in Daniel's shirt and listening to her father. Eli punched his pillow and said, "Since '53 they've had their eye on the area."

She studied him over the shirt. "The Confederates? Father, by area, do you mean New Mexico Territory?"

"More'n that. See, Jefferson Davis was secretary of war in Pierce's cabinet back in '53. From the beginning he was a man determined to further the interests of the South. Namely slavery. Davis had a dream of securing a commercial route across the southern section of the country for the purpose of more closely tying the West Coast to the rest of the country. Coincidentally, he was interested in the California gold fields. To further this dream, he knew the United States must obtain land from Mexico."

Amy ducked her head to hide the smile. When Eli adopted his "teacher voice," he was unconscious of all except his subject. Amy interrupted, "You mean 1853? Father, are you telling me there were problems that far back?"

"Of course." Looking at his excited face, she recalled the last time he had discussed politics with such fervor. It had been in Central City with Lucas Tristram.

The memory of that man's face surfaced in Amy's mind. She moved her shoulders uncomfortably as she began to wonder why he was in Santa Fe. *Had he been there when the Confederate flag was raised? Why did the memory of his face cause such discomfort?*

Eli's voice overlapped Amy's thoughts. With relief, she turned to listen. "Right now, both sides are blaming the other for the problems leading to the war. The Union is blamed for restricting the rights of the southern states—they called it freedom to allow slavery to exist. The Confederacy is accused of trying to split the Union apart. Neither one will bring out the real issue. Slavery has been a wound in the side of the whole country almost from the beginning, and it's going to have to go!"

Amelia stacked dishes on the shelf. Nodding she said, "Because of the Constitution. Any man with a lick of conscience would declare his obligation to support it. Without a doubt it advocates freedom for all men."

She spun around, and Amy saw the bright dots of red on her cheeks as she lifted her chin and added, "White superiority smells to high heaven!"

"Now, Amelia," Eli chided. Amy watched the red fade from her mother's cheeks as she turned back to the dishpan. She also noted the once-proud shoulders were drooping.

Caught by the difference and intrigued by her mother's passionate statement, Amy dropped the mending into her lap and studied her. Somehow the words seemed to belong to the woman called Silverheels. Uncomfortable with that thought, Amy tried to push it aside, but it lingered.

Her father's voice faded into the background as she looked at her mother's faded blond hair twisted into a discreet knot and the unadorned face still marked by the ugly red scars.

She could see Amelia's eyes were still flashing and her lips compressed as she bent over the dishpan. *Mother is not just a former dancehall madame. There is something more, and I want to find out what it is.*

Amy glanced at her mother, feeling a new excitement as she

thought of the strong statements she had made.

Her father was silent. Amy stuck the needle back into the fabric and asked, "Father, you said slavery was a wound. Why?"

He brooded over the words as he said, "Because man could neither live with it or without it." Leaning forward to shake his finger at Amy, he added, "It's no secret that the North, for the most part, would rather the whole situation just go away. They fear losing their jobs to the black man. There have been enough Negroes willing to work circles around the lazy white man that we've learned to fear the results of true freedom for all."

The words slipped past Amy as she watched her mother move about the little cabin restlessly. Her shoulders still drooped, and when she turned, in the moment before her smile, Amy saw the sadness in her face.

Amy realized her father was no longer speaking. She saw his eyes were closed. Amelia whispered, "Let's go. I want you to meet some of the women."

Carefully Amelia closed the door behind them and said, "There's still a number of army wives here. I thought you might like to make their acquaintance."

"I wonder what is happening to Daniel," Amy brooded as she kept pace with Amelia's long strides.

"No doubt he's having a good visit," Amelia smiled down at Amy and drew her arm through hers. "I can't believe that silly charge will persist. A clergyman spying!"

Silently Amy pondered the problem of Matthew. Tentatively she probed. "What are they going to do with the prisoners?"

Her mother studied her. "I don't know what they do. There's still a war going on. Amy, you're too sympathetic. Leave the war to the men."

She studied the ground. "Do they let people visit them?"

"I would think so." They stopped in front of another cabin and Amelia rapped on the door. "Katherine's husband is an officer. They—"

The door flew open and a tousled head appeared on a level with the knob. "Mama isn't here. Nanny says come."

They stepped into the room. A tiny girl was seated in the middle of a cot. She sobbed soundlessly as she scrubbed at the tears on her face. A tall, ungainly figure leaned against the broom she held and peered into a shadowed corner.

"Set, if you wish. There's a rat behind that barrel and I aim to be ready when he comes out. Now hush yourself, Elizabeth; it won't do no good to fuss." The sentence ended in a squeal and Amy watched the woman launch into action.

Elizabeth screamed and Amelia picked up the child. The broom stopped its flailing and the woman backed out of the corner. "James, hand me that shovel. I declare, this killing the varmints is getting to be a daily affair."

"The poor child," Amy crooned as she stroked the baby's cheek.

The woman shook her head. "She just doesn't want me to kill them."

James added, "Elizabeth likes varmints." He sat down and folded his arms. "Me, I don't. I'm going to be a soldier like Pa; only I'm going to shoot rats."

"Well, I hope by the time you're growed this war'll be over." She faced Amy and asked, "You're new. Husband in the Army?"

Amelia said, "Daniel's a clergyman."

"I think we need soldiers instead. Let me tell you, I lived in Texas until Missus Horton hired me away. Came from Georgia first off."

"Why did you leave the South?" Amelia asked.

The woman studied them just long enough for Amy to note the careworn face and the calloused hand sweeping back her hair. "You say that like you think the South is good. It is if you live on a big plantation and have nothing to do all day but eat bonbons and do fancywork. When you're poor whites, you scramble to make a living, just like the slaves."

She returned the broom to its corner and added, "The big plantation owners are buying land as fast as they can beat a poor fellow to market. And they don't want it for growing corn and beans, no sir. It's for planting cotton so's they can get rich. How's a poor man to feed himself? We went to Texas, and now they've sold us down the river. Surrendered to the Confederates without a fight. No common man had a chance to say whether or not he wanted to be a part of their fight for independence." She studied her frayed apron before adding, "Pretty soon there'll be no room for any but the rich."

Katherine didn't return. Amy and Amelia soon left the cabin, but Amy continued to mull over the conversation. She was thinking about Amelia as they hurried back across the parade ground.

Looking at her mother, she said, "I'm learning things about this war I'd never thought about until today. I knew slavery was the cause of the war; didn't stop to think how wrong it is. People need to be free, don't they?"

Amelia looked down at her with a slight frown, and for a moment Amy wondered if they were talking about the same kind of freedom.

Daniel followed the orderly into the commandant's office. With a flourish of his hat, the orderly waved at the man behind the desk. "This here is Colonel Paul."

The man lifted his head. "So you're the fellow picked up for aiding the enemy."

Daniel hesitated. "Yes, sir, I suppose that's about it. This fellow—"

"This is war. Why aren't you in the Army?"

"Sir, I'm a missionary for the Methodist Episcopal Church. My wife and I came to New Mexico to look—"

"Never mind. I'm more interested in the charges against you. Do you have anything to say for yourself?"

Daniel pulled out the letter. "I was given this letter to pass on to you. I don't know the fellow's name who gave it to me. He asked us to call him Hal."

Paul quickly scanned the letter and looked up at Daniel, "Describe the man."

"Tall, thin, with white hair."

"The letter is from a man who doesn't fit the description. Also, the information is worthless. Our men have already engaged the enemy at Glorieta Pass." He tossed the letter to the desk.

"This is war. Your actions indicate a hostile mind, favoring the enemy. You are under arrest. Because of the crowded conditions of the prison, you will be allowed the freedom of the post, but under no condition are you to leave the fort. Good day, sir."

Daniel stood on the porch of the colonel's office and took a deep breath. "Well, that is that. Until Chivington gets here, that is." He studied the concrete walls of the prison and a grin tugged at his mouth. "Oh, boy, is Chivington going to be surprised!"

He walked slowly past the prison. The tiny cubicle was windowless, except for a narrow band of barred vents near the top of the wall. Taking a quick glance around, Daniel circled the prison. The parade grounds were still empty. Once more he passed behind the prison. With another quick glance behind him, he walked close to the wall and said, "Hey, you in there. Is Matthew with you?"

There was a pause and then a weak voice. "That you, Daniel?"

"Yes, how ya doing?"

"Fever's come back." Daniel chewed his lip and Matthew spoke again. "Haven't had the rag changed today."

"You oughta be in the hospital. I'll see what I can do."

Walking back the way he had come, Daniel examined the various small log buildings. There was one larger than the others. As he hesitated, the door opened and an enlisted man appeared. "Is this the hospital?" Daniel asked.

"As such," the youth replied. "Infirmary is the name. Want to see the doc? He's just come out of surgery."

An older man appeared in the doorway. His face was lined with fatigue, but his tired eyes were patient. "Doc," Daniel said, "we arrived yesterday with a soldier. He's in the prison and I don't think he's doing too well—"

"And you want me to check on him," the doctor said with a tired sigh.

"What I'd really like," Daniel hurried out the words, "is for you to release him to me. My wife and I spent a couple of days nursing him along. We'd be glad to continue caring for him as long as we're here. We'll be leaving as soon as Major Chivington arrives, but until then—"

"It will be a blessing to me. I know the fellow and he'll make it if he has someone to dress that wound about six times as often as it's getting it right now." He came down the steps. "Come along, I'll have him out of there in a minute."

He cut briskly down the row of buildings and stopped at the commandant's office. Daniel's heart sank, but by the time he reached the steps the man was inside. He was addressing the young lieutenant. "I've a volunteer to nurse that Reb with the hole in his arm. Please release him to—"

"Gerrett, sir."

When Amy returned to their cabin, she opened the cabin door and gasped. "How did you get here?"

A grinning Matthew was propped up on a bunk built into the wall. Daniel turned from the stove. "Simple, my dear. We're all prisoners of the United States Army. Somehow it didn't seem to matter to them whether we have bars around us, just as long as we don't intend to go anywhere. I think the doc was convinced Matthew wasn't anxious to run."

"We are prisoners too?"

He nodded. "But just until Chivington arrives. Meanwhile, we have a pile of bandages and some strange salve to use on Matthew. Also, I have a piece of deer meat and some potatoes and carrots—prisoner's rations."

With a smile Amy said, "I can only claim one wild story about rat hunting. I suppose that doesn't impress you at all."

"And that's all you've done all day?" He grinned wryly and winked at her. "Come cook this stuff while I take care of Matthew, and you can tell me all about it."

By the time Amy had the vegetables cooking and the meat ready to go into the skillet, Matthew was comfortably drifting toward sleep, and Daniel returned to the bench.

"You look a mite uneasy, Amy—what's the problem?"

Amy glanced at the bunk and saw Matthew's arm was across his face. She took a deep breath. "Uneasy? I guess that's what I'm feeling. I was with Mother and Father. Some things were said, but that wasn't as important as what I'm feeling," she brooded as she carefully placed the meat in the melted fat.

She studied Daniel's face. "It's Mother. Daniel, all the spunk has gone out of her."

"She's different than when you knew her at Buckskin Joe? Amy, life's dealt her a pretty hard line this winter."

"I don't think that's it." She turned the meat and came to sit beside Daniel. Seeing the concern in his eyes, for a moment she nearly regretted speaking out her thoughts.

He prodded, "Go on, I'm listening."

"She—seemed to feel deeply about the war, more than that, about reasons behind. I could see it was important, and Father—"

Daniel sighed and nodded, "I see. Amy, I don't want to criticize Father, but I get the feeling he's walking on pins and needles, fearful—"

Amy said it slowly, "That Mother is going to disgrace him?"

"At least entertain ideas he can't handle." But immediately, he added, "Don't forget, we haven't spent much time around them."

Amy spoke slowly. "Mother thinks, and she isn't afraid to own her thoughts. I'd like to be that way. Sometimes the words burst out of me, and then I'm sorry. Not sorry I have them, just sorry I said what I did. It . . . causes problems, especially with Father."

Matthew stirred and said, "That meat sure smells good."

"And I'm not about to burn it," Amy declared, jumping to her feet.

Their opportunity for real conversation was interrupted by Matthew's waking, but Daniel rose and went to stand beside Amy at the stove. "Give it time, sweetheart," he whispered as he put his arm around her. "Both for your mother and yourself. God's still on the throne."

CHAPTER 15

Two more restless, pain-filled days passed before Matthew's fever subsided and the wound began to heal. On the day he was up and wearing the tattered gray uniform for the first time since Amy had washed and mended it, he asked the question they had all avoided.

"Your friend Chivington will be through here any day now. I suppose you'll be heading for home. Have you heard what they intend doing with prisoners of war?"

"No," Daniel said. "I've tried to find out. Mostly there's just a shrug and a vague wait-and-see answer. Frankly, I don't think the fellows around here know."

"Have you any news of what's happening out there?" Matthew asked the question with a jerk of his head.

"The Confederates have pulled back to Santa Fe and Albuquerque. I'm guessing, since they're still there, it's an indication neither army is giving up." Daniel paused, then added, "I've had a little more information about the attack on Johnson's ranch.

"Major Chivington started out with a detachment of four hundred men. He had orders to approach the Confederates from the rear, and that's what he was doing when we saw him. It was only by accident he discovered the supply train and destroyed it."

Matt's face twisted. "Any details?"

"The fellows behind the cannon were shot. That accounts for the abrupt silence. It was confirmed that eighty wagons loaded with supplies were burned. They said it was all of their guns, ammunition, food and clothing."

"The idiots," Matthew muttered. "Foolhardy and over-confident to have brought them into the canyon."

"All this might be why it's taking Chivington so long to get back here," Daniel stated.

Matthew continued to sit with his chin resting on his chest. "The fellow that got away—" Daniel said, "remember we saw one flying out of there early on? Well, he carried the news to the battle going on up the way, where our men had just about lost out when the Confederates got news of the battle at the ranch. That was a blow they couldn't recover from. Your man, Scurry, sent a flag of truce, and that was that."

Amy joined the conversation. "Katherine's husband has just left to join Colonel Canby's men, so there's an indication something is being planned." There was silence. She added, "Katherine said the quartermaster in Albuquerque destroyed all the food and arms stored there. He did it to prevent the supplies from falling into Confederate hands."

Matthew sat up and looked at Amy. His eyes were dark, unreadable. "The Indian agent in Santa Fe opened up his stores to the Confederate troops. So it sounds like there's a little sympathy for the cause."

"It seems," Daniel spoke slowly, "the territory is equally divided in their loyalties. Perhaps that's why there's been so much apathy on the part of the people. Can't make up their minds who should be supported, Union or Confederacy."

"Did you have that problem?" Matthew asked, studying Daniel with the dark question still in his eyes.

Amy caught a glimpse of movement as Daniel's head jerked. "Because I'm not in the Army? No, Matt. Matter of fact, for a time I thought maybe it was God's will for me to enlist, seeing nothing else seemed to be coming together for me. It was back last year when the fighting began." Amy sucked in her breath and Daniel looked at her with the expression in his eyes softening.

In a moment he began to speak again, but Amy was thinking, *Daniel didn't know where I was. He thought I'd left forever. What if—*

Then Amy realized Daniel was speaking and turned to listen. "That was when the verse in Ezekiel began to mean so much to me. There the Lord tells Ezekiel the nation of Israel has become sinful, from humble man to king. He reminded Ezekiel that when He didn't speak, the people turned away to do evil.

"The Lord summed it all up by saying He looked for a man to stand in the gap before Him to build up the crumbling wall of defense against spiritual enemies. I was convicted by His words, 'I sought . . . but I found none.' " Daniel's chin sank down against his chest.

Studying his brooding face, Amy began to feel a new emotion, something apart and separate from their life together, and yet somehow linking them. The feeling blossomed in her with a strange joy. She could not restrain the hand that had to touch him. *Is it love or a deeper kinship—something that comes through knowing God?* She couldn't answer the question.

"Found none," Matt echoed the words as he lifted his head, sighed and said, "Those are terrifying words. I'm glad I didn't live in Old Testament days."

"Is there a difference?"

Early the next day, they were at it again. Words were parried back and forth, building up questions and answers Amy couldn't understand. When Amy had the dishes washed, she sat down to listen and watch their faces. She wanted desperately to pick apart their words, to understand the ideas about slavery and God and fellowmen and freedom they were tossing around. The arguments built up until Amy's head was in a whirl and she wanted to flee.

But before she could move, Matthew was on his feet. Although a head shorter, and nearly frail compared to Daniel, he shouted with a strange anger that left Amy trembling. "Who is the adversary; who is responsible? Who separates brothers? Why must there be this ugliness? Do you realize, my friend, we'll never heal this wound as long as the country exists?"

"You are wrong." Daniel paced the room. "I don't know politics, and I've no book learning, but I know God somewhat. This is a great nation. He will not let us down if we sincerely want the right."

"Right? What is right?"

"I guess if you believe there is a God, and if it follows that He's loving, just, and righteous, then we find right by aligning ourselves with Him."

"Simplistic. No educated man would buy that."

Heavily, Daniel said, "Probably not, that is until he's tried everything else. But I want to be around to say the words over and over. There'll be a day—"

Matthew was speaking as if he had not heard. "We are both smug, both sides, thinking we are right and that our way is Christian. See, Daniel, that's why I had to go back home. There's too much behind me. Traditions. A hundred years of believing in a way of life. You can't throw over loyalties and family ties just like that. You don't toss out all the values you've cherished simply because someone questions your beliefs." With hard, quick steps, Matthew paced to the window and stood with his back to Daniel.

"I know how you feel," Daniel said slowly. "But, Matt, at some point we both have to sit down and struggle through our beliefs. I hope we're both man enough to admit errors and throw them out."

Amy jumped to her feet. "I see Mother coming. You men are on your own; I'm leaving." She swished through the door and forcefully closed it behind her.

For a long minute there was silence in the room. Then Matthew slowly turned from the window. "Daniel, that woman, what is her name?"

"Mother?" Daniel stopped and looked at the strange mixture of curiosity and dismay on Matthew's face. He hesitated a moment as he paced back and forth across the room. *This is the situation we've all dreaded. The past has come back to haunt Silverheels.* He faced Matthew again, saying, "Her name is Amelia Randolph. I would appreciate your saying no more."

Matthew threw him a startled look, and immediately Daniel realized the man had no intention of saying more.

"Sorry," Daniel muttered as he resumed his pacing. The conversation was flattened and their words stilted. In a few minutes, Matthew headed for the bunk, and Daniel said, "I'm going over to see the folks, to give you a chance to rest."

"Do me a favor?" Matthew's voice was muffled. "Don't mention my name to her."

"Sure, fella." Daniel carefully closed the door behind him.

Amelia had been at the well on the edge of the parade grounds when Amy rushed forward, crying, "Oh, Mother, it is terrible! Those men have been arguing for two days now. At least when Matt was ill he didn't feel obligated to defend the whole Confederacy."

Amelia blinked with surprise. "Amy, what are you talking about?"

"That Confederate soldier we've been taking care of. You've been so concerned with Father that you've paid no attention. Is Father feeling better today?"

"That's why I'm here. The fever is gone and he's been fussing for food and you. He wanted me to bring Daniel too, but since he's occupied, we'll see him later." Linking arms they strolled down the path together.

Eli was dressed and seated on the edge of the bunk. Amy hugged him and then sat down beside the bunk. "The gripe," he explained. "Didn't want you and Daniel to come down with it. The doctor is saying I'm well enough to travel about any time."

"You mean your leg is healed?"

Amelia interjected, "The doctor is willing for him to travel as long as he does so in a wagon and without putting his weight on the leg. Come see the contraptions they've built for him. Because of the fighting, they've run out of crutches."

Amy examined the crude crutches. "Then you won't be able to continue visiting around the territory like Father Dyer wanted you to do?"

Eli said, "No, it'll be months before I can sit a horse or do much walking. Besides"—he hesitated as he looked at Amelia—"I'm thinking of filing for a piece of property. A homestead claim. In Colorado

Territory. We'll be eligible for a section big enough to support us."

"Father, you a farmer?" Amy cried. Then turning to her mother, she asked, "How do you feel about this?"

Amelia averted her face but Amy saw the dismay as she looked toward her husband, "Eli, I thought you'd forgotten about that." She caught her breath and faced away from Eli. "It was bad for me to come back, disrupting your life; but this is worse, knowing I've taken you from your first love."

"Amelia," Eli's face flushed, "we've gone through this before. Please, no more."

"But—"

"Father," Amy protested, "don't Mother's feelings matter? I mean, I don't think you're being fair." She saw the frown on his face and turned her back. "I'm supposed to be grown up, yet I can see you think I've no right to express how I feel. But for Mother's sake, let's talk."

"Please, Amy." Amelia's hand was warm on her shoulder. "I'm just sorry I spoke. I've no right to dig up the past. It was just that I was taken by surprise. That's all. It is his decision; it's only—"

"You don't like it because of what it means," Amy said bitterly. "And we're not allowed to voice our opinions."

There was a tap on the door and Daniel pushed it open. "Thought I'd join you." Amy saw his puzzled face as he looked from her to Mother.

"We're having an argument," she explained. "Father's decided to take up farming." Daniel's eyebrows went up. "You don't think he's a farmer either," she added, while Daniel moved his shoulders uneasily.

"Well, since I'm not the one doing the farming, how can I complain?" he said with a shrug.

"Daniel." Amy saw him wince, but she pushed on. "It's because of Mother, and she doesn't want him to give up the ministry. Why can't he see it is only making matters worse? I know how guilty I would feel. That is, how I did feel when you said you'd give up preaching all because of my selfishness."

Eli protested, "Amelia, I didn't say you were forcing me."

Amy wheeled around. "Father, this is a bad situation, but don't make it worse!"

"Daughter!" His voice cut through hers, and Amy stopped. It had been a long time since she had heard this stern note. When he had their attention and the room was so quiet that they could hear only the crackle of fire in the stove, he said, "This is not a bad situation. It is a promise fulfilled. One that the Lord gave me years ago, and one that sustained me when I didn't think it was possible to keep going."

He hesitated a second, dropped his head and then began quoting softly, " 'Therefore, behold, I will allure her, and bring her into the wilderness. . . . I will give her a door of hope.' "

Slowly Amelia got to her feet. Amy was surprised to see the tears on her cheeks. Softly she murmured, "Eli, I didn't realize—"

Daniel said, "Amy, let's go home."

When he closed the door on Eli and Amelia, he pulled Amy's arm through his. "You're blinking. Have a bug in your eye or do you want to have a good cry?"

"Daniel, if you push with one more word, I shall cry in spite of myself."

"Then I'll talk of something else. Amy, I think one of those situations we've feared has come up. Matthew has recognized your mother. He didn't explain, and I let him know I hoped he wouldn't. He did request we not mention his name to her."

Amy sighed and rubbed at her eyes. "Most certainly. After this afternoon, that would be the most terrible thing that could happen to her. Oh, Daniel, do you suppose it will be this way for the rest of our lives?"

From the weary shake of his head, she guessed her question was answered. After walking in silence, he turned to grin down at her. "Mrs. Gerrett, is life getting more confusing, or am I just getting old?"

"Old, at twenty-one!" She patted his hand. "You mean because of the way we were acting back there? Daniel, do you suppose it will be possible for them to ever—"

"Be sweethearts again?" He pursed his lips for a minute before saying, "At times I think your father is a mite stuffy—now, Amy, don't jump to conclusions. I admire and respect him, but I think he needs to have the starch washed out of his soul."

Amy collapsed against his arm, laughing up at him. "Daniel, my dear! Some times I think you resemble my father more than you realize. But then, in this family, I think someone needs a little starch."

CHAPTER 16

At breakfast the next day, Daniel drank the last of his coffee and pushed the cup to the middle of the table. Amy reached for the coffeepot. "Matt," he said, "I heard a rumor yesterday. I've been pondering whether I should pass it on. I guess that's the thing to do. It's about prisoner exchange.

"Some of the officers were talking at the armory; it sounded like reliable information to me. They told me they heard a contingent of enlisted men is scheduled to head east with prisoners for exchange."

Matthew dropped his spoon; slowly Amy put the coffeepot down and looked at him. Matt's pallor surprised her, but a glance at Daniel's sober face kept her silent. Finally Matt looked up. His voice was even and controlled as he said, "Well, I guess that's none of your concern. I'd appreciate time to adjust to the idea."

Amy blurted out, "What will that mean to you?"

He shrugged. "It's a straight trade. You get a man and they get a man. Soldier, if you please. I get another chance to have my head blown off." With another shrug, he struggled to his feet and paced the cabin.

"Your arm's not healed yet, and you're still limping on that leg,"

Daniel said slowly. "I'm of the opinion you won't be sent into action again. Right now, I'd like to talk to the doctor. Could be he won't think you're up to travel."

"Thanks, friend, but I'm certain you've pushed as far as they'll let you. I appreciate all you've—"

"Hey, fella, you're not done with us yet!" Daniel exclaimed.

"I only wish the whole matter of war were behind us," Matt muttered as he began to pace back and forth. "What ugliness! I don't think Jeff Davis foresaw it dragging on like this. The suffering it causes!" He looked up at Daniel. "In the beginning the idea behind the show of force was simply to underline the fact that the Constitution supports freedom. That's a subject that attracts men, but I'll admit"—he paused to shoot a quick glance at Daniel—"it's starting to look as if we've tried to carry it too far."

Daniel said slowly, "Freedom seems to mean different things to different people."

Matthew's voice overlapped Daniel's. "Supposedly there was to be a big rallying cry for freedom, a show of arms, and then we'd all be satisfied. See, Daniel, the issue is freedom for mankind to live as he pleases, not—"

"Freedom for the slaves?" Amy couldn't keep the words back. She had been thinking of Aunt Clara Brown, and the way her face saddened as she talked about her people. Abruptly she shoved the last dish on the shelf and rushed to the door.

For a moment there was silence in the room as Daniel watched Matthew. He turned from the window. "You'll be glad to see the last of me—I've done nothing except cause conflict. I've sent her flying off again, for the second day in a row."

"Don't take it personally," Daniel grinned. "Besides not liking the gentle discussion, she has a bigger need right now, and it's to be with her mother." As quickly as he said the words, he regretted them. Matt's face was a puzzle of unvoiced questions mingled with a strange sorrow.

It was Daniel's turn to pace while he hunted a safe topic. With his voice rumbling with emotion, Matthew said, "You've managed to poke religion at me; now answer a few questions."

Daniel watched Matt carefully sit on the edge of the bunk. "It's about the cause."

"You mean North versus South?"

"If you want to put it that way," he replied roughly, adding, "Daniel, this isn't an argument for fun."

"I didn't think it was." Their eyes met and Daniel was surprised at the relief washing across Matthew's face.

He said, "You're a parson. I was raised in the church, but there's still much I don't understand about religion." He added, "I've always considered myself Christian, even when I was pulling the trigger on a Yankee brother. Daniel, what's bottom line for Christianity?"

"You mean, what must you believe? Matthew, that's easy enough to answer, but I doubt I can make my answer clear without a great deal of talk. See, I'm not a scholar."

"I'm willing to listen." For a moment Daniel was caught by the unexpected humility in the man's voice. He studied the bowed head and cleared his throat.

"Matt, the Bible lays it straight. Christian faith isn't belonging to a church or hugging a list of do's and don'ts. It's loving the Lord your God with all your mind and heart. It's believing Jesus Christ was God, come to die for your sins."

"I know all that. But what does that mean?"

"Accepting the fact you can't be righteous on your own, but you can let Jesus Christ clothe you with His righteousness. Just accept the gift He gave you when He died for your sins. My sins too."

"Daniel, I did all that long ago. It's dry ashes. Why do I still feel I'm the worst of sinners in God's sight?"

Daniel studied Matthew's face before answering. "Let's put it this way. If I were feeling the same way, I'd know there was a reason. First, I'd want to check myself. Do I really believe God meant it when He said that Jesus Christ died for my sins? Do I believe that the only condition, the only way it is possible for me to really believe, is by accepting the sacrifice and then obeying God? And that it's not just for me, but for all who accept Him and obey?"

Daniel saw the shadow and gently said, "I had a big struggle at that point—wanting my will instead of God's. Matt, is that a problem?

I've been around you long enough to know you're as strong-willed as I am."

"Fighting cock, my dad called me."

Daniel kept on. "Also, I had the wrong slant on life. Took a while for me to learn I was to listen to God's ideas on how to live."

Matthew was lying on the bunk now. His good arm was under his head, and he stared at the ceiling. Daniel continued. "Then, too, I found out that an important part of Christianity is that God is concerned about more than just forgiving sins. He's in the life-changing business."

There was silence from the bed; for a moment Daniel wondered if Matthew was asleep. But he kept on. "And this isn't just to please himself and get the work done; there's a bigger part. It's to save us from ourselves and help us be comfortable with life. To tell the truth, Matt, I discovered it's mighty hard to live up to God's easiest requests—like loving our fellowman."

Daniel nearly forgot Matthew as he said, "The Apostle Paul talks about knowing the right way to live, but being unable to do the good instead of the evil."

He got up to pace the room. "I don't think this part of Christian living is talked about all that much. But it can happen, when we recognize our powerlessness to change and begin to ask the Lord to change us."

Matthew moved restlessly and Daniel quickly added, "Dependence on God must become a way of life. Dependence also helps us grow. The psalmist said, 'I will run the way of thy commandments, when thou shalt enlarge my heart.'"

Matthew sat up. Bitterly he said, "But it's too late."

"Not as long as you're still alive." Daniel studied the twisted face and added, "Matt, I don't know what's bothering you, but I do know that after asking the Lord's forgiveness, I had to forgive myself. I know it isn't easy, and sometimes it's impossible to change the pain."

Matthew sat for a long time with his head in his hands. Finally he said, "Look, back when this all started, I made some bad choices, and they can't be changed."

"Would it help to talk about them? I probably can't do a thing about it, but I'll listen." Daniel sat down, while Matt got up to pace the room.

"Big hero me," he muttered. "I guess I was swayed by my emotions without thinking through all my beliefs." He wheeled on Daniel. "But maybe I didn't have any—real ones, that is. I left a wonderful cause, and all of it happened when I allowed a strong-minded man talk me into endorsing things I didn't really believe.

"I'll have to admit I understand that now. But at that time I didn't comprehend it all, and I was willing to let him do my thinking for me." Daniel blinked and shook his head, but Matthew didn't see him.

He continued. "I can't talk about it all—it's too personal. But the worst part of it all is that I fell in love with a beautiful woman and married her. She was Creole. In addition, after we were married she told me some other things about her—things that made it impossible for my family to accept her. I guess you have an idea what it means to belong to an old southern family; good blood means a lot." Daniel winced, but Matthew hurried on.

"I wasn't at home when all this happened. When I got my head on straight, I started thinking about what I'd done to my family. Mind you, I still loved my wife. But I knew it was an impossible situation."

He turned to face Daniel. "I suppose I was an idealistic fool in the beginning. Crystal was lovely and loving. I thought it would all work out. Of course it couldn't. But I take blame for the failure of our marriage.

"When this fellow helped me get my thinking straightened out, I realized there was only one solution. I had to go back the way I came. That meant home and my responsibilities. Crystal—well, we parted under the worst of circumstances. It's been several years now. I'm older and wiser. I know there's no way I'll ever be able to get rid of the past. Right now I'd give anything to see her and just say I'm sorry. But there's no way. I doubt she's even going by the name Crystal Thomas now."

Daniel started to his feet and then stopped. He was busy pondering Matthew's statement and didn't hear him add, "If only I could find Clara Brown, she could tell me."

Creole—Crystal Thomas. There's no mistake; that's his wife! As the thoughts ran through his mind, Daniel recalled the last time he had seen Crystal. From dowdy maid to beautiful woman. *That dress, those feeble protests. How can I tell him I think she's a prostitute?*

Matthew faced him. "Pretty bad, huh?"

Daniel took a deep breath. "Might say I need to do a little thinking about the whole situation."

Matthew blinked. "You think the Lord won't forgive me?" For a minute Daniel paused. He studied the arrogant face in front of him, and for a moment distaste twisted through Daniel. Looking up, their eyes met and now Daniel saw the pain, the honest questions.

He sighed. "Matthew, we don't think alike, even hold dear the same things. But no, I didn't mean that! Matt, of course He forgives. I know that from personal experience. Sin is sin, and He forgave mine."

"I have an idea you've asked Him that a million times. Now's the time to begin to trust His promise to forgive."

The lines of strain began to lift from Matthew's face. Daniel hesitated and then said gently, "What God wants for you—for both of you, I have no way of knowing. Seems you might need to find her and make the bad things right."

Hastily Daniel added, "But you'll have to accept the possibility you'll never see her again. Sometimes the past can't be changed. Who knows what her circumstances are now?"

He nodded, "She's probably divorced me and remarried; it's been a long time."

Daniel watched as Matthew continued to pace the room. The strain was showing in the lines creasing his forehead. Once he glanced at Daniel, opened his mouth and then turned away. Just as deliberately Daniel pressed his lips together.

Finally Matthew headed for the bunk, muttering, "I'm going to try to sleep now."

"I guess I'll go look for Amy. See you in a couple of hours."

Eli met Daniel at the door, hobbling around on the new crutches. Nodding at the contraptions, he said, "I want to be up to traveling when the next wagon train heads for Colorado. Can't say I'm too content with this serving as an extra leg." Slowly he crossed the room, saying, "Amy and Amelia are off visiting with the women folk. Might as well come sit."

"My patient is sleeping," Daniel explained.

After they were both seated, Eli asked, "What do you think about trying to get some homestead land?"

Daniel studied the sharp eyes before answering. "I thought your getting out of the ministry was something you two had agreed upon."

He shrugged. "I decided. Amelia isn't resting easy with it."

Daniel pushed his back against the rough log wall and said, "I don't think I ought to be passing my opinions around. Isn't it enough to have two women pushing at you?"

"Then you do agree with them." Surprisingly, Eli sighed and grinned jauntily. "Well, Danny boy, since you admitted, then pretend you're a stand-in for Father Dyer and hear me out. I've been doing a lot of thinking about this whole situation. Decided I've been too rigid, or whatever it is that Amy was thinking. I guess I need to quit worrying about all the rules and regulations of the church and start thinking about people." He threw a quick glance at Daniel. "Maybe I've been . . . self-righteous. Might be the reason Amelia and I've had troubles."

He sighed and took up the dialogue. "People. I need to help people. Not pointing a finger at their sins; I can let the Lord do that. But I guess I can offer my arm—once I get free of these crutches." He grinned wryly, then lapsed into thoughtfulness.

Daniel rubbed at his furrowed brow and waited. Eli added, "Seems what I need to do is to find a way to help people learn to be comfortable with the Lord Jesus Christ."

Tentatively Daniel asked, "What's the problem?"

Eli blinked. "Why, not a thing, except that Amelia doesn't realize I need a way to support us while I'm going about the real business."

"Then you really are finished with the church?"

He moved uneasily, then posed a question. "You think I'm still unwilling to face an investigation?"

"Looks that way from here."

"Is it possible to think the Lord's leading me another direction? Think I could do the work just as well behind the plow? As a farmer instead of being a preacher?"

Before Daniel could think out an answer, the door opened and

Amy entered. "Daniel! So you and Matt did run out of talk."

"Matt was sleeping when I left. I think I wore him out."

"Mother and I have made the rounds. So, Husband, shall we go home?"

Outside the cabin Daniel remarked, "I'm beginning to think you're really enjoying being this close to Mother and Father, even if it's with your husband under guard."

"Well, I can't take your arrest too seriously." She paused and added, "Mother and Father—yes, it is a treat to be here with them. But I promise you, I'm not getting soft. I'll be ready for Oro City when we get there."

"How's that?"

"I don't really know, except I find myself thinking and wondering about the place and people. Maybe it's just the home feeling that's starting to grow on me."

"The place? Or is it me and you?" He leaned toward her, his eyes fixed on hers.

"Daniel, don't kiss me out here where the neighbors can see!"

"The cabin is getting too crowded," he muttered before opening the door.

Amy walked through the door, saying, "I thought you said Matthew was sleeping. He isn't here."

Daniel went past her to the bunk. "There's a note," he said. Sitting down he unfolded the scrap of paper. He read the note slowly, then handed it to Amy and dropped his face in his hands.

Amy studied the scrawl and read aloud: "Thanks, both of you. It's only fair I tell you. I've slipped the noose. Please don't say anything until morning, my friends. This one last favor, please. I want to get as far as possible before they know." She carefully folded the paper. "Daniel, is it because of what you heard?"

"Of course. I should have realized this would happen. But then I would have been obligated to—"

"Report Matt? Oh, Daniel, I'm glad you didn't guess."

"Amy, you don't understand. Matt is injured. Alone he's not going to make it anywhere. It isn't possible for him to survive. In that uniform, he runs the chance of being shot rather than questioned."

"You don't really believe that."

"I do. This is war." Daniel stood up and reached for his jacket. For one moment Amy studied his face and then threw herself at him.

"Daniel!" she cried, "don't leave me here alone—even for a few hours! I can't stand it."

"I'm sorry, sweetheart. Just don't say anything. I promise I'll be back as soon as possible. Before morning. But whatever happens—if I'm delayed, stay with Mother and Father."

She went to shove food into a bag. He followed her. "Remember, I'm under arrest, too. Don't say anything."

She watched him through the window. He casually wandered behind the line of cabins and disappeared into the trees. Leaning against the window, Amy whispered, "Before morning."

CHAPTER 17

Daniel walked slowly around the buildings bordering the stockade. He hesitated, waiting for a challenge. There was only silence. He stepped through the broken fence and waited for another moment while he casually studied the parade grounds. Taking a deep breath he straightened his shoulders and walked out of Fort Union.

Daniel kept his steps slow and measured as he headed up the mesa. The hair on the back of his neck prickled as he continued to anticipate the guard's shout, the gunfire.

Just below the crest of the mesa, he reached a line of trees and stopped to catch his breath. When he turned to measure the distance he had traveled, he was surprised to see the whole of Fort Union spread before him.

Shading his eyes from the late afternoon sun, he studied the terrain, looking for a sign of movement near the guard post. The sentry marched slowly back and forth. He could see the flagpole with the stars and stripes whipping lazily in the breeze.

As he turned to begin the final climb, he hesitated. Just to his right, down the steep slope, lay the star fort. Slowly he muttered, "It's a good thing the Confederates didn't make it this far. The slope of the hill has left the entire fort open to view. A howitzer could drop a half dozen shells right in the middle of the star fort before the fellows could move." Shaking his head, he started the steep climb to the top of the mesa.

Daniel walked through the trees, stopping every few minutes to listen and study the peaceful scene at the foot of the mesa. "Well, Matthew, my friend," he muttered, "it's easy to guess you had an unchallenged exit from Fort Union, just as I did." And then he added, "God, help me catch up with him before they do."

The late afternoon sun slipped behind the distant hills, throwing Daniel into shadows. He quickened his steps, muttering, "It's going to be dark in less than an hour. My chances of picking up Matthew's trail are fast disappearing."

Just before breaking out on top of the tree-covered mesa, he paused to look around once more. To the west the pattern of light and shadow seemed to move. For a moment he froze. Was that a movement in the trees to his left? He studied the terrain for a long time before he began to move again. This time he kept his eyes focused on the dense wood in front of him.

Daniel had been walking for nearly an hour up the plateau and down the other side into deep woods. The shadows had deepened when he heard a twig snap. He paused, then eased into the shadow of a fir and waited. When he was nearly ready to step out again, he heard another snap. Now he could detect the low murmur of voices. As he continued to stand in the shadows, he heard a crackling noise, then a flare of flame caught his attention.

In the deepening dusk it became a beacon, and he edged toward the light—step, wait, step, wait.

The smell of roasting meat drifted up to him, tightening his stomach with hunger pangs. Slowly Daniel shifted his position, trying to see down the incline. A rock slipped and he froze. Just below him two men were talking. As one fellow repositioned the rack of meat strips, his unseen partner said, "Sibley's going to be pleased. Didn't expect this bonus."

The cook turned on one heel. "Goes to prove a general lack of intelligence and foresight when they built that fort. Might say it points up the super intelligence of our forces." The man snickered, adding, "Planting that fort underground without checking the terrain." He paused to shake his head before saying, "Seems tightening up the Army's loose spots will be first priority after we take over—and that's your job, Wood."

"You're confident, Ellis," the other voice mused. "This war isn't over yet."

His friend chuckled softly, "I know, but I don't think I'm counting chicks where there ain't no eggs." Again there was a pause and then an impatient, "I hate this waiting. Why wouldn't Tristram let us rendezvous with him?"

"Sometimes it doesn't pay to ask questions," Daniel heard the mild-voiced man reply. He watched him look toward his partner before he added, "He's the boss this trip. We follow orders. That meat done?"

After his initial reaction to the name, Daniel began lining up the facts. Tristram, Confederates. He couldn't believe his ears. Were they saying Tristram was involved with the Confederates? He measured the idea against the picture of Tristram in Santa Fe. Remembering the background of gray uniforms, Daniel started to ease himself to his feet when he heard the horse. Slowly he sank back in the bushes and waited.

"Lucas, that you?"

"Who else?" From the sound of the heavy voice, Daniel guessed the man to be extremely fatigued. He peered around his screen of trees as the man approached the fire. While he tethered his horse, Daniel studied the drab miner's garb, realizing he wouldn't have recognized Tristram in a crowd.

Good thing that fellow named him. Sure doesn't look like the dandy I saw in Santa Fe.

"Supper'll be ready in a few minutes. Didn't want to smell up the whole hillside with smoke and meat."

The cook inched closer to Tristram. "Have a good trip?" Tristram nodded. The fellow persisted. "Well, what did you find out?"

Tristram grinned across the fire. "Might say I'll wait for dinner and the right person to hear me out." With a grin he rubbed his fingers together.

"At times, Tristram, I get the feeling you're more interested in the gold than the cause of the Confederacy," the other man said. Daniel detected a note of authority in the man's voice and he tried to peer at the face hidden by the smoke.

Tristram's voice was mild. "You're paying me for a significant job. Might be that just keeping you hidden behind the shield of that dirty shirt is worth the gold it costs the Confederacy."

There was silence. Daniel held his breath, trying to avoid giving away his presence by the surge of excitement and curiosity he felt.

"Wanna tell us who the contact was?"

"No." The reply was terse. Tristram helped himself to the pot of coffee, drank and then added, "The less you know the better—for all of us. The information you have is enough, and the only other item you need to know is that he's an important political figure. When the Confederacy runs up their flag over Colorado, then will be the time to let you men meet him."

"Well, give us some details. And it had better be good."

Tristram nodded, sipped his coffee and said, "Better than it was a month ago. You know the leaflets have been spread in every mining camp of size. There's been good support. The only negative thing I have to report is that Gilpin's still throwing his weight around, so much so they're starting to say Lincoln's taking notice. Already he's talking replacement."

"What's been happening?"

"Well, you know Gilpin was responsible for getting the true blues riled up to the point the Colorado Volunteer Army was organized. Now everywhere our fellows go, trying to buy up arms and powder, there's a crowd jeering along behind, calling them traitors and cop-perheads. It's making things uncomfortable. Our men were run out of Oro City."

There was a terse string of oaths. Tristram spoke out of the si-lence. "I'm trying to cover that negative reaction with a good image.

Pays to keep friends in a camp as significant as Oro City. Gilpin. Now he's pushed his way in without waiting for Lincoln's orders. He's issued drafts on the United States treasury to support his army, and in addition he's buying arms without Washington's permission."

"Well, if Washington doesn't put a stop to this in the next few weeks, we'll have to help them out."

"Washington might not be in a position to issue orders of any kind," the fellow beside the fire sneered.

"What do you mean?" Tristram shifted on his heels and faced the man beside him.

There was a faint smile on his face as he said, "Guess this far from Washington it won't do any harm to drop a gem. For the past year there's been plans afoot to blow up the capitol. So far Secretary Walker has put the plans on hold, but we're not ruling it out yet."

There was a long silence. The meat continued to sputter over the fire and the aroma drifted up to Daniel. Finally Tristram spoke. His voice was mild, even gently chiding as he said, "Well, something is going to have to happen. It's general knowledge any place the Confederacy congregates—money's the biggest problem we have. It will continue to be so. Obviously it's to our advantage to get this war over as soon as possible. President Jefferson Davis soon will be without funds unless he can stir up a little more loyalty."

The cook grumbled, "Heard from back home that he's getting the money by grabbin' up—"

The rock beneath Daniel started to slip. Quickly he made his decision. Lurching to his feet, he called, "Hallo down there!" With giant strides propelled by the sliding earth, he plunged into camp.

He was nodding and smiling as he strolled up to the fire. "Your supper smells mighty good. You fellows have an extra hunk? One of the dear sisters sent me on my way with a loaf of fresh bread."

From a sitting position they spun on their heels and the cook pointed his knife as Daniel hurriedly said, "Methodist Episcopal Church—name's Daniel Gerrett. I make it a habit to preach wherever I put my foot down."

The man stood and introduced himself. "I'm Wood; the cook there is Ellis."

"Glad to make your acquaintance," Daniel said.

There was silence and then the cook nodded. "Yer welcome, especially with bread, but you can forget the preachin'. I've a feeling north and south preaching is a mite different."

Wood drawled, "Now, Ellis, that's not hospitable. 'Sides, it's the same God. We're Christians, Parson." The cold gray eyes studied Daniel.

"Ya come from the fort?"

"Yes, headed out Taos way."

"Better stay clear of Santa Fe. They're sticking loose white men in prison, uniform or no."

"Why?" The firelight revealed the quick, shrewd glance of Wood.

"War time," the cook replied. "Where's that bread?"

From the corner of his eye, Daniel saw Tristram stir. He turned casually. "Well—we meet again." He addressed the group around the fire. "Met Lucas Tristram in Santa Fe a couple of weeks ago. Surprised to see you. Figured you'd be back home by now."

Slowly Tristram got to his feet. He teetered back and forth on his heels as Daniel explained. "I'm headed toward Taos. Saw the fire and smelled the meat. Gets lonesome, this traveling by yourself."

"Alone? Where's your mount?"

"We came to a parting of ways. I've left my wife with her parents." He paused, then hurriedly added, "Sure didn't expect the forest to yield such a high number of travelers."

When Daniel pulled out the loaf of bread, he saw the slight nod Tristram gave. Handing over the bread, he tried to breathe more slowly.

As he hunkered down beside the fire, he was thinking of Matthew and mentally surrendering him. *Lord, only you know where he is; please take care of him.*

The sky had begun to show signs of dawn when Daniel awakened to hear the cook whisper, "Lucas, I can stick him with my knife."

"Not yet. I've a feeling he could be useful."

Daniel tried to keep his breathing slow and even as he waited for the dawn.

After eating the rest of the meat and bread, washed down with coffee, Daniel said casually, "Well, I guess I'll just say my goodbyes and head over the hills."

Just as casually Tristram said, "Might as well ride along with us. The packhorse will accommodate a rider. At least we'll see the parson gets fed."

After reflecting on the stony faces surrounding him, Daniel shrugged and said, "Be better than depending on shank's mare. Are you heading toward Taos?"

"By way of Santa Fe." Daniel looked at the speaker; it was the cook, the one who had warned him away from Santa Fe.

"Maybe I'll just avoid Santa Fe."

Wood's voice was soft as he said, "It'll be safe with us along."

Daniel nodded slowly. *Two or three days' travel. I'll never catch up with Matt.* He turned away to hide the dismay he felt.

That day, as they rode, the cook sang. It was a tuneless montage of sound that grated on the nerves, but no one except Daniel seemed to notice it.

The day passed slowly as Daniel jogged down the trail on the bony packhorse. In the evening, around the fire, Tristram drawled, "Gerrett, for a preacher, you're mighty quiet. I thought preachers were instant in season and out."

He kept his voice light. "I don't preach before supper, but I'll be glad to entertain you as soon as we eat. Tonight I can contribute a small sausage."

Later, around the fire, Tristram said, "You are too young to have been a preacher for long. You had a mining claim in Central City. Why didn't you stick to it? Digging gold pays better than preaching."

"I guess I feel my job now is more important. God is calling me to guard the gold in men's lives."

The cook stirred and adjusted his hat. "What's gold in a man if he doesn't have it in his teeth?"

"The freedom to choose without being forced. God gives us this gift. Unfortunately some men are more than eager to take it away from others. In addition I see Christianity as gold in men's lives.

Sometimes it's hidden away by the care of living. I reckon it needs to be taken out and polished."

The cook snored deeply, and ruefully Daniel said, "I guess it's time to end this sermon."

"That's all right," Tristram drawled. "You've tomorrow and the next day. Maybe you'll have polished all our metal before this trip is over."

CHAPTER 18

That night Daniel tossed restlessly, wondering what lay ahead of him, and worried about Amy. The small fire had burned away to warm ash before he was able to surrender the troubling thoughts of Amy.

All too soon, it seemed, they were back on the trail. Dawn was lighting the sky with a touch of pink when they pulled out. But in the eerie quiet of the shadowy mountains, Daniel felt as if night had become part of him. As they rode, the sun rose above the trees and bathed the group with warmth. Then Daniel began to realize the trip was half over.

He eyed the cook slumped in his saddle, singing the tuneless song, and the questions cropped up again. Why had the man warned him against going to Santa Fe?

Late in morning, just as Daniel made up his mind to talk about Taos again, Tristram turned to look at him. The perplexed frown on his face brought Daniel out of his musing. "Something wrong?" he asked.

Tristram nodded. Jerking at the reins, he turned his mount. "I hear horses, more than just a few." He dug his heels into his mount.

"I'll go take a look—just keep on and don't stop for anything." His orders encompassed them all. The men watched as Daniel nodded and slapped the reins smartly. Their horses moved out at a trot while Tristram cut up the side of the bank, away from the road.

As they rode the sound of hoofbeats grew louder, and the men began exchanging worried glances. When they frowned Daniel's direction, he pulled even with them and said, "Do you suppose it's Indians?"

Wood had been remote, saying little as he kept his distance from Daniel. Now his eyes were uneasy with concern as he rode Daniel's direction. "Too many." He frowned but he held his horse, continuing to study Daniel. Finally he confided, "I don't know why Tristram said to keep on going, but I think we'd better do what he says."

With a curt nod, he dug his heels in the horse's sides and galloped ahead. Ellis jerked his head, and Daniel nudged the horse under him. Within a short time, the road in front of them wound up a steep hill and the horses slowed.

Daniel looked back as they took the next curve. His heart thudded. The horses were coming fast. He could see the dust and guessed there were many of them. Soon the thunder of the horses' hooves on the road blocked out all else. The cook lashed at his horse as a cloud of dust rose in the canyon. As Daniel started to slap the packhorse, he paused. Down the hill, coming around the curve, he saw the group pursuing them. All the riders were wearing blue uniforms.

Wood whirled on Daniel. "This is your doing?" Daniel had only time to turn his head when the man's whip lashed out at the packhorse. The horse reared, then plunged sideways against the Ellis's mount. Both horses stumbled. With a curse, the man yanked his horse away. Daniel saw it was too late. He jumped just as the three horses lunged into each other.

The sounds of hooves and warning cries mingled. Daniel sprinted away from the road while the plunging horses circled the group and stopped.

Daniel ran toward his horse just as the first soldier dropped from his mount. The pistol was cocked, pointed at Daniel. He heard the words. "Gerrett, you're under arrest. Men, get those friends of his."

When the dust settled, the three were aligned in front of the young lieutenant from Fort Union. He waved the pistol at Daniel and said, "You nearly cost me my commission. These are your contacts? I suppose you've had this planned all along. Well, come on. The prison in Santa Fe will be less crowded."

"Santa Fe?" the cook sputtered. "That's—"

"Shut up!" Wood snarled out the words, while the lieutenant watched. As his prancing horse stepped sideways, the lieutenant pulled it under control and said, "I'm Dayton, United States Army, in charge of this detail. You men will fall in ahead of me. We're riding into Santa Fe as fast as we can get there."

An enlisted man circled back to Daniel and grinned. "Lead out. This is going to be interesting," he crowed. "I can't wait to get to Santa Fe. Our men are shoving at the Confederates right smart like."

Daniel climbed on the packhorse and led the way. The cook snarled, "Preacher, huh? Jailbird. You had us fooled. What did they get you for?"

There was silence from Wood, but later, when they camped for the night and Daniel was placed under guard, he saw the speculative look the man turned on him.

Daniel aimed a broad grin back at Wood as the guard tied his wrists together. The guard saw the grin. With a quick glance toward the others, he said, "Lieutenant Dayton, these fellows are friends; maybe—"

"Keep them under guard," Dayton said hastily.

After the mess of beans and bacon, Ellis smirked, saying, "Well, Parson, how about the evening sermon?"

"Promise you won't go to sleep on me?" There was a snort of laughter, but some of the men moved closer to Daniel.

"So you're a parson."

One fellow teased, "Let's hear you. I wanna know if rebels have a man who can preach worth a pinch of gold dust."

Behind the curiosity, Daniel saw the same dark look he had been encountering so often lately. "Be glad to oblige," he said.

Hastily the fellow added, "Just as long as you don't have to have your hands free to wave."

Awkwardly Daniel got to his feet and looked around the circle of faces, lighted by the flicker of the fire. Taking a deep breath he quoted, " 'Come now, and let us reason together, saith the Lord: though your sins be as scarlet, they shall be as white as snow; though they be red like crimson, they shall be as wool. If ye be willing and obedient, ye shall eat the good of the land: but if ye refuse and rebel, ye shall be devoured with the sword: for the mouth of the Lord hath spoken it.' "

In the silence the men moved uneasily. Daniel continued, "These words were spoken not to the North or South, but to us all. The dividing line in this life is not locality or politics, but the human will. Not a one of us stands faultless before our Lord. Beating our swords into plowshares will not destroy the conflict within our breasts.

"Neither President Abe Lincoln nor President Jeff Davis can give us peace. Only at the feet of Jesus Christ do we learn to be the true seekers of peace.

"Where I come from, men are all seekers of gold—miners and Methodists alike. For some it is the treasure of the earth; for others it is the treasure of the heart. I challenge you to examine your treasure now. Will time and circumstances pare it away? Will it stand the corruption of the grave? The Lord Jesus said, 'I counsel thee to buy of me gold tried in the fire, that thou mayest be rich.' "

Later when Daniel awkwardly lowered himself to his bedroll in the New Mexico dust, he realized not one soldier had dozed beside the fire.

The next day as they rode into Santa Fe, Daniel began to sense the difference in the town. There was a murmuring current of excitement sweeping through the people on the street. Skirts and mantillas swished, curious dark eyes peeked around water jars, while burros twitched their ears.

Until they rode into the town plaza, Daniel couldn't identify the reason. Then he saw the flag cracking in the breeze over the Palace of the Governors. "It's the Star Spangled Banner!" he exclaimed softly. His guard wrinkled his brow as he looked from the flag to Daniel.

A uniformed officer standing in the portico moved and Daniel blinked. He was wearing blue. Looking around, it began to sink in.

Every uniform he saw was blue. "Tell me," he urgently addressed the soldier at his side. "Tell me about it."

The soldier began to grin. "Canby. Colonel Canby gathered his forces and started pushing. He's chased Sibley to Albuquerque, and I hear he's still going.

"You should have been there. The Rebs and Canby shot it out with cannon. Quite a boom! Quite a mess; those cannon balls were plopping all over the place! It's going to take a time to repair all that adobe." He paused and with narrowed eyes he studied Daniel.

"Man, where've you been? You didn't know! The war is over in New Mexico. Colorado, too. There ain't no way the Confederacy will get a toehold in the place now." He paused as the perplexed expression came back. "But how come you're so glad? I thought—"

Then he shrugged and turned. "Come on. It's Fort Marcy and the guardhouse for the likes of you."

Daniel protested, "Listen to me first. You've got to let me talk to someone—even Lieutenant Dayton."

"If it's so important, why didn't you say so a couple of days ago?"

"Because I thought we were walking into rebel territory. I had no idea Santa Fe was free."

"It's just a trick. You and your friends are up to something."

"They are. That's why I need to talk. See, there's another one and he—" Daniel stopped. Finally he grinned, "Maybe his news isn't important after all. If the threat to Colorado Territory is over, then I guess I needn't worry. But say, is Major Chivington in town?"

"Chivington, of the Colorado Volunteer Army?" The soldier shook his head. "I don't know where he is."

"Well, see if you can find out. He knows me."

"What good will that do?"

Daniel took a deep breath and said, "I'm Daniel Gerrett, missionary of the Methodist Episcopal Church, I—" The soldier was grinning.

When the door closed behind Daniel, he found his prison mates were his trail companions—all except Lucas Tristram.

He sat down and studied their dismal faces. "What's happened to Lucas?" They shrugged.

Wood studied Daniel. "What does it matter to you?"

"Now it doesn't," he said softly. "I just thought you might care."

The man shrugged. "Might be the Indians will get him. I reckon not, though. Lucas always seems to land on his feet. He's probably back in Colorado, hatching up some new scheme to rake in the gold."

"You've known him for a long time?"

"We grew up within six miles of each other, down in Mississippi Delta country." Wood seemed disinclined to talk. He settled his hat low on his forehead and leaned against the cold stone wall.

At breakfast the following day, Daniel said, "You fellows know we're apt to be prison mates for some time. How about getting acquainted?"

"Sounds like a good idea," Ellis said eagerly. "I've been curious. Tell us who you really are."

"Well, you'll never believe this," Daniel said slowly. "But I am a missionary in the Methodist—"

Wood stopped chewing and Daniel shrugged. Finally the man said, "I can see we'll never find out. Mind telling us where you're from?"

Daniel sighed. "Colorado. Oro City."

The man shook his head and then added, "I suppose I'll not have anything to lose if I introduce myself. I'm Colonel Jeremy Wood, most recently from Texas."

"I thought you were an officer," Daniel muttered.

Wood replied, "I guess my powers of observation aren't as acute—" He shrugged.

Ellis said, "I'm from Georgia, but I've been living in Texas since '57. Got so's we couldn't make a living in Georgia, so we homesteaded in Texas."

"Why couldn't you make a living there?" Daniel asked. He saw the quick glance the man threw at Wood.

There was a flicker of contempt in Wood's eyes as he said, "Cotton. Most of the poor whites were being bought out. Ellis was one of them."

Ellis continued. "Texas isn't like home, but the womenfolk are working hard at helping out."

"I'm surprised you're fighting to—"

"Support the way of life that ruined him? Slavery," Wood said. "You forget we're fighting for our freedom, not—"

"But that's part of it," Daniel said softly. "At least that's the story we get. You want your freedom to push slavery. Man, can't you see it yet? Slavery will never make it as long as there is a Christian in the States."

Wood snapped, "That is a bigotry if I've ever heard it!" He took a breath and went on. "Has it occurred to you that we have churches and Christians in the South? Also, we care about our people. We take good care of them. There's medical aid, and schools. There's—"

"Everything but freedom."

"One of these days we'll be able to convince you that these people don't want freedom; they want someone to take care of the them—"

"You'll have a hard time convincing me of that," Daniel snorted.

"One of these days," Wood said softly, "you'll have no recourse but to accept what we've known all along."

"And that is?"

"With all these black people here, there's nothing that's going to work except the shelter and help they have now."

"Slavery," Daniel retorted. "Man, I don't know too much about Negroes, except that God created them, too. They are human, just as I am. Seems they ought to have every right I have, including freedom and the opportunity to live as they wish. Especially in the United States of America."

"But not in the Confederate States. We're the only ones smart enough to know it's not a gonna work."

By morning Daniel was able to put out his hand and say, "Wood, I apologize. Not for my position on slavery, but because the Lord convicted me. I was being a pigheaded judge. I ought to know by now that it is only God who knows the heart. It's only the judgment day that'll strip away our faults and prejudices to the place where we can see ourselves the way the Lord does. Meanwhile, God forgive us all for the ugliness we're inflicting on each other."

Ellis spoke up. "At least the Union's feeding their prisoners a sight better. Back in Texas—" He paused as Wood got to his feet and paced the narrow room.

The following week Ellis and Wood were led out of prison. The guard told Daniel it was prisoner exchange. Daniel watched them go and felt the heaviness settle around his heart, thinking of Matthew, wondering where he was. In addition he recalled that last glimpse of those men's eyes. There was nothing in their expression to indicate they were happy with their lot.

Finally Daniel settled back against the cold stone wall and muttered, "Well, with all this peace and quiet, I'll have plenty of time for prayer." Again he found himself wondering about Matthew. That same troubled expression had been in Matthew's eyes. Were these men beginning to have doubts about the war?

And Crystal—had he done right by not telling Matthew about Crystal? What were those final words she had said to him? He frowned, shook his head and then went to lean against the bars shutting him away from sun and freedom.

CHAPTER 19

Amy paced the floor for most of that first night. She tried to tell herself it was no different than being in Oro City. "Alone is alone," she murmured, looking out at the dawn. But deep inside she knew it was different. There was a feeling of finality to it all. At the moment she watched Daniel stride leisurely around the end of the log enclosure, despair dropped on her like a cape she must wear—a dark, dismal gray.

Two more days passed before Amy could accept what she had been seeing mirrored in the eyes of her father and mother. Each day Amelia had come to urge Amy, "Please, dear, gather your things and move in with us. You mustn't stay here alone."

At first Amy had turned away from her mother, but on this day, she faced her with a new concern. "Mother, what was that noise just before dawn?"

"The cavalry moving out. Eli and I were up to watch them—all dressed in their uniforms and fully armed. Does that tell you something?"

Slowly she spoke. "The Army. Something bad has happened. If Daniel were coming back, he would be here by now." Her lips were wooden and Amelia reached for her.

Finally she allowed Amelia to help her gather up their belongings to carry down to her cabin. Slowly folding Daniel's shirt, and thinking that he didn't even have a blanket, Amy gave in to tears. Amelia put down her load and came to Amy. Amelia lifted Amy's face, and with her palms she wiped the tears from her face, saying, "Daughter, you've been strong before, you must be again. Don't give up hope until—it is necessary."

Amy crumbled against her shoulder. When she finally raised her face and scrubbed at her eyes, she managed a smile. "I'll try to be confident, Mother. How thankful I am that you're here!"

"Now let's have some breakfast and then go to the sewing circle over at Trina Dayton's place."

Eli turned as they walked through the door. He was leaning on the crutches, and Amy guessed he had been hobbling around the cabin. There was a white line of pain around his mouth and Amy saw the expression in his eyes. She stopped in the doorway, wondering about that expression.

Is it possible Father cares more deeply than I've guessed? It's also possible they have news.

She winced. Hastily Amelia said, "There's been no word; I just can't have her over there alone. What trouble that young rebel caused when he violated Daniel's friendship and ran away!" she said as she went to put on her apron.

Eli nodded his head in agreement as he hopped across the room and patted her hair. "Maybe you'd better be thinking about moving out with us next week. There're several wagons headed for Colorado, and we've been offered room."

"I wondered why you were working so hard with those crutches." Amy turned away, adding, "I suppose if Daniel isn't back I'd better go. That's what he wants me to do, only it's so—" She gulped and took a deep breath. It was impossible to say the word *final.*

Eli shook his head, saying, "Well, with all the activity—the Army moving out and the prisoners being traded, it doesn't appear to be a good idea to hang around much longer. Who knows what'll happen?"

After breakfast Amy and Amelia gathered up their mending and walked across the parade grounds to the line of officers' quarters. A distraught Trina met them at the door. Two crying toddlers clung to her skirt. Amelia handed the sewing to Amy and scooped up the nearest child.

Trina rubbed at her brow. "I'm sorry. It always affects me this way when the men ride out. I can't forget the bad times.

"Even before all this started, it was bad. One day last summer a fellow rode in with news that the settlers up the Santa Fe Trail were being harassed, so the men all rode out. A bright shiny day like this. I still thank God that my husband's horse threw a shoe. Of course he had to stop to take care of it. By the time he caught up with the men, it was all over."

Trina's words threw a clear picture in front of Amy. The sunshine, the plunging horses, and the hills erupting with shouts and dust as the Indians swooped down upon them. A bright summer day, while some women were forever plunged into winter. *Winter of the heart,* thought Amy. *A gray, dismal cape to wear forever.*

Half the morning had disappeared behind the murmured conversation before Amy asked the question. "Do you know why the men were called out this morning?"

Trina looked surprised. "Don't you know! Canby's men have the Confederates in retreat. They are running and our men are chasing."

"But that's good!" Amy exclaimed, sitting up straight and pushing her fingers into the corners of her eyes to stem the tears that threatened. "There won't be any more fighting."

Amelia spoke gently. "Not here—but Amy, the war isn't over. This is just one little battle."

Now Amy's voice was dull as she voiced her fear. "And other women will keep on facing this. Back there. War—why can't we get along with each other?"

Trina cuddled her little girl against her shoulder. Her face was sad, remote, as she slowly said, "That isn't all. There's other parts of war that are bad. It tears at the hearts and minds of people. In '61, just before the war started, this place was torture. People were being torn apart by all the conflicting views.

"It's bad to have to decide against everything you've been taught to believe is right. We saw that here. People were going south, leaving the Union and the Army, because of the pull between family and home."

Amelia added, "But there was conflict. How it must have torn the families apart."

Trina nodded. "We tried to be polite and continue to be friends. But it sure does tear a person apart inside, knowing that some of our dearest friends will soon be fighting against us."

From across the room the quiet little woman spoke. "Sometimes it isn't easy to do what you really want to do, deep down." For a moment sadness pulled at her mouth; then with a sigh she straightened and smiled and continued briskly.

"For months the only topic discussed was the right and wrong of it all. North and South. It ruined even the most joyous of occasions. Finally, when war was announced, there was a rip right down the middle of us. It's one thing to talk, but it's another thing to be faced with the fact of war.

"Now we were friend and enemy. The feeling was there, even among dearest of friends. It became impossible to speak your heart. See, this wasn't all because of politics. It was blood loyalties that swayed the men and their families. I tell you, there were some sad partings as men packed up and went south to fight a war they didn't endorse, simply because family was in the South. It was in their blood, to believe family was more important than anything else."

There was silence in the room. Amy saw that Amelia was bent nearly double over her sewing. Her voice was muffled when she finally spoke. "I daresay not a one in this whole nation hasn't been touched in much the same way. Men fighting when they don't want to fight. Men and women ripped apart because of all the ugliness. Some not even understanding why. I've seen it happen, and how I wish I could have prevented it! At times I wonder if we will ever again be whole."

"But it hasn't been going on all that long!" Amy exclaimed, bewildered by the pain in her mother's voice.

Amelia looked at her. "It has been going on for a long time. Too long. Since the beginning, when the first Negro was brought into this country in chains and that first white man looked the other direction, the trouble began. We can't turn away from things like this and still continue to be whole people."

There was silence in the room as each woman busily worked at her sewing. Trina broke the silence. Her voice was low and thoughtful as she said, "There were other things, too. I was raised in the South. My family was poor, struggling to keep food on the table. Just struggling to keep the few acres we had. There were eight of us children. I remember chopping brambles and fighting weeds before I was old enough to go to school." She paused and looked at Amelia. "There was not one thing we poor people could do to get ahead. The big planters around us, with their army of slaves, just plain took every acre they could get their hands on. Standing there, with a grin on their faces, they waited for us to fail so that they could grab our land."

Later, when they stood to leave, Trina said, "As long as there is war there will be an army. My husband and men like him will have a job. The power and the glory. Sometimes I think they close their minds to the rest and see only the horses and uniforms. The glory of it all." She shuddered.

Amy cried, "But if you hate it so, why did you marry him?"

She saw Trina wince before she said, "Because I love him." Taking a deep breath, she added, "I asked Colonel Wainswright's wife the same question. The colonel was killed in the skirmish with the Indians." She watched Amy as she stated, "I guess there's no way we can avoid pain in this life."

Amy recalled that statement the day their group of three wagons left Fort Union. With Eli cushioned on the bed of blankets in the rear wagon, and Amelia on Daniel's horse, they rode out as soon as the sun was above the horizon.

Amy avoided looking behind as she prodded her horse and searched for something to say to her mother. Finally she said, "We're not a very big wagon train. I heard the men talking. They're saying the Indians are starting to give the settlers plenty of trouble."

Amelia was smiling as she asked, "Did you and Daniel think of that before you left Colorado to look for us?"

"No. It was too early for the Indians to be doing much. Besides, I think we were young and foolish then." She had to stop to steady her voice.

Amelia said, "Amy, if ever faith is important, it's important now."

"You think that if I just pray, God will bring my husband back to me?"

"You know I don't mean that. Daniel's been saying it pretty strongly to me. Faith means having confidence that God is in control, and also that there's nothing in His creation which doesn't fit into His plan." Amelia smiled gently. "See, I'm learning my lesson. I said this over and over the day the accident happened."

"I know," Amy replied soberly, "and I also know God's plans could be completely different from the plans I hold in my head. But somehow I didn't think we'd work out all our troubles just to end up losing—having something like this happen." She faced Amelia, unable to keep back the rush of words, "Oh, Mother, I'm so frightened. I love Daniel and I just can't see life going on without him." Amelia's head was bowed. She didn't reply.

The wagon train turned northeast out of Fort Union. Finally Amelia said, "This is the way we came down from Raton Pass after the accident. It was a steep hill; now we'll have to climb it."

"What happened to the team?"

"One of the horses had a cut on his leg. We decided to sell them both. The wagon was a pile of firewood."

They rode all that day through the arid desert flatlands. Ahead of them the line of blue mountains promised relief from the dust and burning sun, but they seemed to keep their distance. When Amy pulled Daniel's old hat forward to shade her eyes, she remarked, "Seems hard to realize Colorado is still having snow. Another week of riding and we'll be wishing some of this warmth back on us."

Amelia's sharp glance made Amy straighten in the saddle and smile. "Well, can you recommend the scenery, Mother?"

"It gets better as we go. Amy, you haven't asked about the wagons ahead of us."

"Father told me there's some wounded Colorado men riding along. I wonder why."

"They are going home. But they are still soldiers. I understand their injuries aren't serious enough to prevent them from protecting the wagons."

Late in the afternoon one of the men came riding back to Amy and Amelia. Cheerfully he hailed them. "Name's Downs. Guess I'm in charge. How are you ladies? Are you enjoying the scenery?" Amy nodded and he added, "Just wanted to let you know we'll soon be stopping for the night. We're getting pretty close to the Maxwell ranch." He explained, "A fellow by the name of Lucian Maxwell has been acquiring a sizable hunk of the territory. Just ahead is Cimarron, and the settlement is part of the Maxwell ranch. This means we'll be under the protection of the ranch for another day or so."

There was something guarded about the man's manner, and Amelia asked the question Amy dared not ask. "Are you thinking we'll have problems with the Indians?"

"The chances are more than likely. Ever heard of Taos Lightning?"

Amelia nodded and Amy said, "I hear it's bad liquor. They sell it in Colorado Territory."

"Well, there's some ranchers and settlers hereabouts who've discovered there's a good profit in selling the stuff to the Indians. Having the Army distracted by the war isn't helping matters any."

Amy could think only of Daniel. "Has there been anything happening—with the Indians, I mean—this past week?"

She saw the sympathy in his eyes as he shook his head. "No, ma'am. As far as we know there's not been trouble like that recently. The Indian agent, Arny's his name, seems to have a good handle on things right now. Soon it's time for the men to be getting crops planted. That helps." He hesitated and then added, " 'Course, it could be a different situation when we reach Colorado."

Amy watched Downs' brisk salute as he rode away from them.

"Shall we catch up with the wagon and see how your father is doing?" Amelia asked.

CHAPTER 20

Two days after leaving the Maxwell land grant, the wagon train reached the summit of Raton Pass. Since early morning heavy clouds had billowed over the mountain. Now it was snowing. Amy and Amelia were huddled in heavy coats, but the wind-driven snow lashed at their faces.

"Stay close to the wagon," Amelia called as they rode along. Amy nodded and clung to the reins. The snow in front of the horses swirled, making Amy dizzy as she strained to see the trail in front of them. By the time they reached the crest of the mountain, the snow had nearly obscured the wagons. With heads down, the horses slowed to a walk, while snow piled a crown of white on their forelocks.

"Hey there!" Amy heard Downs long before she saw him. He appeared out of the storm like a white apparition. His hat and coat were plastered with snow while moisture dripped from his eyelashes as he said, "How about tying those mares to the back of the wagon? It'll be warmer inside."

"Eli needs all the space," Amelia said tersely. "We'll manage."

Amy's teeth were chattering as she asked, "Will we be stopping soon?"

There was a worried frown on Downs' face. He shook his head, saying, "Not until we get down off this mountain. Rate this snow is falling, we won't be able to find the road by morning. I'm guessing another hour will see us out of the worst of it. Welcome to Colorado Territory, ladies." He touched his hat and rode away.

"Amy, there's room in the wagon for you," Amelia offered, guiding her horse close and peering down at Amy.

Amy saw the worried frown and shook her head. "I'll be fine, Mother. I'm just as tough as you are. I just hope—"

Amelia reached across to Amy. "Please, dear, don't worry; instead let's pray that he's not out in this."

By late afternoon, they had dropped down to the lowlands. The snow stopped and the Colorado foothills were nearly as warm as the New Mexico flatlands had been. Amy looked at the sagebrush decorated with a frosting of snow and said, "I didn't think sage could possibly be this welcome."

Amelia pointed ahead, saying, "I'm of the opinion that's the ranch we're bound for. The first wagon is turning off the road, and I think I see buildings in the distance."

"I wonder if there are Indian troubles ahead," Amy mused.

"Because we're stopping early?" Amelia asked, shaking the wet snow off her scarf. "Well, I'll be grateful for shelter for any reason."

Lights were appearing in the windows of the long, low adobe building as they rode up. Amy watched the men lift her father to the ground and then hand him the crutches. Amelia gave the reins of her horse to Amy. "If you'll take her to the barn, I'll go with Eli."

After taking the horses to water and giving them grain, Amy turned them out to pasture and headed for the house. When she reached the farmhouse, she followed the sound of voices and the clatter of dishes. She discovered the other travelers had gathered in the low-beamed main room.

Briefly she stood in the doorway looking around the pleasant twilight-filled hall. At the far end she could see tables being set for a meal. Logs blazed in the stone fireplace stretching across the opposite end of the room. Already the members of the wagon train were lined close to the fire, and the steam was beginning to rise from their sodden garments.

Amy unwound her scarf and pulled off her coat as she walked across the room. The wan faces of the wounded soldiers lifted, and they shuffled down to make room for her. Her father was on a bench on the far side of the fire.

She glanced around and then asked, "Where's Mother?" The injured soldier sitting close to the fire shrugged. "Is Mother changing bandages?"

The soldier beside her answered, "No, ma'am, she's talking to that fella over by the kitchen door. Don't know who he is, but she headed straight over there as soon as we came in. I'm guessing it's someone she's known elsewhere."

Amy followed the man's pointing finger. In the shadows she saw the two with their heads close together. She recalled the soldier's statement and turned away. Moving her shoulders uneasily, Amy said, "She'll be back to help," nodding at the soldier's bandaged arm.

"We appreciate it," the soldier murmured softly. "It's good of her, and not a one of us expected that of a lady."

Apologetically he added, "It isn't pleasant. Thornton over there is missing the most of his hand. Your mother's kept it from poisoning on him. Not many supplies to work with, except the turpentine." He added, "Better that than nothing."

"I'm surprised," Amy said softly, "that they'd let you travel without medical supplies."

The soldier raised his eyebrows. "Ma'am, compared to most, we don't need anything."

Amelia came toward the fireplace with the stranger in tow. "Amy, I'd like you to meet—"

Amy gasped, "Matt!" Amelia dropped her hand and looked from the stranger to Amy. "Mother, this is the fellow who stayed with us— the wounded soldier Daniel went to find."

Turning back to Matt, Amy blinked as she studied the pale, weary face, and only then did she become aware of his ragged, soiled assortment of clothing. She blinked again when she saw it was topped with an old horse blanket. She opened her mouth to ask about his uniform, but his quick glance caught her attention. It was that haunted, trapped animal look. Was he pleading for silence?

Amy gulped. "Fancy meeting you here."

"So you know my daughter?" The look Amelia turned on Matthew was sharp, questioning.

Matthew's face was stamped with defeat. He admitted, "I was the one staying with them at Fort Union." He turned to Amy with a perplexed frown. "Did Daniel stay behind?"

The implication struck Amy and she could only stare at him. Matthew was safe, but Daniel wasn't with him. She turned away, saying dully, "As soon as we discovered you were missing, Daniel went looking for you. He didn't come back."

Matthew backed against the wall. For a moment he sagged there, slowly shaking his head. He lifted his head when Amy turned to face him. The twilight shadows of the room slanted across his pale face as he whispered, "Ma'am, I'm sorry. Will you give me your horse? I'll go looking for him."

"Where?" Amy stared up at him while the question settled into him. He shook his head with the futility of it and Amy stated, "Your wound needs attention. How did you walk this far in such condition?"

"Indians. That's where I got the clothes. They were wanting information in exchange for food and shelter. But I was getting a bad feeling about it all. Uneasy is putting it mildly. Slipped out during the night."

Amelia stepped closer to Matthew. Amy watched her intent study of his face. When Amelia turned from Matthew, her eyes had narrowed. *Mother knows that man, and from her look, I don't think she likes him at all.*

Amelia's voice cut through Amy's thoughts. It was even, strangely controlled as she said, "Come meet Amy's father."

Later Amy confronted her mother, saying, "Mother, I don't want to pry. Maybe I shouldn't ask. How did you come to know Matt?"

Amelia frowned as she faced Amy. "I was living in Pennsylvania, working for a group of people who were helping the slaves run away from their masters." She hesitated, and her voice softened as she went on. "Amy, when there's more time, I'll tell you all about it."

She touched Amy's cheek and said, "It's strange we never met the Reb—the person staying with you. Surely my name was mentioned. But I can guess Matthew didn't bother telling you that we've known each other for years. He has some unhappy memories of that time."

"Oh," Amy replied, her eyebrows raised.

Amelia turned quickly and snapped, "It's not what you think!" Abruptly she squeezed Amy. "I'm sorry. It is nothing more than I deserved, but it wasn't that at all. One of these days, when I can—" She paused. "For now we'll just have to wait for our talk."

After supper Amy helped with the dishes while the wounded travelers huddled around the fire. By the time the dishes were finished, the soldiers began to disappear. One by one they carried their blankets off to the sleeping quarters. When Amy came back into the room, she found Downs beside the fire with her mother and father.

Amy sat down on the bench as Amelia addressed him. "This young fellow, Matt, wants to ride with us tomorrow. I knew him years ago, and I think he's a pretty decent fellow. He told me he's down on his luck, doesn't have a horse, and he needs a ride into Denver."

Downs listened intently, studying Amelia's face as she talked. Amy could see the hesitancy reflected in his eyes. Finally he said, "We've been cautioned against picking up riders. There's rumors of soldiers, both Union and Confederate, cutting out of New Mexico. How do I know he isn't one of them?"

"Does it matter? He's human and needs a helping hand right now. Seems to me that's most important." Amelia delivered the statement in an even, emotionless voice, while Amy sat on her hands to hide their trembling.

Downs continued to study Amelia. Finally he got to his feet, saying, "Might tell the fellow he can join up with us. We may need all the Indian fighters we can get before this trip is over. I hear the Utes are riled and they're headed this way."

"I thought the Utes left the white people alone," Amy said slowly.

"Not now. In the past they've been pretty easy to get along with, but with the war, right now all the Indians need to be regarded as dangerous. Don't forget, the fighting in New Mexico has drained off the protection the soldiers have given us in the past. Like I said, we need all the help we can get." He started to walk away and then he stopped and turned back to them.

"Don't waste time a-worryin' about Indians. There's a string of little settlements all the way up to Denver. Might say we'll plan on hopping from one to the other. The worst that could happen is we'll have to hole up in some little village for a time."

Amelia watched Amy climb the stairs to the room shared by the girls of the house. She turned to see Eli struggle to remove his one boot.

"Wait a minute and I'll help you," she told him. Picking up the pile of blankets and quilts, she carried them to the bunk built into the wall close to the fireplace.

Eli crossed the room on his crutches and helped her straighten the bedding. "Eli," she said slowly, "I've something on my mind; could I tell you about it before we sleep?"

His voice was a low rumble. "I figured as much. Might as well."

"Oh, Eli," she murmured, hesitating, and then said, "Please, be patient with me. It's about Matthew. See, I know him from the past. We were together in Pennsylvania. Right now I have a feeling Matthew needs help from a person who knows something about him. I saw your eyes when I introduced him. I don't deserve your trust, but please, Eli, I must beg this of you. Be patient and don't think wrong of me." With a touch of sarcasm, she added, "How could anyone think me other than what I appear?"

"Well, I do. I nearly thought—" Amelia caught her breath and he added sadly, "Even a joke can't be said."

He seemed to be studying every scar on her face as he added, "And you'll need to be patient with me, Amelia. Old thoughts take a while to die."

"Never mind that now. I'm trying to tell you, this young man needs our help and prayers. I'll do my best to see he travels on with us—clear to Denver City, if possible."

He smiled at her and touched her cheek. "Go to it, my dear, and may you have good success. I promise you I won't act the part of a jealous husband."

"Eli, you are only half serious. I see this as a second chance for Matthew. But he'll need to unscramble the mess he has made of his life. This is a cause for desperate prayer."

Eli studied her face soberly. Finally he said, "Then, my dear, come to bed and we'll pray together. But I think you need to tell me more."

Amelia hesitated. "If I tell you all, then how effective can your ministry be to him? I think he needs to do the telling."

The next morning Amelia decided where Matt would ride. She looked from the crowded wagon to the two horses and said, "I guess we can trade off. Me and you, Matt. Eli needs to keep that leg straight, and you look like you could use a good rest for a couple of days. That wagon seat is only next best to nothing. We'll see if you can squeeze in beside Eli."

The sun was bright as they left the ranch and turned back onto the main road. Amy rode ahead of the wagon. She could hear her mother, riding beside the wagon, talking to her father and Matthew.

Blocking out their words, Amy sighed wearily and rubbed her forehead as her horse plodded along. As she reviewed the tossing and turning she had done most of the night, she heard Amelia's horse cantering up beside her.

"I changed Matthew's bandages this morning," Amelia began. "That was a nasty wound. Did you have trouble with it?"

Amy nodded. "There were two days when we thought the fever would take him. Strange, Matt didn't seem happy about having Daniel pray for his arm."

Amelia gave her a quick glance. "That tells me things I need to know about him."

They rode in silence. Fear for Daniel crept in and possessed her thoughts. Gently Amelia asked, "You having trouble with Matt being here?"

Amy sighed and admitted, "Is it any wonder? Daniel—"

"Dear, I know. Please, Amy, don't let bitterness rob you of hope. Right now that's the only thing that's keeping us going."

Through the tears she looked at her mother. "Us?" she questioned.

"Of course. He's your husband, but we love him, too. Eli just told me he spent most of yesterday praying that things will go well with Daniel, that the Lord will deliver—"

Amy groped for Amelia's hand, and it was there, warm against her face.

Throughout the day they rode in sunshine across the dry, barren end of the territory. Eli explained it all from his bed in the wagon. "You notice it's just like New Mexico land. Well, this part of the territory was Mexican land a long time before boundaries were set. The Mexicans living in this part of the territory didn't get too disturbed when they discovered they lived outside of New Mexico. They've clung to their traditions, and life has gone on just the same for them."

That night the three wagons drew close together for protection, while the horses and mules were picketed within the shelter of the wagons.

Downs had picked a camp just outside a tiny, quiet Mexican village.

By the time Amy was off her horse, the men had taken the horses to water. She watched them hobble the horses and mules close to the wagons on a grassy slope. When they left to gather wood for a fire, Amy climbed the slope beyond the wagons. The little village was spread out below.

A scraggly line of trees marked the river and shaded the village of adobe huts. It appeared the huts had been built close together, with their adobe walls joining to form a solid, square fort.

From the wagon camp, the village seemed too quiet—empty of life. Filled with her own personal melancholy, Amy sat down to study the village. Its strange isolation was making her uneasy, when a small boy approached.

He was herding three bleating sheep in front of him. She grinned as she watched the sheep milling around, trying to elude the youth. Just as the boy's task seemed hopeless, a tall wooden gate creaked open. Abruptly the milling sheep broke into a run, heading straight through the gate.

The bleating faded away. Amy watched with new respect as the little fortification settled back into silence while their suppertime fires began to puff a contented message skyward.

Amelia came up the slope toward her. "Mother, I was getting worried. The village seemed too silent, empty. But now I've decided they are completely secure and contented. That's a nice feeling."

"Are the Indians making you think this way?"

"I suppose so," Amy brooded. "Now, all of a sudden, everything is a threat."

Amelia sighed with her and reached for her arm. "Well, come have your dinner. I'm thinking Matthew's suffering along the same line. He seems to see threats in everything. Please don't be too hard on him tonight."

CHAPTER 21

For that first week of travel after Matthew joined the wagon train, Amy and her mother rode together. Amelia explained the change. "I have a feeling that Matthew needs to talk to your father. He also needs to let that arm heal, and that can't happen while he's riding in the saddle." She added, "Eli needs some man talk too."

Amy felt her eyebrows slide up. Amelia commented, "Does that surprise you? Any man gets tired of the apron strings." For a moment her smile twisted and Amy was caught by the expression.

Amelia added, "Most men don't like to talk about things close to the heart. Your father's that way around womenfolk. It just seems to be the way men are. Raised to be strong, not given to tears and fluttery feelings. Sometimes I think I've always pushed too much." She sighed and smiled at Amy.

"I know," Amy admitted. "I always wanted something more'n he gave out. But Aunt Maude made him uncomfortable at times. Tears just don't set well with Father."

"It isn't tears, so much," Amelia said slowly. "Sometimes I get the feeling that if he'd allow me to say it all out, then it might be he'd trust me more."

"Mother!" Amy couldn't keep the pain out of her voice. Staring at her mother, feeling her heart sink in the old familiar way, she thought, *If she can't be trusted, then what about me? How'll I ever get to the place where I can trust myself?* She thought about God and felt the old, familiar shrinking.

Amelia was watching her. Amy straightened and tried to smile. "I guess I'm not sticking as close to the Lord as I should. It's—"

"Hard when there're troubles?" They rode in silence and then Amelia looked at Amy. "I suppose I should be telling you to have faith and trust, but Amy, I'm only beginning to live there. Now I feel only a happy companionship with Him. I remember the story about the woman washing Jesus' feet and wiping them with her hair. Jesus explained her actions by saying a person forgiven much is inclined to be very grateful. That's the way I feel. At the same time, I'm realizing it isn't so much a matter of how many sins are forgiven but that they are forgiven."

They rode in silence again until the sun was nearly overhead. Amy tucked her shawl behind the saddle and glanced at Amelia. "Maybe I'm not grateful enough; sometimes I forget—"

Amelia looked surprised. "Oh, Amy, that isn't what I meant. I'm not mourning over my sins. I have no right to that attitude. Eli made me know that right off. See, God's love is like showers of gold. When He forgives and pours the forgiveness out on us, it's like being bathed in gold. It sticks to you, reminding you that it's still all there— the forgiveness."

For a time there was only the creak of wagon wheels and the plop of hooves. Finally Amelia spoke slowly, softly. "My past makes me shudder now. Dance-hall girl, madame, runaway mother." She turned a bleak smile Amy's direction. "The only merit in it all is the Lord's willingness to forgive my sins and to allow you and your father the grace to forgive and accept me again." She paused, then added, "When I finally faced my sin under God's eyes, I would have died without having His forgiveness. But that is by faith, because He says so.

"It is just as Eli says, when the Lord pours His glory out on us, we frail humans have golden souls. He keeps reminding me I can polish gold all I want, but it's His business to keep the gold there. By our faith and trust."

When she looked up and smiled, Amy caught her breath. "Mother, you are beautiful! One of these days—"

Amelia shook her head. "Now, Amy, I can see it. The Lord has started His beautiful work in you, too."

The next day they continued to journey away from the mountains while the landscape grew increasingly arid. Amy knew they were heading for the Arkansas River. Beyond that lay Colorado City and even farther beyond was Denver. *Straight north,* she was thinking when her mother remarked, "It seems to be taking us a long time. Since Raton it's been over a week we've been traveling and we haven't reached Pueblo."

Amy nodded. "I said so to Mr. Downs. It's over a hundred miles from Raton Pass to Pueblo. He did say we've been making fifteen or twenty miles a day, and that's good. That's because it's mostly downhill."

Her mother was watching with a puzzled frown. Suddenly she said, "Amy, what is wrong? You seem—"

Amy looked up in surprise. "Why, nothing much. Just tired of traveling. My stomach's been bothering me. Guess it's too much cornmeal and beans. I'll be so glad for home, at least when I don't think about—" She paused, sighing deeply. "If only Daniel would be there!" Then she closed her lips firmly over the worry, and for a time they rode in silence.

Finally Amelia straightened with a sigh. "I fussed at Mr. Downs because the trip was taking so long. He said it's because of the Indians. Can't move very fast with the wounded men and can't travel late because of the Indians."

Amy asked, "Did you have trouble with the Indians when you and Father traveled this way?"

"No, and I can't understand the fuss—we haven't seen a one."

"But Matt said he thought the Indians he traveled with had something brewing, and he didn't seem happy about the whole situation."

"Yes, and I think he said a great deal more to Downs," Amelia added soberly.

Later Amy stirred herself to ask, "You've been through Pueblo; what's it like? The name sounds interesting to me. Probably because we traveled through Taos."

"Well, it has nothing to do with that kind of pueblo. It's a little place, mostly a trading post and a freighting stop. It was settled by the Mexicans a long time ago. Just a farm area then, back before the gold mines were opened. It's situated on the Arkansas River, so there's plenty of water."

"I wondered," Amy murmured. "The past couple of days I've been thinking it looks pretty desolate. Right now I can't see anything except sagebrush and rolling hills."

"Pueblo is interesting," Amelia continued. "Most of the buildings are adobe, just like the ones we saw in New Mexico, except these have better roofs. More rain around here. There's a big church. The Mexicans come from all over the valley to worship."

"Catholic?"

"Yes, but there are white people around who aren't. And there's people passing through all the time. Freighters too." Amy turned to look at her mother, and Amelia glanced at her with a smile. "I don't know why it took our attention. It's not the comfortable place a person would want to live; still—" She sighed. "Your father is excited about it. So much so, I'm guessing he'll find an excuse to come back here later to look around."

Downs was riding toward them. There was a heavy frown on his face as he pulled on the reins. "Report of Indians hanging around. The fellows have been watching them play hide-and-seek in the rocks over there." Amy followed his pointing finger. To the northeast the low bushes and touch of green in the meadows abruptly ended at a rearing wall of rock.

Amy shaded her eyes against the sun and studied the rough rampart of gray rock. The wind moved bushes and bent grass, but there was only stillness in the rocks. She shivered. "I hope the fellows are as mistaken as my eyes say they are."

He threw a quick glance her direction as he curtly replied, "I'm giving the orders to stretch leather. You ladies be certain to keep the wagons between you and those rocks. Indians like pretty women with blond hair."

"Amy," her mother said calmly, "we need to catch up with the wagon. I want to speak to your father."

Matt was awake and seated beside the driver. "Wanna trade places with me?" he addressed Amelia.

She shook her head. "I have more arms than you do right now. Is Eli asleep?"

Eli answered by scooting forward in the wagon. "Amelia, do you want to take this rifle?" Amy watched her mother's face and tried to keep from shivering.

Amelia shook her head. "I need both hands on the reins."

He scooted closer and reached his hand across the side of the wagon. "Amelia, no matter what happens, ride hard for Pueblo. I love you both." The wagon was moving faster now. Amy watched it go. Her throat was tightening with fear.

When she turned, Amelia blinked and smiled. "Come on, daughter of mine, let's stretch leather, like Downs said."

With a nod, Amy grasped the reins and smacked them sharply across the flank of her horse. As the mare moved out, Amy glanced toward the rocks. She caught her breath and studied the rock again. "Mother," she cried into the wind, "I see dust up there!"

"Ride!" Amelia shouted. Amy bent low over the horse's neck, but her thoughts were filled with the facts. *There's just three wagons and a handful of wounded men and two women.*

It seemed they had been riding forever. Only the dry wind chafing her face and the snorting horses existed until Amy raised her head and blinked. She could see a dark slash across the horizon.

A cluster of trees appeared. "Mother!" she cried. Looking over her shoulder, she saw Amelia smiling. They were keeping abreast of Eli's wagon. Amy began to relax.

She heard the shout before she saw the wagon in front of them swerving. "Amy!" Her mother cried the warning and cut away from the trail. Amy's mare followed, plunging down the embankment. Amy was still trying to understand when she heard a sharp crack, a shout. Amelia circled her horse beside her. "Indians! Amy, head for the river."

There was another crack. This time Amy knew it was gunfire.

She clung to the saddlehorn and bent low on the horse's neck. But in the dash toward the river, while wind lashed at her and the horse jumped sagebrush, Amy's mind was filled with another picture—an image of blue and gray uniforms, of plunging horses. The sharp crack of gunfire went on and on in her mind. She heard her mother screaming her name.

Amy lifted her face. The horse had stopped. Amelia and the trees were in front of her. Slowly Amy pried her fingers away from the horse's mane, sat up. Mother was patting her face, "Amy, dear! It's all right. See, this is—"

"Ma'am, this is Pueblo. You ladies need help?" Amy stared at the stranger. He was a white man and his eyes were filled with concern.

Amy pressed her fingers against her numb lips and watched Amelia slip from her horse and turn toward the trees and the river.

She saw the cluster of adobes and the sprawling log building. She caught her breath and focused her eyes on the man. "We're safe?"

A stream of people poured down the dusty street toward them. Amelia flung her arm, pointing and crying, "Indians! Please help."

"Ma'am, look." The man pointed toward the road cutting away from the log building, climbing the hill. "My men heard the commotion, they'll give your menfolk a hand." His tracing finger followed the whooping men on horseback headed up the hill.

He was grinning and at ease as he added, "I'm Bill Whiteside, I run the trading post and stage stop. Now don't you worry about the Indians. 'Tis too close for them to try anything much. More damage jest from those wagons plowing into each other. See?"

Amy turned. In the distance, outlined against the sky, she could see the Indians. They were bare and bronze, with feathers and paint. She watched them circle the cluster of wagons, moving cautiously closer.

The shouting men from the trading post breasted the hill and Amy heard a shot. Like toys on a stick, the Indians whirled their horses. The lump in Amy's throat disappeared as she watched the bronze streak stretch out across the horizon, to be swallowed by the barrier of gray rocks.

It was nearly twilight before the two wagons were separated and slowly pulled down the hill to join Amy and her mother under the trees. They could see the other wagon still on its side with one broken wheel outlined against the sky.

The wounded soldiers and two new casualties were made comfortable on the the grass while the wagons returned to the hill. When her father hobbled toward them, Amy saw his face was white, but he was smiling as he said, "Our driver stopped an arrow. He's in pain and he needs help. There's another fellow with gunshot wounds, though not bad. We can only thank the dear Lord for protection." He paused, adding, "The wagon in front of us broke a wheel and we tangled with them, otherwise we might have outrun the Indians." Amelia moved and sighed. "Amy, are you up to helping?" She blinked. Her mother's face was white, so colorless that the red scars had become brilliant blotches. With a quick lunge, Amy threw herself at Amelia. Finally, with another hug they smiled at each other and headed for the wagons.

From the litter of blankets and supplies the men had dumped on the ground, Amy pulled tents, cots, and blankets. Matthew came limping up to help. His grim face was still pale. She said, "Matt, between the two of us, I think we can get a tent up."

"I'll do the tent. You go help your mother. Here's some bandages, and I guess this stuff is turpentine."

Eli was seated on a box, working beside Amelia. Some of the wounded soldiers came to help Matthew. Another fellow began to gather firewood. Amy stopped, looked around, and took a deep breath. A young soldier with a bandaged head grinned at her. "Good to be alive, huh?" She nodded and blinked back the scalding tears in her eyes. It was Daniel she wondered about.

In the morning, while the members of the wagon train gathered around the fire for breakfast, Downs got to his feet and faced the group. "I've spent most of the night trying to decide what to do. Either we leave supplies, which we can't afford to do, or we leave people. I'm under contract to get you soldiers to Denver pronto." His eyes shifted toward Eli and Matthew.

Eli spoke up. "We're in no hurry to move on. In fact, we're just happy to have had company this far."

A protest boiled to Amy's lips and she pressed her fingers to her mouth, but she could only think, *We've just been attacked by Indians, and Father wants to go on alone!*

Matthew offered, "I'm footloose. I'll stay here and wait for the stage."

She saw the relief on Downs' face. "We can make it with two wagons and most of the supplies. We can also get these men to a doctor a great deal quicker. Thank you, ladies and gentlemen."

The next morning the two wagons pulled out, leaving behind the wounded driver, Will Harvey, Matthew, Amy, and the Randolphs. Matthew said, "The fellow who runs the trading post is an Anglo. He's offered me a bed if I help him out. He's also pointed us in the direction of a Mexican lady who'll take Harvey in and watch after him."

"Harvey don't need no watching," the driver grumped.

"Well, if you've got all summer to recover, I guess not," Amelia stated. "Seems a little attention will get you back on your feet in a hurry. Maybe in time to be traveling when Downs comes back this way."

"Maybe so," Harvey muttered as he carefully shifted his injured arm.

Amy faced her parents. She noticed the hint of excitement in her father's eyes and remembered the conversation with her mother.

Amelia was frowning. "We can't just let you go off by yourself, Amy. Downs said there would be a stage through here in a day or so, but it will be a lonesome trip for you—" She stopped and looked at Amy imploringly. Amy turned away and scuffed her toe in the ground, waiting for the lump in her throat to go away.

Finally her father sighed and said, "How about giving me time to learn how to hang on to a horse with this leg. Then we'll ride up the mountain with you."

"To Oro City?" Amy studied their faces. She saw Amelia's relief and her father's resignation. She also saw the yearning in his eyes as he looked over her shoulder toward the village behind them. Trying to ignore her need to leave, Amy said, "Let's just not decide for—a week or so." Both of them were giving satisfied nods.

Amelia and Amy helped settle Harvey in his room, and then they went with Matthew to the trading post.

Bill Whiteside, the owner of the trading post, said, "Come here. I'll point you the way. There's a woman down by the church." He went to the door and gestured toward the tall adobe church with the sharp peaked roof. "Her name is Maria, and she's willing to take you in."

He turned with a grin. "Matter of fact, she made that very plain to me just as soon as she saw the wagons pull out." He eyed Eli's crutches and added, "I'll get the wagon and take you down there. Might as well get you settled before the commotion begins."

Matthew came across the room. "I'll be glad to help all I can. Ma'am," he said, addressing Amy, "what are you going to do about the horses?"

"You can pasture them here with my team," Bill offered. Amy nodded and turned to follow him. He took the reins of one of the mares and led the way to the corral. "I'll hang your tack in here with mine." As he lifted the saddles from the mares, she saw his curious glance and guessed he had questions she didn't want to face.

Her throat tightened and she turned toward the door. "Thank you, Mr. Whiteside. I appreciate the help you're giving us. My father's leg seems to be healing nicely, so we'll be on the road soon. He had an accident—his wagon rolled on Raton Pass nearly two months ago." She walked ahead of him to the trading post.

As Bill helped Eli into the wagon, Amy said, "What did you mean when you mentioned getting us settled before the commotion begins?"

He glanced down at her. "Penitentes." He flicked the reins and looked at her again. "I see you don't know anything about them. Religious folk. Every year about this time they get together and have their own little crucifixion."

Amy gasped, "Crucifixion! How horrible."

"Well, it gives a white man the creeps, but—well, stick around for a couple of days and you'll see what I mean."

Down behind the church, they followed Bill into the adobe-walled courtyard. A dark-haired woman was sweeping the packed earth with a twig broom. As Amy stepped through the open gate, the woman stopped her sweeping and came toward them. "Maria, these are the Randolphs."

"Sí señor," she nodded and turned to Eli. "Welcome. I will show you the way."

To Amy it was like reliving the trip into New Mexico. The memory of that warm happy time scalded her eyes with tears. She was seeing identical whitewashed walls, with a conical fireplace built into one corner. The firewood was positioned in the fireplace, stacked neatly on end. High above their heads on the wall was a scrap of shiny tin. It was opposite the tiny window, where it could catch and reflect the light.

After the woman left them in the hut, Amelia asked, "Why does this cabin make you unhappy?"

Amy managed a laugh, saying, "It's just like all the other huts we stayed in. Did you notice the string of peppers hanging close up under the eaves?"

That night Amy spread her blankets on the floor next to the fireplace, conscious only of sudden deep fatigue and the need to escape into sleep.

The next morning when a rooster crowed, Amy heard her father hobble out of the hut, but she squeezed her eyes shut tightly. It was a signal to rise, and Amy knew it was morning. She could only bury her face in the blankets and moan.

She heard the rustle of her mother's skirts. Amelia stepped across the blankets as she moved between the fireplace and the table.

With a sigh, Amy carefully rolled over and opened her eyes. "Mother," she murmured, fighting down the nausea as she tried to lift her head. "Oh, Mother, I feel so terrible. What did I eat?"

Amelia knelt beside her and felt Amy's forehead. "Amy, what is wrong?"

"My stomach."

"But you haven't eaten—last night you scarcely touched your supper." She rocked back on her heels. Amy opened her eyes again. She saw the concern on Amelia's face, the beginning frown. Amy rolled away with a moan, but Amelia's hand was insistent. "Amy, look at me. Are you pregnant?"

Slowly Amy opened her eyes. "Oh, Mother, is that what is wrong with me? A baby?" She blinked at the tears spilling over. Amelia gathered her close and rocked her in her arms.

"There, darling. I'm here. I'll stay with you as long as you need me."

"Daniel—"

Eli hobbled into the hut and leaned over the two of them. "Amy, what's happened? Are you crying?"

"She's fine, Eli. Or at least she will be after breakfast. Eli, what do you think of being a grandfather?"

He was silent for a minute and as Amy tried to lift her head, he asked, "Isn't that what's supposed to happen?" He headed for the door while Amy and her mother stared at each other.

"Amy, don't give up now," Amelia urged gently. "Hope, and keep hoping—for Daniel, for you, for the little one."

"Little one," she murmured slowly. She was still struggling with tears. "Maybe that's all I'll have of Daniel now."

CHAPTER 22

Daniel tipped his head to one side and looked up at the square of daylight. Since dawn the sounds coming through the slit of a window were different. Now hope began to replace lethargy as he listened to brisk footsteps and the thump of a broom.

Quickly he stepped up on the edge of the wooden shelf that served as his bunk. By stretching and pressing his face against the stone wall, he was able to see adobe walls and green trees through the bars.

Fort Marcy's prison left a great deal to be desired; but today Daniel was grateful for bars instead of glass, for boards instead of a soft bed.

Since early morning he had been aware of a puzzling rustle of sound sweeping through the fort. Now standing on the bunk he began to comprehend the changes. The lazy walk of the guard had been transformed into crisp, firm steps. A moment later he realized cheerful laughter had become clipped commands, and indolence had sharpened into excitement.

He stepped down off the bunk with a wry smile, realizing that, as usual, his breakfast was late arriving.

When it was shoved through the bars, the guard apologized,

"Sorry. The cook is busy preparing for the bigwigs."

"Who's coming?"

"Don't know for certain; Major Chivington said—"

"Chivington!" Daniel cried. "Hey, I asked you fellows to tell me when he got here."

"Well, he just came two days ago. It's fer certain he has more important things to do than review your complaints."

Daniel sighed and tried to throttle his impatience. "Well, tell me what's been going on."

"Sibley's been pushed pretty near out the other end of the territory by Colonel Canby. Does that make you glad or sad?"

Daniel sighed and again refused the hook. He asked, "How's the war going in the States?"

"Terrible." The grin faded from the guard's face. "Lincoln's just about to lose it there. One good thing, at least they're saying so, General McClellan's now heading up the Army of the Potomac. Some are saying that'll tighten things up a bit."

Daniel looked into the soldier's bleak eyes and said softly, "I pray every day—" He swallowed the lump in his throat. "This slaughter between brothers is a stench and a blemish before God."

"It's also scaring us to death," the fellow muttered. "You Reb sympathizers ever think what it's going to be like if *you* get control?"

The same old protest boiled to Daniel's lips, but he vented his frustration in a quick pace across the cell. He turned to say, "Well, we can throw out the Constitution as a start, because it won't be easy to live with. The way it reads now, freedom must be for all." After a brooding moment, Daniel said, "But regardless who wins, I've got the job of preaching it straight."

The guard was scratching his head, a bewildered frown on his face as he asked, "What do you mean by that?"

"That God's Word is open to only one meaning. There's something wrong with the way our fellowmen are learning to read if it's possible to see two different versions of God's will in the Scripture."

The guard blinked. "You're certain they are readin' it?" Without waiting for the reply, the soldier backed away. "I'll tell Chivington you want ta parley."

Daniel finished his breakfast and began to pace the cell. The monotony of pacing freed his mind, and his lonesome thoughts turned to Amy. Going to his wooden bunk, he looked down at the scratches he had made in the wood. "Three and a half weeks. Has it been only that long? Seems an age since I left Fort Union." He thought about Amy, trying to paint his memory afresh with her laughing face.

Those first days of riding the trail together had been wonderful. He recalled the sunshine, the warm air, and Amy with her blond hair stuffed in his old hat. Daniel began to pace again, this time hard and fast, drumming his boots impatiently against the floor.

While he struggled with the lump in his throat, he pounded his hands together. "Matt," he groaned, "why—"

The question died on his lips. The searching Presence held him. Slowly Daniel sank down on the bunk and dropped his head into his hands. The Scripture was there. How often he had glibly quoted the words, *As ye have done it unto one of the least of these . . . ye have done it unto me.*

"Lord, it's easy to say that while sitting in front of your own fire." He looked at the gray concrete walls and reflected, "Guess this is where the words have to be proved out in life. Also I guess I'd never expected this to happen."

He was still sitting there when the outer door clanged. There were footsteps, two sets of them, and there was the clink of spurs. Slowly Daniel got to his feet. Chivington's astonished face was pressed against the bars.

"Daniel Gerrett—well, I never!" He addressed the guard beside him, "How did a missionary of the Methodist Episcopal Church happen to get stuck in prison?" The guard rubbed his slack jaw and didn't answer.

Chivington opened the bars quickly. "Come along, Parson. I'll have you outta here in a hurry. Where's your wife?"

"Only the dear Lord knows," Daniel muttered, reaching for his coat. "I'm hoping she's headed for Colorado Territory with her mother and father."

When they stepped out into the open air, Daniel paused and took a deep breath. There was a sympathetic nod from Chivington. "Never know until we've been there, huh?" Daniel nodded and Chivington said, "Come this way. I'll sign whatever needs to be signed and you can be on your way."

Together they walked into the low-ceilinged adobe building and were pointed to the commandant's office. While the officer poised the pen over the sheet of paper, he asked, "Sir, what is your business in the territory?"

"I am a missionary in the Methodist Episcopal Church—" Daniel began and then paused. The officer still held the pen suspended while he studied Chivington.

Chivington leaned across the desk. "Why don't you just put down the information and sign it. Don't ask any more questions. Sometimes war does funny things to people." The two men were still nodding at each other as Daniel picked up his coat.

At the door Chivington remarked, "If you want some company, there's a detachment leaving for Colorado Territory via Taos. Might find they have an extra horse." He paused and then added, "The Indians are restless right now. Give my regards to Dyer."

It was spring, definitely spring, even in the mountains. Daniel couldn't get enough of the sunshine, the odor of new life, and the sound of rushing, snow-fed water.

The troops from the Colorado Volunteer Army were just as eager to get home as Daniel, and they rode hard. Daniel discovered they were a silent bunch for the most part. Their haggard faces, fresh scars, and tattered fragments of blue uniform told all that needed to be said. Over the supper fires, with only flickers of light on their faces to underscore their terse stories of battle, Daniel began to fill in the gaps of the battle story as he knew it.

Soberly the men admitted it was Chivington's action at Johnson's ranch that had decided the battle. Together they reviewed the agony of it all. And the glory. They bragged, "I heard a Reb saying they'd a won the territory if it hadn't been for the Pikes Peakers. Didn't know a good scrap until they met us."

"In all fairness," came another voice from the shadows, "I learned Canby's men hadn't drawn a wage fer the past year. Doesn't do much fer a fella's view of himself when Washington can't support him."

"They sure rallied once we got Sibley's men on the run." He turned to Daniel, "See, the Confederates holed up in Albuquerque with Sibley, licking their wounds and trying to regroup. That's when Canby put them to the rush to get home." He chuckled. "Heard they buried the Confederate field pieces in the middle of the plaza down there. Also heard when Canby came down with his cannon, they didn't put up too much resistance. Don't blame them. It's hard to fight when adobe bricks are falling on your head."

From back in the shadows a voice joined the rest. "I heard the Confederates talked the Indians into joining the fight. That's scary. Guess we had more to be fearing than we knew. Indians. If they'd fight in New Mexico, they'd fight in Colorado."

The day they reached Pike's stockade, Daniel shook hands with the men and watched them ride out for Fort Garland. "I'll get this mare to Denver right off," he called after them as he turned toward home.

With scarcely a glance, he rode past all the little settlements that were part of his circuit. Pressed by time and the thoughts of Amy at home, at night he chose to camp beside the trail. Thinking of the welcome he would receive at any fireside, he shook his head. "Right now I'm more willing to risk Indians than the comfort and delay of a settler's cabin."

The day he rode through the long valley toward Oro City, it snowed. Huddling into his coat, Daniel reflected on the capricious weather. "Wouldn't be Colorado Territory without snow pushing at spring. Hope Amy and the folks are safe at home." He nudged the horse again.

It was the middle of the afternoon when Daniel turned up California Gulch. He could hear the clunk of the stampmill and the hollow thump of wood as the rush of water and rock shot through the sluices. Several of the men along the stream straightened to lean on their shovels and wave as he passed up the road.

Before he reached the cabin, he sensed the lifelessness of the place. There was no sign of smoke coming from the chimney. Untrodden snow still buried the path to the door.

As he led the mare to the shed behind the house, he eyed the chicken coop. "From the looks of the thing, someone's either rescued the lot or Father Dyer ate them all before he left." Daniel rubbed down the mare and fed her. Dreading the empty cabin, he delayed until his hands and feet began to tingle with cold.

As he walked around the cabin to the door, he stopped and stared. A wagon had backed up the slope to the door. He could see the wheels were blocked. As Daniel hurried toward the wagon, four men began wrestling an enormous packing crate out of the wagon. "Wait," he called, "you've made a mistake."

One fellow turned and shoved his cap back on his head. "Aren't you the parson? Well, I thought so. We've had this thing in the storage fer a month now. Jamison's been itching to get it outta there. When he saw you coming up the trail he sez, 'There's the parson. Get that dad bloomed thing outta here so's I can move without knocking my knees off.' I sez, 'Sure, Mr. Jamison,' " He shrugged. "Here we are. It's your baby now."

Daniel went to open the door. "What is it?"

The two grunted and groaned as they shoved the crate across the room. It nearly filled the cabin.

The fellow turned. "Want I should knock that crate apart?"

Daniel nodded and the man seized his hammer and a crowbar. With two whacks the side dropped off. The drayman stepped back and his helper tugged at the wadding.

"Say, that's pretty nice fer these parts." There was new respect in the eyes of the drayman as he looked up at Daniel. "Not anybody else, not even the house down the way, has one of these pianos."

Daniel recovered his voice. "Where's the paperwork on this? You've got the wrong name. We didn't order—"

The man thrust the sheaf of papers into Daniel's hand. The writing spelled it out. The order was addressed to Mrs. Daniel Gerrett. The order had originated in St Louis, Missouri, but at the bottom there was another name: Lucas Tristram.

The man was watching him. "Ever'thing all right?"

"I guess this is the place," Daniel said slowly, still trying to think his way through the muddle of facts.

"Guess we'd better be on our way. That crate is big enough to make a chicken coop. Might as well get some good out of it all."

Daniel carried in wood and built a fire. While the cabin was warming, he dug around, trying to find something to eat. "Beans, cornmeal, a can of peaches. Mighty poor pickin's for a man who owns a bright, shiny new piano. At least his wife does, a gift from an old beau."

All the implications behind the gift of the instrument began to build up in his mind. Looking at the flour and lard in his hands, he guessed he wouldn't be able to swallow a flapjack.

There was a tap on the door and he went to jerk it open. "Mrs. Withrop—come in." She did. Still holding the bundle she carried, Lettie slowly walked around the piano. The questions were big in her eyes as she faced Daniel.

"The Missus not back yet?"

"She's with her ma and pa."

She nodded her head in the direction of the piano. "Sure beats all. Guess it's a good thing I took it upon myself to bring you some fresh bread and eggs from your own chicks. I'll have Hank bring over the chickens tomorrow."

"No," Daniel said hastily. "Just keep them and use the eggs. I'll come after them later. It's getting close to conference time, so there's a trip to Denver—"

Lettie nodded happily. "Glad to oblige. When will the Missus be back?"

"I don't know. Her father's had an accident. That's one of the reasons we've been gone so long. When did Father Dyer leave?"

"Afore the last snow. About two weeks now. He's going over to Mosquito for a time. But he said he'd be back shortly." Nodding her head, Lettie started for the door.

The questions were still big in her eyes. Daniel watched her hurry down the slope, glancing behind just once as she passed her own turnoff and moved down the hill to the neighbor's house.

Finally he shrugged and turned to face the piano. Even in the dim light, the dark shiny piano gleamed. "Well, I didn't answer the questions she didn't ask. Guess I'll have to leave that to Amy. I reckon Mrs. Withrop won't be the only one with a question. Might say, dear wife, I'll have a few of my own."

CHAPTER 23

Since dawn Amy had been aware of the voices, the shuffle of feet along the street. When her father hobbled across the room and tried to slip quietly out the door, dust wafted into the hut.

Amy sat up and pulled a blanket around her shoulders. She saw her mother watching from her bed. Amy managed a wan smile. "Good morning."

"Feeling better today?"

Amy nodded. "Except for thinking—" Looking up she saw the tears in her mother's eyes.

Amelia got to her feet. Briskly she moved across the room as she tied her apron. "Come. A full stomach makes it easier to live with the beginning months."

Eli came into the hut just as Amelia remarked, "I don't remember when I've been so excited about a baby."

Eli stood in the doorway for a moment. The sparkle in his eyes dimmed. Heavily he said, "Well, it's a good thing. One thing about a baby, it takes precedence. Over everything and everyone."

Amelia raised her head. There was a stillness on her face that caught at Amy. She turned to look at her father, but he was giving all his attention to the porridge in front of him. Slowly Amelia sat down.

Amy could feel her pain. She wanted to ask, *Is that what happened? Are you saying all the honeymoon feeling is over once there is a baby?*

Even as she was making up her mind it must not be so between them, she remembered. Daniel was gone. Maybe forever.

Amelia glanced at Amy. "Eat your breakfast; remember you're eating for two now."

After breakfast Eli patted her hand and beamed. "Now, let's get out on the street."

"Why?"

"The Penitentes. That's the commotion we've been hearing out there. They're coming from all directions."

Amelia shook the towel and asked, "You mean the people who act out the crucifixion?"

Father nodded. "There are hordes of people on the streets. I'm guessing they've come from all the little settlements around here."

Amy and Amelia followed him out the door. Looking over the village, they could see the people beginning to form lines along the road. The excited chatter Amy had heard earlier was now a gentle murmur.

To the north and east, a cloud of dust was rising from the trails leading into the village. "Let's walk toward the trading post," Amelia murmured. "I can't understand why there is so much dust."

Father replied, "It's the crosses many of the people are dragging. Let's start now; I can't move fast on these things."

Amelia led the way toward the trading post. Amy trailed behind, sharply aware of the oppressive mood of the village. To her father she murmured, "It's as if there's such sadness in the air, and everyone has caught it."

Before they reached the trading post, the first of the Penitentes made their appearance, coming slowly down the road toward the village. A movement in the crowd at the side of the road caught Amy's attention. She saw Matthew in the middle of the crowd.

He looked around and then made his way down the street toward them. Speaking softly when he reached them, he said, "Don't go any farther. Let's stand over here under the trees. I'm thinking we'll intrude if we try to become part of the ceremony."

Looking around, Amy tried to identify the low murmuring sound she was hearing. It seemed to be moving through the people on the street and keeping pace with the approach of the dust cloud. She felt the rhythm of a chant as she backed into the shade of the tree and closed her eyes against the glare of intense sunlight.

In the murmuring music of the Spanish language, there was nothing that she could understand; but the emotion was clear—deep grief. As she listened her own emotions swept up in response.

When her father breathed, "There!" she opened her eyes.

The man was nearly in front of her. He moved slowly, perspiration streaming off his naked shoulders. Immediately Amy's attention went to the heavy cross laid across his shoulders. She could see the muscles on his neck and shoulders bunch in agony while the perspiration poured down his face. *So that's what it was like!*

At the crack of a whip she turned to see a dark-clad figure advancing. When he stood just behind the cross, the whip snapped again. Amy winced and closed her eyes as the man flinched and staggered.

Beside her Amelia's voice was full of horror as she said, "His back! It's bleeding." Amy turned to her mother as Amelia moved and Eli's hand dropped to her shoulder.

"Let it be. Amelia, we've no right to interfere."

Amelia looked up at him, and Amy saw his arm slide around her shoulders. For a moment his lips trembled. He was murmuring and Amy strained to hear as he said, "That part of you hasn't changed, has it? The need to help, to make everything all right."

She was still looking into his face. Amy saw her mother's tears as he pulled her close.

Amy turned back to the crowd and found Matthew there beside her, saying, "Ma'am, Amy, I'd give my soul to bring him here right now."

"Matt," Amy choked, "don't say such things! God himself would never take the trade."

"I—sorry. I suppose it's just an expression. But I do want to do what I can. Believe me, as soon as I can get a horse under me, I'll start looking."

Eli moved closer and touched their arms. "The people. Everyone seems to be headed toward the church. Coming?"

When Matthew and Amy looked, Amelia was standing with her back to them. Her shoulders sagged as she watched the people on the street. Amy went to walk with her mother, and Amelia grasped her arm. Her voice was full of a strange urgency as she murmured, "Amy, look. Do you feel—"

In front of her the crowd of people had begun to walk slowly down the street. The strange heaviness of their mood swept over Amy, and she clung to her mother's arm.

As they watched, the sea of dark heads bowed. The people swayed forward, and the low murmur rose. When the crowd reached the end of the street, the murmuring had became a chant full of pathos.

Amy gasped and stopped. One by one the crowd swayed and fell into the dust of the street. Amelia's arm tightened around Amy. Transfixed by the mystery of it all, they watched the people crawling toward the church. Their tears had dampened the dust on their faces.

When the last one had dropped to his knees, Amy shivered and rubbed her chilled arms. She glanced up at the sky. *It seems fitting that the black clouds are rolling in and the wind is beginning to swirl dust around them.*

Eli spoke. "Let's go before the rain begins."

Amelia looked dazed and Amy took her arm. "Please," she pleaded with her father, not knowing what else to say.

Amelia stirred, then nodding at Eli and Matthew, she said, "You go. Both of you. We'll walk down there. To the church."

Matthew and Eli left. Amy and Amelia watched them and then Amelia murmured, "There."

Amy turned to look toward the church. The chanting was rising to an agonizing plea. Slowly, painfully, the people were crawling into the church.

There was a strange catch in Amelia's voice as she said, "I think I know how they feel. Love. That's what I'm like on the inside, and I don't know how to say it. It's a love too big for anything except crawling on your face."

Amy nodded without understanding; she couldn't feel the emotion, but she knew the rightness of the act. Silently they continued to watch, but Amy's heart was being stripped to its painful core. Daniel. The tears flowed down her face as she murmured, "Yes, Lord, even Daniel. I left him once; now, needing him so much, I must surrender him to you. How can I refuse?"

They continued to stand outside the church. One pilgrim after another entered. Soon the chanting diminished, ceased.

Total silence held the village. Suspended, Amy waited, holding her breath.

Abruptly sound came from the church. It seemed to be a thump followed by a heavy clashing of metal. Shivering, Amy stepped back and collided with the person behind her.

It was Bill from the trading post. His face was troubled and pale. He looked down at her with a shadow of a smile, saying, "Awesome, huh? Chains. Signals Christ going into hell. The noise? Chains are being broken. He's free. Now watch the faces."

The people began to come out of the adobe church. Dust still streaked clothing and faces alike. But on the faces there was a subtle difference. The afternoon had left a mark, a reminder that was reflected on the face of each person.

Bill said, "Now for another year, they are stamped with the sign of Holy Week. They won't forget it. They still sin, but there's hope." He turned away with a sigh. "Must be nice to have confidence like that. To be able to believe in a ritual."

On their way back to the hut, Amelia looked at Amy and said, "You have big questions in your eyes. Are you thinking about what Bill said? Well, it isn't just ritual for some of them. It's something more important. I've sensed it, but I don't totally understand. In some way they are aligning themselves with God."

"But it isn't the way we find God," Amy replied.

"That's true, and it's frightening to see such earnestness."

"Why frightening?"

"Because salvation depends on faith—our willingness to trust God." Amelia paused, looked at Amy and went on. "Amy, back there, during the smallpox, I saw my old friends reduced to pleading and then cursing God. They were the strong ones, the gay, carefree ones.

And they were no longer strong or happy. They were face to face with God, and they didn't have a hope.

"For the first time I accepted the fact that I must someday face God. It was then I saw all the glory of my life recede into shame, even my good deeds. I had nothing. I knew I would never win an audience with Him.

"These people. I can understand their crawling in the dust. I wanted to do it, too. Even when we won't admit it, there's a big need inside us to reach out and touch God. I can say I've seen the agony of a person who's never been told the real way to touch God."

Amy looked up at her mother. Studying every line of her scarred, tear-stained face, Amy knew she was seeing deep into her heart.

They linked hands and walked back to the hut, each absorbed in her own thoughts. The woman, Maria, was there. She had washed her face and it was serene. She explained. "It is our way. By this we say to God more than we can say to the priest." As she turned away, she added, "Pain? It makes us feel good."

Amelia faced Amy, saying quietly, "Now I am beginning to see why Eli feels this way about the town. Oh, Amy, these poor people!"

She went into the hut, but Amy lingered on in the courtyard. Leaning her arms on the low adobe wall, she thought about the day. The wind still tore at her hair, but the clouds were passing over.

Matthew came out and started down the street. She saw his face was troubled. With a sigh she stirred herself and called out, "Matt, did you let Mother change your bandage?"

He came to the wall. "The wound seems to be pretty well healed. No more bleeding, and it's scarring over." He studied her as if he wanted to say more.

She nodded at the clouds. "Guess no rain for us. Did you and Father have a nice talk?" He nodded, but his face was guarded.

Amy spoke over the lump in her throat. "Matt, please don't think I blame you for what happened. Daniel's just that kind of person. He had to go. He wouldn't want you to go around looking like a kicked pup."

He tried to grin and failed. "Is that what I look like? Amy, I do feel guilty. But I have other things on my mind, so don't think it's all—about Daniel."

"The girl back home and such?" She spoke lightly and was surprised by the black look he turned on her. "I'm sorry," she gasped. "I'm not prying. But I'll be glad to lend a listening ear. Even write a letter for you if you'd like."

"Well, I don't have a girl back home. There's no girl, and won't be." She dare not push words past the scowl on his face. She studied the clouds.

"Matter of fact," he continued, "my troubles are pretty much beyond a lady's help." He hesitated and then hurried on. "It's this whole lousy war. Now I'm thinking hard of just slipping over the hill. By rights I should go home and turn myself in, but my heart isn't in it."

"Must be hard to see your buddies getting—" He winced and she said, "I'm sorry. Guess I'm thinking out loud. I suppose all of us Union people have one thought on our mind. It makes it pretty hard to talk to someone on the other side of the fence."

"You could pretend there's no fence." He studied her face and she was struck again by the misery she was seeing in his eyes. He went on. "Aren't we all pretty much alike down underneath? I don't believe in slavery either, as a matter of fact—" Now he was looking into her eyes. She watched the questioning look sharpen and she waited. He seemed ready to say that word, ask that question. Then he turned away.

"Matt, I don't know what you believe about God. But I know I just can't live without Him, praying to Him, asking for help." He moved impatiently, and hastily she added, "I'm not trying to push gospel on you. It's my guess you know all about how Jesus is God and that the only chance you have of making it for eternity is through accepting His sacrifice for sins."

Under the dark expression in his eyes, his grin was amused. "Lady, you just said it all. Just because I'm from the South doesn't mean I'm heathen. Believe it or not, we have the same gospel, the same hymnals, and the same Holy Bible."

"Then what's the problem?"

He looked perplexed. "How's that?" She sighed and he asked, "Has it occurred to you that there are genuine Christians who are also

Confederates? See, Amy, when you believe in a cause, even though there're parts that aren't in line with your thinking, you end up obligated to make the best of the situation and fight for your people."

Troubled, she questioned, "When do the bad parts matter so much that you have to do something about it, like quit?"

He looked down at his white-knuckled hands. "I guess it happens when you can't stand the mess of ugly questions rolling around inside. Is it possible to throw out everything and start all over again?"

His honesty forced her to be honest too. "Seems the score is about even on every side. Those Union soldiers were killing too. Why? Matt, I don't understand much either. What I want to know is, what's going on? What's become so big and important about personal beliefs that we have to kill and tear up the whole country? Daniel says it's selfishness. He says that if we dig deep enough we'll find—"

The bleakness on his face caught her up short. Daniel. His presence was there between them, and it was looking much like a sacrifice. Miserably Amy looked at Matthew and tried to not dwell on the worthiness or unworthiness of the cause behind the sacrifice.

CHAPTER 24

Amy fingered the tin of peaches and addressed Bill. "If these people upset you, why do you stay here at the trading post?"

"I didn't say they upset me. Sometimes the things they do make me a mite uneasy. Take the Holy Week business. Kinda puts me to shame. I consider myself a pretty good Christian, but I can't see myself crawling in the dirt once a year. Matter of fact, all the wild chanting kinda gets under my skin. Not that I'm intolerant. I just don't understand."

The front door of the trading post banged open and a heavy voice interrupted. "You sell beans in anything smaller than twenty-five pounds? I'm on the road and can't carry much."

Amy wheeled around. "Father Dyer! What are you doing here?" She started forward and then stopped. She watched the emotion cross his face. First she saw surprise, and then something like sorrow. Her heart sank. She whispered, "Daniel, it's about Daniel, isn't it?"

She felt her hand slipping across the counter and Father Dyer had his arms around her. "Amy! What do you mean? I saw Chivington last week." He shook her gently as he added, "Met him on the trail; he told me Daniel was headed for home."

"Daniel—home?" She touched his face. "You really are here; he's safe—it's true?"

He pulled her toward the bench. "Sister, I don't know what you're talking about. Chivington said he'd just seen Daniel in Santa Fe. I asked him about your folks and he didn't know anything." He stopped suddenly and bent over her. "I'm sorry. I didn't mean to tell you this way, but—"

"What are you trying to tell me?" Amy cried.

"That your mother and father went to New Mexico Territory. I fear—"

"Mother and Father are here. It's Daniel—" Suddenly she comprehended the meaning of his words. "Daniel is alive!"

He cradled her in his arms and awkwardly patted. "Now, now. Chivington seems to know all about it. Said Daniel started for Colorado with a group of soldiers. Said he was probably back in Oro City now. It settled my worries about leaving the people without a pastor."

Amy wasn't listening and finally he stood up. Bill said, "Want I should go get her mother?"

The door banged and Amelia cried, "What's wrong with Amy?"

"Oh, Mother! Daniel's alive. Father Dyer says he's probably in Oro City right now. I want to go!"

"Well, you can't go in this fuss; you'll lose that baby for certain." The men were grinning at Amy.

Bill hurried away. "Missus, I'll bring you a drink of—water. Guess that's what mothers-to-be are supposed to drink."

Amelia was patting Amy. "Now, you calm down and drink the water. Father and I will see that you get home just as soon as possible."

"I'll take her," Father Dyer offered. "I've no call to go to New Mexico now."

"New Mexico?" Amelia exclaimed. "Why did you send us there to have that accident if you intended going all along?"

For a moment she frowned while Amy mopped the last of her tears. Taking a deep breath of relief and peering at the expression marching across Father Dyer's face, she said, "Oh, Mother, you're making him feel terrible, and it will be worse when he sees Father."

Amelia rushed to him and squeezed his hands between her own. "I am sorry. Still—" She sighed and then smiled sweetly. "How can such a big, tough guy be fussed over a woman scolding?"

"Mother, he was on his way to New Mexico to look for you." For a moment Amelia studied him and then she pressed his hands to her face.

Amy turned to hand the cup to Bill and noticed his face was very red. As he shifted from one foot to the other, Amy looked from her mother to Father Dyer and suggested, "Maybe we should just go find Father, so Bill can wait on his customers." Mother turned and Amy waved at the line of dark eyes watching them.

Later that evening Amy realized Matthew seemed to be the only one who couldn't be explained. As she watched him sitting back in the shadows, she noticed that neither one of her parents seemed inclined to try to explain his presence. With Matthew's troubled eyes watching her, she dared not.

The next day the wagon train came into Pueblo. Bill was stomping around the trading post, putting away boxes and barrels when Amy came for milk. He explained, "This is the first supply train to come through in two months. Between the Indians and the fighting going on in New Mexico, there was just no call for taking more risks."

He stopped and pointed his pencil at her. "You tell Father Dyer to come in here. These men will be expecting a little entertainment. We might as well have revival while they're here."

Amy's jaw dropped. She pondered which question to ask first. He added, "Now don't get me wrong. I'm not all that sold on religion. But these men have to be entertained. If we don't the girls will. I'm the boss here, so what I say goes. The best we can offer right now is revival. Go tell him."

That evening, while the sea of men's faces lifted toward Father Dyer's happy grin, he said, "Mighty sorry I didn't bring my portable organ. But I didn't expect this privilege. Sister Amy will come and lead us in a hymn or two."

Amy came, wistfully thinking of the clunky little portable organ as she faced the men and began to sing. When she finally sat down, her thoughts were full of the memories of revival in Buckskin Joe.

She glanced at her mother and father. They were nodding and smiling as Father Dyer stood to preach.

For a moment Amy had to battle the lonesome lump in her throat, but the lump disappeared as she reminded herself, *I still have a husband, and I'll be seeing him soon!*

Father Dyer's words caught at her. "Oh, children of Israel, children of our God. Would that I could grind your golden calf and make you drink, just as Moses did. But those days are gone forever. There's not a one on this earth who can successfully push your nose into the trough of gold-tainted water. You must be Moses and children. You must do the pushing yourselves. Drink the gold of Jesus Christ's sacrifice if you genuinely desire to drink of the fountain of life."

Amy's thoughts began to drift. She was thinking of the smoke-marked crucible Father Dyer had brought to her. At the time she examined the tiny drop of gold in the bottom of the cupel, she had determined to fill the crucible to the top with all the gold nuggets she would dig herself. What a lark it had been to think of surprising Daniel with a crucible of gold mined from their own rocky soil! Ruefully, she remembered the small handful of nuggets. *You didn't find enough nuggets to buy Father Dyer's organ, let alone a real piano.*

Father Dyer's voice broke through her thoughts. "My friends, are you absolutely certain that the gold you harbor is genuine? Fools gold can sparkle and blind our eyes. Are you hugging your gold so close to your bosom that you can't tell whether it is the genuine article or fools gold?"

There was a heavy silence as he added. "We can have the perfect gold of Jesus Christ in the beginning, but it is possible to allow corruption to creep in. Not a one of us dare guard the gold in our lives, hugging it so closely that Jesus Christ isn't allowed to burn out the dross. This evening I ask: What do you hold most dear in your life? May it never be melted into a golden idol."

As Amy went to lead the final hymn, she wondered if a piano would be considered an idol.

The wagon train loaded with goods departed for Santa Fe. But the village quiet was momentary. Another wagon train arrived. Bill explained the stream of people stopping in Pueblo. "The word gets

around. The fighting is over in New Mexico, and all the folks afraid
to face the trail are out there again. Hope they aren't sorry. The Indians
are mighty brave. They've got it figured out that the white men are
too busy fighting each other to have time for them."

"Is that so?" Amy asked.

Bill carefully measured the beans into Amy's tin lard pail and
looked up. "Of course not. Sure, the soldiers were busy for a time,
but remember the traffic across the trail stopped for a time, too. The
last wagon train through here brought the news that California's gearing up to send troops this way. Just in time for Indian problems."

She gave him the coins and turned. "So matter-of-fact," she murmured, shaking her head. Matthew was stacking miner's picks and
shovels against the front wall. She stopped. "Are there gold mines
around here?" He nodded and went on with his work. She studied his
face. Impulsively she said, "When you aren't laughing and having fun
with the others, your face is so sad it makes me ache."

The grin he turned toward her was crooked. "Thanks for the
sympathy."

"What are you going to do?"

"Your folks have asked me to stay with them for a time. They'll
be starting for Central City to gather up their belongings and they
need help." He shrugged. "I'm not in a hurry to do anything, so I'll
stick around."

Amy couldn't think of anything to say, but she continued to
watch him as he finished stacking merchandise. He turned. "Come
into the back room. I want to show you a saddle. It's Mexican, and
too costly to be out front." He led the way, saying, "I doubt you've
ever seen one."

"Well, I don't know," she said hesitantly.

"You'd know if you saw one. Tooled leather, and shaped more
like a throne than a hunk of leather to keep you from falling off a
horse." He led her through the shelves. Stopping in front of a shrouded
object, he carefully lifted the blanket.

Amy's eyes could scarcely take in the grandeur. "Oh, Matthew,
it's beautiful." She touched the design of flowers and leaves cut deeply
into the mahogany leather, while her fingers followed the hammered

silver mountings set with turquoise. "This is the most beautiful saddle I've ever seen, but I can't imagine anyone actually riding on it."

"Bill says he's had it for a couple of years. I don't think he's ever used it."

"Well, he doesn't have it hanging in the tack room in the barn."

As Amy turned to leave, the door of the trading post banged and she heard a chorus of voices. Matt said, "French. Who is speaking French out here?"

The voices ceased abruptly and Bill's slow voice came, "Good day, gentlemen. Lucas, I'm surprised to see you here. Guess I expected you to be long gone."

Amy heard his reply just as she started forward. At the same moment, Matthew blocked the doorway. He whispered. "Stay here! I don't want that fellow to know I'm back here."

Amy heard Lucas's low laughter as fragments of the conversation reached her. " . . . not done yet. Be patient, my friend, and don't forget we are friends." He stressed the words and added, "That carries its own reward."

Amy looked at Matthew and mouthed, "But I know him—Matthew, I want to at least greet him. He's a member of Father's church."

Matthew's lips twisted; he kept his voice low, saying, "He's a Confederate of the worst kind, and he'll kill me if he has the opportunity."

"You're not serious," she whispered, moving close enough to see his eyes in the dim room.

Matthew's hand signaled silence and she listened. Lucas said, "I need fresh mounts. I can have your horses back in three weeks, but for now you'll have to trust me. It's imperative I get to Denver as quickly as possible." There was an undercurrent of meaning in the words that caught Amy's attention. She saw Matthew tighten his lips.

In a moment Bill said, "Go to the stable and have Joe give you what you want." His voice was devoid of its usual friendliness as he added, "I'll hold you to your word or else—"

Lucas's voice was just as flat as Bill's when he answered, "You're not in a position to make threats—that is, if you're interested in a decent future."

Matthew and Amy waited until the door banged again. Matthew gave Amy a gentle nudge. "Tell Bill I'm working back here. Go home and don't make any effort to see Tristram. I don't know what will happen if you do. To me, that is."

"Matthew?" She questioned, trying to see his eyes in the dark room. His face twisted as he pressed his lips together. She hesitated and then touched his arm, "Matthew, I won't reveal you. Please—" He shook his head and she went through the doorway.

Bill looked up in surprise when her footsteps echoed across the puncheon floor. The surprise faded into a questioning discomfort. "Didn't know you were back there."

"Matthew wanted to show the saddle to me. He said to tell you he's working back there." Bill nodded and turned away. With a sigh of relief Amy headed for the door.

CHAPTER 25

Amy, are you certain you can tolerate this trip home? Horseback is hard enough when you're feeling good."

Amy met her mother's troubled eyes. "You're thinking about the sickness? Mother, it isn't as bad now. Besides, both Father Dyer and I want to get back to Oro City. I'll never rest until I see Daniel with my own eyes. And Father Dyer—"

She turned to smile at the sandy-haired square block of a man seated at the table with her father. He scarcely tossed her a glance as he went back to pounding the newspaper in front of him.

"Eli, the war news is grim. Our men are leaving the circuit to enlist at a rate that scares me. I sympathize. Any red-blooded young man wants to do his part. Even your Daniel struggled with his call. He told me so. He nearly bolted a year ago, wanting to pack a rifle in the Army if they wouldn't let him pack a Bible."

Eli continued to shake his head. "You're wrong to think the church will find a spot for me. I'm finished as a preacher in the church."

Amy saw her mother wince and blink tears out of her eyes. Quickly she turned away from the table. "Father," Amy protested, "you know Mother doesn't believe that, and she certainly doesn't want you to quit preaching. I can't understand why you think it's necessary, particularly now. Like Father Dyer says—"

Eli's face reddened, and he moved uncomfortably on his bench. "Daughter," he rumbled, "I think there're some topics you've no call to push."

"But, this isn't just—" Amy argued. The anguish on her parents' faces made her stop.

Father Dyer's expression was stern as he turned from one to the other of them. "Eli, what about the promise? You told me you had absolute confidence the Lord would intervene in your life. Do you think He did?"

Eli nodded. With his hand resting on the Bible in front of him, he closed his eyes and quoted softly, " 'Therefore, behold, I will allure her, and bring her into the wilderness, and speak comfortably unto her. And I will give her vineyards from thence, and the valley of Achor for a door of hope: and she shall sing there . . .' "

"But, Father, can't you see? Mother isn't singing," Amy pleaded. "She isn't happy. I know the before and after woman. For these weeks I've been watching her. It's like she can hardly keep back the tears sometimes—"

"Amy," Amelia said sharply, "you've no call to talk to your father that way. Let us work this out."

"I've lived with him longer than you have." Amy's words were cutting in over Amelia's. "He gets his mind made up, and there's no changing it at all. Now, I won't let him hurt you this way."

Unable to stand it any longer, Amelia burst into tears. Trembling, she faced them. "There are problems, but it is nothing you have any right to address. This is between the two of us. Please—"

Eli straightened. "Why, Amelia, I didn't know." The hurt note in his voice triggered Amy's anger.

"Father! Now you're trying to heap it up to make us both feel guilty for—"

"Daughter." Eli's injured tone sharpened; "you need to go pray about this. Seems you're not living up to—"

"Not being holy, like you? Say it, Father!" The tears were running down Amy's cheeks as she continued. "And I despair of ever being able to measure up to your standard, no matter how much I love you."

Amelia's hand was on her arm, tugging. Now her voice rose. "Eli, I must say this: you are pushing down both Amy and me. Defeat. I've seen it in your eyes. You expect me to fail again. Are you so caught up with forgiving that you've forgotten to expect a miracle?" She was sobbing openly now. "Eli, the two of us need a miracle. You talk about change, a deep-down spirit change, but it won't happen until you're pulling with us, not against us."

Eli began to talk, and the words came out in his preachy voice. Amy heard the stern words, the anguish in his voice. Again she protested, "Father, you throw up a curtain of words. A wall. They've always stood between us. And the way you say them is louder than what you say. Do you know? For years I thought you didn't love me; now I know all the words—the curtain of words—were because you suffered over Mother."

Amelia was caught. Her hands stopped short of her tear-stained face as she asked, "Did you, Eli? I didn't guess."

Father Dyer rumbled, and they all turned to look at him. Amy quaked before the man's stern face as he said, "Eli, you are less than a man of God if you fail to make this woman the Lord gave you feel like the most beautiful, most desirable woman on earth. You have no right to judge her by the past. She is your wife, your sister in Christ. Her salvation is your responsibility; you judge her with open arms."

He started for the door and turned. There were tears streaming down Eli's face, but Father Dyer ignored them. He said, "About being a minister. The Lord called you. If the church won't have you, then find a street corner. But don't diminish your wife by failing the Lord."

The door shook as he forcefully closed it behind himself. Eli wiped the tears from his eyes. He looked at Amy. "Daughter, why don't you go pick daisies 'til dinner time?"

When Amy and Father Dyer rode out of Pueblo and turned on the trail pointing over the mountains toward Oro City, Amy gave a huge sigh of relief. Father Dyer grinned at her. "Wanna explain it?"

"Mostly I'm just glad to be heading home, back to Daniel."

"Well, just take it easy. You mind your mother and don't be rushing this trip."

Amy slanted a glance at him. "Mother and Father, they seemed pretty—"

"Lovey-dovey?" He grinned. "Romance doesn't die when you reach thirty, my dear."

"I suppose you are going to be preaching all the way home."

"To you or when we stop for the night?"

"Well, I was thinking of the nights."

"Of course. Think any circuit-riding preacher would dare head outta town without delivering his soul?"

"I suppose not. At least Daniel had that hungry look on his face when we stopped in villages, even the Spanish ones." She paused. "I'll be so glad to see him."

Father Dyer tossed her a sympathetic glance and then asked, "Think you can handle my preaching at you all the way home?"

"Guess I can, if you can handle my tears." He harrumphed, and Amy continued. "Sometimes people get pushed by life until they come out feeling like they've been living out a sermon."

"That's not going to get you off the hook, but how's that?"

"The hymn you sang to me. About God refining our gold." She was silent for a moment, and then with a gulp she said, "Before Daniel and I started this trip, I was desperate with loneliness. Now, well, I guess I've done more praying these last couple of weeks. Somehow I feel . . . well, not so desperate about it all. I've even gotten to the place where—" She stopped and glanced at Father Dyer. "Is it possible that being in the bad places can help you love God more?"

"Seems to me," he said slowly, "human nature being what it is, a body has got to come out of them either loving the Lord more or not loving Him at all. Now mind you, this doesn't mean we understand all the experiences we've been put through, or even that we particularly relish having gone through them, but still the end result shows our true mettle."

The following day Amy was able to ask the question: "Father Dyer, when your wife died, did you feel abandoned by God?"

He was silent for a long time. Finally he lifted his head. "I suppose

I wouldn't be quite honest if I said no. Time dims the emotions, but I suppose there was the feeling of being dropped flat on my face. Is that what you meant?"

"I was angry when Daniel didn't come back, when I didn't hear. That made me feel terrible and then guilty. I told the Lord I was sorry."

Father Dyer was grinning at her. "The Lord lets you apologize even when you don't have to." She blinked. He added, "At that point in time, He knew how you felt, and He also knew it was to be expected."

"I know what you mean, but Father Dyer, it was more than my attitude. It was lack of trust. Now I'm ashamed. He does work things out, doesn't He?"

"Not always the way we think He should." His voice dropped and Amy remembered the story of his unhappy second marriage.

Softly she said, "I'm sorry. I'd forgotten." She hunted for words, "You had all those children to raise." He grinned his crooked grin. "Those children. Amy, I couldn't get along without them. Maybe having them and being forced to my knees on a regular basis made it possible to learn to trust Him in a better way."

"I suppose that's good."

"Considering we learn trust a little at a time."

Father Dyer was correct about the preaching. Amy discovered it the first night they stopped at a cluster of cabins. She also discovered that he need not introduce himself. The word was passed; by the time the dishes were washed, the wagons and horses began to arrive.

The night was duplicated over and over—too many times, it seemed to Amy, as she counted out the days.

Midpoint in their travel, Father Dyer brought up his favorite subject. At noon they stopped to eat beside the river. Later, while Father Dyer rested with his hat pulled over his face, Amy walked up the bank of the river. She had found three nuggets in the spring-freshened stream coming down the hill when Father Dyer joined her.

He nodded his head. "It's a good time of year to find nuggets easily. The freezing breaks up the ground and the water washes them loose. He rolled the nuggets in his fingers and said, "Nice. They'll keep bread on the table for a time."

She admitted, "After all the sermons and talking about the true gold, I feel like a grub."

He sat down on a rock and assured her, "There's nothing wrong with pulling out a nugget. I've spent considerable time digging out gold, especially when the offerings have been sparse."

Amy admitted, "Since you gave me the crucible, I've found a good handful."

"What are you going to use them for?"

"A piano. Oh, Father Dyer, more than any one thing on earth, I want a piano. Is that a bad reason to look for nuggets?"

"As long as you don't take up playing for dances again, it isn't."

Amy flushed. "At the time it didn't seem wrong, but now just thinking about it makes me so ashamed. When I think of Buckskin Joe, and the way the smallpox hit right after revival, I wonder if it would have made a difference if I had said no." She gulped and stood up.

Back on the road, he leveled a searching look at her and warned, "Might as well get yourself geared up for this. There's nobody working for the Lord with an ounce of seriousness in his bones who isn't a seeker after Experimental Religion. Running after God with a questing heart. In the 1850s, to an uneducated miner struggling to find peace with God, it was probably mostly an experiment. It goes this way, just like the Apostle Paul said in his sixth chapter of Romans, as well as the seventh chapter: you can take all you want from the Lord—salvation, grace, and all the other good gifts—but sooner or later you're going to have to start giving back."

He settled into his coat collar, and for a short time they rode silently. Finally he sat up and said, "Getting Experimental Religion is like bursting the skin of human nature. Early on, after we first encounter God's saving grace, we begin to get the idea our humanity just isn't big enough to hold all He wants to put inside.

"Well, when you burst the skin of human nature, then we're to the place where we can begin to allow God to shape us into His image. But it takes trust. Trust means you acknowledge God has better ideas than you do, and it's best you give in to His will."

Again they rode quietly together until he straightened, grinned, and said, "Sometimes I feel like God is pulling me through a knothole backward in order to accomplish His purposes in my life."

Amy laughed. "Knothole! Father Dyer, when I was very young we had a little kitten. Too young to be left to roam outside. One day we left him in the lean-to. Unfortunately there was a knothole in the bottom board."

"Knowing how a cat's head is shaped, I can guess what happened," Father Dyer replied. "How did you get him out?"

"Pulled, greased him down, pulled again. Finally Father decided the kitten *had* to come out, so he pulled again. It was a happy ending for all of us, particularly the cat."

Later in the day Father Dyer returned to his subject. "Amy, you know, religion isn't worth a working dollar until God is gifted too."

He paused and looked intently at her. "Are you having a hard time doing what you make up your mind needs to be done?" He squinted. "And what about the other issue?"

Amy was quiet for a moment as she studied his face. "Why don't you tell me?"

"That you're walking a tightrope, scared to death you're going to fall? Amy, if a person has a ten-cent pinch of that kind of insecurity inside himself, then the old devil is going to push it to the limit. You'll end up afraid to make a move for fear you'll fail.

"Would you like to get beyond that feeling? Would you like to have the absolute confidence the Lord will be with you all the time, pouring His strength and His power into you, so that no matter what you face, where you go, He's there with you?"

When she didn't answer, he added, "I know it sounds like a fairy tale if you haven't put it to the test. There's one catch."

"What?"

"The Lord isn't in a position to do anything like this in your life until you've decided you'll sign over the whole mortgage. He gets all of you—signed, sealed, and delivered. Now and forever. You get God in control of you, walking hand in hand. And then you start trusting. See, this is a provision for living.

"I'd like to see you and Daniel make a go of it. He's a mighty fine preacher boy, but he can't make it without all the help you can give."

Soberly Amy revealed her anxiety. "Father Dyer, there's something that frightens me. Mother was in the same position I'm in, she—" She found the words impossible to say; silently she looked at him.

"Amy, God never asks us to do what He will not enable us to do, but we must ask. For strength, for wisdom, for courage—nearly every day I ask for the whole list. His word tells us He'll make us more than conquerors, but there's something preceding this.

"We've got to let the Spirit set us free from the tight skin of human nature—the fears, the ugliness. Amy, it's a way of life. That's why I call it Experimental Religion. You start out with God's Holy Ghost help, but you have to keep at it every day of your life."

On the day they rode up the mountain, Father Dyer met her grin with a smile. "You're right. The down slope on this mountain marks the beginning of Daniel's circuit. You're on familiar territory now."

"Except that I haven't traveled this part of the circuit with him."

"Better do it before the young'uns are born, because you'll be too busy afterward. You notice these people are mighty proud to meet the parson's wife."

"Daniel said so. I guess I didn't give it as much thought as I should have. Guess I didn't really think he wanted me along."

When they dropped down the other side of the mountain range and stopped for the night, they discovered Daniel had been through on his circuit the week before.

The rosy-cheeked miner's wife beamed at Amy and said, "Didn't know you weren't at home. Met your father at conference time a year ago. Sure do like him. I also like that young man you're married to. He's getting more spunk about preaching, and he's got a sympathetic ear that nearly gets pulled off every trip he makes this way. Guess we shouldn't take up so much of his time, but it's good to have a parson to listen."

When they reached California Gulch, Amy nudged her horse with a sharp heel. Father Dyer grinned at her as they took the road winding through the jumble of buildings and turned toward the mouth of the gulch. Amy noticed that spring had come. In the midst of the mine dumps green grass had laid a carpet for the early yellow and purple of mountain blossoms.

She also saw that the frantic activity around the mines continued unabated. Although it was late afternoon, the sluice boxes were full and the wagons continued up and down the road.

She measured the height of the disgorged earth and rock around the mouth of the mine shafts and the line of men along the sluice boxes. With a nod she said, "There's progress. I've been gone a long time. It's good to be home."

Amy's mare quickened her steps as they started up the slope toward home. Father Dyer called, "Hold up. I'll just give you the reins of this filly now. Don't suppose you need me around this evening, so I'll head on up to my cabin. Tell Daniel I'll see him down Granite way next week. Tomorrow I'll be heading out before the sky's light." He grinned up at Amy as he handed the reins to her, saying, "So long!"

She nodded. "Thank you, Father Dyer, for the company and the sermons." She watched him cut up the side of the mountain to the little cabin tucked back in the trees. He waved and she dug her heel in the mare's side. "Come along, you gals. I want to cook a good dinner for Daniel tonight. Even cooking on that funny little stove sounds good!"

As Amy rode past the Withrop cabin, Lettie appeared on the stoop. "Hello there! Daniel said you'd be home soon. Too bad he couldn't wait around for you. Just missed him."

Dismay washed through Amy. She sighed and asked, "Where's he gone?"

The woman shrugged. "Didn't get it all clear. Either on the circuit or else to Denver City. He came for supper two nights ago and said something about a conference time in Denver City. I supposed you'd know all about it."

"Oh, dear," Amy murmured. "Guess I forgot. I'll be heading for home. I'm tired." She flipped the reins and let the horses trot up the hill.

Amy dropped the bedroll and bag on the front stoop before leading the horses around to the corral. The chicken coop was still empty. Amy stared at it and addressed the empty roosts, "Well, that means he's going to be gone a time if he didn't bring the chicks home. Probably Denver City."

She pulled the saddles and bridles off the mares and shooed them into the corral. Slowly she mounted the steps leading to the front door. With a weary sigh, she unlocked the door and tumbled the bedroll inside. As she turned to pick up the bag, she noticed the twin ruts from wagon wheels. They had cut deeply into the soft soil of the lane leading up to the front door.

"That's strange," she murmured, "a heavy wagon's been in here. Hope it isn't been someone stealing the stove and Daniel's books. 'Tis certain that's the only things of value." With a shrug she pushed open the door and entered. She stopped and blinked.

Nearly the whole cabin was filled with a dark, gleaming piano. "Daniel!" she cried. "Oh, my darling Daniel, a piano! But I know we can't afford a piano now."

Her fingers ached to touch the keys. Forgetting her tiredness, she dropped the bag and went to pull the stool close. Amy ran her fingers across the keys and trembled with excitement at the rich sound filling the cabin. "Oh, glorious! Beautiful dream come true," she whispered, blinking at the tears in her eyes. "At least until Daniel returns to the scolding he shall get for being so extravagant, I shall play to my heart's content."

She ran her fingers across the keys, touching every chord and running the scales until she realized her cold, stiffened fingers were numb. With a sigh of pure joy, Amy went to build up a fire. She filled a pan with water for tea and then turned back to the piano. There was a scrap of paper on the table.

"Ah, a note from Daniel." Leaning across the table for the paper, she backed close to the stove. Except for the glow of the fire, the room was nearly dark. Amy looked for the matches and lighted the lamp. Settling on the bench close to the fire, she opened the paper.

With a frown she studied it. "Why, this is a bill of lading. It's very strange. The piano is directed to me, but the sender is—" She gasped, "Lucas Tristram! This is unbelievable." She started up from the bench and then stopped. She began to laugh and the tears rolled down her cheeks. "Silly girl. You should have guessed. It isn't yours at all." She wiped at the tears and tried desperately to deny the hurt. "If you just hadn't jumped to conclusions! Besides, why didn't you guess Lucas had something like this in mind instead of a practical gift like Bibles or hymnals?"

The thought caught up with her and she turned to stare at the piano. "This is a very expensive gift for a church he doesn't even attend. Why?"

There were the obvious answers. "Lucas, you are still trying to make a splash, to impress everyone. Or, is it possible you are trying to say something else, something about me?" She moved uneasily on her bench. The memory of that horrible day still burned into her mind—the day Lucas and Daniel had faced each other in Central City. She could still see Lucas's arrogance contrasted with Daniel's shabby coat and hurt brown eyes. Slowly she admitted, "I have a feeling, Lucas, that you aren't above sticking a dagger in a person and then twisting it for the joy of seeing him writhe!"

The question was still in her mind when another thought occurred. She remembered the handbill Lettie had shown her. Lucas had been in Oro City at the same time. And there was Lucas, dapper and smug, standing on the plaza in Santa Fe, nearly under the Confederate flag flying over the Palace of the Governors.

Finally Amy got to her feet. "There is a possibility that I have judged Lucas harshly. One thing is certain; I'll not let him make a statement with this piano. There's not to be one hint of a tie between Lucas and me."

But in the next breath she said brightly, "However, I'll give him the benefit of a doubt. It is possible the piano was misdirected, and that Lucas intended it to be simply a gift to the church. Tomorrow, first thing, I'll find a man to move the piano to the church. Quickly, before Daniel has a chance of seeing it here and being hurt by whatever devious thoughts Lucas may have had in mind."

Going to the piano, Amy pulled her fingers across the keys, listening with her thoughts overlapped by Daniel's sad brown eyes. She sighed and started to turn away. Now something else caught at her thoughts, a violet velvet dress.

Slowly her hand crept to her lips. The memory was impossible to deny—after she had fled Buckskin Joe, in that terrible suspended time when she had been running away from Daniel.

Amy paced the room. Pictures piled up in her mind. Lucas laughing down at her, with that expression in his eyes. Amy winced. *That is when I should have sent him away. But I didn't. I liked the flattery, the gifts, and all he represented: money, position. He was building a house for us. I didn't say one thing to discourage his advances until that kiss.*

She moved close to the fire and tried to warm her hands. The old fear surfaced. *Like mother, like daughter.*

With a sob she threw herself across the bed. "Oh, Father, at the time it was ugly; now I see it as you do. Sin I couldn't face long enough to really confess. Buried and ignored." She sank her head into the pillow and wept, her heart breaking at the revelation.

When Amy finally got up and went to the stove, she knew the ugly sore spot was gone.

The water in the kettle was boiling, but for one final time, Amy went slowly to the piano and sat down. Her critical ear continued to applaud the deep, melodious tone of the instrument, but already her emotions had flattened.

She tried to feel happy. Now there was a piano to be played. Now the miners all up and down the gulch would hear the music each Sabbath day. Perhaps they would come, at least to hear the music.

Amy stared down at her hands resting on the piano keys, and the sure knowledge surfaced. "I have to do it, don't I, Lord? I have to send this lovely piano back, so that there will be no ties between Lucas Tristram and me. And there's more. Things won't be right until I tell Daniel how I've been false to him."

CHAPTER 26

Early the next morning, just after the sun had broken free of the mountaintops, Amy took the mare and headed down the gulch. She planned as she rode. "Seems somebody at the livery stable could give me a hand." At the same time she shook her head, "A piano is heavy. I remember watching them move the piano into the boarding-house in Central City." For a moment she mused over that scene. *What an awesome event it was! Little did I dream there'd be one like it in the middle of my house!*

Amy swallowed the lump in her throat, flicked the reins, and tried to forget the glory of that one moment of ownership when she thought the piano had truly been hers. Impatiently, she urged the horse into a trot.

Halfway down the road Amy saw the Withrops' wagon just in front of her. With the problem of the piano and the jumble of emotions fighting through her, Amy looked at her neighbors with a sinking heart. "Least of all," she murmured, "do I want to be pressed by Lettie's questions."

For a moment she held back on the reins and then nodded. "But maybe Hank can answer a question for me." She pulled even and hailed them.

Hank stopped the team. Lettie beamed at her as Hank said, "Morning, Missus. Sorry you've missed your man. 'Spect he'll be back pretty soon."

She nodded. "I might just take the stage down to Denver City and meet him there. Hope those hens are still producing for you. Mr. Withrop, I have a question. Just before we left, Lettie showed me a handbill you'd picked up at the mines. She mentioned there was some activity around the mines, with someone trying to raise money and arms for the Confederate cause. Is it still going on?"

His eyebrows lifted in a surprised arc. "Well, I didn't think a parson's wife would be interested in that. No. Seems the fellows around the mines kinda gave the gentleman in question a push in the right direction. I don't think they were too riled, though. It's hard to regard a dandy like that as being serious. Some were saying they thought he was more interested in padding his own pockets, anyway. I'll tell you that didn't set too well with the fellows."

Amy nodded. "I guess that answers my question. Thank you."

"Where are you going now?" Lettie asked.

Amy hesitated and then said, "Just a bit of business. When I have more time, I'll tell you about it. Good day."

By noon the piano had been shifted from the Gerrett cabin to the little log church up the hill. Amy offered the drayman a handful of coins, but he shook his head. "My contribution to the church, seeing's I can't afford to give a fancy piano."

There was curiosity in his eyes and Amy said, "Well, come hear the music on the Sabbath."

"You kin play the thing? My missus will like that." He nodded his way back to the cart, and Amy watched him glance at the church again. With a wave, she walked back into the church.

Her intention had been to only touch the keys, but when she finally looked up, she found the noontime sun had slipped westward. She looked around and sighed, "Oh my, the day's almost gone—but what a joy!"

Getting to her feet, she noticed the sinking sun had laid a pattern of light on the piano. With her arms akimbo, she studied the piano and murmured, "That'll never do. Up here the sun'll ruin the finish in no time. Guess I can give a shove, at least enough to get the sun off it."

Amy put her shoulder to the piano and pushed. She stepped back and looked at its bulk and tried again. This time she felt it teeter slightly on the uneven floor. "Come on, you beautiful thing, just move a bit," she coaxed. She pushed again.

Now panting with exertion, she braced her feet and strained. "Oh!" The pain shot across her back and she dropped to the stool and leaned against the piano. For a moment the room dipped and swayed around her. She moaned and tried to cling to the slippery surface of the piano.

"Ma'am! You're ill?"

Without looking up, Amy whispered, "I'll be fine in a minute. Pushing the piano made it all come back. The sickness."

The woman's hand was warm on her back and finally Amy was able to sit up. "My back still hurts." She straightened and looked up; then she blinked. "Crystal Thomas—the Lord sent you for certain."

There was an amused smile on the woman's face. "I was riding past when I heard the music. Actually, I was clear down the gulch. Just couldn't help wondering about the music, though. Pretty nice piano for a church like this," she murmured, looking around the room before turning back to Amy. "And you are a good pianist. Didn't expect that of a pastor's wife, especially a pastor in the Methodist Episcopal Church. Changed their view a little?"

Amy nodded, but couldn't find strength to mention the piano at the church in Denver City. She continued to rest against the piano. As Crystal talked, Amy became aware of her slight accent. It reminded her of the last time she had seen the woman.

The pain stabbed and Amy straightened with a moan. "Oh, Crystal, I'm afraid. Do you suppose pushing the piano would hurt the baby? I didn't think."

The woman bent over Amy. "Baby? Might be. How far along are you?"

Amy shook her head. "I don't know about such things. But

Mother said I was most certainly pregnant."

Crystal was quiet for a moment. She sighed and said, "Well, if you can walk, I think we'd better get you home and to bed. A day or so will settle it for good or bad. Maybe I'd best go after your husband."

"Daniel is gone."

Crystal pondered for a moment. "Then let's start walking."

A wave of nausea swept over Amy as she got to her feet. Crystal slipped her arm around her. In a few minutes Amy was able to lift her head. "I'm feeling better; let's go," she murmured, taking a step forward.

After Crystal had Amy settled in her own bed, she built up the fire and casually said, "Guess I'll stick around for a time. I'm used to this. There's a saw-bones down the hill, but right now I think I'll do you more good."

"You think I'm going to lose my baby?"

"Like I said, we'll know soon."

Crystal stayed the night with Amy, sleeping beside her on the bed. In the morning she said, "I think you'll make it fine. Since the pain in your back's letting up, I'm taking that as a good sign. Mostly I think you just pulled muscles, and the pain gave you the nausea."

She added, "I'll stay awhile if you want." Her mouth twisted in a wry smile. "I've nothing else to do right now." Amy looked at her and wondered. Today Crystal's gown was unadorned cotton. After breakfast she said, "You've big questions in your eyes, Amy. Let's clear the air. What do you want to ask?"

"I'm wondering what's been happening to you. When I left Buckskin Joe, you were still living with the Tabors. What happened?"

"The smallpox. When the Tabors moved into Denver City, they took me along. I stayed there after they returned to Buckskin Joe." The expression in her eyes was open and honest as she went on. "I worked at the hotel Charley started. Now I'm up here."

"What have you been doing?"

Crystal didn't answer. Her eyes frankly appraised Amy.

Finally Amy answered, "I suppose I shouldn't pry. But you invited me to clear the air."

In a moment she took up the subject again. She had been watching

Crystal as she moved about the cabin. There were the same tidy, efficient motions that had first attracted Amy's attention as she watched the Creole work in Augusta's kitchen. "You know what I remember most about that time?"

Crystal quirked an eyebrow. Amy hesitated and then pushed. "Seeing you at the burying ground, at Lizzie's funeral. You were singing. Your head was tipped back, and it was like sunshine was coming out of your face. You know, Crystal, I kept that in my mind. Somehow it made all the religion I'd been seeing suddenly come across all shabby."

Crystal continued to work around the room. After she created order from Amy's chaos, she mixed bread and used the broom on the floor.

Amy watched and thought about the Crystal in Buckskin. The scene she had recalled brought back the uneasy questions. Now she was left wishing for answers, as if putting words to the scene had stripped her down to a bleakness of soul she didn't know she had. Were these the feelings Father Dyer had referred to when he talked about her fears? Finally she asked, "Why this now?"

Crystal looked at her and her eyes narrowed. "I 'spect you've got things hidden in your life. Want I should dig at them?"

Amy sat up in bed. She snapped, "Crystal, you're talking like you did in Buckskin Joe—that is, when we were around to listen to you. Since I've been here, my friend Lettie and I have heard you speaking a foreign language. Yesterday and today, you've let it slip. When you forgot to be careful, I heard the same sounds in your words. Who are you? Where did you come from?"

The quick look Crystal threw at Amy was dark and heavy with hidden secrets. Her voice was light. "You already had it figured out. Fancy clothes, fancy lady. I saw it in your eyes."

"I wasn't judging, but I was disappointed," she said slowly. "Crystal, don't you see? If you can fall that far, what is going to happen to me? I'm afraid."

"Mon ami!" The words bursting from Crystal were followed by a sharp exclamation.

She turned, hesitated, and then came slowly to Amy. Carefully she said, "I want to help you, but you mustn't dig at me. When you can accept me as I am, then we can be friends."

Amy spoke slowly and deliberately. "That first time I saw you here, there was a man with you—a gentleman. It took me a long time to figure out who he was. But now I know. I saw you with Lucas Tristram, didn't I?"

Crystal's back straightened, and she turned a smile on Amy. "Yes, you did. What is so alarming about that? Mr. Tristram is an old friend. I might ask how you made your acquaintance with him."

"He was in Central City when I lived there." Watching Crystal's face, Amy added, "Mr. Tristram presented the piano to the church." Crystal's eyebrows raised.

"But you knew him before coming to Colorado Territory," Amy guessed. The woman's dusky features froze, as if cut from ice.

"Yes, but does that make a difference? I could remind you that you are prying. Amy, it is you I want to discuss now."

"Am I going to lose my baby?" The horror was back and Amy raised herself to look up at Crystal.

"No. You are not. Stop worrying. I'm sure it was just a pulled muscle. Now—" She came to sit on the edge of the bed. "Amy, does it matter whether I know Lucas? What does that have to do with your problem?"

"Can't you see? You were dressed like a fancy lady, leaning on the arm of a man I know to be—well, less than honorable."

For a moment Crystal narrowed her eyes. When she spoke, her voice was mild and nearly amused. "Tell me why you said that."

Amy rejected all her mental images of Lucas in Central City and said, "We saw him in Santa Fe, for one thing. It was in the plaza and the place was filled with Confederate soldiers. Why was Lucas there?"

For a moment Crystal was startled. Then the expression in her eyes sharpened and became veiled by something Amy couldn't understand. Slowly she said, "Amy, I don't keep track of the man. But I do think you ought to keep this information to yourself. At least for the time being."

She got to her feet and paced the room. Suddenly she came back to the bed and grasped Amy's arm. "Do you understand? I think it is important that you say nothing about this. Can you trust me?" She paused and then added, "The information could be dangerous to you."

The next words tripped out of Amy, and she regretted the mocking statement even as she replied, "You're threatening me. I'd guess you either love Lucas or hate him." Crystal's face tightened into an unreadable mask as Amy whispered, "I'm sorry."

"And you can't accept the questions I won't answer. All right, Amy, I'll tell you. It isn't love. I've been married to a wonderful man. But I watched that man warped, twisted into a pawn. I'll tell you no more about the subject. You've guessed I'm from the South. What does that spell to you?"

"Rebel, Confederate. That you have no business being here, trying to—" She drew a breath and realized she was only guessing. "But you're . . . not white. Crystal, what do you really hold dear?"

"I believe mankind was created to be equal and free, and we're not. None of us, not even the pawns. They think they are free and strong. They think they own their minds. But they have been used, just as surely as they are using us."

Amy tried to puzzle out the strange words. She guessed, "That means you are against slavery. That means—Crystal, what were you doing with Lucas?"

Crystal continued to study Amy's face. Her eyes became sad as if she were seeing something twisted and ugly moving between them. Amy sensed it. She knew that no matter how much she denied it, Crystal's words had created more problems than they solved. And they also confirmed what Amy had guessed.

Crystal got to her feet. "I suppose I might as well go on home. Your Daniel will be back soon. You're past danger." She hesitated. The dark expression was still there.

Finally she smiled at Amy. Arching her eyebrows she said, "Just like you think, huh? You think I'm owned by Tristram? You think ah'm one of the massa's other chill'n, bought and paid for. Amy, it don't matter what you think, about me or my morals. But one thing I'll tell you. We're proud people; we don't like being owned like cattle."

"That's ugly, Crystal. You're trying to shut me up, digging out that talk so I won't see the real you. I'm not a baby. You're raising a dust storm so I can't see. Why? I'm not telling you how to live. Not even judging. Right now I'm confused." The two studied each other.

Amy turned her head on the pillow and tried to sort through the jumble of feelings. She said, almost to herself, "In a few days my heart will be breaking over all this, and it won't be because of what I'm thinking."

She turned back to the woman. "See, Crystal, I am growing up. I'm worrying about you. For some reason, I can't get you out of my mind, and this started in Buckskin Joe. Daniel says we hadn't ought to be pushing religion, but instead we should be pointing to Jesus. Crystal, you'll still be having to face Jesus one of these days."

Crystal's voice was light as she walked to the door. "And, dear parson's wife, you are a self-righteous prig."

By the next day Amy felt well enough to be out of bed. She baked a loaf of bread and began to wish Daniel would forget the spring conference and just come home.

On the second day, Amy determined she would waste no more time or tears fussing over Crystal. But the scorn in the woman's eyes and voice still stung Amy. "Self-righteous prig," Amy said slowly. As she stared at the door, she was thinking of the velvet frock and the prayer she had prayed. *There are two things I must do. I must see Lucas Tristram and find Daniel. Unless Lucas can give me a better answer than I can think of right now, he must take the piano back.*

On the third day, Amy began to pack her valise. Lettie came to call that afternoon.

When Amy opened the door she said, "You've come just in time to bid me goodbye."

"Where you off to now?"

"I've decided to take the stage into Denver. I haven't seen my husband for over a month, so I'll just go surprise him."

Lettie offered, "Hank and I'll give you a ride down to the stage stop."

"The stage leaves at two this afternoon. I'll be ready."

Amy nearly missed the Denver stagecoach. It was pulling away from the hotel at the bottom of the gulch as they rode up. Hank shouted while Lettie and Amy waved their arms.

The driver stopped and climbed down. "Didn't wait around none. Seems not many are hankering to ride into Denver City this trip. I'll stow your bag up here." He took the valise and helped Amy into the stage. She waved at Hank and Lettie, and turned to sit down.

As she settled into the seat, the one other woman turned. "You!" The word burst out of Amy.

Crystal's smile was bitter. "Fancy that. We'll be stuck with each other for two days of hard riding. Are you feeling able?"

Amy nodded and leaned back in her corner. "I'm fine now. Sorry to have inconvenienced you."

The other passenger, a man, was seated across from them. His head was moving from right to left as they talked. Amy noticed his eyes were getting brighter with each brittle sentence.

Crystal looked at him. With a nod of her head, she said, "Might be wondering how the parson's wife comes to know a fancy lady?" And then her amused grin moved from one to the other.

CHAPTER 27

Amelia walked behind the trading post and approached the livery stable where Matthew had his room. When she spotted him leaning on the corral fence just beyond the stable, she walked quickly toward him.

"Matthew." He turned at her approach. Seeing the wary expression in his eyes, Amelia held up the bottle. "I've brought my vial of olive oil. Let's go see if we can rub a little life back into that arm."

He moved uneasily and looked embarrassed. "Mrs. Randolph, it isn't doing badly all on its own."

"Stop calling me Mrs. Randolph. We've known each other too long by our first names. It seems like—"

"Hypocrisy?" She nodded and watched his eyes as he struggled. Finally he sighed. "I was tempted to cut out of here." When she said nothing he continued. "But it seems a dirty trick after all you've done when I was helpless. Taking me into your wagon."

"The wagon belongs to the Army," she reminded. "You've no obligation if that's what you want. Eli and I can stay here until he throws the crutches away."

"That's making it hard on you. You know I can't show bad

manners that way." She couldn't keep back the grin, and the easy smile slipped away from his face. "You're amused. Let me guess. Could it be the times you've caught me with a display of . . . bad manners?"

"Like our last conversation in Pennsylvania. Seems I remember an argument. I should say brawl. But anyway, I remember we had an audience. What was the fellow's name?"

She could see he had no intention of answering. She added, "It's long forgotten; I do remember he was some dandy. But the thing I remember most, Matthew, was his devilish smile. He acted like all the cards were stacked in his favor. At the time that made me very angry. Maybe that's why I fought to keep you from going." She paused and then added thoughtfully. "Looking back, I think they were—the cards." Amelia turned to lean on the corral fence.

Slowly Matthew spoke, and a kind of sorrow came through the words. "Maybe so. At least time hasn't handed me a better place in life. I've had many an occasion to regret not taking your advice." He studied the cows along the fence before he turned to face her again.

"Yes, of the lot of us, he was the only one to land on his feet."

Quickly he glanced at her, "Begging your pardon, ma'am, you seem to have done all right."

Amelia's head dropped. For a moment she toyed with the idea of satisfying the curiosity in his eyes, but then she rejected the notion. It was Matthew's problems that needed to be addressed.

"I'm guessing the reason you want to take the stage is to avoid all the questions I want to put to you. I've already concluded that you're not in the least happy with the choice you made that day."

"Look, Amelia, all that's behind me. The day I made that decision, I thought the fellow was offering me the chance to undo all the grief I had caused my family. And the rest . . ." He shrugged, but Amelia saw the pain in his eyes. "My wife? Don't forget—she played a part in it all."

Amelia started to protest, but she caught herself and said, "I'm not going to get caught up in that again. Meanwhile, Matthew, there's that arm. Take off your shirt and let me massage it. If you don't start working those muscles, you'll never be anything except a cripple."

Fumbling at the buttons, he turned to look out over the barren hillsides, "So this is Colorado Territory. I wondered what it would be like."

Amelia asked, "Why? What have you heard about the territory?"

"Not territory—at least not then." He looked at her. "Crystal and I had talked about going west when we were back in Pennsylvania. There was starting to be rumors about gold. Seems some of the men heading into California had done enough prospecting in the Cherry Creek to encourage consideration. It was Clara Brown who had first mentioned it to Crystal."

"Who is she?"

"A former slave. Crystal has known her for years. She bought her freedom and told Crystal she was heading west. Last we heard she talked about settling in Kansas. But we knew her intentions were to move into this end of Colorado soon as the gold fields opened."

"Matt, from Pueblo you can ride east with some of the freight wagons."

"Well," he said reluctantly, "I guessed I'd just go on into Denver City. Thought I'd ask around about Clara Brown."

"Mind if I ask why?"

He glanced up. "Thought I'd ask if she's heard anything about Crystal."

"Maybe she doesn't want to see you. Matt, you said some ugly things to her." Matthew didn't answer. Finally Amelia sighed and said, "The shirt, Matt."

He looked down at his arm. "Or I'll be a cripple. One advantage. I wouldn't be expected to fight again."

She looked at the painful twist of his lips and said, "That's a different tune you're singing. All the yelling we did to each other that day started because you couldn't wait to get back home when you thought things were gearing up to a fight. In '58, wasn't it? About the time all the rumbles were starting over the states rights issue." She sighed and shrugged. "The arm, Matthew. That's the issue now."

She tugged at his sleeve and he remarked, "Maybe Eli won't like your playing nurse to me."

"Eli and I have discussed it." Her voice was mild and she continued to ignore the questions in his eyes. Slowly he began to remove his shirt. With a slight smile, Amelia mentioned, "You know, many people have a tough time recognizing me with these scars."

"And the dowdy dress and skinned-back knob of hair." There was a touch of amusement in his voice. "That's a good disguise."

The grin disappeared from his face. "I'm sorry," he said. "You've acted so lighthearted about it all. I know it's been difficult. I've had a hard time guessing how you must feel down inside."

Amelia poured oil into the palm of her hand. With her other hand she slowly pulled Matthew's arm away from his body and straightened it. She watched the white line of pain around his mouth as she began to massage the scar and knotted muscle in his arm.

When the perspiration drenched his face and streaked his undershirt, she released his arm. "I think that's enough for today." She added, "Might be to your advantage to stick with Eli and me. You need that arm massaged every day." She watched him wince as he thrust the arm back into the shirt.

Matthew muttered, "You didn't pull any punches about letting me know how you feel about me, yet you've been dressing my arm. Now you're trying to make it work again. Why?"

"Sometimes you do things for people because you love them, not because you like the things they do."

While he fastened the buttons, she said, "About my scars. Matthew, would you believe I'm to the place now where I can rejoice in them?"

She sat down on the woodpile. Matthew pulled up a log. He moved his shoulders under the warmth of the sun and then squinted up at her. "Maybe you'd better tell me how. I think there's a few things in my life I need to learn to rejoice over."

"Or change," she said. They sat in silence for a few minutes. Finally Amelia leaned forward to look at Matthew.

"Back in Pennsylvania days you knew I'd left my husband. Until this past February, I've been living in Buckskin Joe, over on the other side of the mountains. At the time the smallpox epidemic hit town, I'd been struggling with a lot of things. But mostly just me. I guess I discovered then that approaching God is an impossibility if the pack on your back is too wide to fit through the door."

Again they sat in silence while Amelia sorted through the thoughts pressing at her. Finally she lifted her head. "Having smallpox was more like God reaching down and pulling off the biggest pack on my back. The thing I couldn't surrender without a miracle was the thing smallpox snatched. Me, my beauty. Overnight, pride was stripped from me. I was left with the choice of accepting what had happened or destroying myself.

"Matthew, a long time before the smallpox, I wanted badly to be able to accept God's forgiveness, but by then I had hit the very bottom of life. You know the kind of person I was. Later, it seemed like a cheap shot to be crawling to Him, on my knees, after I was ruined.

"It took a lot of thinking before I realized part of the sacrifice of Christ's atonement is this final mile. For me He not only provided the way to himself, but He allowed the burden of life to roll in upon me and crush me until I realized there was no escape except into His arms. A begging Lord with the sacrifice in His outstretched arms." Slowly she got to her feet and looked at Matthew. He was still on the chunk of firewood, staring at the ground.

The next day Matthew came to the Randolphs' cabin. When Amelia opened the door he said, "I've come to have you massage my arm. Also, I've been thinking. I'd like to ride into Denver with you. I'll be ready as soon as you want to leave."

Eli nodded. "The sooner the better. I saw an article in an old *Rocky Mountain News* I'd like to investigate. It's about the Homestead Act that's taking effect in the Territory now." Amelia was shaking her head as Eli added, "I'd like a hunk of land for myself."

Two days later Eli was still talking about the Homestead Act as they rode out of Pueblo. He was stretched out on the bedding in the wagon while Amelia and Matthew shared the wagon seat. "You know the Act is a chance in a lifetime. No money for acres; just work the land. Make improvements."

Finally Amelia sighed and said, "Do you think that's what the Lord wants you to do?"

Reluctantly Matthew put in, "Plowing fields and feeding livestock is hard work. Are you sure you are up to it? If you go to preaching again, Amelia will be left with most of the work."

They rode along silently, each absorbed in his own thoughts. The weather along the eastern slope of the mountains was pleasantly warm. The road they traveled led from one small community to the next. Farming and mining still seemed equally important to the villages they passed through, but the farming seemed to be getting the most attention.

There were flocks of sheep and cattle, and the fields were scraped into neat furrows along the rivers and streams. Already fingers of green traced out the length of the furrows.

Each night they were able to find a place to camp close to the security of a farmhouse. Most nights their hosts came visiting with fresh produce or milk. Their faces were always swarthy, and usually the exchange of English was limited.

One evening Amelia watched the farmer walk out of sight, and then she turned to Eli. "Why are most of these people of Mexican descent?"

"Because this section of land originally belonged to New Mexico Territory. Last year when Colorado became a territory, the boundaries were changed. How would you like to get up one morning and discover your house is no longer in New Mexico, but instead you're a resident of Colorado Territory?"

"Guess I wouldn't."

Amelia went to wash the tiny beets and carrots. Eli turned to look at Matthew stretched out on a grassy patch beside the grazing mules. Matthew tilted his hat off his face and looked at Eli. "Mind telling me a little about Denver City?"

Amelia bent over the pan of water as Eli replied, "Not much to tell. It's still a bunch of log cabins and milled lumber business houses. There's a handful of hotels and a triple handful of saloons. Charley Harrison's made good. He's just about been running the place."

"He's the mayor?"

"No. Runs a couple of saloons, has a couple of the best hotels in town. Doesn't have too good a reputation. He's just about half outlaw."

"Half?" Amelia questioned, dumping the pan of water and dropping the vegetables into the pot of beans and meat. She added, "Harrison might come across as a good fellow, but that gang of outlaws hanging around him gives his whole establishment a bad flavor."

"The Bummers," Eli said. "They've been blamed with everything that's happened, and rightly so, it seems. Soon after Gilpin became the territorial governor, he put together a volunteer army. They took up the name Pikes Peakers. The soldiers' first assignment was to get rid of the Bummers. That made Charley pull his neck in a little."

Matthew was silent. Finally he sat up and said, "I'm getting the feeling there's not much of a job market in Denver."

Eli replied slowly, "I don't think that impression is valid. After all, the territory has been bled of young men to fill up the Colorado Volunteer Army. Just what did you have in mind?"

Matthew shrugged. "I was trained as a lawyer, but I'd do about anything."

Eli looked as if he were about to ask a question. Amelia hastily said, "Well, most of the newcomers try their hand at gold mining. Now's a good time of year to start. Matter of fact, if you'd want to follow Father Dyer around, he could point out some likely spots. He's been to most of the gold camps in the territory."

After they had eaten and the fire burned low, Amelia could see Matthew was still hashing over the subject. She watched him take a deep breath. There was something about his face that caught Amelia's attention. From the expression, she guessed that he had reached a milestone. With a headlong thrust, he began to talk of all the things he had been avoiding for the past weeks.

The fire flickered shadows across his face. She felt like applauding him as he said, "I don't know how to say all this without it seeming as if I'm looking for sympathy. But, I just can't go home. The bottom line is, I don't believe in the Confederate cause any longer. As long as the war is being fought, I won't be welcome there."

Finally Eli prodded, "Son, do you feel like you'd like to enlarge on the subject?"

Matthew shot a quick glance at Amelia. "At one time I thought

I was for the cause, a Confederate all the way through. I did have a lot of pride in the South. But what really happened was that in a weak moment, I let a fellow talk me into seeing my duty to family and home. I went home. Shortly after that I began to have serious doubts."

"Oh, Matthew!" Amelia cried in dismay. "Fighting is bad enough when you really believe, but—"

"Let's not talk about the fighting. That was not of my choice. It's the other. You know," he said heavily. "As well as I do, you know. I listened to the wrong fellows. But to begin with, it was my spoiled brat nature. I got all hotheaded about something I shouldn't have."

Amelia finished softly. "About her? You believed the lie, and your foolish pride wouldn't let you listen to reason. Love does strange things to a person and you were no exception. If only you'd given Crystal a chance to explain."

"But she couldn't," Matthew said slowly. "I'd said things that she'd never forgive."

"About her race? Matthew, I'd wondered."

There was silence around the fire. Matthew went to the wagon for blankets and came back to spread them beside the fire.

Amelia got to her feet. She could see Matthew's face was lined with the kind of agony that struck a response in her own heart. *Dear God, help me to be able to say the words that will help,* she found herself thinking. *I know how he feels—it's like a dead-end tunnel.*

She watched Eli pick up a crutch and limp toward the wagon. She followed him and said, "Let me help, Husband."

"I can make it." He touched her cheek, then hoisted himself into the wagon.

After they were settled in the blankets, Eli spoke hesitantly, "Matt seems without hope."

"His wife was Creole. As long as I've known him, Matthew has been a hotheaded, spoiled child. So different from his sister." She sighed. "I think most of his early life was just a pattern of following one whim after another. Guess that's all right for a young'un. But when it starts hurting others—"

She stopped and Eli fumbled for her hand. She whispered, "That's what I did. I am so sorry. But that isn't going to change the past."

Eli bent over and kissed her before pulling her into his arms. "You and I both know there's mistakes that only the Lord can make right. And it does take a miracle—as well as a commitment to a lifetime of working at problems."

Her voice was low as she said, "Certainly I don't deserve a second chance. It is only the mercy of God that forgives sin, but a second chance at life is like being handed a fortune."

Minutes passed in silence, and Amelia thought Eli was asleep. Then he spoke. "Amelia, a fortune is to be spent."

"Am I hoarding it?"

"Nearly. It's as if you're afraid it will run out. The Lord doesn't do things in a halfhearted way. And I do trust you, my dear."

She wanted desperately to ask that question, but she pressed her lips together. He moved beside her and bent over her again. "Are those tears on your face?" He touched his lips to them.

"Remember, God changes the heart, even mine, and it isn't a halfway job. Also, I'm taking Father Dyer's advice seriously. I've a feeling I'm going to enjoy spending the rest of my life telling you how much I love you and want you with me."

In a moment she heard the amusement in his voice as he said, "Maybe in another twenty years, you'll see there's not much difference between scars or wrinkles—on either one of us." Amelia laughed softly, and Eli cuddled her head against his shoulder.

CHAPTER 28

When the stagecoach stopped, Amy sat up. She had been trying to sleep in her corner while the stage bounced over rocks and swayed around corners. As she peered out the window, she sighed with relief. Under the cover of her shawl, she pressed her hand against her stomach.

It was late and very dark, and the only thing Amy could see was a cluster of lights down the street.

The driver swung down from his perch, making the coach sway. "All out!" He barked, stopping beside the window. "We're here for the night. There's a hotel down the street. Be back by daybreak. We want an early start. It's a long ride into Denver City."

The male passenger pried himself out of his corner and disappeared. Crystal gathered her shawl and valise. She looked at Amy. "Come along. The accommodations aren't luxurious, but the driver won't take the coach through the mountains in the dark."

She waited for Amy to climb out of the stagecoach, and then she started down the street. Glancing at Amy she asked, "Feeling better now?"

Amy nodded. "You noticed?" She followed Crystal into the hotel.

The room to which they were directed was lined with crude cots covered with a straw tick and a blanket. Crystal carefully shook both items and turned with a look of distaste. "Oh, my mother would have heart failure if she could see me now!"

Amy blinked with surprise as she went to shake her own bedding. *Strange. Why have I never thought of Crystal having a past, other than the one at Buckskin Joe? She has a mother, a family— and they are probably wondering about her. Worrying.*

Crystal carefully removed her gown and hung it on a peg. As she wrapped herself in a shawl she looked at Amy. "Those questions in your eyes! Sometimes I get the distinct feeling you proper white ladies forget we're human."

Amy felt her face getting warm as she carefully lowered herself to the cot and smoothed her frock. "I'll freeze if I take off my clothes. At least cotton doesn't wrinkle as badly as—whatever that is."

"Moire. Watered silk."

Amy winced. "I know I'm ignorant of such."

Crystal turned carefully on her cot. Her voice gentled as she said, "Being Creole isn't that bad. I know it's hard to believe, but my family is well respected in New Orleans." In a moment she added, "I'm sorry. I guess I'm still touchy."

"About our argument? Crystal, I've been judging you. But without facts it's hard to think otherwise. When I saw you first in Buckskin, you didn't even have a warm wrap. Now, well, you dress like—"

"A prostitute. And they are the only women in the territory with decent clothes. Good night, Amy."

In the morning there were more passengers. The driver helped them in until Amy felt the stagecoach bumping against its springs. By the time they started down the canyon, dawn had painted the clouds apricot, and Amy feasted on the view.

One of the men tainted the air of the coach with his alcoholic breath as he asked, "Heard any more about the Confederates holding up the stagecoaches?"

Amy caught her breath and fumbled with the tiny money bag

stuffed with gold nuggets—all of them. They were intended for a piano when their volume had doubled, tripled, and doubled again.

She was lost in thought, measuring Father Dyer's sermons against her secret desire. Were the nuggets a golden idol? *When this trip is ended, there will be neither nuggets nor piano.*

A man laughed. "Confederates, don't give them credit where it isn't due. One incident blown twice its size."

The woman next to Amy nervously patted her bag and said. "I thought the war was settled by Chivington's men. Didn't the Confederates go home?"

The man opposite her said, "Lady, nothing's settled. As long as there's shooting, this territory will be in danger." He shot a quick look at the man who had laughed. "Contrary to some, there's far too many incidents of stages being held up. Might not be much gold lost, but it's leaking out of the territory, and it'll be buying guns to shoot our young men."

It was late afternoon when they reached Denver City. The line of buildings along Cherry Creek blossomed with light as they rode down the street. When the stagecoach turned on the road leading to the livery stable, Amy could see the final glow of color over the mountains.

She watched the clouds tumble and change shape and color, murmuring, "Beautiful!" Crystal looked at her. "When we came out here, the mountains and the sunset were the first things I noticed," Amy explained. "Beginning then I thought the territory was bound to be something special. The mountains, the sunsets, all of it made it seem destined for great things."

Crystal's smile was amused. "Do you still feel the same way?"

Amy thought and slowly began to put words out. "It's hard to see people with hungry eyes and shabby clothes still looking for gold and not finding it. I hurt when I see others hurt. It almost seems to drag me down, and keep me from remembering the beauty. But the feeling's still there." She looked at Crystal. "It's terrible not to hope in a brighter tomorrow, not to expect—" The word flashed through her thoughts: *Piano.*

She took a deep breath. "I guess I'm older. I no longer expect gold nuggets to fall out of my rugs when I shake them. But even if they did, the good of the people is best. Somehow, I can't stop *believing* in good."

The woman seated across from Amy watched her. Her eyes were curious, suspicious. Her double chin moved gently with the motion of the swaying coach.

When they turned to follow Cherry Creek, Crystal said, "It's dark. Amy, I'm going to the hotel. Why don't you come too? Tomorrow you can search for your Daniel."

By the time the coach stopped in front of the hotel, Amy had sorted her thoughts and surrendered her dream of finding Daniel waiting for her. She nodded and followed Crystal to the hotel.

Amy handed over one of her gold nuggets to the man at the desk and climbed the stairs to the tiny room on the top floor. While she unpacked the valise and shook the wrinkles out of her frock, Amy mulled over the events of the past week. But the most pressing was the piano.

I must take care of it tomorrow. I must clear the air with Daniel and let him know that there is nothing—nothing anymore—between me and Lucas Tristram. Whatever else happens, I don't want Daniel to be hurt by suspicion—

Finally she lifted her hands to her throbbing head and said, "All this thinking is only confusing me. I'm tired and hungry." She looked at the door and decided. "First thing, I'll find Crystal and we'll have something to eat. I know she's down on the next floor."

Amy picked up her shawl, the key, and the little bag of gold nuggets. She balanced the bag of nuggets on her hand and said, "I thought I was saving these nuggets for a piano. I never guessed I'd be spending them on a trip to Denver City to find Daniel. Neither did I think there would be a beautiful piano sitting in the church this very minute."

She was still thinking about the piano as she locked the door and started down the steps.

When she reached the next floor, she stopped and looked at the line of numbered doors marching down each side of the hall. "I don't know which room is Crystal's," she murmured, "without going down to the desk. How'll I find her?"

With a shrug she turned toward the stairs and then stopped. There was a burst of excited words coming from one of the rooms. As she paused, she realized she couldn't understand the words. Amy waited, and when the rush of words came again, she knew they were foreign.

A heavy voice replied. With a shock of recognition, Amy took a step toward the door. Both of the voices were familiar. Now they were speaking words she could understand.

Lucas—and Crystal! His voice dropped as he said, "Don't despair, my darling china doll." Amy stepped close to the door and listened. "This war isn't over by a long shot. I still need you, and you will be handsomely rewarded. I must have every scrap of information you can give me." He paused. There was a quiet murmur, and scornfully he added, "Who are you to judge whether or not the information is important? Now come, let's go to dinner and then we'll talk about this later."

Amy flew up the stairs.

As she sat on her bed panting, her fear of discovery changed to outrage. "Crystal, you lied! You are everything I guessed you to be— and more! Lucas was talking about the war. Daniel and I saw him with the Confederates."

Amy's breathing slowed. She leaned back on the bed and tightened her shawl around her. She began to relax, to push the lies out of her mind. Turning over on her back, Amy looked and then sat up to look more closely at the ceiling.

The neat white ceiling was only canvas tacked to the rafters, Amy began to giggle. "Fancy hotel, 'til you look up. You get what you pay for. Were you trying to buy us, Lucas?"

Amy concentrated on the hazy ideas that seemed about to slip away from her. She tried to sort out the jumble of thoughts: Lucas. Crystal. The war. The piano. But as understanding escaped her and exhaustion took over, she fell asleep.

When she awoke it was cold. The lamp was smoking, and its light was dim. It took Amy several moments before she began to remember. "Daniel," she murmured with a sinking heart. And then she added, "Crystal, Lucas. The piano."

The morning was half gone before she awakened again. The now-familiar nausea was there to remind her she hadn't eaten.

She bathed and dressed while she counted off all the facts. "Without a doubt Lucas had a reason for giving us the piano, and it had nothing to do with his charitable instinct. Now I think he was trying to win my favor and silence."

She was still thinking as she went downstairs to the dining room. While Amy ate her breakfast, she thought about the effect the piano would have on Daniel. Crumbling the last bite of bread, she decided, *One thing is certain. I must tell Lucas to get that piano out of the church, take it back. I am ashamed to admit I know a man like that. Dear Lord Jesus, to think I've let him blind me to the real Lucas all this time! I can't allow Daniel to see that piano on top of the other hurt. Please help me have this all settled without Daniel having to know about it!*

She sat staring at the coffee cup in front of her. *Why does this seem all wrong? I'm trying to protect him from any more hurt.* Amy winced as she thought of the words she must say to Daniel. As she got up and went to pay her bill, Amy still struggled with the uneasiness she felt.

With her valise firmly in hand and the shawl clinging to her shoulders, Amy set out from the hotel. Thinking of Crystal, she muttered, "Right now I don't feel like confronting any more lies. Sorry, Crystal, I just can't take more of you right now."

It was a long walk to the church. When Amy arrived it was time for services to be over. Still thinking about Crystal, Amy reached the steps of the log church and stopped. Bewildered, she looked around. There wasn't one buggy or horse to be seen. The door was tightly locked and not the slightest sound disturbed the stillness of the day.

With her face puckered in a puzzled frown, she went down the street toward the Goodes' home. The silence of the cabin was evident before she reached the door.

Turning away, Amy walked down the road to the next house. She found a woman hanging laundry on the bushes. Amy said, "The church—aren't they having services?"

The woman shook her head. "You're thinking of the conference next week. I don't go there, but Mrs. Goode was telling me all about it just before they left."

"Where have they gone?"

She shrugged. "Visiting someone. Said they won't be back until the Sabbath. Want I should give a message?"

Amy shook her head and turned away, trudging back down the way she had come. She reached the hotel before she managed to push away the confused thoughts. There was only one thing to do. Amy approached the desk. "May I have my room for another day or so? Just until I finish my business and get ready to leave for home?"

The man behind the desk shook his head. "Sorry, ma'am, I've let it out. Might be you could find a room down the street." Slowly Amy turned away. She thought of her dwindling store of nuggets. She also thought of Lucas and the message she must deliver.

She straightened her shoulders and turned toward the stairs. "Ma'am?" the man called.

"I'm going up to see Crystal Thomas," she said, continuing on her way.

When Amy reached the second floor, she stopped in front of the room she guessed to be Crystal's. Last night it seemed the voices she identified as belonging to Lucas and Crystal had come from here. She tapped.

A moment before the door was pulled open, she looked at it in horror. What if Lucas were still there? The door was wrenched open and a surprised Crystal peered out.

"I thought you had left."

"I found the meeting isn't until next week. I don't know whether to stay or just go home."

Crystal pulled the door open. "Well, I suppose you can stay here. It'll save you money. I guess that's a consideration, isn't it?"

"Yes," Amy said slowly. She swallowed her pride. "I would appreciate it very much. I must see Lucas Tristram before I return to Oro City."

"Lucas Tristram?" Crystal said slowly. "Why?" Amy lifted her chin, and Crystal said, "Sorry, I didn't mean to sound like a scolding mother."

"Well, I suppose you might as well know. It's the piano. I'm starting to mistrust his motives, and I want to have a talk with him."

Crystal blinked. "Motives? Amy, I don't think—you mean why he gave you the piano? Surely the fact that he did is most important. Can't you leave it there?"

The expression in Crystal's eyes changed from questions to uneasiness. Amy hesitated, trying to muddle through the implications wrapped in last night's conversation. Slowly she said, "I'm not free to say much. It's just that—well, maybe I shouldn't have accepted it. I need to talk to him. If it's all wrong, then I must get it out of there before Daniel comes home and sees it."

The expression in Crystal's eyes sharpened. "I find it interesting that a parson's wife feels she can't confide in her husband."

"You don't understand." Amy turned toward the window and tried to control the rush of words that rose to her lips. She struggled with her thoughts. Perhaps if Crystal knew more of her suspicions, then she would understand.

"There seems to be something strange going on in Lucas Tristram's life. Something about the war. It began when he was in Oro City the first time. Handbills were passed to the miners. I need to know whether or not he was involved in that."

"And what will you do if you find out that he was? Amy, there's cause for suspicion in nearly everyone's life, if we dig far enough. Why were the Gerretts in Santa Fe, New Mexico Territory, a couple of weeks ago? See—even you could come under suspicion."

Slowly Amy said, "Crystal, there are other things. We met a—" She caught herself before she said Matthew's name, and as she hesitated, she wondered why it seemed important to keep a rebel's name secret.

She continued. "A man who recognized Tristram. The accusations he made against Lucas are interesting enough that I feel I must do something about them. At least to satisfy myself."

She looked up and was surprised by Crystal's expression. The questions were gone from her eyes, and something very nearly like hope shone there. Crystal turned to pace the room. Finally she said, "Amy, I can help you find Tristram, but do you want to ruin your reputation searching out a man in Charley Harrison's saloon?

"Why don't you just go home and forget the whole thing? When this war is over, if Tristram is still around, you can ask. Meanwhile, you will have the joy of that beautiful instrument in your church."

"I can't do that, Crystal. I mustn't have any more hidden things in my life. Daniel is too important to me. Certainly, I could pretend I don't know where the piano came from, but I don't want to live that way." She started to turned away and then hesitated as she studied Crystal's face and measured the risk.

Slowly and deliberately, Amy said, "Why don't you bring him here, like last night?"

Crystal was very still. Amy felt her heart thudding out the seconds as she waited, studying the changing expression on the woman's face. Crystal stirred. "Very well." She quickly crossed the room and picked up her hat.

She stood in front of the mirror and adjusted it carefully. Amy watched, wondering why Crystal's hands were trembling.

Picking up her shawl and handbag, Crystal headed for the door. "Why don't you lie down and rest. I'll be back before you've had time for a good nap."

She waited beside the door. Amy got on the bed and pulled her shawl over her. Crystal nodded. With a smile she said, "Now be quiet, like a nice girl."

Amy burrowed into the pillow as the door clicked. It clicked again. Puzzled, she lifted her head. The heavy door and the solid walls had muffled all sound of footsteps, but she guessed Crystal had left.

She lay down again, but her eyes were wide. Why would the door click twice?

The answer had Amy off the bed and across the room. As soon as she touched the doorknob, she knew. Slowly she crossed the room and looked out the window. "Too high. I'll never get out of here until Crystal wants that to happen. What did I say that caused her to do such a thing?"

Below her, the wagons and carriages were moving up and down the street. She tried the window. There was no way she could lift it. A man dressed in white came down the street. He disappeared from sight, but a moment later he reappeared. This time there was a woman clinging to his arm, and Amy recognized Crystal's bonnet.

CHAPTER 29

The late afternoon rain began to turn to snow. Daniel hurried his mare along. "Old girl, let's get down off this mountain. Come on, move it. Might be we'll find Amy at home tonight, the good Lord willing."

Daniel prodded the borrowed mare and settled deeper into his coat collar as he addressed the mare. "Need to head into Denver City with you before the Army comes looking for their property."

He patted the mare and squinted at the sky. A May snowstorm wasn't a surprise to anyone living in the mountains. With the cold wet flakes melting down his neck, Daniel considered the possibilities. There were cabins along the way where he would be welcome, but his thoughts were reaching toward the cabin in Oro City.

The snow thickened into big soft flakes. By the time he reached Oro City, the storm had hidden the high road above the gulch. He dropped the reins across the horse's neck, saying, "You're the boss; your feet are better than mine on this road. Take us home." He settled back and let the mare plod her way over the road. When they reached the lane, he guided her toward the shed behind the cabin. Daniel peered toward his windows, hoping for a hint of light.

He shook his head and sighed, "No one, and they won't be coming home in this storm." He rubbed down the horse before he poured a measure of oats for her. As he hung the saddle and bridle out of the reach of mice, he muttered, "Can't understand why it's taking them so long to get home. Father's leg seemed to be healing nicely." He patted the horse and added, "Girl, we might just have to take a few days and head out after them."

He was in the cabin, building a fire in the little stove before he realized the piano was gone. Settling back on his heels, he studied the room by the light of the leaping flames. Not only was the piano gone, but the cabin showed evidence of a woman's touch. The floor had been swept and the tumble of towels had been washed and folded. He looked in the covered tin and found a loaf of bread.

Daniel was grinning as he sat down and studied the room. "She's home! At least she was." He studied the empty spot where the piano had stood, then turned to the table. The paper was gone. The piano and the bill of lading were missing. He folded his arms and watched the fire flicker.

Finally he shoved back on the bench and sighed. "Well, this is a mystery. Why is the piano gone? Does it have something to do with the names on that piece of paper? Where's Amy?"

There were no answers in the cabin, only silence except for the crackling fire.

In the morning Daniel walked down the hill to the Withrops' cabin. Lettie opened the door and frowned. "Back from conference already? Wantin' your horses. I'll call Hawk."

"No. Please keep them here. Conference is a week away. Have you seen Amy?"

"She's come and gone. Only had a few minutes with her, and that weren't much of a visit. When she found out you'd gone to conference, she packed up and headed for Denver. Oh!" She paused. "You didn't go."

"Next week," Daniel said patiently. He studied Lettie's puzzled face and considered asking her about the piano. But there were all those shadowy things connected with the affair. Not only was the piano a mystery, but Lucas Tristram's name was on the bill of lading.

Why would Tristram send a piano—and why would it be specifically addressed to Daniel Gerrett's wife? Daniel moved his shoulders uneasily and held back the questions.

He turned away. "Well, I guess I leave early for conference so I can find my wife."

"Won't you come in for dinner?" He shook his head, and she called after him, "Hope you find her."

Amy heard the key in the lock. She yawned, momentarily wondering where she was. Crystal. Amy sat up and waited for the door to open. The woman glanced quickly at her as she entered.

She closed the door and leaned against it. "Sorry I had to lock you in. It seemed best."

"You had to warn Lucas?" Amy's sharp words wiped the half smile from Crystal's face.

Slowly she said, "No. He still doesn't know you are here. Amy, I—" Crystal's voice trailed into silence as she paced the room. When she stopped beside the bed, she said, "I don't know what to say or how to say it all. And there's a lot that needs to be said. Can you trust me for a few days?"

"Few days! Crystal, are you planning to keeping me locked up? I want to have my say to Lucas and then get out of here. I want to go home to my husband. Do you know, he doesn't even know we're going to have a baby! I haven't seen him for a month now."

"Why haven't you seen him?" Amy opened her mouth and then closed it. She nearly mentioned the young rebel soldier again. Crystal shrugged. "We do have our secrets, don't we?"

Slowly Amy replied, "There are quite a few of them. Crystal, why are you holding me here? I can't believe the questions that I have to ask Lucas are of any concern to you."

Crystal paced the room again. Her steps were short and agitated; the clicking of her heels grated on Amy's nerves. Slowly Amy said, "I'm beginning to get the picture, and my assumption is right, isn't it?"

Amy sat on the edge of the bed and lined up the thoughts that had been floating around in her mind all day. She carefully designed hard words in hopes of getting Crystal to admit her feelings. Taking a deep breath she said, "You're in love with Lucas Tristram. That doesn't surprise me. I know another dancehall girl who let her feelings show too clearly. I have an idea Lucas was the father of the child she carried until she tried to abort it."

Crystal whirled. "Dancehall girl! Where did you get that idea? I've never been such in my life."

"Ah, Crystal! Don't you remember referring to yourself as a soiled dove that day we met on the streets of Buckskin Joe?"

Crystal's expression lightened. "I did so, didn't I? But do you remember I was talking about getting a job cooking?"

"Then why did you use that expression?" Crystal's face became stony as she studied Amy. She turned to walk to the window.

With her hand on the curtains, she said, "To answer that forces me to talk about things I'd rather forget. Amy, you're an innocent. I can't expect you to understand a deep hurt. Will you just not push for a reason behind the word?"

"Yet you ask me to believe you, trust you? Crystal, I don't want to hurt you, but I'm getting more confused by the minute."

Crystal came to sit beside Amy on the bed. "Do you remember I also told you I knew the madame of the brothel across the way?" For a moment Amy closed her eyes. *How could I forget? She led me to my mother!*

Heavily Amy answered, "I remember, but what does that have to do with—"

"I have known her for years. Although I was never a prostitute, we were good friends. You might say we became even better friends when I quit trying to reform her. She was kind to me. When I've been in need of a job, she's always found a position for me. Sometimes it was cooking in her kitchen. I'll always be grateful that Amelia's kindness kept me out of the brothel. You know, it's hard for a young Creole woman to find work except in the houses."

Amy's face rested in her hands. "Crystal," she said brokenly, "Amelia Randolph is my mother."

After a long time there was a whisper, "Amy, I'm sorry."

"Don't be. Remember that day? You mentioned her name. Later

that turned out to be the confirmation I needed to accept the hard facts." She lifted her head. "About her. You don't know what happened? She had smallpox."

Crystal nodded. "After the Tabors took me to Denver City, I read the papers. I met her about two months ago."

"Then you know she and Father are back together again."

It was a long time before Crystal whispered, "Does he know about her?"

Amy nodded. "For all of us it was a difficult time. Crystal, if it hadn't been for the way the Lord helped us, none of us would have been able to accept her back. Even Daniel struggled. But not as much as Father and I did."

Suddenly drained of energy, Amy leaned back against the pillows. Crystal moved restlessly around the room. Finally she said, "That nearly gives me hope. If Amelia could make all that happen, then there's hope for me."

Amy was too tired to ask the questions the statement raised.

During the night Amy awakened. Beside her, Crystal's breathing was deep and steady. The night sounds from the street were muffled by the thick log walls of the hotel. Amy listened to the hollow clop of horses' hooves against the packed soil of the street. She heard the murmur of voices. Curiosity roused her out of bed, and she leaned against the window and watched the dark figures move against the pale log buildings.

Restlessly she wondered, *How long will she hold me here? Daniel could come and then leave without me. I would forget Lucas if only—*

Crystal spoke out of the darkness. "Amy, why are you standing beside the window?"

She came to the bed. "Oh, Crystal, please let me go. I promise I won't go near Lucas."

"Where will you go?"

"Looking for Daniel again. He could think I'm not here and leave without me."

"I'll see that he knows you are here. Amy, trust me. Just a few more days."

The words echoed through Amy as if a sad refrain tolled like a bell in the depths of her soul. Over and over she heard the words. And in her dreams Daniel slipped away from her reaching arms.

In the morning, while they were at breakfast, the words sounded their gong again. Amy choked as she tried to swallow the dry crumbs of her breakfast.

Crystal looked at her while Amy dabbed at her eyes. "Are you all right? Shall I go get—"

The words waved a flag high in front of Amy. She whispered, "Water." She watched Crystal walking rapidly toward the kitchen, pushing her way through the crowd as she went. One second more. She was out of sight.

Amy got to her feet and strolled out of the room. When she reached the boardwalk, she glanced quickly around, *Amy,* she urged her sluggish mind. *Out of sight; get behind the hotel.*

Forcing her feet into a rapid stroll, she left the hotel door. She was nearly running as she rounded the corner and saw the trees. Behind the hotel a grove of cottonwoods and willows swooped down over Cherry Creek. Amy paused by the back door of the hotel to look both ways and then she dashed toward the trees. Breathing hard, she stood in the shadows and contemplated her freedom with a shaky grin. The grin faded. *There's no one at the Goodes'. Where shall I go?*

A door banged, and she heard sharp heels clicking on the wooden walkway. Amy caught her breath when she saw Crystal hurrying up the street. "She's nearly frantic," Amy murmured as she watched Crystal plant a hand in the middle of her hat. Her hoop skirt was swaying from side to side as she headed toward the Methodist Episcopal Church.

Slowly Amy walked to the street and turned her back on the direction Crystal had taken. Her steps quickened. For once she was grateful for the prim dark cotton she wore. She knew it was nearly invisible on a street filled with shabby, dark-clad men.

Within a few minutes, Amy realized she had passed the last hotel. She slowed down. Ahead she could see the garish sign hanging out from the wall of the building. "Criterion Saloon," she read. That was the name Crystal mentioned in connection with Charley Harrison. *A no-good guy, they said. Maybe he knows where I can find Lucas.*

At the saloon she found one man. He stood behind the split-log bar, in the rays of the early morning sun. Bracing his arms on the bar, he said, "Lady, what'll it be?"

Amy looked at the line of bottles behind him. A battered string of tin cups stood beside them. "Lucas Tristram, please," she said.

He blinked. "That's one drink I've never heard of. How about Taos Lightning?"

"Oh dear, that's liquor. I mean the man."

He shook his head. "I was funnin'; Lucas doesn't appear before sunup. Come back about three this afternoon."

"Where can I find him?" This time he blinked twice. She said, "I have business with him." He eyed her handbag.

He continued to study her and then his brow cleared. "He has rooms in the hotel down the street. Why don't you just—"

"I just came from there!" she cried impatiently.

"All right, lady. He usually plays keno every morning. Go in the back room and wait. I'll tell him you're here."

In the back room Amy looked at the green felt-covered tables topped with a shaded lamp. Biting her lips nervously, she paced the room. Too many things could go wrong. Lucas could be gone. Crystal could find her. Father Dyer could choose to do his preaching in a saloon today.

Amy went to one of the tables and gingerly sat down. As she considered Daniel, she found herself praying, "Dear God, please help me get this settled with Lucas before Daniel finds out about that piano. He will be hurt terribly with that piano on top of the other. Please—"

She faced her commitment and bit her fingernails. Studying her fingers, she murmured, "It's something like this, isn't it? Jesus Christ, I promised to let you be Lord of my life, and I've been running too fast for you to catch up." She folded her arms and waited. The peace was there, but it didn't seem to reach all the way through. "Just like always, huh? I keep forgetting, and then I start off running as fast as I can." She caught her breath. "Please, rescue me again. Next time, I promise, I'll think and pray before I start running."

There was a quick step behind Amy, and she turned. "Crystal!"

Her arms were folded like a scolding schoolteacher. She was still panting. She said, "There's not too many places to check this time of morning. Did you get over your choking spell?"

"I honestly did choke," Amy stated, resisting the urge to cross her heart.

Crystal dropped into the chair opposite Amy. "Going to find him and spill it all before I got here? Have you any idea what it might net you?"

The expression in Crystal's eyes stopped Amy. She wasn't angry, she was afraid. "Crystal, I am not making myself clear. There's only one thing I want of Lucas, and that's for him to get that terrible piano out of the church before Daniel sees it."

"Do you expect me to believe that? Why would your husband object to Lucas giving the church a piano?"

Amy couldn't answer. The dark expression was still in Crystal's eyes when Amy got to her feet. Crystal said, "Where are you going now?"

"Where will you let me go?"

Slowly Crystal dropped her head. Amy watched as she wrung her hands together. When she looked up at Amy, she said, "If you'll come back to the hotel with me, I'll talk. Amy, I'm begging now. Please, my life as well as yours depends upon our walking out of here like the best of friends—and having that talk immediately."

CHAPTER 30

When they reached the hotel room, Crystal placed the key on the washstand. "Amy," she said, "I'm sorry for treating you this way. I promise you that what happens after we have our talk is up to you. I won't pressure you to stay."

Crystal turned away from Amy and began to pace the floor. Finally she stopped and asked, "How much did Amelia tell you about me?"

Amy tried to hide her surprise. "Nothing—she's never mentioned you to me. Why?"

"I was wondering how much I must tell you now." She paced, then turned with an apology in her smile. "Didn't want to bore you with my problems."

"I'm confused," Amy admitted. "I keep coming back to what I see, and that's you and Lucas together. I can't help thinking you two make a very handsome couple."

Crystal wheeled around and crossed the room to Amy. Bending close, she hissed, "I detest that man! Were it not for—" She gulped and steadied her voice. "Amy, I don't know how God puts up with me. I try, but at times even I wonder what motivates me. Is it possible to think we are acting out of charity, when in reality our actions are goaded by the ugliest selfishness possible?"

Amy could only shake her head and whisper, "I don't know. Sometimes I wonder that about myself. I see myself as being holy and good; then it's like I turn around quickly and see something ugly. And there I am back on my knees again." For a moment Crystal looked at her with a strange expression. She opened her mouth as if to speak; then with a shrug she continued to walk around the room. Amy asked, "How did you come to know him?"

"Lucas?" Crystal was still for a moment. Curiously she asked, "This time? After I left Buckskin Joe, I tried to find a job in Denver City. There wasn't an opening in any of the rooming houses. Seems no one is making enough money to hire a cook. I tried to get on at the hotel here. They didn't need a cook either. Charley Harrison liked my looks and tried to hire me at the saloon. Wanted me to deal cards for him.

"You know the story. Pretty girl attracts customers. Boss wants girl to pass out favors on the side. I didn't go for that." She moved restlessly and said, "Sometimes having a pretty face is a disadvantage. It makes it twice as hard to convince people that you're moral—especially in the mining camps."

Amy cringed and whispered, "I'm sorry. I judged you falsely. Crystal. I nearly lost my head over the whole thing."

"Why?" There were honest questions in Crystal's expression, and the words nearly flew out of Amy.

"Because I was caught by you. Nearly from the beginning. You were shabby, and I was too. You seemed—abandoned. That was the way I felt. All alone."

"But you had a husband and a father."

Amy shook her head. "I didn't really. I'd left them behind. See, I was fighting God. And I had to do it all on my own. Have you ever felt that way? The hurting and misery is deep enough to make you want to crawl in a hole, away from everyone who doesn't feel the same way. Besides"—she paused to catch her breath—"when I saw you, standing there in the snow beside Lizzie's casket, singing with sunshine on your face, I started to hope again."

"I didn't know," Crystal murmured. With her head low, she walked around the room again. It was a long time before she turned back to Amy with a bright smile.

But to Amy the smile seemed pasted on. Crystal continued. "Well, it turned out all right. At least until Lucas came along. Charley hired me to sit behind the desk at the hotel. I think it was mostly because he could get me cheaper. I saw a lot of interesting things in the months I worked there. The Bummers, Charley's gang, were in and out all the time."

Slowly Amy said, "I heard about them. A bunch of cutthroats, the newspaper called them. Hired thugs. What did Mr. Harrison have to do with them? I thought he was honest."

"So did lots of people," Crystal replied. "But there's a taint hanging over the whole organization—not only the lawlessness of the bunch of men drifting in and out of Charley's presence, but the whisper of secession floating around over it all. Too often I saw Lucas in the crowd. Mind you, not snuggling up to the Bummers—just close to them."

Amy thought about Lucas standing in front of the Palace of the Governors in Santa Fe. She opened her mouth and then firmly closed it. Crystal restlessly paced the room and then stopped to look out the window.

She turned unexpectedly. "You heard Lucas here that first night. He may come again. If he does, keep quiet. I'll slip out. But I'll have to lock the door. He'd be suspicious if I were to fail to do so."

Amy nodded, aware of the anxious shadows in Crystal's eyes. "You still haven't explained why you are afraid of him," Amy stated.

"Afraid." She looked startled and then thoughtful. "I suppose I am." She looked at Amy. "Lucas is a strange man. I've watched him gamble. It's like he suddenly becomes a cold, cunning machine. You can feel a difference; even his muscles seem turned to metal. Amy, I get the feeling that there's nothing that will stop him from going after what he wants."

"What does he want?"

Crystal's forehead creased into a frown. "I'm not absolutely certain. It could be power. I thought so once. For a long time I thought he was moved by an ideal. A high and nearly sacred one. Now, these past years seem to have shaped him differently. The lofty emotion I thought was idealism now seems like cynicism. It's as if deep down inside he cares nothing about anyone."

She sat down beside Amy on the bed. Amy found herself admiring Crystal's long frame and the fragile hands as she clasped them together. Crystal went on. "He wants to seize everything attractive. But at the same time, there must be an advantage in it for him. It must work for him. At one point I was dreadfully afraid of him. But when I repulsed his advances, I made the most astonishing discovery."

Amy bent forward. "What was it?"

"He listened to me. I convinced him that not even the most casual of feelings must interfere with his goal. It was as if I managed to dangle a golden carrot just beyond his most primitive human instincts and he no longer wanted me.

"The discovery? I was only a means to an end. If you please, an envelope to carry his messages—nothing more."

As Crystal's words continued to pour over Amy, the woman began to change before her eyes. She must say it. "Crystal, when I first met you, I saw a bundle of rags. A shivering, frightened human. Now you've grown up in my eyes. You are an actress. The longer we talk, the more I see, even believe. You make me think your thoughts after you." Even as Amy said the words, she saw the bitter smile.

"And you're wondering if I'm spreading the talk to win you to my side. Yes and no. I don't ask you to believe me; just listen and make up your own mind. I don't like using people. Either their minds or their bodies." She paused, then whispered, "See, I've enough Negro blood in me to want freedom more than anything else. And not just for me, for everyone. That's why I feel so sorry for locking you in this room."

"Crystal, you still haven't told me."

"Freedom. I'm caught up in the passion to buy freedom for every man. My money is my tongue and my hands. Nothing will stop me."

"What does that have to do with Lucas Tristram?"

"Until Lucas and every man like him is stopped, we won't know freedom from slavery. One by one they must be exposed. See, Amy, all of this is related to man's greed. You can't have greed and freedom. They fight each other. I believe the Bible—it teaches us to love one another. That's the only way to freedom."

Amy frowned. "You talk as if Lucas has done something to you."

Crystal hesitated before speaking. "He has. But for the present, let's concentrate on what is happening right now."

"We saw Lucas Tristram in Santa Fe, New Mexico," Amy said slowly, thinking aloud. "With that Confederate flag snapping in the air over his head. He looked like I've never seen him look before. Like King Midas with his hands full of gold."

Crystal nodded. "That's so. I believe in causes, but not in using causes for financial gain. Amy, I left the South at the time the rallying for freedom began. You see, it was the rich landowners who were shouting most loudly." Twisting her hands, she added, "But the word freedom made me hungry. And I saw that hunger in countless other eyes. I had to leave to find out what freedom really means."

"I'm beginning to understand," Amy voiced. "Freedom means we can't live that way—being a slave or owning slaves." She looked at Crystal. "But you still haven't said what he did."

Her expression was veiled. "I'll get there. Long ago Jefferson Davis scouted out these gold-rich areas. He decided the Confederate cause would best be served by having this gold in their coffers. Tristram has been in the territory since that first summer after gold was discovered. Does that tell you anything?" She paused as Amy gave her a puzzled look.

"He has been busy mapping out all the heavy gold-producing areas. Now he knows where the gold is, and in addition, he's trying to get this gold committed to the Confederate cause. See, the cause wasn't born overnight. Freedom was the handwriting on the wall. It was absolutely necessary the war happen."

"Absolutely necessary? Crystal, the battle in New Mexico took care of their problem. Don't you know that General Canby chased the Confederates right back into Texas?"

"But the war isn't over. It won't be over until the final shot is fired. Meanwhile, Lucas won't give up his position. He'll go on winning the confidence of men. My job is to be courier for Mr. Lucas Tristram. See, I'm Southern. You might say I've had my arm twisted behind me, but in reality it is something different. Anyway, I look as if I belong to the slave class. But I don't—in fact, my family owns property and slaves in New Orleans. The white Southerners look down on us because of our mixed blood, but we have money and power. That is respected."

She added, "Tristram's job? He gathers the reports and the information and I deliver it all to a key person here in Colorado Territory. Amy, Lucas is a spy and I am his stooge. He is here to garner everything he can that will harm the Union, whether it is gold or information."

Slowly Amy said, "Spies are shot during wartime, aren't they?" Crystal nodded, and Amy continued. "You were afraid I would say something about you, about your past. But I still can't imagine what I could possibly know that would harm you."

Crystal was standing beside the windows. Amy couldn't see the expression in her eyes, but she was quiet, waiting. Finally Amy asked, "Is it because there is someone important who must not see you as a spy? Someone you care for very much?"

More minutes passed, and then Crystal sighed heavily. "I believe you. I don't think Amelia has told you anything about me. Also, Amy Gerrett, I trust you. Only the dear Lord knows how badly I need someone in whom I can confide. Someone who'll help me muddle though this mess." As she turned to walk across the room, Amy saw the glint of moisture on her cheek.

When she sat down beside Amy, she asked, "Have I made myself clear? I loathe Lucas Tristram. To smile at him, to laugh up at him and to tuck my hand in his arm and chatter in French because it pleases his vanity to be cast as a gentleman of noble character and good breeding—" Abruptly Crystal broke off and snorted.

Amy snickered into her hand, "Oh, Crystal!" she whispered, "you know him so well!" A sharp object rapped against the heavy door. Crystal clutched Amy's arm. They waited.

There was a low, urgent voice. "Crystal, open up."

They stared at each other. Amy scrambled to her feet; she needn't be told it was Lucas. Across the room the large, dark mahogany armoire stood open. She threw a questioning glance at Crystal and slipped into the armoire.

"Just a moment," Crystal called softly as she closed the doors behind Amy.

Amy heard Crystal's step, the scrape of the key, the creak of hinges.

Carefully she dabbed at the perspiration on her forehead. *What am I doing in here? I want to see Lucas—I have to discuss the piano with him.*

She reached for the door, but at the same instant she remembered the expression on Crystal's face. Crystal was afraid. Amy shuddered and strained to hear.

Lucas was speaking. "I've a message for you to pass on. This time the stage will be stopped halfway up the canyon. You'll recognize your contact by the turquoise amulet on his hat. Make certain the message is in with the gold."

"Lucas, why must you go to such lengths to pass along the message?" Crystal's voice was loud.

"Keep your voice down," Lucas remonstrated. "I have a feeling there's someone watching me. Funny thing, I ran into a fellow in New Mexico. Twice. It seemed a casual contact. My guess is they're using preachers as spies. Good cover, isn't it?"

Crystal's reply was inaudible. Lucas continued with a chuckle. "I've just given the fellow a new piano for his church. If they haul me in, he may have a difficult time explaining the piano."

Crystal asked, "Isn't this all a lost cause? It's been in the papers that the Confederate Army has been pushed back to Texas."

"My dear, as long as we're winning the war in the East and South, it behooves us to keep a strong hand in here." He paused and then added, "I'll admit the chances of taking Colorado Territory aren't good. The Pikes Peakers made a name for themselves in New Mexico. But there are other strategies under consideration."

"That takes good imagination." Her voice was mocking. "I can't guess."

Lucas was quiet for a moment. "New Mexico set us back, but

we're not out of the game yet." Then he added, "It's gold. Gold by the bagful, if nothing else. While we're waiting for another push against the gold fields, we'll continue to win support for our cause and at the same time drain away as much gold as possible. We need it desperately if the Confederacy is to survive."

"You mean you'll pack the ore out of here?"

"Not ore. With a few good contacts, we'll know when the pure stuff is being shipped."

"And they'll never know how much you take?"

There was a pause and Lucas's heavy voice questioned, "You think you're not getting your share?" After another pause he said, "Don't become an expendable commodity, Crystal. You are only valuable as long as you cooperate with the cause. If for one moment I thought your sympathies weren't totally for the Confederacy—"

"And why do you think that they are?"

"Because you made a bad mistake a long time ago, and I know you'll spend the rest of your life trying to win back the favor of your husband."

"You act as if you know where he is." There was a long pause. Crystal's voice was low as she said, "You deliberately compromised me. You carefully planned the scene so that my husband would believe I was unfaithful. Is it possible you had planted additional thoughts before you staged the scene?"

Lucas's low laugh was followed by the teasing words. "Perhaps. And perhaps he only wanted an excuse to follow his conscience instead of his heart."

Crystal's voice was cold. "At least you've used the word *heart*. I can nearly forgive you for implying he was wanting out. That he was a—"

Her voice choked off the words. Lucas's voice made Amy shiver as he finished the sentence. "Nigger lover? Crystal, that makes me wonder what else you have on your mind. Unfortunately, I'll need to address the question at a later time. Meanwhile, here's the bag of gold. Be careful—it's heavy. The message is in the bottom of the bag. I want you on the stage for Central City tomorrow morning."

CHAPTER 31

When the Randolphs rode into Denver City, Eli was sitting on the wagon seat, holding the reins. Matthew sat beside him, listening to Eli as he pointed out the landmarks. "This is the main section of town. That building out in the middle of the creek is the *Rocky Mountain News* building. The little town of Auraria is on one side of the creek, and Denver City is on the other. See over there, that's the famous Criterion Saloon. But then, maybe you haven't heard about Charley Harrison. Gave up on gold mining and has taken to strong-arming his way around town while he runs the saloon.

"The Methodist Episcopal Church is off yonder, down Cherry Creek and through those trees. Conference will be coming up. We might as well stay around for it."

He slanted a glance toward Matthew and added, "You've made it clear you want to go God's way. Might be that the best way to cement the agreement is to hang around conference for a time."

From her seat on the pile of blankets and quilts behind Eli, Amelia watched Matthew. She noticed that he looked uncomfortable with the suggestion. *Was all his talk of going God's way a sham?* The uneasiness was beginning to grow in Amelia when Matthew glanced at Eli. "Sir, begging your pardon, but do you want to stay?"

Amelia caught the question and she held her breath. This would be the final answer to all the long conversations she and Eli had carried on night after night.

He hesitated, then finally answered, "I think I do. I'm still sorting it all out in my mind, but I need to have a talk with the bishop from the Nebraska-Kansas conference." Amelia caught her breath. Without turning, Eli stated, "Now, Wife, I haven't made any decision."

Matthew was grinning over his shoulder at her. Amelia smiled back as she said, "I'm not pushing, Eli."

They turned down the main street of Denver City. Matthew studied the log buildings as they passed down the street. The wind blew dust into their faces, and Amelia smiled at the hint of distaste on Matthew's face.

"We're not too neat around here yet," she stated. "There's a sawmill getting started up, so in another year we should see a good share of planed lumber buildings. Meanwhile, the old cottonwood buildings will have to do."

Matthew looked at her curiously. "You don't sound as if you object to this cow town."

"I don't," she said softly. "I rather like the feeling of a new beginning, whether for people or for towns. You know, Matthew, I've come to one conclusion. Colorado Territory seems to be the land of new beginnings. You get to talking to your neighbors and you find they're fleeing something. It's either bad work situations back East or they're looking for the elephant."

He turned to look at her. "I gather you aren't referring to the structure they call the Elephant Corral?"

"Not hardly. It's a catch phrase. I guess it can best be described by calling it an elusive dream." She was silent a moment before adding, "Some neighbors are just the restless type. They're looking for something new. I don't expect them to stay here long."

"So you think I might try gold mining?"

"Only if you're looking for a diversion. There's a pack of men around. I'd suggest you head for the high country. You might have a few dollars before the snow falls. Then again, you could come out of the hills a millionaire."

Matthew asked, "That's a pretty big business establishment over there, what is it?"

"That's the Elephant Corral."

"Well, it sure isn't elusive. Can't hardly miss the place!"

Eli pointed. "Over yonder are all of Charley Harrison's businesses. I mentioned the Criterion Saloon. There are two hotels in addition and at least one more saloon—see, over there next to the general store. I understand the big saloon has gaming rooms upstairs, and who knows what else. All this was built up after we went to Central City, so I haven't kept up with things. Back in the beginning, us fellas from the church did our preaching in the saloons on a regular basis. Guess they won't cotton to it anymore, now we have a church built."

"Eli." They both turned at her strange cry. Amelia pointed toward the saloon. "Isn't that Amy going into the saloon all by herself?"

Eli leaned forward to peer toward the saloon. "Sure looks like her, but I can't imagine my daughter entering such a place, particularly alone. Besides, Amelia, we saw her head off with Father Dyer. She ought to be home with her husband right now."

"Unless he's come to meeting," Amelia commented. Slowly she added, "I can't imagine what she would be doing in a place like that."

"Might be Father Dyer's having services and she's going in to play the organ."

"In a saloon? Eli, I think we should go after her."

He nodded. "But you'll have to wait until I get this rig around to the livery stable."

"Just let me off, I'll go by myself."

"No—it isn't a fit place for a lady to be seen." Amelia blinked at Eli's back.

Matthew turned to grin at her. "Now, Mrs. Randolph, a pastor's wife—"

Eli's shoulders twitched. "Sorry, dear."

"Eli, that's the nicest compliment you've paid me. Certainly I'll wait. Couldn't be Amy, but if it is, we'll find her."

Eli flicked the reins to hurry the team along. At the livery stable they left the team and wagon and started down the street together, walking slowly for Eli's sake. He was using one crutch and Amelia linked her arm through his as he limped along.

Matthew walked in front of them. When he stopped in the middle of the street, Amelia sidestepped him and lifted her head at the incredulous question, "Is that you, Daniel?"

"Daniel!" Amelia scooted around Matthew, exclaiming. "You've grown a beard! How nice."

Eli smiled. "Good to see you, son. It was a big relief to get news of you through Father Dyer." He clasped Daniel's hand and then added, "We think we've seen Amy just ahead of us, and we're following her. I suppose you know why she's gone into the saloon alone."

"Amy, in the saloon? I've been looking for her ever since I got here. Two days it's been since I rode into town. Had to return the Army's horse, and now I've walked my feet off looking for Amy." He shook his head. "Not Amy, that's not like Amy to be going into a saloon all by herself."

Amy heard Crystal close the door after Lucas. The key turned in the lock, but the minutes stretched as Amy listened, and waited. There was only silence from the room. Cautiously Amy tapped at the door of the armoire.

Crystal opened the door and stepped back, and Amy sighed with relief as she stepped out. "Forever, it felt like," she whispered. The room was filled with late-afternoon shadows. As Amy smoothed her tousled hair, she watched Crystal cross the room to light the lamp on the table. "I suppose you heard it all," she remarked as she touched the match to the wick.

"Yes," Amy said quietly. "Crystal, what are you going to do?"

"First I need to get a message out, and then I'll do just as Lucas has instructed."

Amy caught her breath. "With the stagecoach being held up? You can't; it's dangerous."

"Amy, it won't be the first time. This is an old plan. You heard those men on the stagecoach talking about secessionists holding up the stage? Well, I've been held up several times. Each time I'm relieved of my bag of gold and a message."

"Who gets the message?"

"I have no idea, but I do think it's some key figure in Colorado Territory. Someone so well known that even Lucas isn't allowed to know his name." She paused and then added, "Makes you think all this is very important to someone."

Amy nodded and asked, "Have you read the message?"

"No. It's sealed and I wouldn't dare break the seal."

"You said you have a message for someone."

Crystal nodded. "A contact close to the new governor. It is someone who needs to know every time Lucas sends gold and one of these messages." She added, "By the way, the new governor, John Evans, is a former abolitionist, as well as a member of the Methodist Episcopal Church. Does that tell you something?"

Amy studied her for a moment before saying, "It says something about Lucas, and it also makes what you are doing seem very important." She looked at Crystal, feeling a new respect as she added, "How are you going to deliver a message?" Crystal looked steadily at Amy and didn't answer.

"I—I'm sorry. I didn't mean to pry; it's just that I am worried."

"Don't fret." Unexpectedly Crystal hugged Amy. "It's nice to have someone here. "Do stay on while I'm gone."

"How long will that be?"

"Just long enough for us to be robbed. The driver always heads back to Denver City."

"Is there—do they shoot?"

Reluctantly Crystal admitted, "Yes, sometimes. Mostly it's the stage driver. The secessionists have a reputation for being perfect gentlemen. Quite a reputation," she added with a touch of irony in her voice.

After mulling over Crystal's statement, Amy remarked, "I'm surprised they haven't caught them, or killed someone."

"There's not enough men left to fight our own private war. I suppose you read the *Rocky Mountain News*, and know that the new army's first job was to clean out the Bummers.

"Since the Army's headed south, we've had to take care of ourselves." She glanced at Amy. "This business with the stagecoach is getting to be a gentleman's game. We hand over the money, the gold and jewels; they tip their hats and off they go. I get the feeling the law is looking the other direction since they can't do anything about it." She paused then added, "Or won't until someone is killed."

For a long time, Amy studied Crystal and thought about the situation. She noticed the lamplight emphasized the planes of Crystal's face and heightened the sad droop of her lips. Finally Amy asked, "How much longer are you going to do this? You could be killed."

"I—I guess I don't have much to live for." There was a catch in Crystal's voice. Immediately she apologized, "Sorry, at this stage of the game, I always get dismal."

"You need something to eat; shall we go down to the dining room?"

Crystal shook her head. "Right now I don't feel like being in public."

"Shall I bring food up here?"

She thought a moment and then sighed. "Would you? I know I need to eat. There won't be much time for food tomorrow. Also, will you drop off this message at the desk?"

Amy nodded as she watched Crystal sit down at the table. Taking out a sheet of blue paper she began to write. Amy asked, "That's the contact?"

Crystal nodded and held it out. Amy took the little scrap of blue paper and picked up her handbag. Crystal warned, "You should take care that no one is watching when you go to the desk. Also, make certain you give it to the old man." The concern in Crystal's eyes made Amy pause.

Finally she nodded and left the room, carefully closing the door behind herself.

In the lobby Amy looked around. There was only the old man behind the desk. The lobby was empty. Amy handed over the message and noticed the man seemed to know what to do with it. She watched him tuck it carefully into the pigeonhole behind the desk before he smiled at her.

Suddenly aware that she was shaking with hunger, Amy crossed the lobby to the dining room. It took her a moment to adjust to the dimly lighted room, and another moment to see the room was nearly empty. She settled into a corner and gave her instructions to the youth who came to take her order.

Amy was beginning to think she had been forgotten when the waiter returned with the carefully wrapped tray of food. He apologized. "Sorry for the delay, ma'am; the cook is in a bad temper. Shall I carry it upstairs for you?"

"Thank you, no. I'll manage fine."

As Amy started to leave the room, she glanced through the doorway and stopped abruptly. Taking a step backward into the dining room she leaned into the shadows and watched the man approach the desk. Without a doubt it was Lucas Tristram.

Amy looked at the loaded tray. What a time for Lucas to return! Just as she decided to sit in the dining room, she saw Lucas was turning away from the desk. He held a slip of blue paper.

While Amy watched he read the paper, thrust it into his pocket, and quickly walked out the front door.

"Ma'am, is everything all right?" It was the youth again. Amy nodded and smiled as she hurried toward the stairs.

Crystal turned quickly as Amy burst into the room. "Crystal—was that message intended for Lucas Tristram?"

The answer was written in the sudden pallor of her face. She bit her lip. "Amy, I've considered this possibility. I even suggested it to—All he would have to do is bluff his way into the clerk's confidence by mentioning me." She paced the room, pounding her fists against each other. When she came back to Amy she said, "I'd no idea! Tell me what happened." She listened as Amy described the scene in front of the desk.

"Crystal, all I know is that the paper was blue."

"And the gentleman behind the desk gave it to him?" She nodded and Crystal sighed and turned away. "Looks as if I've been discovered."

In the morning both Amy and Crystal were heavy-eyed from tossing all night. Amy studied the circles under Crystal's eyes and asked, "What are you going to do?"

"I don't know. The stage leaves at ten o'clock. If I'm not on it,

Amy, he'll know I've betrayed him. If I go, then—"

"Crystal, have you thought, I mean have you considered the implications? Is it possible he will have you killed?"

They looked at each other. Slowly Amy said, "I got an idea. But I will have to know where to contact Lucas."

"During the day, most days when he is in town, he can be found in the gaming rooms on the top floor of that big saloon down the street." She paused, asked, "What are you going to do?"

Amy hesitated. "Well, first we are going to have breakfast downstairs. I understand expectant mothers need to eat regularly."

"You did last night—your own dinner and most of mine."

Amy grinned and took Crystal's arm. "Don't look so sober; everything is going to be just fine. Even better than you can guess. But I think you need to buy more than you can eat."

Crystal studied Amy's face for a minute before the smile began in her eyes. "You are a dear friend. But if it doesn't work, don't feel bad. I—" She shook her head as they left the room.

After breakfast they quickly returned to the room, carrying the bundle of food. Amy asked, "What time is it?"

"Past ten. I think I hear the stage leaving. What are you going to do if Lucas comes charging up the stairs right now?"

Alarmed Amy asked, "Does he come to see you off?" Crystal shook her head. Amy went to the dressing table and picked up her handbag and the large key to the room.

She turned to Crystal. "Have a nice nap. When I visit you later this afternoon, I am going to find you bound and gagged, with your bag missing. Of course, everyone in Denver City will know about it before nightfall. Including Lucas Tristram."

The questions were big in Crystal's eyes, but she only smiled. Amy wagged her fingers as she closed the door and carefully locked it.

In front of the hotel she looked up and down the street. The early morning crowd was mostly housewives and rough-clad miners. There was no white suit among the throng of people. Grinning with satisfaction, Amy started her trip along the street. Now that she had started on her mission, panic began building up inside of her. *Dear Jesus, please help me! I'm afraid; so much could go wrong.*

Walking slowly, Amy stopped at every shop and studied the merchandise. It was nearly noon when she reached the end of the street. She quickened her steps, crossed the street and walked through the door of the saloon.

The man rearranging bottles glanced her direction.

"Please, tell me which room Mr. Tristram is in."

He studied her, then finally said, "Maybe he don't want company."

"Might be he does."

"Go up the stairs, turn right. Second door. Don't know about this, but be quiet. Lucas don't like noise when he's with the cards."

Amy followed his directions. As she walked into the room, Lucas quirked an eyebrow at her and continued to deal cards. "What's your business?"

"I've come to talk about the piano." She reached into her handbag and pulled out the bill of lading. "Lucas, you've directed the piano to me. What do you think my husband is going to say when he sees this?"

"Whoopie?"

"You're insulting. Lucas, Mr. Tristram. You said you wanted to donate a 'gift for the church.' I found that piano in my house when I returned home."

He paused. A grin creased his face. "You did? How did that happen?"

"I don't know. But under the circumstances, I think you'd better take it back, unless you can contact my husband and convince him—" Amy stopped and listened. There was the shuffle of feet and a curious thumping coming from the stairs.

Slowly Lucas got up. "Hey, what's going on?" She studied his tight-lipped face and darkening eyes.

"Why, I don't know," Amy frowned, feeling as puzzled as Lucas looked. "But I can't imagine why you are upset by a little noise like that. Lucas, what is—" She gulped and closed her mouth.

She watched Lucas edge around the table, moving his head, as he glanced uneasily around the room. Was he searching for something?

He seemed to consider the window. Just as he backed away from the table and reached for his jacket, the door burst open.

She stared at the people filling the doorway. Lucas backed quickly to the window. "Wait, hold it!" Amy stared at the man rushing through the door. It was Matthew. "Tristram! What are you doing here? You and I have a score to settle."

A white-faced Tristram glared at Amy. "A trap. Crystal is in this somewhere."

"Crystal! Don't even mention her name." Matthew's voice rose. Amy turned and could only stare at Matthew's livid face. With one big step, his hand lashed out and fastened on Lucas's brocade vest. "What have you been up to? You bought me into bondage. Is that what you are doing with my wife? And don't tell me any of the old lies. I don't believe them now. I've started doing my own thinking."

Amy was conscious of others pushing into the room. She forced her fascinated gaze away from the two men and turned. But she needed to blink before she really saw the three. "Daniel!" She dashed to him.

For a moment she felt his resistance, and then he was kissing her. In his arms she patted his beard and pressed her hand to his face. "Oh, Amy," he groaned. "What now?"

"Watch out!"

Tristram plunged through the group with Matthew limping after him, grasping for that white coattail. Daniel dropped Amy and fled after them.

Amy staggered against the wall. She heard a shout, followed by the thud of feet on the stairs and then there was silence. Amy ran to the window, only to find it opened on an empty side street. Bewildered, she turned and looked at her parents. "Gone! Again my Daniel is gone, just like last time, when he went running after Matthew."

She sighed heavily and slumped against her mother and father as they encircled her with outstretched arms.

CHAPTER 32

Amy was panting by the time she reached the hotel. She took a moment to arrange a smile on her face before she crossed the lobby to the stairs. *One, two, up the stairs, around the landing, there, they can't see me.* She took the rest of the stairs and dashed down the hall. With a quick dab at the perspiration on her face she fumbled for the key with a trembling hand. She shoved in the key, twisted and pushed.

Crystal pulled the door open and caught Amy as she burst into the room. "What happened?"

"Nothing." Amy gulped and tried to steady her wavering voice. "Someone came and they—ran. Crystal, who is Matthew?" Slowly Crystal pressed her hands to her face. Amy took her wrist and said, "I think you had better tell me all about it. Crystal, it is important, because I don't know what to say until you do."

Slowly Crystal sat down. Amy bit her lip to keep silent as she waited. Crystal was watching Amy's face as she whispered, "Don't hide it from me. Just one thing. I must know—is he dead?"

"No, he's very much alive. Now, it's your turn."

"Matthew is my husband. Amy, the story is confusing, but you must believe one thing. I love him with all my heart."

"I believe you."

"I was involved in the Underground Railroad; do you know what that is?"

"I've heard Mother mention it, that's all."

Crystal paced the room, twisting her hands together as she talked. "You'll never understand unless I go back to the beginning of all this mess. See it started before Matthew and I were born; the problem was slavery.

"After Nat Turner's time, back in the thirties, the slaves and those who wanted to see them free knew there was only one way this could be accomplished. It was by escape, running away from slavery. Escape into freedom, Canada.

"All these years there's been a movement to filter the slaves out of the South, but it has been growing in intensity since the talk of war started." She stopped and looked at Amy, searching her face.

Amy shook her head, saying, "Crystal, you're rambling. What are you trying to say? What does this have to do with Matthew?"

Crystal ducked her head and paced the floor. When she finally faced Amy, she said, "I've only told a half truth about myself. I am Creole, but in addition, I am illegitimate. My grandparents adopted me after I was born to their daughter and a man who was of both Negro and white blood, a mulatto.

"I've never met my mother; I understand she has married well and is happy. But I feel a tie to the slaves. It's blood deep." She went to the window and looked out.

When she turned she asked, "Have you heard of Harriet Tubman?" Amy nodded and Crystal added, "In the South she's nearly venerated among the slaves. I've heard of her for years, and her story caught fire in me—even before I knew about my father. I can't tell you the details, but I was thrown in such a position that not only could I help these people, but it was imperative I do so." She glanced at Amy. "In Pennsylvania I finally became well acquainted with your mother and became involved with her in the movement."

She went back to her pacing. Amy could see the strain building on her face. When she stopped to wipe the tears from her eyes, she said, "I'm sorry. But this is bringing back things that are very difficult for me to talk about. Amy, will you forgive me if all this seems incomplete?

"Matthew? He was part of the movement, too. But I don't think he was ever a true believer. His sister and a friend were deeply involved, and Matthew was just caught up in the tide of it all. That was unfortunate, because misery is doing something your heart doesn't really own.

"At that point in Matthew's life, I think the only valid part was the love we had for each other."

She faced Amy. Her voice was without emotion as she lifted her chin and said, "Matthew left me. This I'll say for him, even as angry as he was, I know it was a difficult decision for Matthew to make. I can't blame him. It was my fault. There was a moral issue involved. A lie he couldn't forgive.

"See, I allowed him to know part of the details of my life. He knew the family name of my adopted parents, and he knew of their prestige in the South. That was important to him. What he didn't know was about my father's bloodline. I dared not tell him."

Amy watched her compress her lips before she added, "It caused us both a great deal of heartache; Matthew is a proud man. In addition, our marriage created a problem impossible to resolve."

"What is it?" Amy asked slowly.

"Matthew's family was old South. The family had been slaveholders and plantation owners since the 1700s. Their position was important to them. Pure blood.

"Matthew really sympathized with the slaves. In the beginning he helped them escape because he was their friend. Later he was torn by their yearning for freedom. But complicating all this was the pull of his family ties.

"In the end the South won my husband away from me. To be honest, I can't blame him. I was living a lie." She stopped for a moment, and Amy could see her struggle to hold back tears as she added, "Perhaps if I had been brave enough to tell him, and to trust the God I claimed to serve, then things might have been different. I like to think that, anyway. Amy, I still love Matthew very much. Until just recently

I dared hope that someday he would come looking for me."

In a moment she continued. "As the only son, he was to inherit the land. And he knew it was impossible to run a cotton plantation without slave labor. In the South it would be impossible to uphold the family traditions if slavery were abolished.

"Early in our marriage I began to realize this was a problem. But we were foolish and young. He ignored my dark skin and I forgot everything except loving him." Crystal was silent as she slowly walked back and forth across the room.

At last she lifted her face and said, "Amy, I believe, if it hadn't been for the threat of war—" She stopped and continued slowly, "It is possible, if he'd had enough time, if we could have talked without so much hurt and anger between us, he might have stayed with me."

"I'm guessing there was pressure. Was his problem the plantation?" Amy asked.

"Partly. But also politics, and position in the community. It is not easy to be a Southerner and be different. The pressure was money. The South desperately needed his wealth."

She was quiet. A gentle smile touched her lips as she added, "But this I will say for him, there was a love in his life stronger than these loves of family and home—me. At least for a time."

Abruptly she turned. Amy watched the warm, gentle expression harden and turn cold. Her words were sharp as she added, "I like to think that in the end I would have won out if it hadn't been for the war and Lucas Tristram."

"What did Lucas have to do with it all?"

Amy watched bitterness twist the beauty out of Crystal's face. Her angry pacing underlined the ugly passion in her expression.

Finally she stopped. "Lucas? You know he's trained as a lawyer. So is Matthew. They were in school together. See, there was another strong tie pulling them together. Money. Matthew's money. The Confederate states desperately need it, and I'll believe until I die that Lucas was drafted to get that money."

When Crystal spoke again, she said, "Back in Buckskin Joe I really misled you, and deliberately. I had just left Pennsylvania. True, I had worked as a cook just before coming to Buckskin Joe, but the rest—" She shrugged. "I couldn't bear talking about my past. Matthew had just left me to return home, alone of course." She took a deep breath. Her voice was bitter. "The truth had come out and—Amy, I can't talk any more about us."

Amy crossed the room and wrapped her arms around the woman as the words burst out of Crystal, "Lucas wouldn't have succeeded in his mission without a lie. I was trapped in a compromising situation set up by Lucas. It appeared I had been caught in adultery. That was the final blow to our marriage."

Pushing away Amy's arms, Crystal got up to walk around the room before saying, "Matthew has always been an arrogant, proud man with a terrible temper. He left angry, and Tristram was right there to escort him through every decision he made.

"At the time, I knew he would join the Confederate cause, and I never expected to see him again. It was the end of our life together. I had to accept it and go on with living. That's all." Crystal's face dropped in her hands as she added, "But how could I convince my heart to accept it?"

Amy went to sit on the edge of the bed. The despair wrapping Crystal was spilling over on Amy. As she trembled and blinked tears out of her eyes, she recalled her conversation with Matthew. The regret Matthew had expressed, and the darkness in his eyes as he talked about his wife, seemed like genuine remorse.

Amy looked at Crystal and shook her head, saying, "With those kinds of circumstances, I can't imagine you wanting to know anything about Matthew now. To me he sounds like a perfect scoundrel."

Her head came up. "But he wasn't! Matthew was confused and torn. It isn't easy to deny everything in your past. I heard Lucas talk. He goaded Matthew with everything that could possibly give him a guilty conscience. That included the strong belief supported by the southern churches. I was there; I heard it taught from the pulpit that God sanctioned slavery." Crystal jumped to her feet and paced the room.

Her anger was evident when she stopped and whirled around. "If all that Lucas said to Matthew was born out of his own deep personal convictions, I believe I could accept the man. But, Amy, he is a sneak and a liar. Lucas Tristram embraced this war wholeheartedly for one reason. That was the opportunity it offered him to become rich by sinking his boot heel in the faces of the men whose lives were being torn apart.

"Amy, I have no idea how much damage the smooth tongue of Lucas Tristram has caused, but I can guess. I live now to make certain Lucas is exposed and prosecuted.

"Pardon me for sounding patriotic, but I see it this way. A good and honest cause is hard enough to die for. A cause warped by a smooth tongue and personal greed makes every death a national outrage."

As Crystal spoke, a jumble of sounds caught Amy's attention. Shouting rose from the street and grew louder. She cocked her head to listen to the clatter and bang of metal. When they heard the snorting and neighing of horses, Crystal jumped to her feet and they both ran to the window.

Pulling back the heavy draperies, Crystal cried, "Look! It's a fire! Something big—see the way the flames are shooting up? There, I saw fire bursting out windows!"

"Crystal," Amy whispered, "that's in the section down Cherry Creek, by the saloon where I was."

Crystal turned her horrified face to Amy. "Oh, Amy, let's go!"

Outside, they found the street filled with women and children running toward the fire. Men on horseback plunged past. "They are going to fight the fires!" came the cry from the woman running beside Crystal and Amy.

Behind Amy came the panting reply, "If they don't get it stopped, the whole town'll go up in flames." Amy quickened her steps, not daring to breathe out the thought. *Where were Daniel, Matthew and Lucas?*

They were within a block of the fire when the wall of men surged against them. "Go back!" they shouted. "The fire is spreading and we need room for fighters and a bucket brigade. Go home."

Pressed against the store windows, the women watched and retreated a step at a time. Amy met the questions in Crystal's eyes and replied, "They must be fighting the fire."

"They?" Amy shook her head; it was impossible to say the names.

"Is it—" Crystal turned troubled eyes toward Amy. She didn't finish the sentence, but the names were in their thoughts. Joining the women standing on the street, they waited in silence. Before their eyes the fire consumed the saloon and the buildings on each side.

As the fingers of fire reached out the top-story windows and threaded up the roofline, Amy's aching heart recalled, *Just an hour ago Daniel and Matthew were in that building with Lucas.*

With their arms linked, Amy and Crystal stood surrounded by chattering women and children. It was dark when the rafters broke and the roof collapsed in a shower of sparks. The murmur of awe rising from the crowd made shivers run up Amy's back.

Crystal's face was very sober. With a sigh she turned, "Amy, let's go back to the hotel; there's nothing we can do here. In your condition you need to rest."

As she watched the sparks fly from another shower of timbers, Amy murmured, "My mother and father were there. I didn't tell them where I was going when I left them."

Crystal turned to snatch at a passing sleeve. "What about the livery stable?"

The man answered, "The horses and wagons were taken out hours ago. If you're looking for your animals—" He shrugged as Crystal turned away. "Lady," he called after her, "if you need a place to stay, the Methodist Episcopal Church is open."

Crystal shook her head and he went on down the street. "Amy, I think we'd better go back to the hotel, just in case there's a message for us."

"Watch out!" At the shout, Lucas and Matthew ran past Daniel. For a moment, Daniel was caught off guard. Then he tore after Matthew, leaping up the stairs. Ahead of him Daniel could see Matthew lurching and crashing against the wall in the narrow stairway as he tried to keep up with Lucas. When Daniel caught up with Matt, the two of them jumped down the backstairs together, trying to catch the sprinting figure in white.

Out in the open street Daniel took the lead. He could hear Matthew panting behind him as he tore around the corner of the dry goods store. The two of them nearly collided with a woman carrying a parasol. "Stop, thief!" she cried, pointing to the stairs leading to the top floor of the store.

Daniel saw a white trouser leg disappearing up the stairs at the end of the building. With a lunge he reached the stairs and sprinted after the retreating figure. Halfway to the second floor, a heavy object flew past Daniel's head and crashed against the railing. He ducked and pressed against the wall just as a chair tumbled toward him.

"Matt, get back! Find help!" Daniel yelled as he started up the stairs again. He reached the landing at the top just as the door in front of him slammed shut. He threw his shoulder against it and pushed, but it was wedged closed.

Just as he braced himself to charge again, there was a crash, followed by the tinkle of glass. Backing against the railing, he looked toward the window. From below came a cry, "Fire! There's fire—get down!"

As Daniel hesitated, the shouts became desperate: "Get down, fire!"

He was halfway down the stairs when he heard the explosion. The concussion threw him to his knees. Grabbing the railing, he scrambled to his feet and finished the stairs in a leap.

On the ground he backed into the circle of faces. "Is there another stairway? I saw a man go up there." There were nods and a finger pointed toward the store front.

Daniel ran, but just as he reached the door, it was flung open and a man wearing a white apron flew past him. "Fire! There's fire in the storeroom. Gunpowder." He disappeared around the corner.

Matthew came limping toward Daniel, his face ashen. "Daniel, let's get out of here. The fellow says there's gunpowder up in that storeroom."

"Lucas?" There was another explosion. Matthew shoved at Daniel. With the hot air burning their lungs, they ran. By the time they stopped under the trees by the creek, the street was full of rearing horses and the clatter of wagons loaded with buckets.

"You fellas, give us a hand." Daniel stopped and a bucket of water was thrust into his hands.

It was dark when the last bucket had been emptied trying to save the nearby building. Daniel looked at Matthew and said, "For a wounded Reb, you did enough work to get your face well smoked. How's the arm?"

"I think I'll feel it in the morning. Right now, it's just numb."

At that moment the shout came. "The roof is going!" Running across the street, they watched the crash of timbers and the shower of sparks flaring against the darkening sky.

While they stared at each other, Matthew asked the question, "Do you suppose he was still up there?"

"I don't know. I felt bad about not getting in, but I have an idea he shoved something against the door and took out of there through the front door."

"How did the fire start?"

Daniel shook his head. "I heard glass breaking. That's all I can tell you."

They started down the street together. Amelia and Eli came out of the shadows. "Amy is not with you?" Daniel asked.

Amelia stepped close to them and looked from one to the other. "She ran out practically on your heels. It sounded as if she said something about going to Crystal's hotel room. I have no idea where that is."

"Crystal!" At the exclamation Daniel turned to Matthew. He watched the disbelief change to a wary hope on Matthew's grimy face as he asked, "Crystal is here? I can't believe it."

But hope fled as quickly as it came. Daniel watched a twisting bitterness on Matthew's face change to an expression of defeat.

As Daniel studied him, he saw an echo of the emotions he was feeling inside. *I know how you feel, my friend. Now Amy and I must face this Lucas problem. Oh, God, will it ever go away?*

His voice was heavy as he said, "It's late. Want to find her tonight, Matt, or shall we wait until morning? I'm guessing they're in a hotel down the street," Daniel added.

Matthew turned away. "First thing I want to do is get this smoke cleaned off my hide."

"We've pulled the wagon down Cherry Creek a ways," Amelia said. "You could come down there and take a dip if there's any water left in the creek."

Matthew was already nodding. They followed Amelia and Eli down the street, away from the smoke and the crowd. When they reached the wagon pulled back in the trees, Amelia handed out towels and studied their faces by the light of the candle she held. "Might just be a good idea if you fellows let me fix some food. Need to get some nourishment in you before you tackle any more lions tonight." She looked at Matthew, who tried to grin.

"Fine, Mother," Daniel agreed. "Have some soap?"

When they were submerged nearly to their ears in the creek, Matthew said, "I'm still reeling. Can't believe Crystal is here." He brooded, "Not once did Amelia let on to me that she was in the area."

"I doubt Amelia knew it," Daniel told him. Then he admitted, "But I did. Just before we left for New Mexico Territory, I saw her on a stage going from Oro City to Denver. So I knew she was around somewhere, but I didn't rightly know what to say at the time you told me your wife's name. I figured it was the woman I knew. I was still pondering telling you, but before I could say anything, you took off."

Matthew muttered, "I can't just go charging in on her. We split under some mighty hard circumstances. Daniel, I'd never have left her if things hadn't just fallen apart. I loved her more than family, more'n—"

"If you still feel that way, why don't you just forget everything else and tell her so? From what you said in New Mexico, I take it you've no claim to press with her. That it's all up to her."

Matthew was silent for a moment. "There's another reason to keep away. I have a strong feeling the Lord's going to have me back in the Army. Only it'll be the right one this time."

"Matt, I'm proud of you." Daniel paused and added, "But no matter what, I think you need to see her. You need to tell her the things you've told me." He took a deep breath. "Matt, the thing about love, about marriage, is that sometime we have to forget everything in the past and just get on with living. Even the worst parts."

Daniel sighed and settled back in the water. The words were ringing through his ears, but he didn't want to believe they applied to him as well.

As they dressed and returned to the wagon, Daniel found himself faced with the very words he had spoken to Matt. *I judged her without giving her a chance, didn't I? Also, I hear you, Lord. No matter what she's done, I forgive her. I'm saying it now, Father. I guess it's a seal on my intentions.* The burden lifted one moment before he looked up and saw Eli and Amelia waiting beside the fire.

He stopped in the middle of the path to look at them. He grinned, pleased at what he saw. Their faces reflected a new peace and oneness. He found himself marveling at the changes as he looked from Eli to Amelia. Taking a deep breath, he said, "Matt, I'm thinking it won't be too late when we finish eating. I don't think either one of our women will be upset with a little touch of smoke on our clothes."

Amelia's eyes brightened. She nodded and began ladling up the beans. "It's a good thing I fixed enough beans for an army last night. Just warmed them up with a little bacon."

CHAPTER 33

When the knock came, Amy couldn't move. Across the room, she watched Crystal face the door as she pressed her hand against her throat and waited. At the second knock, she glanced at Amy and moved to the door. Softly she asked, "Who is it?"

"Daniel Gerrett. Is Amy there?" Amy rushed to her side as Crystal unlocked the door and stepped back.

"Oh, Daniel!" Amy flew at him, kissing, stroking his beard, and pressing close. "Ugh, you're all smoky!" She leaned back to look at him, to study his serious eyes. "It's been so long. Oh, your beard, I love it!"

Then she sighed as she collapsed in his arms. "Until we met Father Dyer, I had given up," she whispered. "I didn't think you were still alive."

He blinked and tried to grin as he looked down at her. Stroking her hair back from her face, he asked softly, "How about our taking off for a week, just the two of us. Then I'll tell you all about it."

"Daniel, it's conference time—"

"Wife." While she blotted her tears on his shirt, he looked up, exclaiming, "I forgot! Crystal, Matthew is downstairs and he wants to see you."

Amy caught her breath. Taking Daniel's hand, she turned and together they waited for Crystal's reply. The expressions on her face were changing. There was a brief flicker of joy followed by fear. As Crystal walked restlessly around the room, a touch of elation replaced the fear. But when she turned back, Amy sensed a strange flattening of her spirit. Amy's heart was filled with pity as she watched the last flash of hope disappear.

Finally she nodded, saying slowly, "Yes, I suppose that would be wise."

"You don't look very happy about it," Amy remarked. With a shrug Crystal moved restlessly around the room.

Daniel suggested, "We'll wait downstairs. Then if you wish to talk—"

Panic swept across Crystal's face. "Please, Amy, don't leave me!"

"Do you want Daniel to stay too?" Amy asked. Crystal nodded. She wrung her hands as Daniel left the room. They heard his boots clatter down the stairs.

Troubled by the change she was seeing in Crystal, Amy helplessly watched her agitated pacing around the room. She was still trying to think of something to say when they heard quick steps in the hall.

The men came into the room, first Daniel and then Matthew. Amy looked with consternation as she saw Matthew's drooping shoulders and his expression as hopeless as Crystal's.

Slowly Crystal turned, her face filled with astonishment as she studied the cast-off clothing, still tattered and smeared with smoke stains. Matthew threw them a quick glance before he addressed Crystal. His voice was dismal as he spoke. "I take it you want me to get down on my knees in front of both of them."

"You needn't get down on your knees at all," Crystal retorted crisply. She pointed to the one chair.

But Daniel was saying, "Might not be a bad idea at all. Amy and I can leave."

Simultaneously both cried, "No, don't!" Crystal blushed and dropped her eyes. Matthew looked at her while he shifted uneasily from one foot to the other.

Amy began to study them with interest. Noticing a flicker of hope on Matthew's face, she prayed, *Father, they said they love each other. Please do something before they make another mistake.*

Crystal's back was rigid as she carefully sat down on the bed. Amy hesitated and then went to sit beside her. Daniel leaned against the wall. "Well?"

The couple chorused, "I—"

Crystal stopped. Finally she threw a quick glance at Matthew. "Amy told me you were hurt." He nodded, moved restlessly, and looked at Daniel.

"I'm ready to leave any time Crystal says so," Daniel suggested. Crystal picked at a thread on her skirt.

Matthew said, "I remember that dress."

Caught off guard, she studied him a moment before turning to Daniel. "The fire—what happened?"

While the men stared at each other, Amy said, "It has something to do with Lucas, doesn't it?" She saw the discomfort on their faces before both of them dropped their heads. "Do you suppose he started it?" They glanced at each other and shrugged.

In a moment Amy asked, "But why did he run?"

Matthew shifted uneasily from one foot to the other. She looked at his embarrassed grin. "Well, I guess he got the idea I was pretty hot under the collar."

"The way you lunged at him—" Amy interrupted.

Matthew added, "I don't think he was glad to see me." Crystal looked at Matthew as if she were really seeing him. For a fleeting second, Amy thought she was going to smile.

Crystal turned toward Daniel, saying, "That must have been the proverbial straw. Things have been going badly for him in the territory." She was speaking rapidly, "He had a lot of men angry at him. Good, solid Union men who'd been watching his less than ethical ways with the miners."

Amy saw the new expression of despair move into Matthew's eyes as Crystal talked. Now she blurted out, "Matthew, Crystal's been working to undermine Lucas's attempt to win support for the Confederates. You might as well know, she's—"

Amy stopped and looked from Matthew to Crystal. *She doesn't know he's a Confederate soldier, and he—oh, dear, it looks bad.*

She waited. Crystal looked at Amy with a puzzled expression. She seemed to be pondering Amy's statement. Now there was a gleam in her eyes. Amy gulped and waited.

Slowly Crystal went on. "I understand Lucas has been pushing his fingers into every pie he can find ever since the gold fields opened." Now she looked at Matthew as she added, "Lucas wasn't a Confederate at heart. He was merely an opportunist. He twisted everything to his advantage— situations, people." Amy was mentally applauding Crystal as she continued. "My biggest desire was to see him stopped, and all his shabby tricks exposed."

She took a deep breath and held it for a moment as she looked at Matthew. "I don't have a quarrel with anyone who's honestly following his convictions. It's just that war is horrible, and for a person to be concerned only with feathering his own nest, well—" She stopped and shrugged.

Amy could feel the tension building in the room. She pressed her hands together and waited. Matthew didn't reply. Finally Daniel spoke. "We know Lucas was in the vicinity of the fire when it started."

Matthew glanced at Daniel. "Vicinity—that's a gentle way of putting it. He was throwing chairs and other stuff down the stairs, trying to keep Daniel from coming after him."

Amy pressed her hand against her mouth as Daniel admitted, "Just about the time I got to the door I heard glass breaking. I wonder if it was a lamp. Kerosene could account for the way the fire spread so fast. It's likely he had something to do with it." He took a breath and looked at Amy. "It is also possible he didn't make it out."

"Oh," Amy gasped, "that's terrible! Now I'll never be able—" Daniel's face was a thundercloud, and she whispered, "Daniel, I have something to tell you—now before we go home."

Crystal straightened. "You mean you haven't told him yet?"

"No, I haven't had time. I wanted to take care of it first. Now I'm forced—"

"Amy!" came Crystal's low, horrified voice. "You wouldn't! I thought you wanted a baby."

"No! I'm talking about the piano." She turned to Daniel. His face was stony. As she studied his face, she began thinking back to the trip. *All they had talked about—was he fearful? Could he trust her? Could she trust herself?*

Heavily Daniel said, "What does all this have to do with the piano Lucas Tristram sent?"

She stopped and studied his face. "Piano? Daniel, you know about it. How—?"

"The night I came back from Santa Fe, there was a fellow trailing me, trying to deliver that piano. What I want to know is, what happened to it?"

"You knew about it all along!" Dismay swept through her. She looked at him intently. "Oh, Daniel," she sighed. "I can explain. Please. If only Lucas were here. See, while you were gone I met him."

She stopped. Daniel's face was rigid. "Go on. I still trust you to straighten this mess out."

She was whispering. "He said he wanted to make a gift to the church. I thought he meant money or hymnals or some such. When I came home and saw the piano and the bill of lading, I had it moved to the church so you wouldn't think he had given it to me." She stopped and pressed her fingers to her lips. "And you had already seen it! Oh, my poor darling. What did you think?" She ran to him and threw her arms around him. She could feel him relaxing and then he tilted her chin.

There was a strange expression on his face as he asked, "But there's one thing that doesn't fit in the story. What's all this about a baby?"

"Us, Daniel—we're going to have a baby." He grinned and she saw him blink his eyes. Amy threw a quick look over her shoulder. Matthew and Crystal were in front of the window, standing close together and talking quietly. With a sigh Amy slipped away from Daniel's arms.

"You still don't quite trust me, do you? Daniel, I love you even more than I love this little baby. It's—" She paused and then added slowly, "I feel so at home when we're together, just the way I felt when we were riding all over New Mexico Territory. Just being with you is all the home feeling I need. Do you understand?

"I don't need a house or a place. The only need I have is for your arms. It doesn't matter where we live. As long as you're doing what the Lord wants you to do, I'll be happy."

Daniel sat down on the chair Matthew left vacant. He pulled Amy onto his lap. "Sweetheart, you make me ashamed."

"It's the past. I—oh, Daniel, I deserve every bit of your distrust. But I'm determined to show you I'm different." She glanced at Matthew and Crystal, heard the murmur of their voices. Facing Daniel, she said softly, "Daniel, I need to ask for your forgiveness. It's very ugly—about Lucas."

Daniel placed his hand over her mouth and pulled her close. "Hush, my darling. I've already guessed he was competition. And I've forgiven you."

He snuggled her against his shoulder. Finally Daniel sighed. "There are a couple other questions I have. First, why would Lucas give the church such a costly gift?"

"I've wondered too," she admitted. "The only thing that makes sense is that he was trying to buy our favor. You know, get us so happy with the piano that we'd look the other way." She tipped her head to see his face. "He was trying to get gold for the Confederates."

Daniel pondered and then nodded. "Now," he said, "the other question. What were you doing upstairs in that saloon?"

"Talking to Lucas Tristram."

"I noticed. But—"

"I was trying to give the piano back to him. I was also trying to—"

"Why were you trying to give the piano back to him?"

"Because he put my name on the bill, and I was afraid you would be unhappy. He said such terrible things in Central City."

"About all he wanted to do for you? Amy, my darling." She saw the tears in his eyes and pressed her face against his.

"It's all right," she crooned. "I didn't want anything Lucas could give me. I was so angry. The way he acted that day just made me love you more."

Daniel touched her cheek. "That is all I need to hear. Amy, let's forget the past."

Amy turned when Matthew spoke. His voice was heavy as he said, "I'm getting a picture of Lucas Tristram. Could be a better one than a thousand words. For me it's nigh on to being too late."

From out of the shadows Crystal added, "Sometimes there's no going back and changing the past."

"But sometimes it's possible to just go on," Matthew ventured. "At least if people want that." Shaking his head sadly, he added, "I guess there's too much that's happened."

"For you to trust me again? Or are you referring to the past?"

"No, neither. I can't forget the anger, ugliness, the slur I made against you."

"The one you made because you believed the lie?" She paused, steadied her voice and said, "Are you waiting for me to tell you it was a lie? Matthew, I don't think we have anything left to believe in."

Slowly he spoke as if thinking aloud. "Love? I've heard it doesn't just go away. I'm not certain. Is there a love that forgets the past—the ugliness and the hurts?"

Crystal's voice was low. "I did my share of wrongs. I started our marriage that way because I was afraid you wouldn't want me if you knew the truth. It isn't an easy thing to forgive."

Amy was nearly asleep against Daniel's chest. She heard the rumble of his voice. "It's nearly time for a sermon. Now, you two, sit down on that bed and listen. Speaking from my vast experience of less than a year of marriage, I'm getting the idea marriage isn't just a happily-ever-after story.

"It takes a bit of work. Guess the problem is we don't realize how much it takes until we mess things up a bit." He settled Amy against his shoulder and touched her cheek. "Thank God, problems can be worked out. Both the spiritual and the human. And I believe it's worth all the pain and trouble it takes to smooth out the rough spots."

Daniel paused and then went on. "The pain of the love story between God and man is reflected back at us when we look at the ups and downs of the marriage relationship. Only with God and man, it's always man who's unfaithful to his vows.

"Now one thing I learned not too long after I became a Christian is that you can't always feel God's love. Sometimes you just have to have faith in it and get on with living. I'm beginning to get the idea marriage is like that, too. When you don't feel love, then you act in a loving way.

"All hurts are bad; they leave scars. In the relationship with God as well as with the husband-wife relationship, our actions leave scars. We can recover from a bad marriage, but—"

"You mean go off and leave it?" Matt said. "Is that what you're advising us to do?"

"Is that what you want, or has your pride decided that's the less painful solution? I get the idea that in marriage, sooner or later the honeymoon is over. At that spot, you need to tighten up your suspenders and make up your mind that you *will* love. A marriage will be good if you deliberately make it so."

Amy sat up. "Daniel, do you mean the honeymoon is over for us just because we're going to have a baby? That's a terrible thought! You're still important to me. Why am I—"

"Whoa!" Daniel laughed down at her. "I don't think any dinky little baby is going to ruin the honeymoon feeling. But what I was going to say is that I have a feeling this is the situation Mother and Father are finding themselves in.

"Marriage doesn't work unless you want it to. With Mother and Father it seems to be working out just fine. It might be because they decided marriage is more important than any one personal feeling they have about the past."

"When you get your back up against the wall?" Matthew mused.

"What do you mean?" Daniel asked slowly. "Back against the wall? I don't understand."

Matthew shrugged. "It was something Amelia said. Talked about the smallpox forcing her to make up her mind about how she was living. Could you say God might love people so much He pushes love at them until they realize their back's against the wall? Then there's no place to go. You either cooperate with God, or—"

In a moment he looked at Daniel and grinned. "But Amelia said that getting her back against the wall was the best thing that ever happened to her. That God did for her what she wasn't able to do for herself."

Daniel rambled on contentedly. "There's a great deal to be said for letting God smooth out the rough spots of a man's nature. Make's getting along a sight easier."

Amy sat up and faced Matthew. "Father Dyer calls it Experimental Christianity."

Matthew nodded. "He told me about it. Said man can't fight the devil and old sinful nature all on his own. He said God was there with the provision to do and the love to go with it. He also said that God has a plan for our lives, and it's necessary for us to live as God intends we should. Took me a while to get that through my head." He looked at Amy. "Your father helped, too. But he had to get me down on my knees, pounding me on the back, before I'd really started believing such a thing could happen."

He was silent for a moment and then he faced Crystal. "Eli pointed out—and I must admit it was painful to have to agree—that all my problems stemmed from incomplete Christianity. He said I was typical—just too happy to take all the Lord had to give me without being willing to give God what He wanted of me." He paused and gently touched Crystal's face with one finger.

"Eli said God wanted me—ugly disposition and all. All the anger and hate, all the pride and selfishness. When a man who's been there talks like that, it's pretty convincing. He finally made me see it was worth unloading all of me on God, even when it seemed too good to be true."

Abruptly Matthew slipped to his knees beside the bed and touched Crystal's hand. "I don't deserve another chance, and I won't even ask for it. But, Crystal, I want you to know I love you very much. Please forgive me."

Daniel and Amy watched Crystal hesitate. Finally she held one hand out toward Matthew.

Daniel stood up and carefully set Amy on her feet. "Come on. Sweetheart, let's go home."

"Home? Where—"

"Remember you said anywhere. Let's go down and see if they have a room for us." Daniel picked up Amy's bag and they tiptoed out, closing the door behind them.

CHAPTER 34

Crystal looked at the closing door and then at Matthew. He was waiting, and she couldn't meet his eyes. Getting to her feet, she paced to the window. In the distance the last of the fire colored the sky with a burst of bright smoke. The fire made her think of Lucas.

With a shrug she turned to Matthew. "I suppose Lucas is off somewhere, laughing because he has won again. He's left a heap of human wreckage behind him while he's running across the mountains with his bag of gold clenched in his dirty fist."

She couldn't avoid Matthew's eyes. He said, "You sound bitter."

"Do you not think I have a right to be?"

"Justifiably." His voice was rough. "But need we spend time talking about him?"

"You asked me to forgive you."

"And you can't." He made the flat statement. Getting to his feet he paced the room.

She watched his limping gait, studied the ragged garments he wore, and waited. Finally she spoke. "Matthew, you are so strange. The limp. You've lost weight. Those terrible clothes."

He turned and she began to see glimpses of the old Matthew in his twisted grin. "No longer the dandy? I'll never be again. Suddenly it isn't important. It's nothing."

He came to sprawl in the chair. With his head tipped back and his eyes nearly closed, he hesitated. When the words came they were in chopped phrases, leaving Crystal bewildered with the gaps. "It's been long. A person's bound to change. No idea it would be so much until I saw me reflected in you. Did you inherit the bitterness from me?

"Crystal, life moves on. Values change. I thought we'd pick it up from where we left off. Like a half-forgotten chapter in an interesting book. Impossible. It will be a learning over again.

"You married a Southern gentleman. I'm fast becoming a stubborn Yankee, like Garrison, Mott, and some of the others."

"An abolitionist?"

"No, simply a man who believes so strongly that he dares stand on the hard side of a cause. For God, for a united country, for freedom for the slaves—"

Crystal interrupted. "Matthew, I do forgive you. Now please go."

"You don't believe me? I expected that." He got to his feet.

"That isn't quite so. In the past you had strong words, but without this much conviction. It's just that somehow you've grown up and away from me. We're no longer able to measure minds."

"You're diminishing yourself. I've always thought you a fine woman, worthy—"

"Matthew, please." She turned quickly, her hands waving off his words. "Talking convinces me we no longer walk the same road." Getting to her feet she moved restlessly around the room.

In a moment he was beside her, touching her arm. She trembled at the unexpected contact. "I'm sorry," he murmured. "It's just that you seemed almost like a dream. The kind of dreams I've been having since Pennsylvania days. Near enough to touch, yet—" He paused, adding, "Not real. Will you please come sit down and tell me what has been going on in your life? Did you stay in Pennsylvania? I remembered we talked about going west." He hesitated. In a rush of words, he said, "I wanted to inquire about Clara Brown while here, just wanted to know if she could tell me about you."

Crystal had been watching Matthew. "Your arm," she said. "You were wounded—in a battle?"

"Yes, that's where I met Daniel and Amy." His grin was twisted again. "It won't keep me out of the Army."

Crystal stood up and walked around the room again. "I'm sorry you were injured." For a minute she faced him. "That does change a person, doesn't it?"

His face was puzzled. "I keep thinking you are trying to dig me up like a flower patch, to see what's buried."

Their eyes met. Matthew came across the room to her. "Crystal, it's late. I won't trouble you any longer with my presence."

She put her hand to her face, but it was too late. On his face she could read the hope. For a moment she met his eyes, knowing all the forgotten things were alive and life was possible. Turning, with a shaky voice, she admitted, "I guess habits are hard to break."

"Habit? I don't think you're telling me it was all just a comfortable old habit, loving."

His hand was under her chin in the warm, familiar touch. She closed her eyes and tried to move away. "My dear, I won't force you. But I would think that if you didn't love me still, then a sisterly kiss would be no more than a common courtesy."

He was smiling, confident. His hand on her shoulder was warm and gentle. It had always been that way, warm and gentle.

"Why are you crying?"

"Because it is so impossible."

"That shouldn't bring tears if it is what you really mean." He was still waiting and his presence was overwhelming. "Will you talk with me? It seems like the three of us deserve a chance."

"Three?

"You and me and Love."

"Matthew, did you mean those things you said about God and praying?"

"I did. Crystal, I didn't realize the state of confusion I lived in when I considered myself a Christian. You've guessed, of course, that

God didn't consider me a true follower." Abruptly he said, "Crystal, what's wrong? All this talk—it's like I can't reach you. I would rather you lash out at me, say what must be said, rather than this cold formality."

She went to the window. "I had a mission. I suppose it is finished now. Cold? One must put restrictions on one's mind and emotions if there is to be success in such an endeavor."

"Mind telling me about it?"

"Lucas and I have been working together. Naturally, he bought me with the promise of telling me your whereabouts. But I do believe he thought I was a genuine Confederate. For some time, that is. Right at the last he caught me passing a message to my contact."

He moved restlessly. "Would you believe, I'm not interested in hearing about Lucas? Why are you telling me this?"

She cried, "I'm trying to make you understand!"

"That you've been working with Lucas—or is it something more?" His face was still, remote. Once before he had looked that way. Despair moved through Crystal, and suddenly she was weighted with fatigue.

"I only want to get this interview over," she murmured through heavy lips. In a moment she added, "I chose to work with him. I didn't expect him to take advantage of the situation. Matthew—" Now the words were coming in a rush. "Lucas raped me, and for the past months, since February, I've lived with one desire. That is to kill him."

She paced the room and returned to see the effect of her words on him. Not anger, not outrage. There were tears on his face. She backed against the dressing table. "Matthew, it really is finished. It is an impossible situation."

He sat down and rubbed his palms over his eyes. "My darling, another failure. Now I understand the bitterness, the ugliness I was seeing. Will there ever be an end to the suffering I've put you through? Crystal, I dare not ask you to forgive me for this. I can't bear to hear you say no, but I understand. As soon as I walked into the room tonight I could feel the oppression. Naturally my conceit had it marked out. All you needed was my love and the sure promise I have turned over a new leaf."

"You don't understand, Matthew. I'm trying to explain why we can't just take up our life again. It isn't lack of love. It's—"

She straightened the objects on her dressing table. With flat, hard words she stated, "I don't believe, any more than you or Daniel, that Lucas is dead. I still have the passion to track him down, to kill him for all of the ugliness he has heaped on me."

Her controlled voice broke, and with a burst of passion she cried, "For hurting you and twisting your mind with his selfishness, for the outrage of rape. See, Matthew, I'll never be a whole person. I'll never be able to hold my head up again until I've rectified the disgrace by killing him."

Matthew sat down on the edge of the bed. She knew he was watching her face as she moved around the room. Then she returned to the dressing table. Right to left she began again, laying the objects out and then pushing the array to the center of the table. He was very close, and the warmth of his body, the intensity of his eyes moving with the changing pattern of her fingers wrapped her into a cocoon with him in which the movement of her hands united their spirits.

Startled, she looked up. Again there was the impression of his gray eyes channeling between them. A bridge.

"There's another solution." He paused. "Do you know I felt this same kind of outrage in battle? The violation of my person, my mind, my body—given unwillingly. Strange, I thought it the most unendurable situation I had ever faced. It was Eli Randolph who made me realize the violation of my spirit was worse."

Matthew moved away from her. With his thoughts far away, he paced the room. The distance between them stretched the sense of oneness until she felt she must follow after him. He turned to look down at her. "He said the violation of the human spirit creeps upon us without our knowing it. A seduction by thought and action."

"Without agony? I can't believe it so."

"The agony comes not at the rape of the soul, but by the deliverance. A kind of birth agony."

She felt the jarring note of his words and realized he had severed the thought pattern her mind had said was inevitable. Coldly she faced him. "And of course you have an answer. Dare I guess that it is to be a good girl and love my enemies?"

"That is an utter impossibility."

"I could have told you that."

"On your own. Just as the remedy for me was workable, my dear wife, it will be workable for you. I know. Since it came from Eli, and I have seen the pattern in him and Amelia, I can assure you it works. I've started on the course myself."

"I heard you say something about being on your knees and being pounded on the back." Her voice was still cold and he was grinning at her, thawing the ice.

"That's right. Crystal, I was serious about me, you, and Love. That's the only way we'll be able to handle life. It starts with accepting Jesus Christ as Savior, but the momentum really picks up when you take Him as Lord of your life. Of course it isn't easy to surrender hate, but I'll be there to help you—by pounding you on the back."

He reached out to touch the tears on her cheeks. "You are my precious wife. How I look forward to spending the rest of my life telling you that!"